Greig Beck grew up
Sydney, Australia. H
sunbaking and reading
went on to study computer science, immerse himself in the financial software industry and later received an MBA. Today, Greig spends his days writing, but still finds time to surf at his beloved Bondi Beach. He lives in Sydney, with his wife, son, and an enormous black German shepherd.

If you would like to contact Greig, his email address is greig@greigbeck.com and you can find him on the web at www.greigbeck.com.

FROM HELL

Sometimes Hell rises to the surface

GREIG BECK

momentum

First published 2019 in Momentum by Pan Macmillan Australia Pty Ltd
1 Market Street, Sydney, New South Wales, Australia 2000

A CIP record for this book is available at the National Library of Australia

From Hell: Alex Hunter 8

EPUB format: 9781760786984
Print on Demand format: 9781760786991

Original cover design by Danielle Hurps

Cover images: iStockphoto.com

Macmillan Digital Australia: www.macmillandigital.com.au
To report a typographical error, please visit www.panmacmillan.com.au/contact-us/

Do not ask of Hell, for a little piece of it burns inside all of us.

— Greig Beck

PROLOGUE

The Roman city of Pompeii, 79 AD

Mateo's father gripped his hand tightly and turned to stare. The boy was only eight years old and short for his age, but he too sensed the danger, and moved closer to his father's stout legs.

Around him, people ran, bumped into each other, fell over, and yelled in both fear and anger. The ashes had been falling for over an hour now: hot, greasy. At first they fell lightly like a warm snow, but unlike snow, these flakes didn't melt, instead their weight grew until they made roofs groan, clogged the nostrils, and coated the tongue in a sulfurous-tasting oiliness.

The mountain had been throwing up a column of dark smoke like the trunk of a mighty olive tree whose black and gray branches had sprouted as far as the eye could see, turning noon daylight to an evening twilight.

But now, something else was coming.

Mateo followed his father's gaze – a dense black cloud was rolling toward them, pouring forth from the mountaintop and spreading over the earth like a flood of ink. His father seemed frozen; for the first time, Mateo felt a tremble in the man's big hand.

The crowd became more frantic and his father pulled them both off the road into an alley as it surged, a rushing river of wild eyes and yelling mouths. Panic turned people to maddened beasts, and some were trampled while others beat their neighbors out of the way.

His father held up a burning torch, trying to get his bearings. Just inside the alleyway was a dog chained to a door and, on seeing them, it whimpered a mournful greeting. Mateo crouched to pat its head, wiping away greasy ash. It blinked up at him with crusted eyelashes, and licked his hand once before laying down to curl up as if to sleep. Soon the ash was covering it over again.

When he wakes, it'll all be over, Mateo thought confidently.

Then the black flood overtook them. Darkness fell, an absolute nothingness, as if one's lamp had been snuffed out in a sealed and windowless room. Even from where Mateo and his father sheltered they could hear the people's shrieks, which now sounded like a cacophony of damned souls in the pits of hell. Infants called for their parents, others screamed for their wives or children, trying to find them by their voices alone. Many appealed to the gods, but still more wailed that there were no gods left, and that everything was now an eternal darkness, everywhere, and for all of time.

"We must get to the harbor," Mateo's father declared and pulled Mateo with him.

Mateo's father was a man of importance, and the keeper of the ancient texts. When the ground had shaken and the mountain began to spew its contents, he had rushed to gather several of the most valuable tablets. He still held them, tucked up under one arm.

The ground shook again. In the distance spots of light began to appear, but it wasn't the healthy light of the sun, rather the deep red glow of a titan's oven. That, too, was blacked out as the darkness came on once more and ashes fell again, this time in even heavier showers. Mateo and his father continually shook them off, otherwise they would have been buried and smothered beneath their weight.

People came and clung to Mateo's father as if he were some sort of oracle, the last bearer of light. But the torch spluttered, and Mateo heard his father curse; the heavy ash was killing everything, even these remaining fingers of illumination.

There came a change – strange even among the already strange – an absence of sound as if they had stuffed cloth into their ears. People stopped, listened, waited, and then Mateo heard them: shrieks. This time they were different. These weren't just howls of fear but of an unbearable pain and terror. And then they too were shut off as if a hand had been thrust across mouths or clamped around necks.

The torch finally went out, leaving Mateo and his father in a darkness blacker that Hades itself. And then Mateo finally did see something that froze his blood – eyes, clusters of them, not all human, and twice as high as the tallest man.

As the eyes floated toward Mateo and his father, his father slowly drew his silver gladius. The nobleman's stout sword was two and half feet long, heavy, and razor sharp. He pushed Mateo behind him. More and more eyes opened on the looming shape, and fixed upon them.

There came a low moaning as if from a dozen mouths in torment. His father took a step back, but then must have realized they could not escape together. He planted his legs and held his ground.

"I love you, my son. Run, Mateo. Run like the wind," his father commanded, and Mateo hated hearing so much fear in those few words. "*Run!*"

The shout broke Mateo's spell of horror and he did as he was told, running blindly into walls, tumbling down steps, and tripping over fallen bodies.

The agonized scream he faintly heard a few moments later could not have been his father. *Please, not my father.*

Mateo trailed a hand along the brick wall and turned a corner to run smack into people blocking the laneway. They had linked arms, and though he could only make them out when he was up against them, he saw they had featureless masks pulled over their faces and strange symbols and eyes cut into their naked torsos, and some even had what looked like hands and other limbs strung about them.

They pushed him backward, forcing him back the way he'd come.

"I can't!" he yelled.

"She comes again. She must be fed," they intoned as one.

They lashed out with fists and feet, and Mateo turned and ran. He was spent and sick with fear and fatigue when he finally slowed. *How will I find my way out?* he wondered. *How will I find my father*?

In the end he just sat down and put his hands over his head. *I'll just go to sleep like the dog*, he thought. *And then just like him, when I wake up, it'll all be over.*

The small boy screwed his eyes shut, and almost immediately the ash began to get heavier on his body. It was hard to breathe, but it was so warm and soft, like a blanket. He let himself drift away.

PART 1

"Long is the way and hard, that out of Hell leads up to light."

—John Milton, *Paradise Lost*

CHAPTER 01

Pompeii, excavation site 343B – today

Maria Monti pushed strands of thick, dark hair behind one ear as she leaned in closer to her computer set up on the field table. A smile spread over her face at what she was seeing on the small screen.

"I think we have another one."

The scanner picked up the signals from the thumper they'd installed. The device sent a small impact blast into the ground, not enough force to disturb the soil and potentially damage hidden antiquities, just enough to push vibration waves down into the earth. These waves bounced off buried objects, and their software programs would read the seismic echoes and return a 3D image of the item they found there.

About three-quarters of Pompeii's nearly 800,000 square yards had been excavated already, and hundreds of bodies had already been discovered. Many of the plaster casts of the men, women, children, and animals of Pompeii were primarily made in the mid-1800s and were scattered among museums, research institutes, and universities throughout the country. There were many famous casts like the hugging lovers, the dog on its writhing back, or the heart-rending small boy that was sitting, head resting on arms placed over his knees as though he had simply stopped to rest and never got up.

To Maria, they were wonders upon wonders. But to the general public they were now only of mild interest. Over 200 years of being on show had made the casts lose their historical, cultural, and financial significance.

But getting permits to excavate on one of the Vesuvius sites was excruciatingly hard, with the labyrinthine bureaucracy to navigate – all the necessary networking, ass-kissing, and mountains of paperwork. And all that was before the process of determining how any significant finds should be dealt with.

The other problem Maria and her team had to deal with was the actual excavation. Pulse technology had made finding the bodies simpler: they could be located without turning over a single shovel of dirt. But the actual bodies were gone, of course, and they were now just bones in a body-shaped void. In the past, this cavity would have been pumped full of plaster of Paris and left to set for a few days before a life-sized statue was dug up. The upside was the statues were easier to handle as the remains were now solid. The downside was their contents were lost, as bones, jewelry and any fine detail were subsumed within the heavy, mud-like mixture.

But Maria had been granted her permits by demonstrating a new technique her team had perfected called "cavity glassblowing". They drilled down to the cavities, carefully punctured them with a hollow probe, and then sprayed a lightweight composite resin mixture into the void as a gas. It filled the air pocket, coating the inside of the shell and hardening on contact, becoming like toughened glass. The bodies could be safely removed, then washed down and polished, creating a see-through representation of the person, animal, or biological object. Details could be observed right down to individual hairs, clothing remnants, buttons and jewelry still hanging around skeletal necks or decorating fingers or toes.

The added bonus was, if they needed to remove the resin casing, then a warm water solution made it simply melt away.

"Not a big signature." She bobbed her head. "Maybe only four- to five-feet long."

"Depth?" Andreas Katsis asked. The young man had coal black hair, eyes, and matching dark eyebrows that met in the middle. Skinny forearms dangled from a dirty, sweat-soaked T-shirt, and he used one to wipe his brow.

"Three feet down, northeastern edge of quadrant five." Maria stood, grabbed a small flag on a metal spike, and walked among the rows of string lines they'd made to cut their work area up into ten by ten–feet squares. She carefully strode to the one designated quadrant five and stuck the small flag on the far edge. "About here."

Andreas brought the pick, shovel, rake, and an assortment of brushes.

"I'll prep the resin mix, and you, sir ..." She grinned.

"Yeah, yeah, start digging."

The mixture only took around twenty minutes to prepare but the excavation was where the time and effort came in. The digging progressed fairly quickly for the first few feet, but as they neared the cavity under the earth, the process slowed to taking a thin layer at a time, until Maria estimated they were within a few inches of the space left behind by the once organic material.

She and Andreas gently inserted the spike into the soil, turning it and easing it down until they just breached the cavity space with a pop.

She flicked a hand up. "Stop."

"Phew." Andreas recoiled, and waved a hand in front of his face. "Whoever this was must have died farting."

He continued to wave away the escaping gas then lifted the delivery spike, which was like a giant hypodermic needle, and held it while Maria attached a tube to the end, screwing it down and sealing it. She stepped out of the hole and walked to the pump that contained a couple of large tanks of their liquid resin composite mixture. The delivery system would atomize the mixture and force it down in a pervasive mist.

"On the count of three, two, one ..." She switched the machine on and it hummed, and the pump jumped as the mixture raced along the tubing to the spike. She watched the dial indicate the rate of resin dispersion.

After just a few seconds, she shut it down. "That should do it."

Andreas nodded and carefully eased the needle out then jammed a thumbnail-sized blob of putty over the hole. Maria tossed him a metal dinner plate that he laid over the top of the putty.

"How long?" he asked and handed her back the spike.

She took it and wiped the end clean. "That size, probably only an hour, give or take. We'll leave it for two just to be sure."

The pair gathered their equipment and headed back to the open-sided tent they used as their makeshift office. Underneath the canopy was a table, chairs, a few iceboxes, and coffee mugs.

Maria grabbed a thermos and poured two black coffees, then sat down heavily. She raised her cup. "Cin cin."

Andreas did the same. "Salute."

Maria sipped the lukewarm brew and let her eyes wander over the site. Around them, columns and walls rose up from dusty soil, and further back, entire tiled floors. Even perfectly preserved buildings had been revealed.

The area they excavated had once been a collection of labyrinthine alleyways that ran like arteries through the busy city of Pompeii. Maria drew in a deep breath, let it out slowly, and tried to take her mind back to see that time, imagine what it must have been like, first in all its magnificence, and then in those claustrophobic lanes when the sun was blotted out.

The beginning of the end for the city was midday, 24 August 79 AD; perversely, the day after the Roman holiday of Volcanalia, dedicated to the god of fire. At noon, Mount Vesuvius roared to life, spewing ash hundreds of feet into the air for eighteen hours straight. The choking ash rained down on the cities in the surrounding countryside, filling courtyards, blocking doors, and collapsing roofs. But that was only the beginning of the nightmare to come.

When the cone of the volcano collapsed, it triggered an avalanche of mud and ash that rushed down the slope toward the city of Pompeii, just a little over five miles away.

The molten river of death obliterated everything in its path. Pompeii and the smaller neighboring village of Herculaneum disappeared completely. Anyone not frightened away by the previous day's ash fall would have been smothered, coated, or cooked by the 2000-degree layer of volcanic mud.

Perhaps the cities would have remained a legend if not discovered by accident during the construction of King Charles III of Spain's palace in 1738. Miraculously, the two cities were nearly perfectly preserved under the calcified layers of ash – layers that in some places were up to 150 feet thick.

Maria had memorized the ancient city's layout and knew that just a few hundred feet away from where she sat was the Garden of the Fugitives, which held the largest number of victims found in one place: thirteen people had sought refuge in a fruit orchard there. Not far away, nine sets of remains were found at the House of Mysteries, where the roof had collapsed, trapping them inside. A plaster cast of a fallen man could be seen inside the Caupona Pherusa tavern, where the guy might have walked in to have one last drink or maybe to give a final toast to the gods.

The Stabian Baths, the fish market, the granary, and the Olitorium market all contained casts of victims, including animals, and tucked in an alley was the cast of a dog in a collar looking like it was simply sleeping, not far from the cast of the tiny, resting boy. *Did they know each other?* Maria had wondered.

She checked her wristwatch, counting down the seconds until her resin set. Every time a new body was found, the excitement rose – who or what would it be? What story would it tell? And sometimes there was frustration; perhaps frustration with the supposedly perfect record keeping of the Romans. It was said that only a few hundred people remained behind to be covered alive by the ash, pumice, and rivers of magma. But there were other records that said not just hundreds, but perhaps thousands had remained, and their bodies had either vanished or were still hidden somewhere below their feet.

But so many? Thousands ... where are they all? Maria blew air between red lips powdered with dust. The missing bodies were one of the mysteries of Pompeii, and every researcher hoped that they'd be the one to find some sort of grand hall or basement overflowing with the lost dead, solving the nearly 2000-year-old mystery.

Maria checked her watch again and then let her eyes drift to the scanner screen – the signature's cavity space was smaller than that of an adult, and she both did and didn't want it to be a child. There was nothing more heartrending than seeing the forlorn shape of an infant – twisted in agony, bent in confusion, or just looking like it had drifted off into an eternal sleep.

But there was so much to learn from every character they uncovered, and unfortunately, the museums valued Pompeii's children the most – morbidly, they proved immensely popular with the public, and especially with today's children. Perhaps when a youth sees the shape of a petrified child they somehow identified with them, and could feel their fear, pain, and loss.

Maria checked her watch again – a few more minutes to go. The resin dried quickly.

"How we looking?" Andreas squinted at the computer screen.

Maria got to her feet. "I'm thinking we're looking good. Let's bring it up."

She lifted a shovel and walked to the shallow pit, with Andreas following with his tools. They confirmed the object was roughly four and a half feet long and around eighteen inches wide, so they would excavate around it and also down several feet below it. Then they could gently scrape away the matrix until the body or body part was fully revealed.

Maria put further pegs in the ground indicating the shape of the object, and then a dig line around it for them to follow. They shovelled away the earth, but after only fifteen minutes, and before they even reached the object, Andreas became excited.

"Whoa! Got something else here – seems it was lodged in the first object and now has comes loose." He went to his knees and used a brush to wipe dirt from an object revealed beside their primary cast.

Maria straightened, watching him clear the soil away. "What is it?"

"Maybe, yes ... *ooh* ... magnificent." He dusted some more. "A gladius – solid silver, I think. A very high-status weapon." He whistled. "Who or whatever is in that cast must have dropped it."

"Well, the biological object is not big enough to be an adult," Maria said. "Perhaps some young slave was carrying the gladius for their master, and got caught out in the open."

"Yeah, maybe." Andreas had cleared the debris from around the sword and gently lifted it. The blade was heavily pitted and dull, but the ivory handle still bore ribbing of gold and studs of iron. "Big one – coulda done some real damage with this baby." He laid it on a cloth and covered it from the sun, then went back to his excavation.

He grinned again as he found something else. "A treasure trove." He gently dug out the square object and brushed it down. "Ha! A writing stone. Which is odd, as the Pompeians usually used wax on wood." He shrugged. "Guess that's why it survived – wood and wax certainly would have been incinerated or dissolved long ago."

He handed the stone to Maria, who looked at the inscriptions and frowned. "I'll need to study this later." She stepped over the string lines to take it to her desk.

They returned to carefully excavating the resin-filled void. They used small picks, spoon-sized shovels, and tiny, coarse-bristled brushes to remove dirt as they got closer to the object. Though their resin gave a strong finished product, there was always the chance some appendage could be damaged during removal.

It took them another hour for the cast to finally surface, and then Andreas used a rough cloth to wipe it down.

He peered through the cloudy resin. "I see a bone in there, thick, maybe too thick for it to be human, I think. Damn." He continued to gently pick, scrape, and brush at the resin.

"Might be an animal; quite a few horses and bullocks were left behind." Maria felt her enthusiasm plummet. She sighed and continued with her work, and then leaned in close to the cast. She laid a hand on it.

"Ouch!" She jerked her hand back. "It's hot."

* * *

He felt it.

He sat up in bed, light-headed but elated, and felt the tingles run from his scalp to his toes – She had awoken – and now She called.

He knew exactly what he must do, and he would answer, like hundreds of others across the country.

He threw his legs over the side of the bed, headed to the small bathroom in his disheveled apartment, and stood in front of the cracked mirror. He didn't see his reflection, hear the constant drop of the broken faucet, or smell the ammoniac stink from the blocked toilet. All of those stimuli were recorded by senses he no longer needed.

Like an automaton, he opened the cabinet and took out the things he required, laying them out neatly on the sink.

Then he began.

The razorblade traced the flesh of his torso, carving the runes and unholy symbols in deep. His body ran with warm, sticky blood, but he didn't feel it. Next he picked up the large curved needle used for sewing leather and threaded with catgut twine. He pushed it into the corner of his lips and continued sewing until his mouth was closed tight.

He breathed calmly through his nose, staring straight ahead, not seeing himself, but instead something that was buried deep in the Earth and sang a siren song that was the most beautiful thing he had ever heard. He was impatient to finish and go to Her.

With a steady hand, he reached up to pinch the corner of his left eye together and drag the lids forward. The needle went through the thin skin with ease as he began to sew his eye closed. Then he did the same to the right eye.

Only when he was finished did he see clearly what She wanted him to see.

* * *

"It's damned hot." Maria shook her hand and then carefully touched the object only with her fingertips. "Did the sun do that?"

Andreas also touched the cast in several places. "Yeah, you're right, it is very warm. Must have been the sunshine; we better hurry and remove it from the matrix and get it covered. It's been in the darkness for nearly 2000 years, so exposure to UV rays will degrade it in minutes."

Though the specimen could be polished down to glass-like clarity, for now it was still smoky, and clearing away some of the crusting with a rag allowed them a partial glimpse inside the package.

Maria squinted into the murky shell. "I can see it. And yeah, the bone's way too thick for a human even if it was the femur. This thing looks three times the size of a human thigh bone."

Andreas sat back on his haunches. "I have no damned idea what I'm looking at."

The thing, the bone – or maybe bones – had been sheared off at one end, and was probably the last thing the gladius blade had severed.

Maria frowned at the remains. "It's not a horse or a bullock."

"No shit," Andreas scoffed. "I mean, could the heat have done that?"

"I … don't know," she whispered.

At first she had thought it was going to be the leg of a large animal, but the single bone-shaped thing seemed to have been made up of lots of bones – lots of bones that looked melted or fused together. And at the end closest to Andreas, the bones seem to end in a type of claw that would have looked more at home on a raptor than on a terrestrial animal. Though again, the claw wasn't made up of single digits, but what seemed to be the tips of multiple fingers, human fingers, pinched and then melted together. Maria could see that there was a tiny animal hoof melded in there as well.

"Well?' Andreas asked.

"Huh?" She lifted her head.

"Do you think the heat could have fused the bones together like that?"

"No. Maybe. I don't know." She shook her head. "In extreme heat the fat in the flesh can melt together. But bones don't act like that; they just carbonize."

"Well then, what the hell did that thing come off?" Andreas laid his tools down and then exhaled loudly. "Okay, this is gonna sound dumb ... but it looks kinda like some sort of dinosaur." He shrugged and gave her a crooked smile.

Maria pursed her lips. "It's millions of years too young for a dinosaur." She put her hands on her hips. "But I can tell you what it certainly is – a mystery. And if there's one thing that fuels the grant-money train, it's finding something unique, weird, and mysterious." She grinned.

Andreas smirked. "And this fits the bill on all three."

Maria felt a chill run up her spine as she looked down at the deformed giant arm, wing, front leg, or whatever the hell it was. For some reason it was the first discovery she'd made that she wished had remained buried. *Odd*, she thought, *for an archaeologist to even think that.*

"So, the sword," Andreas said. "And the clean cut at the end. My guess is someone hacked this off before they were covered over."

"Yeah, maybe." Maria's eyes went to the pitted gladius sword. "Jeez, as if these poor souls didn't have enough to worry about back then."

"Well, I'll tell you one damned thing: I'm just glad that whatever was wearing that arm isn't around today." Andreas sat back, glancing down at the bone, before lunging forward again. "Hey, wait a minute. Look – was that there before?"

"What?"

"Looks like spore growth on the bone. Don't remember it being there when we first uncovered it."

"Maybe the light has moved, so we can see it now." She leaned so close her nose almost touched the casing. "Or maybe mineral discoloration. Nothing could be growing on the specimen – it's airtight."

"The light might have triggered some mold spores." Andreas shrugged. "I'm guessing."

"You know what? I have no idea who to consult on this – a zoologist, biologist, paleontologist, microbiologist; all of the above?"

"Mythologist," Andreas muttered.

"What did you say?"

"Want to hear a dumb theory? I mean, *another* dumb theory."

She nodded and rested back on her haunches.

"Well, what if the thing that wore this came out of the volcano, and what if— "

Maria chuckled and held up a hand. "We're scientists, right?"

He nodded.

"Okay, just checking. So my *scientific* theories are that geological compression has forced them to become bonded, or somehow the heat has fused the biological material." Maria stood and brushed herself down. "So, we'll start with a biologist. Cover it over. Oh, and check the scanner to see it there's anything else that gladius might have lopped off."

Andreas nodded. "What'll you do?"

She stepped back over the string line. "I'm going to take a look at that stone tablet. And then I'm going to speak to an old friend."

CHAPTER 02

USSTRATCOM, Omaha, Nebraska

In the darkened war room, Colonel Jack 'Hammer' Hammerson stood with his hands clasped behind his back. One wall was entirely taken up with a huge screen, and on that screen there was a satellite image of the nuclear power plant. Down the side within smaller image boxes were 3D computer graphics, thermal representations, and night-vision displays of the site.

"Enlarge thermal."

His order was carried out by one of the technicians in the room and he saw the orange bodies lying on the ground. They were rapidly cooling in the night air and in just a few more minutes they'd be purple-black as they attained the same temperature as their surroundings. It told him what he already knew – these deaths were recent.

What he also knew was that at 0800 hours, a group of twenty heavily armed men and women had infiltrated the Robert Emmett Ginna Nuclear Power Plant – commonly known as Ginna – after executing the external guards.

Hammerson felt his gut twist as he thought about those guards, who had gone to work that day thinking the most they'd needed to contend with was a few lost hikers, or perhaps even boredom. None of them would have expected to be caught in an ambush. There were only twenty-two employees on duty as the plant was undergoing some downtime for refurbishment. Hammerson had no idea how many – if any – were still alive.

"They better be, you sons of bitches."

Just before the plant went dark it was reported that a group of the infiltrators were heading for the reactor, their motives and objectives unknown. It didn't matter to Hammerson; as far as he was concerned, they were as good as dead the moment they killed their first citizen on the site.

Once again, the Hammer and his HAWCs had been called to action, as no one else had the skills – or was crazy enough – to enter a fortified facility with twenty heavily armed and dangerous adversaries possibly bent on nuclear destruction. *Impossible*, anyone else would have said. But Hammerson was a believer in the World War Two motto of the U.S. Army Corps of Engineers: "The difficult we do immediately. The impossible takes a little longer".

Except at that moment he was given just six hours to do the impossible. Then the state of New York would be evacuated. Hammerson grunted. The orders from General Marcus Chilton were clear: *Go in fast and hard, and cleanse the damned site.*

Hammerson's response had been simple: *They started the war, we'll finish it.* He smiled grimly at the thought, and folded brawny arms.

Around him was the soft babble of the intelligence officers and technicians drawing data, assessing it, and assembling it to create a battle-plan mosaic for him to use.

All that chatter dropped to silence when the deep and controlled voice came over the speaker. "In position. On your word."

Hammerson had been waiting on him – Alex Hunter, the Arcadian. He and his team of HAWCs were now hovering well within the maximum operational ceiling of their stealth helo. The sleek, night-dark Blackhawk helicopter wore a cloak of radar absorbing material, a coating that rendered the craft invisible to the eye as well as to any radar. In addition, the engine shields, rotor covers, and extra main rotor blade – used to slow down the rotor speed – made the machine as quiet as the evening breeze.

Hammerson's eyes were unblinking as he watched his screen. "Proceed, Arcadian. Confirming, engagement is level five." Hammerson had no qualms about giving the order. The fifth engagement level was the highest level of lethality – no prisoners, no negotiation, no adversaries to escape. The HAWCs were now judge, jury, and executioners. There would be no record of the mission, or of the kill count, or even that they existed.

"Roger that. Engagement level five, confirmed."

"We are the shield," Hammerson said evenly.

"And we are the sword," Alex Hunter replied. "Out." The line closed.

Hammerson looked at the timer on the screen – they now had a little over four hours remaining from when Chilton's call came through. On the satellite image he saw the outline of the chopper, and then four shapes drop from it.

Release the dogs of war, he thought, and stood like he was made of stone, his battle-hardened eyes never blinking, never leaving the screen. They narrowed as he saw that the guard's bodies begin to vanish from the thermal imaging as they cooled to the ambient temperature. It was as if their souls had finally departed.

He clenched his teeth. "You sons of bitches think you're bringing me Hell? Then I'll send you the devil."

* * *

Alex and his three HAWCs leaped head first from the chopper, dropping like missiles.

A HALO drop was required, but standard night chutes were a problem as they had no idea what surveillance tech the intruders had. The chutes the HAWCs used were batwing canopies blown open by compressed air, power-assisted models that only deployed several hundred feet from the ground. The chute packs would also engage airbrakes of a short downward thrust to slow the HAWCs from a terminal velocity of 120 miles per hour to a survivable landing speed. The change was short, sharp, and painful, but it was one they could walk away from. They'd also do it near invisibly – their armored suits were covered in a similar RAM coating to their helicopter so had zero radar image or heat signature. And their bioshell armor plating was tough enough to withstand the impact of a shotgun blast.

Alex and his team came down in the birch forest half a mile from the facility's perimeter fence. Each member knew to come down in a crouch on one knee and both fists to defray the impact. Their chutes disengaged, and they pulled rifles from their backs and put the scopes to their eyes to begin scanning the terrain.

Alex clicked his fingers once and the HAWCs turned to him. He made a sweeping gesture and then pointed forward: *Spread, go fast.* The black-clad figures began to sprint away.

Captain Alex Hunter ran hard, but not enough to outpace his team. They worked into a V formation with Casey Franks as the tip. They were within their schedule, and level five engagement took pressure off the HAWC Special Forces soldiers because if they encountered resistance, they would simply smash through or run over the top of it – they had the firepower, expertise, and fortitude: everything they needed.

Each HAWC was worth half-a-dozen professional adversaries, therefore the four HAWCs should have had the twenty intruders easily outnumbered.

So far, the intruders hadn't made contact with the outside world. They hadn't listed any demands, and their origin was unknown, as was their firepower or other tech. All they'd done was infiltrate, and proven they were prepared to use lethal violence. The site was heavily shielded, rendering X-rays and other long-range imaging techniques useless. So where the intruders had made their way to inside the nuclear facility and what they were doing was a mystery. However, if they were planning to detonate the site and create a lethal cloud over the state, then they would have to get close to the core. If they were there, then Alex and his team would follow. Alex knew he had two real adversaries to contend with: the intruders and time.

What they did know was the number of intruders and, from the body shapes picked up by ground surveillance when they breached the fence, that there were both men and women. Alex would assume they had significant firepower, and he would also assume they would be prepared to fight to the death. He would cut his cloth according to those assumptions.

Casey Franks went to one knee and raised a fist. The team stopped and went to ground. Casey was one of his most trusted lieutenants. At five-ten, she was half-a-head smaller than some of the HAWCs, but she made up for it with expertise in hand-to-hand combat, speed, and pure ferocity. She was fearless and one of the most lethal HAWCs he had in the armory.

Alex looked at each of his team members, all watching the facility with wolf-like intensity – hungry for action, eager, and deadly as all hell. Just to his left was the hulking frame of Drake 'Hondo' Henderson. The guy was six-six, 260 pounds, but fluid in his movements. He hit like a sledgehammer and was also a crack shot. Out to Alex's right was Benito Zegarelli. The guy was short but broad, with a black stubble that seemed to need shaving on the hour. He was an ex SEAL, tough as boot leather, and an expert in weapons tech and electronics as well as being their demolition guy.

Alex waited as Casey pointed to her eyes and then up past the perimeter fence – there was the tiny lump of a head poking up on the building edge: a lookout. She turned back and jammed a scope to her eye. Alex could see her pressing the tiny studs on its side, moving from telescopic to thermal and then to infrared. She scanned the rooftops, stopping at several positions. She lowered the scope and turned again, this time holding up three fingers – three lookouts. She pointed to several positions.

Alex didn't need the scope to now see each head peeking over the rooftop edge. He bet they'd have infrared, but the HAWC suits masked their body heat and also had reflective camouflage – their armor basically made them two-legged chameleons: in snow they were white, in shadow they were black, in forests they were dappled greens and browns. But Alex knew that even though they were ghosts, they might not be able to cleanly cross the clearing from the perimeter fence with snipers above them.

The rifles they carried were F200s, hyped-up air guns. Except the pneumatics were powerful enough to super-compress air into a ball shape, and then deliver it up to 500 feet at 1200 feet per second, while retaining its destination impact integrity. It was a shorter-range weapon, and had a range of delivery sizes: baseball size would knock a big man cold; pellet size would penetrate steel sheeting at a hundred feet. For now, they'd dialed them back to just penetrate flesh and bone, not steel; if things got nasty inside, which they expected, they didn't want to be rupturing any nuclear shielding.

And if the targets were out of the F200's range, well, they weren't the only weapons they'd brought.

Alex turned to Casey, held up three fingers, then swept a hand across his throat. She nodded, and pulled a stubby device from over her shoulder. She set to telescoping the barrel from the square housing that contained a bulbous belly that acted as a grip. The emitted-light weapon was a battlefield laser, and would shoot a pulse of condensed energy at the speed of light – it was soundless, instant, and had a field of fire that was limited only by the shooter's sight. There was also no need to calibrate for any deviation due to wind or gravity, as the pulse of light was pure energy and not a projectile – basically, it hit where you aimed it.

Casey charged the ELW, waited a few seconds, then held it to her shoulder. She placed her scope on the sliding rail on top of the ELW and locked it in place. Alex turned and watched the rooftops.

Casey fired.

One of the heads simply dropped from sight. Alex knew that there would be a pencil-sized hole in the front and out the back. Seconds later, the other two heads did the same – there would be no noise, no cry of pain or alarm, or any warning.

Casey lowered her weapon and turned to him. She nodded – three down, clean kills. Three threats erased.

They needed to move quickly now; if the lookouts had to call in, then all three going dark would immediately raise an alarm. Casey collapsed the weapon and reholstered it, then led them out.

They reached the perimeter fencing and crouched. It was a double design – the first layer was basic wire mesh, but the inner layer was a line of half-inch metal bars sunk into concrete. It was vehicle-ramming defense. The group made space for Hondo to kneel before the fence. He lifted a pencil-like object and ran it up the steel wire – three feet up, then three across, and three down. The laser cutter melted through the wire like it was butter. He dragged the mesh square out of the way, and moved aside.

Alex reached through the mesh door and grabbed a metal bar in each hand. He flexed, straining for a moment, and then a soft groaning sound came from the steel as the bars opened in a belly and, after another moment, popped free from their concrete base. He bent them up and out of the way, stopping when the hole was wide enough for even Hondo to pass through.

Casey went in, followed by Hondo and then Zeg. Alex paused to scan their surroundings for another moment – all quiet, all clear.

And now we begin, he thought grimly.

CHAPTER 03

Robert Emmett Ginna Nuclear Power Plant – Control Room

Harper Van Owen stood in the center of the large room prophet-like, arms wide, smiling benignly. The technicians, engineers, cleaners, and other workers had been bundled into a small, secure storage room, and the bodies of the security guards lay where they were shot, stabbed, or bludgeoned, pools of blood coagulating around them. Many had resisted. Some had surrendered, but were summarily executed anyway. Better to have a corpse to step over than a point of resistance later on. As far as Harper was concerned, mercy was a weakness.

His soldiers sat in groups or slouched, still wearing their Halloween masks – red devils, Guy Fawkes, or steam-punk goggles. He tried hard to keep a straight face. They were mostly kids from some of the wealthiest suburbs across America – Chesterbrook, Beverly Hills, Hunting Valley, New York City – ideologues recruited from college campuses, rallies, and online chat rooms, whose previous rebellions had been limited to holding up placards or shouting slogans on their college grounds. Though the fire of naïve revolution burned in their young eyes, to Harper, they were just obedient robots and cannon fodder.

Though Harper had a team of twenty, his real comrades at arms were few, but they were battle-hardened anarchists. The bare-faced youth beside him was one of his core team, his Praetorian Guard, who never wore masks. If they were identified, then so be it. If they never went home, then it would mean mission accomplished. They also came from sickeningly rich families, but Jasper, William, Carter, Felix, Finn, Olivia, Amelia, Grace, and Harper's lover, Charlotte Rochester, were willing to sacrifice their all, and basically, everyone else's all. To his Praetorians, capitalism was the devil's rule; that hollow shell of hate, invasion, subjugation, and brutality, and the thing that must fall before true liberation could begin. It just needed a spark, and they wanted it to start here, today.

But Harper also had deeper motivations. His actions were directed by a higher power, or perhaps – he suppressed a grin – a *lower* one.

Manipulation was Harper's forte, and he winked and nodded to one of his Praetorians. All of them had undertaken weapons training in Syria, and worked with several Jihadist groups to hone their skills and fervor. His Praetorians and the Jihadis shared many values and goals, and both groups were enthusiastic about bringing down the U.S.A. – the terrorist groups from outside, and Harper and his team from within. Harper had received millions in funding, access to high-tech weapons, training, and logistics – he had been amazed at the number of wealthy financers, both local and foreign, who couldn't give money quick enough.

Harper chuckled softly. Why was it that every group that wanted to burn it all down believed they'd be the ones to rise from the ashes afterwards as the new global rulers? *Insects, all of them*, he thought with disdain.

He folded his arms and drew in a deep breath of satisfaction. It had taken years of planning, hundreds of thousands in payoffs, and a few grains of good luck, but they'd made it inside. The fools outside would soon learn that his objective was not to unfurl a few banners, take hostages, and make petty demands.

To his soldiers, this mission was to deliver some real education to the oppressors. But to Harper, it was to initiate meltdown and burn a hole right through the Earth's crust. And when it was achieved, he would receive the ultimate gift, of becoming one with She.

She had told him herself. She had been whispering and singing to him now for as long as he could remember. He rubbed at his chest, feeling the raw scars there. *Soon.*

Harper had done his homework on the strengths and weaknesses of the site, and his soldiers had everything they needed, from M16s to fragmentation grenades. He had learned that the Ginna Nuclear Power Plant was a Westinghouse 2 Loop Pressurized Water Reactor, with capability to generate up to 490 megawatts of energy – she was old, but damned powerful. Ginna, like all modern and upgraded nuclear facilities, had numerous fail-safes – multiple emergency cooling systems to safely remove the decay heat in the event of a disaster, plus backup cooling systems, and automatic as well as manual override processes. Taking out just one would do nothing but cause temporary structural damage. Therefore, every single one of them had to be taken out at once, as well as all the electronic alarms and human operators. When the cooling system totally breaks down, and only then, will a nuclear meltdown occur.

Harper wanted to make a big statement, and he also wanted to punch a hole in the Earth. Every nuclear power plant produces an amount of radioactivity equivalent to a Hiroshima bomb per megawatt of electric power. In a plant like Ginna, with nearly 500 megawatts, the radioactivity of approximately 500 Hiroshima bombs would be created. Any resulting "incident" was called a "maximum assumed accident", or MAA.

Today was MAA Day. Jasper, his demolition guy, had already planted C4 strings along the control rod housing, plus several other little surprises for any would-be saviors who tried to retake the site.

He checked his wristwatch; they still had thirty minutes before the international media would receive their statement. Everything had been planned, war-gamed, and prepared for. The world would be watching. His chest swelled with pride – his father said he'd never amount to anything. His smirk broadened into a wide grin – just look at him now.

Charlotte caught his eye, fluttered her eyelids, and grinned. His cannon-fodder kids all thought they'd be arrested, have their day in court, and be heroes to their campus peers. But the core team knew that they would die this day – a glorious and liberating self-sacrifice – an immolation to end all immolations.

Many on his team had wanted him to kill the facility workers immediately. But Harper knew that the hostages bought them time. They'd pretend to negotiate, just to stop a bunch of SEALS, Rangers, or Green Beret Spec Forces trying to crash their party. But by the time the pigs in authority realized they were being played, and certainly when they read the media statement, they'd know it was too late.

Harper's one regret was that he wouldn't be able to watch the coming nuclear flower bloom over New York. A meltdown and the ensuing radioactive cloud would cover two-thirds of the most populous state in America. Millions of two-legged sheep would die, agonizingly, over the days, weeks, and months to come. And from within, the heat and cloud of the meltdown hole would rise those who serve.

MAA Day, he thought. *Yeah, very cool.*

"Lookouts have gone dark." Felix frowned as his eyes slid to Harper. "All of them."

Harper snorted. "Well, well, well, looks like our guests have arrived early. This party is about to get hot, *red* hot." He turned to Charlotte. "Bring the lambs up; the entertainment is about to start."

Whoever their guests were, he bet they'd head for the reactor room. He had a surprise waiting for them – a little bit of Russian tech that'd fry their minds, literally.

The hostages were brought in and pushed against the wall. Many of them had been beaten and sported blood-crusted noses, swollen eyes and lips, and multiple abrasions. They looked either sullen or subdued.

One of the men glared defiantly at Harper.

"*You.*" Harper pointed at the man. "Can help."

The man gritted his teeth as he was pulled out of the line. Harper lifted the strange-looking device he had leaning against his leg. It was rifle shaped, but had a bulb at the end and a coiled metallic cylinder wrapped around it. Chinese characters were imprinted on its casing.

"What we have here is your basic miniaturized atomizer – a gift from some supportive friends in the Far East." He held it out, looking along its length. "It's supposed to scramble the cohesion between atomic particles, rendering them, uh, less cohesive." He cradled the weapon and pointed it. "And I think its time to see what this baby can really do."

Charlotte clapped like a child at a birthday party.

"What's your name, sir?" Harper feigned interest.

"Fuck you." The man stared back with a volcanic hatred and a clenched jaw. He went to lunge at Harper, but the men holding him kept him in place.

"Okay, Mr. Fuck You." Harper swung the barrel toward the man and pulled the trigger.

There was crackling sound and one side of the man's head vanished. In the space where it had been was a red mist of organic matter – the atomized remains of his tissue. The other half of his head looked like an anatomy model of the brain, nasal passages, and mouth. The single remaining eye looked shocked for several seconds before rolling back.

The men holding the arms dropped the body and stepped back in disgust, the mist already settling on their faces and clothing.

"Holy fuck!" Harper whooped, and looked at Charlotte, who squealed and danced on the spot.

The other hostages screamed, fainted, or tried to edge backward.

Harper's eyes were wide with excitement as he looked down at the gun. "I fucking love this thing! I'd say test totally successful."

"Do another one," Charotte said.

"Don't worry." He aimed at the heavy door. "I think we'll be doing lots real soon."

* * *

The HAWCs breached the first door with ease. From the outside, the huge green building was a windowless monolith. Inside, it was a labyrinth of super-reinforced concrete and steel that housed the interconnected processes of nuclear energy production.

They gathered at a junction of corridors, the team crowding around a kneeling Alex. He engaged a small computer pad on his forearm and opened the plant's schematics – by now, they'd all studied them so much they could have drawn them in their sleep. They had two main targets and he pointed at the first – the containment center where the radioactive fuel rods were utilized. It was here that any explosives would undoubtedly be deployed. It was unknown if they'd be timer based, remote detonated, or even motion activated, but it was Zeg's job to find, dismantle, and destroy them. Hondo would provide cover.

Alex moved his finger to the second objective, and then looked up at Casey. He indicated the operating control room, where the intruders were expected to be, and also where any living hostages would be held – if they could be saved, good, but they were of secondary importance. It might also be where the charges would be detonated from, so rapid neutralization of the bad guys was the primary objective. Alex and Casey would take that one.

"They know we're here now, and we know what we need to do." Alex looked briefly into each of his team member's faces. "*You* know what's at stake. Let nothing stand in your way."

"With our shields, or upon them." Hondo stuck out a huge fist.

Three more fists came forward to bump knuckles, and the armor plating over the hands made a clacking sound in the confined space.

Hondo and Zegarelli took off along the western corridor. Their suits' camouflage dappled from white to dark as they moved in and out of shadows along the sterile corridors.

Alex and Casey sprinted along the forward corridor. There'd be limited – or no – element of surprise, but there'd also be no hesitation. Their plan was to go in fast, hard, and violently. That approach always froze an adversary, and if it did that for even a half-second, then they'd mop 'em up.

As a precaution, evacuations were being quietly undertaken across the state. But these were only the portion of people who were seen to be at immediate risk. Trying to move the entire population of 20 million calmly and quickly was an impossible task, and even the best planning would still result in hundreds of deaths, looting, and the possibility of large-scale fires.

Alex knew the original strategy had been to deploy a targeted bunker buster to take out the command team. But though the strategists were confident they could pierce the site's shielding, even a one-in-a-thousand possibility of breaching the fuel rod section and rupturing the core was too great a risk.

That left a frontal assault. And the only group that was fearless, ruthless, had the skills, and was deniable, was the HAWCs.

Casey Franks jinked at a corner, turning into a new passageway. Casey was like a jackrabbit as she went hard and fast, her rifle cradled in her hands. Alex could always count on her to kick a door down and go in, teeth gritted and kicking ass. But sometimes she led with her chin, rather than her head.

The female HAWC was only ten feet in front of him and coming to another juncture when Alex spotted the anomaly. To her, it might have looked like a set of power jacks at floor level, painted white to blend into their surroundings, but Alex's extraordinary vision picked up the super-condensed beams of light that created a crisscross mesh of lasers.

In the split seconds remaining before she sprinted into them, his mind accelerated through what was about to occur. It was probably a laser-triggered claymore: you break the beam, the fragmentation device detonated – right at you. They were usually packed with ball bearings, but the casing itself was designed to break into a thousand pieces of sharp metal and spray them over an area of a hundred feet. If you were right in front of it, it would be like being blasted by several shotguns at once. If you were lucky, you only lost limbs. And if you weren't, you went home in several buckets.

He yelled a single word: "Grenade." But knew she was moving too fast to stop. In two more paces, she'd be right over it – so he dived.

His body landed hard on top of Casey's, crashing down on her, and he covered her head and upper body, just as she broke the first beam. He almost carried them through it, but the explosion was instantaneous, near deafening, and the walls and ground shook beneath them.

Alex felt the bullet-like projectiles batter his armored suit, and the percussive blast smashed at his eardrums. Many of the projectiles penetrated right through the super-tough material of his armor to embed in his flesh. Concrete rained down for several more seconds.

Eventually he rolled off the female HAWC, groaning. He sat back against the wall and held his head. The siren scream of perforated eardrums was agonizing but was nothing compared to the body-wide sensation of raggedness and pulverization from the explosive force and ripping fragments. Smoke rose from his body, and his hyper-strong suit was shredded in places. He opened his eyes as Casey sat up and also held her head.

"*Fuuuck.*"

The scream in Alex's ears subsided as his unique metabolism rushed to repair the damage. "Claymore; laser mesh," he said between clenched teeth, but doubted she could hear him yet. He looked at his hands and arms – the armor was abraded, smoking, and in some places cracked and punctured. Blood leaked from the holes. He grabbed her with one hand and dragged her toward him. "How you doing? HAWC, are you operational?"

Casey nodded. "Bitch of a headache, but I'm fully operational, sir." Then, "Thanks, boss." Her eyes ran over his body. "How the hell are *you* doing?"

He felt at his shoulder. There was a two-inch rent in the Kevlar wrapping, and damage deep in the meat of the trapezius muscle. The armor plating only covered the larger flesh areas, like chest, thighs, biceps and skull, but over the high movement areas were armadillo plates with an additional Kevlar weave.

He reached a finger into the wound, and ground his teeth. Beside him, Casey watched. Alex dug around, pulled free a jagged shard of steel and dropped it to the floor with a clink. He rolled his shoulder. "I'll get the rest later." He quickly sent a message to Hondo, then stood and pulled Casey to her feet. "Payback time."

She nodded. "I heard that."

"This time you stay in behind, there could be more."

Alex headed into the smoke. As he ran the fragments of metal embedded in his skin were pushed out and fell to the ground. The wounds sizzled for a second or two, then began to close.

* * *

Hondo Henderson heard, then felt, the explosion and hunkered down with Zegarelli. A few minutes later, there came a small vibration on his wrist and held up a hand.

"Zeg; hold up." He read the two words on the tiny comm. screen on his forearm they used for silent messaging. "Damn." He snorted. "Laser claymores."

"Knew it," Zegarelli said. "Sounded like RDX packed in behind steel."

"So we expected booby traps and now we know which type." Hondo looked along their corridor.

"And boss just ran into one," Zeg added, and grimaced. "Fuckers are hard to see, even tougher to navigate. And we ain't the Arcadian."

"Shit, if only we brought a demolition expert." Hondo clicked his fingers. "Wait, yes we did."

"Then it's your lucky day." Zegarelli chuckled. "Get moving, ya big moose. You can be my shield."

Together they sped along the corridors, finding numerous puddles of blood – obviously places where some of the security personnel had tried to hold back the inevitable.

In a few minutes they came to the reactor room, and could both feel and hear the hum of the machinery working behind the thick door that carried a nuclear warning symbol on it. There was a security pad, and Hondo keyed in the access code.

He eased the door open a fraction of an inch, and then stuck a small cord in through the gap, turning it in his fingers. The snake camera's image was displayed on his wrist screen.

"Clear." He retracted the camera.

They lifted their weapons and Hondo pulled the door open. Then the big men went in fast, Hondo taking the left and Zegarelli the right, scanning for the slightest movement, human shape, or any potential trap.

They took cover and then switched to using technology – first magnifying every corner and cranny in the large, laboratory-clean room, and sliding their scopes to thermal to check for body heat. However, with so much background heat from the generators it was hard to get a clear reading.

"Jesus H. Christ." Zegarelli whispered.

Hondo joined him. "Yeah, I see it."

What their scanners did highlight were the laser beams crisscrossing the generator room. Shaped charges were packed all along the control-rod housing, the generators, and the cooling water pipes inflow – dozens of them.

"The bastards must have brought it all in a freaking wheelbarrow," Zeg said through clamped teeth.

"What are our chances?' Hondo asked.

Zegarelli let his eyes move over the charges, all of them behind a laser mesh. "If I can get to them, I can disarm them ... but." He began to grin. "The beauty of dealing with amateurs is they assume just because *they've* only got one way in or out, we do too."

"Okay, whatta you need?"

Zegarelli pointed up. Above them, the reactor room's ceiling was filled with pipes, vents, and hoists for moving heavy machinery around. "I'm betting they'll have secured the floor from access to their explosives, but they won't have had time to secure the entire room."

Hondo followed his gaze. The ceiling was high, fifty feet, but about twelve feet up from them there was a large elbow of piping. It ran to the ceiling, and then there were more pipes and railings that led over the floor area and close to the shaped charges.

'Doable," Zegarelli said. "All I need is a big buddy to give me a boost."

Hondo didn't hesitate and bent a knee. He meshed his fingers together. "Going up."

Zegarelli backed up and then ran at him, placed a boot into Hondo's hands, and leaped as the big HAWC lifted his arms, catapulting the smaller man to the first handhold twelve feet above them.

Zegarelli was short but powerfully muscled like a circus performer. In no time, he was at the roof and swinging from pipe to pipe, railing, and chain, and then using anything he could find as a handhold. Soon he was over his objective target area, and he hooked one arm over a pipe so he could remove a length of rope from his pack.

"Piece of cake," he said as he secured it to an overhead pipe, did a quick loop under his arms, and began to lower himself.

Hondo watched as his colleague dropped, going from fifty feet above the floor to twenty in a few seconds. From the corner of his eye he spotted the almost invisible glow of tiny

quickly and cleanly were too astronomical to count. They were probably all as good as dead – the hostages, the intruders, and the HAWCs.

It was a sacrifice they were trained to accept. But Alex couldn't help his mind straying to his wife, Aimee, and his son, Joshua. He shook the images away. This was why HAWCs were supposed to have zero attachments; you had to be prepared to sacrifice yourself, and worrying about others caused hesitation.

He knew that every time he acted, it was to save countless other Aimees and Joshuas out there. He felt the prickling sensation that was like someone in the dark watching him, and he quickly shut down the thoughts, not wanting the boy to pick up on his agitation. Joshua was special; Joshua saw everything.

Alex blinked and turned to Casey.

"New plan."

What Alex didn't know was that the boy was already in his head.

CHAPTER 04

Buchanan Road, Boston, Massachusetts

Ten-year-old Joshua Hunter sat cross-legged on his bedroom floor. Sitting beside him was his dog, Torben – Tor for short. The German shepherd towered over the boy and must have weighed in at 150 pounds if it was an ounce. When they took the dog out walking, some people remarked that he looked more like a bear. Except there was no lumbering gait, just the lightness of foot, deep chest, and muscled flanks that told of immense speed and strength held in check. Plus, unlike the dark eyes of a bear, Tor's eyes were an ice blue and radiated intelligence. The dog was a special type of animal from the Guardian breeding program. Unbeknown to the family, he was a military experiment. A little like Alex, Joshua's father.

The pair sat stone still, staring at a blank wall. Joshua's eyes were pupilless and completely white, just like the dog's now. They didn't see the wall, or the room, or anything in the house. Together they watched what was happening many miles away – in the Robert Emmett Ginna Nuclear Power Plant, in Ontario, New York.

CHAPTER 05

"This is so gonna be fun."

Harper and Charlotte stood on the small landing looking down onto the control room floor. The fourteen remaining hostages were cuffed to railings, door handles, and, in some cases, each other. Harper felt nothing when he looked at their pale, tear-streaked, terrified faces. To him they were little more than human shields – or maybe excess baggage.

He would have executed all of them except for the waste of ammunition, and for the fact that whoever was on the other side of the door right now wouldn't dare use explosives with all the human sheep tied up inside. He smiled as he wondered whether they might knock, as the door was sealed from the inside and the corridor was a little narrow for a battering ram.

Before the corridor camera had gone dark, he'd seen just two Spec Forces operatives arrive. He chuckled softly; he'd pit himself, Charlotte, or any one of his Praetorian team of death dealers against any soldiers the American military could throw at them. They'd trained hard, and trained to kill.

And Harper had one more advantage. He slowly opened his shirt and then took it off, displaying a body covered in the carvings. There were strange runes and eyes, so many staring eyes covering his torso. Some of the wounds were fresh and still weeping.

Yeah, he had one more big advantage: he had a god on his side. He raised a fist. "She is coming!" he yelled over the heads of the people in the room.

The hostages flinched even more, and the eyes of his acolytes brimmed with zeal.

"She is coming," they repeated like an evangelical choir.

He grinned, knowing that they didn't really know what that meant, and he didn't care as long as they followed him. He held up the weapon in his arms and lifted its muzzle toward the heavy metal door before lounging back against the concrete wall. He looked forward to the coming negotiations.

"This is so gonna be fun."

* * *

Hondo joined Alex and Casey, his shoulders still sagging.

"Zeg's gone," Alex said. "This is where we are at. So get your head back in the game, soldier."

The massive HAWC shook himself down like a big dog. "Yeah, yeah." He nodded. "Got it, boss."

Alex explained his strategy, and both Casey and Hondo fell back a few steps to crouch behind him on either side, guns drawn.

Alex felt around the doorframe. He pushed, exerting pressure – there was very little give in what was basically a seven-foot-tall riveted steel plate. He pushed a little more, and heard the telltale groan of the metal hinges, noting where they were: two on one side, and only the bolting mechanism on the right.

He backed up several dozen paces, and began to suck in deep breaths as he mentally ran through his action. He could still feel the tension coming through the door, and also the aggression and confidence of the intruders. But there was also the cold fear of the hostages like waves of static, and their pain, as well as the agony of the dead – their screaming wraiths swirled in the room, demanding vengeance.

He let it all wash over him, and allowed the demand for retribution to soak into his bones. *Make them pay*, something whispered deep inside him. *Make them bleed, make them hurt, and make them know fear. Make them fear … me.*

Alex absorbed it all, letting it fuel him.

He took a last look at the door handle, then the center of the door. He balled his fists, and exploded forward.

In a few paces, he was traveling at thirty miles per hour, and at three feet out he threw a hand to the door handle and lowered his shoulder.

He hit the metal door with an explosive force that combined all of his mass, speed, and great strength. The door blew off its hinges and dragged with it the locking mechanism. He held the huge plate in front of him like a shield.

As Alex's super-charged metabolism took over, time slowed, but only for him.

A split second of shock for the intruders, and then the gunfire started. Heavy rounds peppered the steel door, making it clang like a cymbal against his shoulder. He counted off the rounds, and knew the gun types by their distinctive discharge signatures. There were a helluva lot of weapons.

Casey and Hondo reached around the doorframe to pick their targets with deadly accuracy, bringing them down with centered headshots every time.

Alex lowered his door shield, his own gun drawn, looking for the detonator unit and who was in control of it. He saw two people above him behind a balcony railing. One of them pointed a strange weapon at him, and fired.

Alex quickly snapped the door shield up. The impact, if that's what it was, was noiseless, but he felt the steel shudder in his hands. However, where he expected to see some sort of dent in the door, a cannonball-sized section began to dissolve like the iron was made of gossamer.

Alex couldn't believe what he was seeing, as he watched the steel continue to melt away. He flung the dissolving door to the side.

He stood his ground, unshielded, staring back into the manic eyes of the young man holding the weird weapon. Beside him was a woman, equally as thrilled, aiming what looked like a German H&K FP6 combat shotgun.

Alex began to move, fast. But it was at the same time she pulled her trigger.

Alex was faster than any human being on Earth, but his speed was always going to come off second against a discharging shotgun.

The 12-gauge blast took him in the center of his chest, shattering the already blast-damaged armor panels and slamming him into a concrete wall.

Fool, of course they'd have armor-piercing rounds, a voice sneered at him with disgust. *Now get the fuck up!*

Unbelievably, Alex started to rise. But the shotgun barked again. His face – it burned, and then everything went dark.

* * *

Joshua was thrown to the floor. The huge dog yelped as it, too, was smashed sideways. The dog was up first, shaking itself and blinking its pale blue eyes. Blood dripped from its mouth, but it still moved to use its nose to help Joshua upright.

The boy struggled up and felt his chest and then his face. He grimaced and sobbed – the pain was real, but the physical side was nothing compared to the mental torture of being inside his father's mind when he'd taken the blasts.

Joshua had been assessing the attackers, counting their number and deciding which of them were the bigger threats. But then his father had been blown across the room, and shot again on the ground. Joshua and Tor felt the impact. They both felt the tearing of muscle, sinew, and bone. Joshua knew his father was hurt, *bad.*

Joshua had seen the glee in the faces of his father's tormenters and he knew that they wouldn't be finished until he was obliterated. His father needed to fight back or he'd be killed, brutally.

Joshua had tried to reach him again and couldn't – Alex Hunter was unconscious and had shut down.

The boy crawled back to face the wall, and Tor came and sat beside him. He turned and looked up into the dog's eyes. "I need to go back. I have to help." He swallowed, and then: "I need to go into the dark place."

Tor shut its luminous eyes and lowered its head.

"I know, but I have to. You don't have to come this time." Joshua sighed, but felt his spirits lift as the dog put a huge paw on his shoulder. "Thank you."

Having Tor with him made him feel safe. He turned back to the wall, and the dog whined for a moment, but then its eyes seemed to roll back in its head to become completely white, just like Joshua's.

"This way," he whispered.

CHAPTER 06

"Kill 'em all!"

Casey and Hondo stared in shock and then anger. They were too professional to let Alex's injuries derail their attack, and instead used them as education – they were dealing with weaponry more advanced than they expected. Whatever the pulse weapon was, they needed to make sure it never struck them – if it could do that to a solid iron door Alex Hunter had held, then it'd blow them to pieces.

The HAWC pair fell back on their basic engagement strategy: if your adversary's firepower exceeded your own, then remove their firepower.

Casey took out a hockey puck–sized device from a belt pouch and slid the instrument into the center of the floor. Alex wouldn't have let her use it in the control room, but he wasn't here now, so …

"Fire in the hole!"

Men and women dived for cover, though it wasn't an explosive that was about to be discharged but a magnetized pulse. Every iron-based object in the room would become strongly magnetized for many minutes, and that meant metal objects with moving parts ceased to work – guns, rifles, all the way down to wristwatches. But also much of the nuclear monitoring equipment.

The wave blasted out, washing over everyone and everything. It made their teeth hurt and brains tingle. On the balcony, the guy with the pulse-gun lowered it and grinned, seeing his female comrade click hard on her gun's trigger without effect. He seemed to be relishing the confrontation. He pointed. "Okay, team, old school. Take 'em down."

Casey summed up their adversaries in an instant: the ones they had taken out so far were little more than crash test dummies. They walked into rounds, had crap aim, and seemed to be enthusiastic but being poorly trained ideologues. But the ones remaining were more hardcore, and the way they moved told her they were going to be able to put up more of a fight.

Good, she thought. Right now, all she wanted was for them to stay upright so she could inflict some real damage.

"Kill 'em all!" she yelled as she and Hondo exploded into the room. Hondo took the largest of the intruders head on, lifting him off his feet and slamming him into a wall, and then used his massive forehead to pulverize the man's face. Another of the intruders leaped on Hondo's back and tried to jam an eight-inch hunting blade into his neck, but all he found was impenetrable armor.

Casey Franks came to her feet to immediately block a straight arm strike to her face, lifted her leg in time to stop being swept off her feet by a roundhouse kick, then returned fire with a knuckle jab to the guy's Adam's apple. He went down choking.

The next was a wild-eyed woman brandishing a blade in each hand and whipping them around in some sort of martial arts swing. When she was just close enough in to strike, Casey stepped in even closer, striking her face with the flat of her hand,

and squashing her septum flat with a wet crunch. The woman dropped the knives and sat down, holding her face in surprise.

The man and woman on the balcony watched as half-a-dozen of the hardened attackers came at Casey and Hondo. The other intruders swarmed but seemed content to wait their turn.

For every combatant Casey and Hondo knocked down, another took their place. Armored fists crunched into faces, knives jabbed at torsos and throats, and steel rods came down on elbows and knee joints, all trying to find weaknesses.

"Fuck this." Casey knew they were being beaten back, and in only a few more minutes the EMP grenade's effects would wear off. Whatever gun that smirking asshole above them had used on Alex would be back in full force. She had no doubt he'd deploy it against them, whether or not his own people were in the line of fire.

In the end it was sheer numbers that brought them down. A heavy metal baton clanged against the back of Hondo's helmet with enough power to force the big man's head forward into a fist. He went to his knees. More boots, fists, batons, and knives beat and stabbed at him. The sharp objects couldn't penetrate his armor, but the blows to the armored head would still make the brain slosh around in his skull. He went down flat. Concussion always came next.

Casey tried to fight her way closer to give Hondo cover, just as a perfect roundhouse kick, delivered by a professional with a heavy fucking boot, caught her across the lower face. She saw stars for a second or two and staggered to the side.

Blood was in the water now. She wanted to rip their throats out, but her vision swam, and the guy who kicked out at her was back, raining an avalanche of punches, kicks, and elbow strikes on her. She blocked most, but he was good and a few got through, and then a lot got through, rattling her senses more and more.

Something got jammed into the back of her legs and she went down on her knees beside Hondo, who was lying prone.

The big man managed to open one swollen eye and grin at her, showing bloody teeth. *Bad day*, he mouthed.

An enormous blow from behind knocked her forward onto her fists.

"Stay the fuck down!" someone screamed.

But Casey gritted her teeth and struggled back up onto one knee. "Never!" she yelled as they converged on her. She took the punches and kicks, but refused to go down. She grabbed at a leg, bringing her armor-plated forearm down on the knee to hear the satisfying noise of the joint separating and the leg bending at an angle it was never meant to.

From the corner of an eye now clouded by red mist, she saw the smirking man start to run his hands over a panel on his weapon, and tiny lights blink on along its casing. It was coming back online.

I'm fucked, she thought.

She ripped free her short-bladed knife and slashed sideways into the meat of a thigh as a leg came at her for another kick. She struggled to her feet, but another blow across the eyes from something cold and heavy made her suddenly feel disconnected from her own body.

Casey Franks felt her arms grabbed as she was held up toward the smirker. The people holding her pulled her arms tight into a cross, perhaps so when she was exploded from the pulse her viscera wouldn't splash them.

The maniac lifted the muzzle of his gun, but the woman next to him took it from him – she obviously wanted the pleasure of the kill. She aimed.

"Fuck you!" Casey stared up at them. She waited for her release.

Something exploded behind her, and bodies literally flew into the air. Screams, shouts, and then the smirker and his babe suddenly looked a lot less smug. Casey knew what it had to be. She'd seen that fear in faces before – the Arcadian was loose.

"Welcome to hell, fuckers." She threw her head back and began to laugh.

* * *

Alex was in a deep and dark pit. Pain flared across his rib cage and he knew his armored suit had been obliterated, meaning he must have taken multiple blasts. The open armor meant his exposed and bloody chest was a mess of shredded flesh and splintered and pitted bone.

His face was no better as the second blast had taken him from the chest upward. Raw bone showed on his cheek and forehead, and his top lip was shredded, giving him a skull-like grin. His eyes ran with blood.

If anyone had been watching they would have seen the open wounds begin to bubble at the edges and sizzle as if they were burning. In a way they were, as Alex's body metabolized at a much higher temperature than normal people's bodies did. His freakish metabolism would repair him hundreds of times faster than a normal human being could recover, but every second of it still hurt like hell. The wounds slid together. Bones popped back into place and a few tiny wisps of smoke rose from the torn flesh as the healing process generated intense heat.

Alex tried to rise from the dark pit of pain, but found himself bound – deep in his id there were now chains at his neck, wrists, and ankles.

Noooo! he screamed in the void of his mind. He knew what it meant: he'd lost control of his body. The Other was free.

There was someone with him, though, as a small hand was placed on his shoulder in the eternal darkness, immediately calming him.

Then came a whispered voice: Joshua's.
Let it happen.

* * *

He opened sticky eyes, feeling the pain, and reveling in it. Pain was good, pain meant physical sensation and life ... it meant he was free.

The Other turned his head slowly. He took it all in through bloody eyes – the big HAWC, Hondo, down; Casey beaten to a pulp and being held up, spread wide, waiting for the woman on the railing to blow her apart. The crowd jeered, lusting for the captive's blood.

No one was watching him. And why would they? To them he was just another bloody corpse among the many. He smiled as he saw their hate manifested in their expressions, words, and actions. He drew on it, feeding himself. The red mist of aggression and anger washed over him in a colossal wave of fury.

The Other tested the body. He looked at his hands as if seeing them for the first time, and turned them over, then back. He lifted a hand and made a fist, feeling the armored plating over his fingers and knuckles pop and crackle as he applied pressure. He then moved his toes, and worked his jaw. Good, he was in total control.

He slowly sat up, then dragged himself to his feet. He looked at the crowd and watched the intruders, the infant warriors. These children think they know war? He ground his teeth and his body seemed to swell with energy. These play actors think they know pain?

Alex Hunter's battered body controlled by the Other exploded forward and catapulted into the first of the intruders. He struck the man with such force his body smashed into the wall so hard, all he left was a red streak and a few teeth embedded in the concrete.

The next of the intruders was a little faster and spun, reacting quickly and professionally, swinging an extended metal riot baton. The heavy rod could break bones and definitely put a good-sized dent in your skull if it connected. It was impossible to make out the assailant's expression as he wore a Guy Fawkes mask, but when he brought the bar down, the Other caught it, easily pulled it from his hands, and then swung it back down so hard on the center of his head that it traveled all the way between his eyes with a sickening, eggshell-like crunch. The Other grinned as the Guy Fawkes mask continued to smile. He moved on before the body dropped.

He darted from person to person in a macabre dance, smashing his fists into faces and chests pile-driver hard, so the ribs shattered, collapsing lungs and piercing hearts, obliterating them. Where Alex Hunter sometimes pulled punches, the Other enjoyed inflicting pain, injury, and death. He truly believed that he was what the Arcadian was supposed to be. He was the deadly weapon the military had really wanted.

In the chaos he found it was impossible to control himself – if he'd even wanted to – the frenzy of blood and pain intoxicating. And the looks on their faces when they beheld his nightmarish mutilated visage brought him joy, as their fear and shock were his food and drink.

Then the Other was grabbed from the side, and a stiletto blade sank into the meat of his shoulder where his armored suit had been shredded by the shotgun blast. He left the blade there and spun, grabbing his attacker around the head and ripping it hard to the side, demolishing neck vertebrae. The young man's swarming comrades were shocked into momentary immobility as they saw him staring back at them with a surprised expression on a head now facing fully backward.

The Other laughed as he thrust the body toward them. The attackers began to fall back then, hesitant and unsure. *That's right*, he thought grimly; *hand-to-hand combat can be brutal in a live-or-die game.*

"Oh, for fuck's sake!" the guy on the railing yelled and then showed his teeth in disgust at his warriors' fear. He turned to a group of larger, fitter men and women up on the landing, all in night-black combat fatigues – obviously his elite shock troops.

"Jaz, Will, Carter, fuck this guy up."

The three of them leaped over the railing, two pulling blades, but a third lifting a pair of nunchucks from his belt, the heavy, weighted, wooden sticks on a short chain moving at speed. The woman next to the smirker tried to get a bead on Alex Hunter with the pulse weapon, and the Other was conscious of its power, knowing that another blast with or without his armor shielding would probably melt a dinner plate–sized hole right through him. He thought he'd be safe while he was in the midst of their fighters.

He was wrong. The woman fired anyway.

The Other leaped out of the way far faster than she could adjust her aim, and the released pulse passed through the shoulder of one of the attackers to slam into the concrete wall like an invisible wrecking ball, making a foot-deep crater. The struck man stood upright in shock, his entire shoulder gone, the remains of his left arm flopped at his feet.

The woman cursed through her bared teeth as the weapon recharged. She tried to follow the Other but he moved too fast toward the massive steel door he had used to enter. She gave up, and instead swung the muzzle toward Casey Franks.

* * *

Casey's lips pulled back into a twisted grin as she stared into the odd-shaped bulb that was the barrel of the pulse weapon. It didn't matter: live or die, she knew that soon the Arcadian would annihilate every one of these assholes. There would be no prisoners. There would be only smashed bodies. She knew her death would be quick and painless, but theirs would be a lot more agonizing and bloody.

She reveled in the mayhem she could hear behind her, and she saw the flicker of doubt cross the faces of the youthful leaders up on the landing.

"Harper, check this." The woman lifted the gun, and in the second between her brain ordering the action to pull the trigger and *actually* pulling the trigger, the massive steel door that Alex had snatched up flew from behind Casey to embed itself in the concrete wall – taking the woman's upper torso and head with it. Her upper half smashed flat to the wall like a bug on a windshield.

"Ha!" Casey whooped as the visible remains of the woman's body spasmed then hung there. Body fluids leaked down, her arms dropped, and the weapon clattered to the ground.

Beside her, Harper's eyes went wide with shock, and he fumbled in his pocket for something. Casey could bet what it was – the detonator switch to blow the nuclear plant.

But the split second he fumbled and delayed was all the Arcadian needed. Casey watched the HAWC leader spring twenty feet to the railing to land in front of Harper. The guy's hand came from his pocket holding the detonator, a small black box with a keypad. If he'd planned on typing anything into it, he had missed his opportunity. Alex gripped his wrist, hard, and then harder. Harper gritted his teeth and his eyes began to bulge.

Silence filled the cavernous control room, as all eyes turned to the pair. Even from where Casey was she could hear the bones in the guy's wrist fracture like dry twigs.

Alex stared into the man's eyes as pain contorted his features until the detonator fell from his now useless fingers. But Alex didn't let up, and he continued to squeeze until the hand bulged with fluid and the flesh between it and the forearm was compressed into pulverized bone and sinew held together by skin. The hand flopped.

"You freak!" the man screamed into Alex's mutilated face. "Hell rises and She is coming. And you won't be able to stop Her." The man grinned though the pain still twisted his youthful features. "You are insects, dust – nothing but food for Her larder." He jerked his head forward, catching Alex on the torn cheekbone.

A fatal error. Alex's head didn't budge with the impact, but he returned the favor, launching his own head forward to strike the man's face, causing his head to bounce back onto the concrete.

"You won't need to wait for Hell to rise." Alex let go of the guy's ruined limb and placed his hand over the man's face. "I'll send you to it." He smashed the head into the concrete wall. The first time there came a cracking sound, but Alex did it again, and again, harder each time, the collisions becoming more brutal, a wet thumping until the back of his skull was flattened against the concrete.

"Jesus." Even Casey grimaced.

Alex let him go, and his body slid down the wall, leaving a long red streak. Harper Van Owen's rebellion had ended as violently as he wished. But only for him and a few others.

The men holding Casey's arms just stared, mouths open. Casey snorted her delight at their distraction and used it to jerk one toward her, then swept a leg around to knock him from his feet. He let go of her arm, and Casey dragged her short-bladed knife from its calf sheath, then slammed it down into the side of his neck. But rather than leave it embedded there, she yanked it free and swung it backhanded into the man holding her other arm. The double strike happened in under three seconds and looked more like ballet than combat.

One of the last of Harper's elite force, a muscular young woman with a tattoo of a tear under her left eye, came at Casey with her own blade, a hunting knife with a serrated back. She held it deftly, feinted once and then lunged.

Casey parried the blow and the two short steel teeth clanged together time and again. Casey spun, letting her blade bounce off the woman's, coming back up frighteningly fast, only to be met with matching speed and strength.

From the corner of her eye she saw Alex Hunter watching with excitement. He leaned over the railing. "Kill her!"

Casey tried not to let the words distract her. It wasn't easy, as it hadn't sounded like Alex Hunter at all.

The pair came together, blades locked, and grabbed each other's free arms – big mistake. Casey Franks had trained with the best in hand-to-hand combat, and her skills extended far beyond street brawling, or anything that could be taught by Jihadis or Russian agents.

She used her elbow under the woman's chin, rocking her head back, then jammed her blade into the meat of her throat.

Casey held the blade there, sunk deep, and moved her face in close. The woman's mouth and eyes were wide in surprise. Casey stared into her eyes and saw that her blade gleamed in the back of her open mouth. She grinned. "Yeah, hurts, huh?"

She swept the razor-sharp knife to the side, slicing through the woman's throat. Blood spurted and the woman gagged wetly then fell to the side like a tree.

Casey spun to the remaining intruders. "Get on the fucking ground!"

Around her, a few knives and metal bars clanged to the floor, and the men and women went to their knees with hands on heads. Casey Franks snorted with disdain as she picked up one of the handguns. Her eyes went to the hostages, who seemed even more fearful of her and Alex Hunter than they were of the terrorists.

She crossed to Hondo, who groaned when she lifted his head. "How you doin', sleeping beauty?"

He coughed and blood speckled his lips. "Like coming off a three-day whisky binge."

"You'll live." She let him go. "We're bugging out, so stand tall, soldier." She turned to Alex. "On you orde—"

Casey saw that Alex was staring straight ahead, his eyes vacant. He gripped the railing so hard his hands vibrated from the strain. The metal began to compress with a sound like screaming banshees and then impossibly, began to bend upward.

"*Noooo.*" The railing broke in Alex's hands, and a line of blood appeared from one nostril.

Oh shit, she thought. She should have known from his brutal voice.

"Boss?" She stayed where she was, watching as the man known as the Arcadian tried to pull the demons back into their cage. Or rather, just one demon.

Casey always wondered whether the Other was a totally separate entity, or Alex Hunter himself, the real one, unbound, the manifestation of everything dark about a human being's psyche. His "monster from the id", Colonel Jack Hammerson had muttered once. She wasn't sure she wanted to know and hadn't asked.

She turned to the hostages, who were all looking on the verge of panic at their supposed rescuer's transformation into something more beast than man.

"Hey!" she yelled, dragging their attention from Alex. "You will place your hands on your head, and proceed to the front car park in a single line. Armed officers will meet you there, and you will *not* lower your hands until you have been certified. If you do, you *will* be shot. If you step out of the line, you *will* be shot. If you deviate in any way from our or their instructions, you *will* be shot. Is that clear?"

She waited. "*Is that fucking clear?*" Casey fired the gun she held twice into one of the bodies at her feet. "*Clear?*"

It was enough to terrify them into action, and they nodded jerkily, clamping hands even tighter on heads.

She turned back to Alex. His face was wet from perspiration and his eyes burned like a furnace.

"Wait." His eyes focused and stared down at the remaining intruders. "Zip cuff them, except for that one." He pointed toward one of the intruders. It was the last of Harper Van Owens's elite, the one named Jaz. "Leave that one. He stays."

"We surrender." Jaz's lip curled. "I know the law, and I know our rights." One of the other intruders beside him lowered his hands to pull off his mask. His youthful face was streaked with sweat, but following Jaz's rebellious words, his eyes had also become defiant.

"Fuck you!" he yelled up at Alex.

Others began to follow his lead.

"Shoot him," Alex said.

Casey didn't blink as she shot the young man dead. Hands went straight back onto heads.

Alex leaped over the railing and dropped the eight feet to the ground, landing lightly. His face was healing rapidly and smoke rose from the wounds in curling wafts, but he still looked like something from the pits of Hell. The men and women backed away when he held up the detonator.

"You were prepared to kill millions of people when you blew this facility." He glared. "Men, women, children."

"I surrender." Jaz shrugged. "I'm a lawyer, soon, and I have rights."

His eyes still burned with defiance, and Alex leaned in toward him. "You're in my world now, and in that world, you don't have any rights." He nodded to Casey.

Casey moved among the intruders, jerking their arms down behind their backs. She zip cuffed them all, except Jaz. She leaned around him to sneer into his face, "Enjoy the party. Or what's left of it."

"Take them out," Alex ordered. "I have questions for this would-be assassin."

Casey sneered at Jaz again then she turned to the hostages, her face hostile and in no mood for disagreements. "Everyone else, now, single file, move the fuck out of here."

She helped Hondo up and looked at the small pad on her wrist to read some data. "Helo inbound in four, boss."

Alex nodded. "I'll only need two." His eyes were like death itself, and his face was even worse.

Jaz suddenly seemed unsure of himself. He licked dry lips. "Uh, what … do you want to know?"

CHAPTER 07

Harvard University, Cambridge, Massachusetts – Languages Department

Professor Matt Kearns read his morning messages. The first was from a name he didn't recognise, and he opened a German language mail from a Detective Ed Heisen of the Berlin Kripo – the *Kriminalpolizei* – the equivalent of NYPD Detective Bureau.

He read, his brows knitting. The guy wanted to get in touch about a series of gruesome murders in Berlin, but then it went all haywire with talk of little people from the future, and civilians being disintegrated.

Matt groaned. He hated this sort of stuff, mainly because it always intrigued the hell out of him. He tapped his lips for a moment.

"Okay, Detective Heisen, I'm putting you on the *maybe-list* for now."

He moved to the next message. This one was from his friend at a Pompeii dig describing her work and what they'd found. He then did as she suggested and opened the image file, squinting at the faint scratches in the stone tablet.

Maria Monti was an extremely competent archaeologist, and in past times, Matt had worked with her on several digs and translations; she was like a bloodhound when it came to uncovering artifacts. She worked hard, researched deeply, and then only dug where she knew there was a high probability for discovery. Rarely did she come up empty-handed.

Maria was a little confused by the writing she'd discovered among some Pompeii remains. She had expected Latin, and though the inscription looked a little like Latin and had a number of familiar aspects, there were also many words and symbols that didn't make any sense to her. As she had hit a roadblock, it seemed her plan B was to reach out to Matt.

"Well, let's have a look then."

His brows slowly came together as he leaned forward to inspect the first image. As well as Latin he saw Etruscan, Greek, even Phoenician lettering all blended together. He sat back and folded his arms. "Too primitive for that time." The crease between his eyes deepened. "So why were you there, then?"

Matt knew that seeing the ancient form of Latin at Pompeii was the equivalent of finding a street sign in Brooklyn written in Old English, like the stylized written version in *Cædmon's Hymn* from 650 AD – it was near incomprehensible, out of time, and out of place.

He focused, pulling back a little so as to remove himself from the granular level of identifying the individual alphabet of each language, and instead trying to read the mishmash of ancient tongues as a single message.

There seemed to be disparate words. And some were repeated. Perhaps because some of the text was disjointed, he thought.

"*Τάρταρος* – Tartarus," he whispered the antiquated Greek word for Hell. Tartarus was a netherworld where the souls of the dead were sent. A place ruled by Pluto, their version of the devil, and depending on which cultural time and location, a place of despair and damnation. The Romans had assimilated a lot of words, customs, and even gods from the ancient Greeks, but the word for the Underworld was still rare at that time.

Matt made some notes and then returned to the text fragments. He squinted at the ancient words, trying to draw more from the faint lines. "Could be ..." He wrote more notes, then rearranged the words, turning the scrambled Latin and Phoenician hybrids into a more modern Latin. "*Illa vetus sectae*." He frowned at what he had written, and then translated into English. "The followers, or sect, of Her ... or maybe more like She."

Matt knew ancient Rome had a number of female goddesses – there was Juno, the queen of goddesses, Minerva, Venus, Ceres, Diana, and many more. Maybe these people worshipped one of them. He scribbled down everything he could, and then tried to tease out more, but the rest was indecipherable.

"Okay, let's see what we got." He rubbed his jaw. "A reference to Hell, and some sort of She-worshipping cult. Also, 'beware' ... hmm, or 'be fearful' maybe, 'of them that are of all of us'." Matt sat back. "'Of all of us' – what does that mean?" He rested his chin on his fist – there was more: "'She must be fed'."

Matt sat back. "'Beware them that are of all of us'? Of all men? Is 'them' supposed to be representative of all people?" He sighed. *That doesn't make sense*, he thought. *And if you're going to give a warning, then why write it in a language no one in Pompeii could probably even understand? And what's with "she must be fed"?*

He was sure he was translating the words correctly, but their meaning eluded him. Matt started to type out a response to Maria, but stopped, not knowing how to frame it. He checked his watch. Maria had given him a voice-over-internet address and a good time zone overlap to have a chat about what he found out – much better than trying to lay it all out in an email.

He clicked the icon, and the familiar *boing-pop* sounded, indicating he was online and available. He saw that Maria was there, and selected her smokey-eyed profile. The link popped again, and then the attractive dark-haired woman's face filled the screen as she sat closer.

"Buongiorno, handsome; long time no see." She smiled, showing a row of perfect teeth in an olive-skinned face. "What have you been up to?"

Matt swept his long hair back and returned the smile. "I've been around, just hanging out and waiting for some beautiful Italian woman to send me a dead language or two as an ice breaker."

She sat straighter. "So, it *was* a dead language, not Latin? I knew it."

He chuckled. "Yes and no. Your language fragment would have become Latin in maybe another thousand years or so. Weird, considering the language hadn't been used in that area for that long. Doesn't make any sense." He tilted his head as a thought popped into it. "Hey, what depth was this language fragment found?"

She shook her head. "Same depth as the gladius and the other specimen. The ash and pumice layer showed the same unbroken geological striations, so it hadn't been thrust up, or buried later. Had to have been contemporaneous."

"Damn, there goes that theory."

"Matt, you don't know the half of it. So, anyway, what did it say?"

"Okay, I'll send through the full transcript when we're done here, but in a nutshell, it says: 'Beware', or maybe 'be fearful of them that are of all of us'." Matt laughed. "The local politician maybe?" His face became serious. "Sounds like a warning; does it mean anything to you?"

"A warning, yes, that might make sense." Maria's face remained stony.

"There was a little more," he said. "There were several references to Hell – 'Tartarus'. Plus a few lines indicating they worshipped some sort of female She deity, and also a fragment that translated as: 'She must be fed'. I've checked it several times, and though the words seem right, that sentence means nothing without context."

"Si, si." Maria sighed as she seemed to think it through for a moment. "Well, it was certainly a time of Hell coming to the surface, si?" She looked up, and there was nervousness around her eyes. "Matt, I need you here. There were other ... *specimens* we uncovered. Other things that shouldn't be there – no, no, I think these things shouldn't be *anywhere*." She looked over her shoulder. "Maybe you called too late. They're closing us down, confiscating everything." She licked her lips and leaned closer. "We found bones, but strange, not like human bones."

"Animal bones? Like from horses, sheep or dogs, you mean? Or something more exotic?" Matt knew that the Roman Empire covered the known world at that time and traded in exotic animals. So if she had found elephant bones, he still wouldn't have been that surprised.

"No, I *know* bones, and this is something big and not natural ... unidentifiable. When we tried to get an expert to assist us it seemed we showed our hand. Instead of gaining knowledge we got a platoon of government teppisti, who started sealing off our dig." She lowered her voice. "We managed to save some of the images, more writing, but I can't send it to you as our email and texts might be rerouted. It's only safe to talk face to face; can you come?"

"Maria …" He groan-sighed. "I'm on my spring break."

"Matt, *please*, I wouldn't ask, but this is important. I'll even pay." She smiled anxiously. "Plus I'll cook you your favorite paella."

He laughed. "The one with the big shrimp in it?"

"Of course. A few days holiday, my treat."

He sighed even louder. "So, what about these bones anyway?"

"They –" Her eyes became even wider. "They seemed to be … growing."

CHAPTER 08

USSTRATCOM, Nebraska – debrief

Colonel Jack Hammerson placed a hand on Alex's shoulder and pressed for a moment before letting it drop.

"Good work at the Ginna plant. The information you extracted from the terrorists led us to the local network and financers. We're squeezing them hard to find out a little more about their international accomplices." He looked up and smiled, but with zero humor. "Then we'll pay 'em a visit."

Alex looked at him from the corner of his eye. "Sorry about that last guy."

"It wasn't you." Hammerson waved it away. "Besides, he came to kill. He got what he deserved."

"He surrendered."

"And he still got torn apart; so what? He wouldn't have blinked at the opportunity to kill thousands, hundreds of thousands." Hammerson looked at his protégé. "Don't forget what they did to Zegarelli."

Alex lowered his head. "Yeah, good soldier, gone."

"That is our lot, son. But you all got the result we needed."

"Did you find out anymore about that 'She' character they kept mentioning?" Alex asked. "They seemed to regard it as some sort of powerful person, leader, or even a deity. Might have been their ultimate controller."

Hammerson shrugged. "Nothing in the databases, and never heard it before. We'll open a file on it, and if we get any crossmatches in the future, we'll be ready."

He and Hammerson were on level five of USSTRATCOM's underground research and development laboratories. The huge facility was dug into the bedrock below the base. The first two levels were armor and weapons research plus prototypes, and also firing ranges. Then on the lower levels there was the biological and nuclear research. The lowest level, the one they were on now, had no designated name and was simply marked *classified*. Commander in Chief Jack Hammerson, Alex, and military rank above general knew what went on down here, and none spoke about it above ground.

"Just glad we could save so many of the hostages," Alex said, and stopped before the formidable-looking metal door.

"A good mission. *Almost* perfect." Hammerson turned to face his soldier. "He – *it* – got out, huh?"

Alex exhaled then nodded. "Yeah."

Hammerson grunted. "You've nearly got it under control. Maybe one day we can rid you of the Other forever. But our objective right now is for you to control it, harness it."

"I can and can't control it," Alex said. "So far it returns to its dark place when it decides it's had its fill of blood or vengeance. But I don't know what will happen if it ever decides that it doesn't want to go back."

"Well, you pulled it back, so you're still winning."

"I think I had help this time." Alex jaws clenched for a moment. "But it's getting stronger, Jack. One day it'll be the winner."

"You let me worry about that. That help you mentioned … was it Joshua?"

Alex stared at his commander for a moment before simply shrugging. "Hard to say."

"Doesn't matter." Hammerson slapped his shoulder again. "Like I said, a successful mission is what counts." He went to continue down the corridor, but Alex stopped him.

"Need some time, Jack. Time with my family."

Hammerson smiled broadly. "Of course, take a few days. But after …"

"The Box," Alex finished.

"Yeah." Hammerson's mouth was a flat line. "It got out, and you know what you need to do."

Alex drew in a deep breath and then let it out slowly.

Hammerson walked him to the secure elevator. "Go and give Aimee and Joshua a hug. Say hello to them for me, and tell them we'll all have to catch up for a cookout soon. Come back and do your decompression, and then when it's over, get the hell out of here and enjoy a long break."

Hammerson placed his palm against a pad that traced an outline of his hand and read his prints and DNA. The elevator door slid open. He waved. "Go."

"Okay." Alex entered the reinforced steel elevator and turned. He saluted. "See you tomorrow."

* * *

Hammerson smiled as his protégé was sealed in behind the elevator doors. When Alex was gone, he pulled his phone from his pocket and dialed through to one of the other secure levels above him: PsycWar – the psychological warfare unit.

It was answered immediately. "Colonel."

"You were right – the boy is already displaying telepathic abilities." Hammerson talked softly as he headed back to his office.

"How deep?" The voice got a little more excited.

"Psychic linking at a minimum," Hammerson replied.

"Control?"

"Unknown."

"Can we bring him in?"

Hammerson's mouth turned down. "Not yet. I'll monitor the situation. But it's looking very promising."

"This could be it, Colonel Hammerson; the breakthrough we've been waiting for. Make sure nothing happens to the boy. This is a priority, you understand?" The voice was forceful.

"I'm all over it." Hammerson half-smiled. "And one more thing: don't forget who the fuck you're talking to. Out."

CHAPTER 09

Buchanan Road, Boston, Massachusetts

Joshua Hunter looked deep into the dog's eyes. Torben's unnatural pupils were so pale and blue they seemed to glow like luminous ice. His own gray-blue eyes were like night to Tor's day.

He could hear the animal's thoughts, not just muddled images of warmth, comfort, fun, or hunger, but more complex mental processes. *More like a person than a beast*, Joshua thought. Joshua was also pretty sure that the dog could read him almost as clearly as he did it.

Tor was only two years old but already outweighed Joshua by a good thirty or forty pounds. Joshua smiled; the dog scared some folk, but not him. Often people would even cross the road when they came down the sidewalk. But it never growled, or even acted threatening to anyone, even to other dogs that sometimes yapped. The big shepherd would gaze at them, and then they'd simply stop and back up, as if they suddenly recognized royalty or a leader.

Joshua looked deeper into the dog's eyes. He knew there was the potential for violence there.

In his dreams, the dog spoke to him – Tor told him they were friends, but more than that, they were siblings. Torben recognized Alex Hunter, Joshua's father, as the pack leader, and Aimee as den mother. But Joshua was its pack brother, and as far the huge dog was concerned, all three were to be defended with its life; ferociously, if necessary.

Made sense, Joshua guessed, as Uncle Jack had said Tor came from a program that called the dogs 'Guardians', a special kind of animal bred for their intelligence, strength, and even durability against radiation. Plus they had longer life spans.

Sitting down, the dog still came up to Joshua's chest.

He straightened. "Up."

Tor stood up on its hind legs, towering over the boy. The dog wasn't unstable, or unsure of itself; it seemed quite comfortable standing. Then Joshua nodded and Tor walked around the room on its back legs.

"Cool." Joshua grinned. He never got used to it. "Okay."

He watched as Tor dropped back down and came and sat before him, its mouth split in a normal doggy grin.

"Let's try the link again."

The dog's grin vanished and its face became serious, the pale eyes penetrating deep into his own. Joshua grabbed its large head in his hands and closed his eyes. He concentrated, and in a moment, felt like he was falling, and then there came the familiar sense of rushing along a dark tunnel toward a place of light.

The light intensified into an aura of ice blue, and then he felt the sensation of physical power, and the sounds, smells, and sensations around him became amplified. He opened his eyes.

Wow, he thought. He never got used to this – on the ground in front of him was his own body, laying with eyes open, but pupils rolled back. He turned slowly, and then stood up on Tor's back legs again. It was strange seeing his room from this height, and everything seemed small. He walked to the window and looked out from the second floor onto their front yard and street.

He could see saw Mr. Abernathy watering his lawn. The old man paused and looked up, perhaps sensing he was being watched. His mouth dropped open and he froze. Joshua smiled, wondering what the old man made of seeing a giant dog staring down at him – staring down, but not needing to rest its paws on the windowsill.

Should he wave? His grin widened. Joshua looked at the paws. Another difference between the Guardians and normal dogs – the paw's digits were long, dexterous, and more like short-fingered hands. He waved at his neighbor, and the man's jaw dropped another inch.

Behind him, his bedroom door opened, and he heard his mother scream.

Damn, he thought, quickly dropping down to all fours, closing his eyes and breaking the link.

In a split second he was back in his own body, and Aimee, his mother, was cradling his head,

"*Moooom*, I'm fine. I was just napping."

Aimee's brow was furrowed as she stared into his eyes. Her expression told him she didn't believe a word. He looked past her to Tor. The huge animal sat patiently, watching them. Its grin was back.

* * *

"It happened again," Aimee Weir said with her arms folded tight across her chest.

Alex looked up at the ceiling; above them was Joshua's bedroom, and he bet the boy heard every word they said, no matter how softly they spoke. "You think it's something serious?"

"I don't know, but we need to find out." She began to pace. "It's like he blacks out. His eyes were rolled back and he was non-responsive." She stopped and turned. "And the dog was standing there, freaking *standing* on its hind legs, weird, like a person. It worries me."

"No, the dog loves him, and would protect Joshua with his life. He'd protect all of us; I know it. I can sense it." Alex stood. "Let me talk to him. And then tomorrow we can have the base doctors check him over. Okay?"

She exhaled. "There was something else."

"What?"

She looked up at him, her blue eyes level. "The dog, Tor, its eyes … for a moment they were … Joshua's." She held his gaze as if daring him to disbelieve her. Then she sagged. Alex put his arms around her, and she put her face into the crook of his neck. "I know he's different. But I don't know what's going on anymore," she said almost in a whisper.

Alex kissed the top of her head. "I'll find out."

Aimee looked up at him and nodded. "I shouldn't worry, but …"

Alex chuckled. "You're his mom, it's your job to worry."

"Just talk to him. He opens up to you." She gave him a crooked smile.

He held her at arm's length. "It'll be fine, *he's* fine. In fact, I'll do it right now."

He turned and bounded up the steps to knock on Joshua's door. "Coming in, buddy." He pushed the door open, and found his son on the bed, book open, the one he requested on Norse mythology. *Appropriate*, Alex thought, considering the dog's name, Torben, was the name given to Thor's pet bear. Interestingly, they didn't name him. Joshua had told him that the pack leader, Big Fenrir, had bestowed the name on him.

The huge dog was crouched beside the bed. It sat up and Alex patted its head, noting that it came to his waist now. The thing was already as big as a gray wolf – no, bigger – and seemed to still be growing. Thor's bear was right.

"Jesus, Josh, what are you feeding Tor? I'll need to get him a saddle soon." He scruffed the dog's head again and he was sure it grinned, understanding his joke.

Joshua didn't look up. "Did you know that in Norse mythology, Valhalla is like the Viking heaven, except you only go there if you've died in battle, or died protecting those you love?" He looked up. "Tor said that's where he and all the Guardians will go when they die."

Alex grinned and sat down. "Oh, he told you that did he?"

"Mmm hmm, yep, in my dreams. He said they're like Vikings." His face became solemn. "'Never walk away from home ahead of your ax and sword. You can't feel a battle in your bones or foresee a fight'." He shut the book and sat cross-legged. "That's from the book of Viking wisdom."

"From the Hávámal," Alex said. "I know the quote; it means always being ready." He smiled. "Your Uncle Jack quotes that stuff all the time."

"Be ready to fight, to defend yourself and those you love." He looked up quickly. "But only when you have to, right?"

"Right. And you have the gift of a good brain; always try using that first." Alex looked across at the enormous dog. Its pale eyes never seemed to blink. "Mom says you were unconscious again; blacked out. I think we should –"

"I wasn't blacked out, or even unconscious," Joshua said softly. "You know that."

"I think I do." Alex watched the boy closely. "Tell me about it."

Joshua's brows came together for a moment, as though working through what to tell his father. He shrugged. "It's, um … I can, sort of … get in Tor's head." He looked up. "Become him." He frowned. "No, that's not right; it feels like I'm in there *with* him. He makes me feel strong, brave, and not afraid, when …"

Alex waited. "When?"

"When I see the monster." He looked up, his eyes a little fearful.

"Where did you see the mons …" Alex trailed off. He'd felt the boy inside his own head. He knew what monster he was talking about. "You don't need to worry about that, Josh, ever."

"I know. It's you, but it's not you. I don't fear it when Tor is with me." His eyes watered. "I'm sorry."

"Hey." Alex grabbed him and hugged him. "Nothing, no place, no time, will ever hurt you while I'm here, okay?"

"I know." Joshua leaned back and wiped a sleeve across his nose. "What I can do is cool, but scary at the same time."

"Yes, it can be." Alex had always known that Joshua was different. The Arcadian program that Alex had undertaken seemed also to have had some flow-on effects to Joshua, and passed on many of the physical, and perhaps psychological, differences as well. It remained to be seen whether they turned out to be a good thing or not.

But Alex knew that the mental projection Joshua was able to do was something else entirely. Something beyond Alex's capabilities, unique to his son.

When Joshua had been in his head, it was those times when Alex had been in extreme danger and agitation. In turn, the boy had felt that pain and suffering as if it was his own. *And that can't be a good thing*, Alex thought.

He turned again to the dog, which continued to watch them with its intelligent eyes. Aimee had told him that Torben had also been affected. Was Joshua taking the dog with him on these mental journeys?

Joshua reached forward to lay a hand on Tor's huge head. "I can do it anytime, from anywhere. I can travel into Torben." He turned to Alex. "Watch."

"No –" Alex reached out, but Joshua flopped backward on

the bed. Just like Aimee had said, his eyes rolled back, and his small body was loose like he was in a deep sleep. Alex went to reach for him, but a large paw came down gently on his forearm. He looked at it and first saw that the paw had longer than normal digits that actually gripped like short fingers. He lifted his gaze to the face; Torben's ice blue eyes were now the familiar blue-gray of his and Joshua's.

Alex stared and sensed the duality of the minds in that large head. The dog then rose up onto its hind legs to stand like a human being.

"Holy shit." Alex stared. Tor was easily as tall as he was, and Alex was six-two. The dog opened its mouth, and the jaws worked for a moment, but only low growls and grunts came out.

Thank god. It might have been too much to bear if he heard Joshua's voice coming from the huge animal. Tor smiled down at him, but this time not with the sappy smile of a dog, with just a slight curve of the lips.

"That's enough."

The dog dropped back down to all fours, and shook its head as if to clear it. Immediately Joshua sat up, grinning like he'd just pulled off a cool magic trick.

"See? I'm fine. It's really awesome."

Alex chuckled softly and put his arm around his son's shoulder. "I think, uh, I think we'll just keep that between you and me for now. I'm not sure Mom will think it's as awesome as you do."

Josh nodded. Alex turned to the dog. Tor stared back, and he was sure that it also nodded its understanding to him. No, he *knew* that it did.

* * *

"So?" Aimee waited as Alex came down the stairs.

He opened his arms wide and grinned. "He's fine, just fine."

Her eyes blue narrowed and became diamond hard for a moment as she scrutinized him. "You do know you're the worst liar I've ever met in my life?"

He laughed as he went and poured himself a coffee. "Seriously, Aim, he really is fine. He's just a normal kid. Well, sure, he's a little different to other kids, so his challenges are also a little different. But he's coping, well adjusted, and I think he's got everything under control."

"Why am I skeptical?" she said, moving in closer. "I mean, usually being a little different means he would tend to be reclusive, or likes to sing opera instead of play football, or even be able to play the piano like a concert master at the age of ten. But we already know Josh is physically stronger and smarter than kids his age. And that weird link with the dog seems to manifest whenever you're away on a mission. And that's a mile more than a *little different*."

"Maybe." Alex leaned against the bench. "So, what do you want to do?"

She tilted her head. "Well ..."

He laughed. "You've already got a plan, haven't you?"

She smiled. "You know that conference I have coming up in Naples? The one on new biological petroleum technology?"

"*Yeeees*?" He sipped and waited, already guessing where she was going.

"Well, what about I make it a holiday for the three of us?"

"Naples, this time of year? Sunshine, great food and wine, warm, blue water – sounds terrible." He grinned. "I mean, great idea. And you're taking off Saturday, right?"

She nodded.

"What about you and Josh head down, and I tidy up some stuff here and then meet you in a few days? I've always wanted to drive down along the coast of Italy."

"Sports car, open top?"

"Wind in my hair."

"Yes!" She hugged him, but then held up a finger. "But no dog, okay? Josh needs a break from everything ... just family."

Alex opened his arms. "Well, Torben *is* family. I bet he thinks so."

"Alex ..."

He knew that look, and it had zero give in it. He sighed. "Okay, okay, wouldn't hurt to have Tor take a holiday as well. There are plenty of doggy ranches where he can hang out with some four-legged buddies. Not that he really thinks he is one."

Aimee clapped and hopped on the spot. "I'll need to check Josh's visa." She held up a hand, counting off fingers. "And book rooms, plus flights. Buy some stuff." She bustled off.

Alex laughed softly, knowing Aimee would already be building a to-do list a mile long. He felt good – no, great. A holiday in the sun with the family was just what the doctor ordered.

"Bellissimo," he said, inserting as much Italian accent into the word as he could. Then his face became serious as he stared into the distance. *Just one thing in my way – got to get through the Box first.*

CHAPTER 10

USSTRATCOM, Nebraska
Level 5 – The Box

Hammerson led Alex along the featureless hallway down on one of the deepest and most secure levels of the facility. He finally stopped before a door recessed into the wall. He pressed some numbers into the control pad and the door whizzed and clicked as heavy bolts drew back.

"You know what to do." He pulled the door open. "Rebuild the cage. Seal it in, lock it down. Remember, you're in charge; let it goddamn know that."

Alex exhaled and stood in the doorway for a moment. It was an empty room, solid steel. There was a metal toilet in one corner and a tap for water. On the floor was a mat. There was no light inside.

"Three days," Alex said softly.

"Three days," Hammerson repeated. "See you then, son."

Alex entered the room to sit cross-legged on the mat with his back to the door.

"Good luck." Hammerson shut the heavy door. Locked it.

CHAPTER 11

The Frasassi Caves, Province of Ancona, Marche, Italy

The caves were deep and old, and had always been a place of mystery, solitude, and secrets. It was a long and winding trek through dark forests to find them and the thick growth and obscurity had allowed them to be forgotten. It was probably why the fantastic labyrinth beneath the earth was only rediscovered in 1971.

Along the way you'll pass an eleventh-century Romanesque abbey, and tucked in one of the many cave mouths you'll find Valadier Temple, built in the early 1800s. Plus there's the rubble of some unknown ruins that could even be many thousands of years older. Though the deeper cave system had only been ventured into in the last few decades, there are those who had known about their labyrinthine pathways for many generations. To those few who know about them, the caves have always been a place of worship, and experts think the primitive peoples of the region considered the deep chambers sacred and used them to speak with their chosen gods.

The caves usually contained the silence of the tomb, broken only by the distant drip of water, or maybe the scuttling of some unknown arthropod in hidden corners. But lately from within its deepest recesses there came the sound of chanting, and following that rhythmic sound was a group of worshipers. A group who devoted themselves to something that far predated any concept of good and evil laid down in any religious texts of the last few millennia. The collection of men and woman seemed trance-like as they swayed with the chant. Their faces were covered with otherwise featureless masks dotted with eyes, and around them hung effigies of hands and other limbs, giving them a grotesque, alien appearance. Blood ran from wounds on their bodies, carvings of ancient symbols and the eyes of all manner of beasts.

The language they used would only have been able to be penetrated by the likes of Professor Matt Kearns and his learned colleagues, and if anyone did take the trouble to understand the words, what they would have heard was a somnambulant chant repeated over and over until its vibrations sank into the stone around them and penetrated deep into the Earth.

She comes again – She must be fed – She comes again – She must be fed.

Around them tiny tendrils, whip thin, came up from the rock in a carpet and, one after the other, the people took turns lying down among them. The tendrils waved and swayed and some broke off and stuck to the group, quickly vanishing inside their bodies.

CHAPTER 12

Sicily, Catania, in the shadow of Mount Etna

Aimee smiled as she maneuvered the sports car along the Via Nazionale. On one side of her was the multi-hued town of Catania and on the other the long, golden beach of Letojanni. In the air was the smell of salt and hot sand, and the water was the color of sapphires. Umbrellas dotted the beach, people splashed in the shallows, and further out, sailboats tacked in a gentle breeze.

Aimee leaned out of the car, her black hair whipped back by the wind. "*Yahoooo!*"

"*Moooom.*" Joshua turned and gave her his best 'grow up' look before shaking his head. "So embarrassing."

She laughed and took one hand off the wheel to nudge him. "Come on, Josh, get with it. Your dad will here soon, and we're on holiday; nothing to do but swim, eat, laugh, and then swim some more. We're in heaven!"

"Yeah, I guess." He nodded as he looked away. "I just wish we could have brought Tor."

"He's on holiday too, remember? Large meadows to run in, a creek, and plenty of doggy buddies to hang out with. I bet that'd be his idea of doggy heaven."

"I bet it's not; he's not just a dog," Joshua muttered.

"Coming up." Aimee tracked the house numbers, and finally pulled into the Giarra. "Oh boy." She'd rented the luxury villa for the entire week – sea views, spa and pool, balcony overlooking the coast, and a garden with a gate directly onto the beach. It was everything she hoped for – a two-story building on the hillside that had terracotta tiles, blue and white awnings over a large balcony, and bright red geraniums spilling over the railings. She turned to her son. "You'll feel better once we've had a swim, and then maybe some of the world's finest gelato. Double scoop ... or maybe a triple."

He grinned. "That could work."

"Damn right it could." Aimee felt better than she had in years. And once Alex arrived it really *would* be heaven. The day-to-day mundane jobs, the endless petrobiology conferences, as well as the horrors of Alex's work, would be washed away in the azure waters of a Sicilian beach.

She popped the trunk and shouldered open her door. "Help me with the bags, Hercules."

"Kay." Joshua opened his door and stepped out, but as soon as his feet hit the warm road, he frowned. He tilted his head as though listening to something.

Aimee was at the back of the car, about to lift the trunk lid, but paused to watch him. Joshua crouched and placed a palm flat on the ground.

"Watcha doin, big guy?"

Her son ignored her and continued to stare at the ground. "Bad," he said, and moved his hand over the ground. "Bad things."

Aimee looked around but saw nothing except a beautiful beach, sparkling ocean, their villa, and blue, blue sky. She was about to look away when she noticed all the seagulls heading out to sea at top speed. *Fish*, she guessed, and faced her son again.

His mouth now gaped open, and a line of drool hung from it.

"Joshua?" She came around the side of the car just as he rose to his feet.

He faced her and his eyes were milky white, completely, and his mouth worked for a moment before finally forming words.

"Bad things are coming ... *coming up*."

CHAPTER 13

Sicily, Catania – on the slopes of Mount Etna

Angelo's cups, saucers, and plates rattled on the dresser, and he stopped in his tracks to stare at Gina, his wife. She returned his gaze, her hands stopping their work peeling vegetables.

Their shared look held a thousand questions, and a million fears. They waited. The seconds stretched, and then the plates rattled again, but this time a vibration in the floor that tickled the soles of their feet accompanied it.

Angelo turned to the window, the one that had a view to the volcano. It sat there mute and colossal, dominating the skyline. But it seemed quiet, calm, and dormant, other than a few wisps of smoke escaping from ancient vents.

Mount Etna was a stratovolcano, cone shaped, and like all of them had the characteristic steep slopes, built up by many layers of hardened lava, tephra, pumice, and volcanic ash, and also had a penchant for periodic and explosive eruptions. In that regard, Etna didn't disappoint.

The five craters at the summit could all erupt, spewing toxic gas, ash, and fiery plumes. But it could also erupt from its flanks, where there were more than three hundred vents ranging in size from small holes in the ground to large, cave-like apertures dozens of feet across. Over the last few centuries there had been hundreds of eruptions from both the flank and summit, and in only 2012, the summit had exploded once again. That time Angelo and Gina had endured cracked walls, broken tiles, and sulfur stains on their curtains.

But they knew it was only a matter of time until there was another big one. Some locals sought guidance, forewarning, and protection from science, some from lucky charms, and others from gods far more ancient than any Christian variety.

Angelo and Gina lived on the outskirts of the city, and had a small market garden where they grew huge roma tomatoes, peppers, and grapes for a delicious homemade wine called Montepulciano that was as dark as ink. Their small harvests were always excellent as the volcanic soil was rich and never needed fertilizing. From their eastern window they looked toward the Ionian Sea and the city of Catania, Sicily's second largest city, with a population of well over a million.

As the pair watched, it was like a dark blanket was being pulled over the city even though it was midday. Automated streetlights started to wink on. Angelo rushed over to the opposite window and saw a dark gray mushroom cloud rising up from Etna's summit and spreading in the upper atmosphere to create a thick umbrella.

The ground still tickled the soles of his feet, and he nodded slowly. "It will pass." He watched the plume spread and, as the midday sunshine was blotted out, instead of feeling a growing coolness from the lack of sunlight, he felt a radiating heat, and with it an accompanying whiff of sulfur. He turned to Gina. "It *must* pass," he said softly and made the sign of the cross over his chest.

The explosion that followed made Gina scream and Angelo grip the windowsill. Within seconds, hard pellets started to rain down on their tiled roof, and a dry snow coated their garden beds.

Angelo backed away from the window. He spun to his wife. "Grab what you can. We go, *now*." He snatched up his wallet, his keys, opened the kitchen dresser drawer and found papers, birth certificates, deeds, and other contracts.

Gina scurried from room to room, picking up photographs, bags of food, and some clothing. She crossed herself in front of a small statue of the Virgin Mary and then met Angelo at the front door. He nodded, not knowing what to say, and settled for simply rubbing her shoulder for a second before turning and pulling open the door.

The thing that filled the doorway made Angelo's mouth gape, and he dropped everything he held. Gina simply fell, fainting dead away beside him. He desperately wanted to check on her, but found he couldn't tear his eyes away from the huge lumpen figure.

The thing didn't make sense. It seemed to be made up from pieces of different bodies, arms, hands, bits of faces, with crying, raving, or gibbering mouths covering the slick, red torso. Something that could have been a head leaned in at him on a long rubbery neck like it was a giant finger. Eyes dotted the "head", most human, but some not.

Heat radiated from it, and being so close to it seared Angelo's flesh. Horrifyingly, it reached out an arm that had dozens of hands, each taking hold of him and pulling him close, closer, and then finally right onto its slick body, where he stuck.

"Gina!" was all he yelled as his face was pressed to the hot, wet flesh – and then *into* the flesh.

CHAPTER 14

Hotel Vergilius Billia, Naples, Italy – 365 miles from Mt Etna

Matt stood at the third-floor window and looked east across the sparkling harbor to the volcano. Mount Vesuvius, called Vesuvio here. It dominated the landscape, skyline, culture, tourist trade, and just about everything else in between.

The caldera was still cone shaped, but now its sides were coated in green vegetation, and amazingly, or bravely, the settlements traveled all the way to its very base, and even a little up the slope. Just over the other side of the bay from where he stood were the ruins of the city of Pompeii. The ancient ruins were approximately the same distance from the cone as he was now.

Matt tried to imagine what it was like back then. The daytime sky had turned black, and the volcano had started to shake the ground as the sea of magma beneath it built pressure in preparation for the eruption, the poisoned fluid of a boil about to burst. And when it did, that terrible emanation, called a pyroclastic flow, rushed toward Pompeii, searing, scalding, and burying everything before it. Many of the victims vanished forever, were probably still encased in stone dozens of feet below the surface.

Matt rubbed his chin, feeling the stubble graze his knuckles. He also knew of the legends. Those that were rescued at the docks told stories of people taken in the volcanic fog. Some thought it was the work of the gods or even ancestral spirits rescuing souls from the pain of a fiery death. But others saw it as something darker and more malevolent. Many reported the screams in the fog that were more terrifying than anything else they heard that fateful day.

And if they were taken, why and where were they taken? And most importantly, *who* took them?

Matt loved mysteries of the past, and one thing he had found over the years was that buried inside every legend was a kernel of truth. He believed something strange had happened back then in among the chaos – because chaos was always the perfect cover.

His eyes were drawn to the street below as a little red Fiat cut across traffic and pulled in fast. He smiled as he saw a slim arm protrude from a window to give the finger to a passing car that had obviously leaned on their horn.

"That's my girl."

Maria was fun, and smart, and sexy, and full to the eyebrows with life. He also knew she was pretty unflappable, and their earlier conversaion had been the first time he'd heard confusion and nervousness in her voice. It wasn't the promise of her treating him a holiday that got him here, it was that fear in her tone.

Matt wore jeans, sneakers, and a T-shirt, and grabbed a cotton bomber jacket before finishing with a NY baseball cap over his long hair. He looked in the mirror.

"Could you look any more American?" He chuckled and headed for the door.

Once on the street he found her car, but it was empty. He spotted Maria at a café, ordering coffee. He jogged over.

"Black, one sugar."

Maria turned, smiled broadly, and leaped into his arms. "Buongiorno! My beautiful Americano." She kissed him so hard on the lips he was sure he'd end up with a bruise. *Worth it*, he thought.

She turned, keeping one arm looped around his neck to shout the extra coffee order to the barista. She faced him again.

"I thought I lost you," he said into her beaming face.

"There is okay coffee up at the dig site, but better coffee here. So …" She was handed a cardboard tray that contained three coffees. "One for you, Andreas, and me. Let's go." She kept hold of the tray and took Matt's hand in a tight grip as she headed to the Fiat.

Inside the small car she passed him the coffees, but Matt knew better than to try and take his cup and sip from it. The woman drove as if she was permanently pissed off, in a race, and also well out of control. Better just to hang on and enjoy the coffee when they got there, or what would be left of it anyway.

They screamed along the harbor foreshore, dodging traffic as if it was standing still, with the occasional horn blast and Italian curse hurled from the window. Matt held tight to the coffees with one hand and kept a death grip on the armrest with his other.

Maria took the turnoff to the Pompeii ruins sharply and headed up a steep track on the mountainside. After another few minutes of hill climbing she pulled over under a stand of trees and jerked the handbrake on.

Matt looked through the windscreen. "What are we doing? I thought your dig was down in the ruins."

"It is, and we were." Maria took the tray of coffees from him.

A slim young man with glasses appeared from out of the trees and waved to them.

"Andreas," she said. "Like I mentioned in our chat, you could say our dig has been … commandeered."

"Who by?" Matt frowned. "Why?"

"The government, police, Martians – I don't really know yet. But officials from some federal agency turned up, ordered us to stop excavating, and then kicked us off the site altogether." She bared her teeth. "Then, *poof*! Just like that, our dig permits were cancelled."

She opened the door with a squeal of hinges, stood and handed Andreas a coffee. She took hers out, placed the tray on the roof and then leaned her elbows on the car. "And I'm betting the why is because of what we found."

Matt shook hands with Andreas and then grabbed his own coffee. The man saluted him with his cup and grinned, showing long, horse-like teeth with a small gap at the center.

"I am a fan of your work, Professor Kearns."

"Matt."

"The translation work on Petra stones was brilliant." Andreas' eyes gleamed.

Matt shrugged. "The Nabataeans were a race that was a blend of two worlds: one Arabian, and the other Hellenic. Once you understand that, then you see how it comes together."

Andreas nodded. "The reading of the language was one thing, but the understanding of the inferences is what made it special."

Matt's grin widened and he held up a finger. "Pro tip number one: try and get into the head of the people doing the writing. It makes a difference."

"I'll remember that." Andreas toasted Matt with his coffee again.

"Cut out the speed dating, you two." Maria reached into the car and grabbed a small pair of binoculars. "This way."

She led them further up the hill and then into a thick stand of olive trees, where there was an ancient rock wall. She sat down and lifted the glasses to her eyes.

Matt sat on one side and Andreas on the other. The view over the ancient city and the dig site was magnificent. But there was something down there that stood out among the ancient ruins – a huge tent, possibly the size of a football field, covering a portion of the site.

"*That* used to be our dig site." She still held the glasses to her eyes as she scanned the activity down there.

Matt squinted. "So, seriously, who are they?"

"I wish I knew." She exhaled loudly. "AISI, AISE, DIS, CISR, take your pick, they're all the same. They arrived a few days back in their dark suits, waving badges in our faces, and then started to *assist* us in gathering our belongings ... or some of them. Twenty-four hours later, this circus tent went up, and we weren't allowed back in."

Maria's jaw worked for a moment. "But they've got my notebook, and I want it back. They refused to let us into the site so there was no way to recover my notes, or find out what's going on." Maria turned and smiled sweetly. "Until now."

"You got your permits back?" Matt's brows went up.

"No, something better than that." She tilted her head toward him, still smiling. "We've got the internationally renowned Professor Matthew Kearns now."

"Me? What can *I* do? I don't carry any weight with these guys. Whoever these guys are," Matt turned back to watching a few people milling around outside the large tent. "Not much security though."

"Why would there be?" Andreas said. "No one knows about them confiscating the site. And for that matter, we didn't exactly attract a big crowd."

"Most of the activity is inside, and I know for a fact that they can't fully decipher the tablets they've found." The corners of Maria's mouth drew up. "They brought in Carlo Rembrani, and even he's having a tough time of it. The old fool."

"I know him," Matt said. "He's a good linguist, and no fool. And he's stumped, you say?"

"Yes, and he *is* a fool for allowing us to be kicked out. Scientists should stick together." Her lips turned down in distaste. "So, he's a fool and a prostitute."

Matt chuckled, knowing not to get in front of one of Maria's outbursts. Hot Italian blood ran like fire through her veins.

"I bet Rembrani doesn't even know who engaged his services." Maria's eyes turned sly. "But he knows you, and you can tell him you've been sent to help. Maybe even work *for* him. That would certainly appeal to his inflated ego. He won't be able to resist."

"So I tell the security guards it was Professor Rembrani that sent for me, and then tell Rembrani I was sent by the government to help *him*." Matt bobbed his head. "Double bluff – might work."

"Of course it will." Maria reached up to run a hand over his hair and then tug gently at the locks for a moment. "Tonight, 7 pm, when the day shift has gone home. We – *you* – pay them a visit."

* * *

Just after seven they were back on the hill overlooking Maria's dig site. She opened her bag and withdrew a dark perspex box no bigger than a packet of cigarettes and handed it to Matt. She held up her phone, tapped in some numbers, and an image of Matt appeared on her phone.

"Wow." Matt held the box up. "It's a freaking camera?"

"Hold it up and hold it still." She zoomed in and out, adjusting and focusing. "A little gift from some friends in ArgoTech. You place that close to where they're working and it will pick up images and sound from all four sides." She fiddled some more. "There. Perfect." She switched it off and looked up at him. "Just hide it in among the other equipment, and make sure its line of sight is unimpeded, okay?"

"Clear line of sight, got it." Matt stared into the tiny box for a moment more. "If it's safe to do it, I will." He looked up. "And what about this notebook of yours?"

"Yes, you mustn't forget it." She held her hands a foot apart. "It's a folder, this big, leather, and about an inch thick. It's got *all* my notes, thoughts, and site-sketchings; it's vital you retrieve it."

Matt grimaced. "That's going to be a little harder to sneak out."

"Andreas." Maria clicked her fingers at the young man, who opened his backpack and pulled out a lab coat. He shook it out and then handed it to Matt.

"It's one of mine."

"Seriously?" Matt chuckled. "I'll look like a visiting dentist."

"Yes, seriously," Maria countered. "And it makes you look like a professor, instead of a beach bum student. Besides, it'll work on the guards."

Matt sighed and pulled it on. It had deep side pockets and he knew it would hide the book … if he could find it. *And* if he could manage to get inside without getting chased away, or arrested.

He straightened and dusted himself down. "Well, then, let's see what we can see." He jammed his hands in the pockets of the lab coat, one curled around the miniature camera.

"Good luck." Maria kissed his cheek and then gave him a little push.

How do I get myself into this stuff? he wondered as he trudged down the hill toward the tent entrance. As he got closer he saw the structure was translucent, but he couldn't see any movement inside. *Good, the fewer people I have to fool the better.*

Matt straightened and tried to look as confident as he could manage as he approached the entrance. Two dark-suited men appeared and one frowned and held up a hand to his face. He spoke in annoyed and rapid Italian.

"This is a private facility – you are trespassing."

Matt responded in fluent and flawless Italian. "Just doing my job. Professor Rembrani sent for me to assist in the translations. I'm from Harvard." Matt handed him his business card.

The guard studied the card as if it contained the secrets of the universe, then lifted his eyes to glare a moment more. "I need to check this."

"Tell the professor I'm here." Matt didn't flinch. "Take your time. You're paying me by the hour – and I'm expensive."

The security guard drew out a phone and dialed a number. Matt heard him ask about his credentials, and check his bona fides. He leaned around the other security guy and spotted the silver head of Rembrani. He needed to be past the first line of defense quickly, before everyone got coordinated.

He called out, in Spanish: "Professor, es bueno verte. He sido enviado para ayudarte, trabajar para ti – Professor, good to see you. I've been sent to assist you, and work for you."

The older academic turned, his eyebrows up.

Matt waved, and changed to Arabic: "Matt Kayranz, fi khidmatikum ya saydi – Professor Matt Kearns, at your service, sir."

The guards were nonplussed and, as Matt hoped, they were locked out of the conversation. But Professor Rembrani smiled and waved.

"Yes, yes." The older man kept waving as he approached. As Matt expected, a linguist loved to play the language game, and would ensure that it kept the guards out of their exchange. "Saya pernah mendengar tentang Anda, selamat datang, selamat datang. Masuklah, Matthew. Siapa yang mengirimmu?" Rembrani responded in Indonesian. "I've heard of you, welcome, welcome. Come in, Matthew. Who sent you?"

Matt shrugged and moved past the guards. "Ah, the general."

"Marconi?"

"Who else?"

Rembrani snorted. "No one tells me anything." He brightened. "But I can certainly use an experienced subordinate."

The first guard entered the tent, looked from Matt to Rembrani, and frowned. "Is he authorised, as –"

Rembrani rolled his eyes. "Yes, yes, General Marconi authorised it. Go away." He waved the man off as if he were a bothersome fly.

Matt watched as confusion and conflict crossed the security guy's face. Matt nodded to him and pulled his face into an "everything is fine" expression.

After another moment, the guard snorted loudly and spun, leaving the pair alone in the huge tent.

Matt looked around, impressed. "I was expecting some translation work on tablets, but this, this is like an entire workshop, or maybe a museum." He turned. "Professor Rem—"

Rembrani held a hand up. "Call me Carlo."

Matt nodded. "And Matt or Matthew, please."

"Then Matthew it is." Rembrani cast his arm around, indicating the football field–sized tent. "And for now, this is my kingdom, and also my Heaven and my Hell."

"There's been a translation problem?" Matt asked.

Rembrani bobbed his head from side to side. "Hmm, perhaps not so much a problem with the translation but a problem with the interpretations. I know a lot of what we have found is a mish-mash of Etruscan, Greek, even Phoenician lettering, as you would expect from a form of proto-Latini."

"Mmm, and strange to have that ancient language in Pompeii."

"Yes, and a lot of the phrasing is repeated. Almost as if it was plastered everywhere on that fateful day. It seems to be telling the people of Pompeii to 'Beware them that are everyone'."

"Or perhaps, 'Beware them that are of all of us'," Matt corrected.

Rembrani paused. "You know some of it?"

Matt shrugged. "The general showed me a little."

The old man snorted. "So much for secrecy." He sighed. "And then there's the repetition of: 'She must be fed'. Who is She? And fed what exactly?"

Matt shrugged.

"There are so many oddities and inconsistencies. The writing is one thing, but the physical artifacts are truly ... astounding. They need a team working on this, not one old man. But together, maybe we can work wonders." Rembrani waved Matt to follow him. "Come, a brief tour."

They passed long tables covered in excavated materials. There were boxes stacked beneath them, and Matt saw Maria's name stenciled on some of them. He bet her notebook was hiding in there somewhere.

Rembrani spoke over his shoulder. "You've come just in time. To witness something ... perplexing. A specimen that is confusing everyone."

"You mean an artifact?" Matt asked.

"No, I said, and meant, a specimen. The biologists are very excited about it, and have dispatched a team that will arrive tomorrow. It's one of the reasons they closed down the site – potential contamination."

"Is it?" Matt stopped. "Contaminating?"

"How should I know?" Rembrani stopped at a long table. "But first, my bête noir." He opened his hands to a row of large clay slabs, each with what looked like tiny hen scratchings pressed into them. "Matthew, I am a translator, and a very fine one. I can speak many, many dozens of languages and can read dozens more. But I am not a paleontologist, prehistoric animal investigator, or someone who ferrets around in the words and deeds of the dead." He looked up and smiled. "But I believe that is your expertise."

"Don't believe everything you've heard, Carlo." Matt grinned.

Rembrani looked back down at the tablets. "This, I don't recognize at all."

Matt edged in closer. The clay itself was fire hardened, baked, and he knew that if they took samples, they'd undoubtedly find small pollens, plant fibers, and perhaps seeds that could date it to within a few decades and also be able to place exactly where the clay was drawn from.

There were three tablets, each filled with the cramped lettering. It was the most ancient of Latini letters and symbols, but the way they were put together didn't make any sense. Except for one symbol that represented a name. Matt placed his finger upon it.

"Romulus."

Rembrani frowned. "The story of the first king of Rome?"

"Not just a story," Matt said. "He lived and ruled from 753 to 717 BC. There is a lot of evidence to believe he was real. Before the caesars there were the kings, and he was the beginning of the time of the first great rulers of Rome."

"I remember now; he was the first of the seven great kings." Rembrani waved a finger. "That period rings a bell for some reason." His finger stilled. "Ah, yes. This area exists under the shadow of Vesuvio, and she has erupted many times in the past. Did you know that some of my colleagues made an unusual discovery a while ago? Thousands of prehistoric footprints in a layer of volcanic ash."

"Earlier than Pompeii?" Matt asked.

"Much earlier." Rembrani beamed. "The footprints were made when the cooling ash was still soft and fresh. And strangely, they're all headed in the same direction: towards the volcano. But they're dated from an eruption around 3,800 years ago."

Matt whistled. "Eighteen hundred years before Pompeii."

"And there have been constant eruptions since. The people of this area, all the way back to the Bronze Age, would have known about its geological hostility. Maybe they somehow prepared for it." The aging scientist scowled down at the tablets. "I should be able to read it, but I can't." He turned his head. "Can you?"

"Yes and no. Or rather, not yet." Matt scratched his chin. "We seem to agree it's ancient Latini, but if I had to guess, I'd say it's jumbled or has been rendered into some sort of code."

"Codified? Why?"

"Maybe it wasn't code back then. Or maybe this message, or ruling, or edict, or whatever it was, was never meant to be read by the common folk."

"I see, like some sort of secret message. And you think you can decipher it?"

"Sure. Given time, all linguistic codes can be broken. Just consider it another lost language that needs to be deciphered." Matt fished in his pocket for his phone camera, and took a photo of the tablet's etchings. "I'll look into them."

"Good. Good. Then that will be the first of your tasks, I think." Rembrani grabbed Matt's elbow. "There are other puzzling oddities that may help or hinder. Maybe they're connected, maybe not."

He led Matt toward the rear of the tent. Matt had at first thought it was the end wall of the structure, but now saw a flap leading to another walled-off section. Rembrani went through first, ducking his head, and Matt followed. Inside it was near freezing.

There was a long clear case, like a coffin, ten feet long and four wide. A small generator hummed underneath it, obviously keeping whatever was inside cold.

"We did some more excavation. There were more artifacts and remains, but of the usual kind – human. But they were also limbs, separated – not cleaved, but strangely, they appear more pulled apart." He stepped closer to the tank.

"Holy shit." Matt stared at the thing Maria had mentioned to him.

"And then there's this … and I'm not sure 'holy' is the word I would use to describe it." The small man's eyes were almost fearful as he looked through the clear covering.

Matt reached out to wipe the glass free of condensation, feeling the freezing temperatures against his palm. He leaned closer, seeing the thing clearer.

His stomach spasmed. "Jesus H. Christ."

It was an arm, maybe, and it looked … *wet*. It was roughly six feet long, and the bones were heavy, thick, and ended in a claw that looked to be made up of … other hands and fingers pressed or melted together. Matt leaned closer until he felt the cold against his face. The bones weren't a single organic design, but looked like they were made up of several bones twisted or fused together.

Matt swallowed dryly. "You dug this thing up?"

"It was excavated from this site," Rembrani said. "But not by us."

"It looks like some sort of animal bone, or deformed animal bone. But it seems more like a cadaver, rather than fossilized remains. It's ..." Matt grimaced. "Is that blood and new tissue?" He turned. "You took it out of its cast?"

"No, it broke out as its size increased. It simply outgrew it." Rembrani pursed his lips. "The ... specimen seems to be reacting to the air now. The biologists don't think it's growing or regenerating, but more that there is some type of fungus on it that is covering the bones in a simulation of tissue regrowth," He shrugged. "They'll know more once they've had a chance to examine it."

"You're keeping it cold, freezing, in fact." Matt observed. "So why is it still growing in that environment? Should be frozen solid."

Rembrani's lips pulled up into the semblance of a smile, but there was no joy in it. "Because the specimen is hot. Another conundrum: the remains are generating extraordinary heat. Some sort of exothermic reaction to the air, we think." He paused. "We think, ha! We guess." Rembrani pointed to a small camera with a recording box fixed to the near wall. "We've been watching its growth. At least the cold is slowing it down."

"And if it wasn't slowed down?" Maria had told him that the remains she had found were little more than a few large arm bones that seemed disfigured. This thing was certainly malformed, but it was big and solid. Was it the same thing?

He straightened and tried to imagine what it could have looked like. Given the length of the limb, if it were proportional to a man, it would make it at least ten feet tall. And the thickness of the bones attested to a very powerful creature indeed.

The hand dispelled any illusion of it belonging to just an overly large man as it wasn't even close to human shaped. It was hard to clearly make it out through the frosted glass, but in anybody's book, this thing was a freaking monster ... or had been. He remembered the translations: *Beware them that are of all of us*, and *She must be fed*. He shuddered.

"Professor Rembrani, do you think it's possible that this specimen is from a different time zone? Maybe it's some sort of mega fauna species that was somehow blown to the surface by the eruption?"

"I hope so," Rembrani said softly. "But I don't know for sure, and I think it's unlikely. I have a friend who is a geologist and he has told me before that igneous rocks form from molten rock and rarely have fossils in them. Fossils don't survive volcanoes. Too much pressure and heat. It's really only sedimentary rocks that contain fossils." He stroked his chin. "You know, Matthew, I just can't imagine this thing being alive at the time of modern man."

Matt shook his head slowly. "Surely we would know about it? The Romans were diligent in their note taking, and had impeccable records."

"I agree, I agree." Rembrani's lips curved down as he stared at it.

"She must be fed," Matt said softly.

"Excuse me?' Rembrani half-turned.

"Nothing." Matt said and backed up a step when Rembrani turned back to the case. He still had that bad feeling in his gut as he exited through the flaps and continued to move toward an adjacent table. He dropped a hand into his pocket and grabbed the small camera box. He removed his hand and leaned back against one of the tables, secreting it in among some other equipment, before placing his hands back in the lab coat.

Rembrani followed him out and Matt smiled innocently.

"This way, Matthew, we have much work to do." Rembrani headed back to the tablets, but Matt remained, first to check he had the camera angles right, and then to stare a little more at the remains.

He didn't believe for a second that it was a fungus growing on the misshapen bones. He could make out tendons, ligaments, and the buds of muscles growing along the giant skeletal frame. In addition, the end that had been severed now had an inch of brilliant white bone – *new bone*. There looked to be something akin to white, hair-like filaments at its end.

What would happen if it kept on growing? Would it grow shoulders, a head, a brain? Would it grow an entire body? And then what? Matt felt his heart rate kick up a notch and a coil of something unpleasant knotted in his gut again.

The translation came back again: *Beware them that are of all of us.* He shivered and turned away from the tank. Suddenly he regretted taking up Maria's offer of a trip to Italy.

* * *

That evening Matt, Maria, and Andreas reviewed the video footage from the camera, and Maria pointed out the objects she said she needed. Matt pushed his hair back.

"Jesus, Maria, all of that? I'll need a wheelbarrow." He exhaled loudly. "I'm going to wear out my welcome real fast."

"Matthew, this is important. And what they did was professional theft."

They watched as the flaps to the end cool room opened and closed. Maria paused the footage, and she craned forward to peer at the partly obscured images from inside.

"From what I can see, the specimen seems bigger than when we uncovered it," Andreas whispered.

"Professor Rembrani thinks it's some sort of fungal spread on the remains," Matt said.

"Impossible; those remains were nothing more than desiccated bone." Maria straightened. "But I agree, they seem different now. Might just be the light or the angle."

"Well, looked damned revolting to me, whatever it is," Matt said. "The biologists are due in tomorrow morning. They're going to start their analysis."

Maria paced for a moment before turning back. "Matthew, you need to move the camera ... inside the cool room. We need to see what it is they're doing in there."

Matt groaned as he tilted his head back. He had come down expecting to help Maria out with some sticky translations and also to check out some historical anomalies, not to get involved in her espionage activities. "Maria, I'm getting in a little deep here."

She smiled, grabbed his shirtfront, and pulled him close, looking up at him with her dark eyes. "Last thing I ask, I promise." She kissed him quickly and then pushed him back. "This is the most intriguing find of my life, so I'm not going to let it be whisked away from right under my – *our* – noses."

Matt groaned even louder.

She tilted her head. "Matthew, you know very well if I could do it myself, I would."

Matt held up a finger and waggled it at her. "Last thing – you promise?"

She nodded solemnly as she slowly made the sign of the cross.

He sighed. "Okay."

After a late supper of seafood pasta, ouzo until midnight, and then coffee and sweet cakes for another hour, Matt had crashed at Maria's. Next morning he surfaced at around nine, blinked puffy eyes and felt a deep throbbing in his head. Maria and Andreas were already up, and looked as fresh as teenagers.

"Erk." He rubbed his face as he stumbled into the living room, cradling a cup of syrup-thick coffee. "Damn ouzo. I think I swore last time I was here I'd never drink that stuff again."

Maria grinned. "You sure did. And you promised the time before that as well. You're a man of fantastic will power, Professor Kearns." She gestured with her head. "Come see. Something has happened."

Matt crossed to where she had her laptop open on the table, receiving the feed from the camera down in the dig site tent. She rewound the footage, then paused it for a second to give him some background.

"The biologists came early. Just on dawn and Rembrani was already there to meet them." Maria reran the feed, and it showed two men in disposable biosuits following Rembrani into his cool room at the end of the tent. The counter clicked over for minutes and then Maria sped it up as hours flew by with zero activity.

"What are they doing in there?" Matt asked.

"Wait," Maria said as she slowed it down to normal speed once again. Her eyes were wide. "Watch ... *now*."

Several hours had gone by. There was no sound, but suddenly there was a flurry of activity. The two guards who had been stationed outside ran past the camera as if they'd been summoned and pushed through the flaps into the cool room.

After a few moments the flaps were agitated as if by a breeze or someone bumping up against them, before hanging still.

"Wish we could hear," Andreas said softly.

Matt exhaled through pursed lips. "What the hell just happened?"

"Exactly." Maria turned to him. "That was hours ago, and still no one has come out of that room."

"But that's – how many? – five grown men in there now? That'd be standing room only. Hard to do for all those hours." Matt frowned. "And there's no back door on that tent."

Maria pushed back from the computer screen. "We must check it out, yes? Now, while security seems to be occupied."

Matt was intrigued, but didn't want to go back in there even though he had no good excuse other than an uneasy feeling. "This is getting out of hand, Maria. Maybe it's time to call in someone from the authorities."

She scoffed and pointed at the screen. "Those guys *are* the authorities." She spun and clapped her hands together. "Andreas, grab a bag. We're going down to see for ourselves what's going on at *our* dig. And recover our property."

* * *

Maria's car skidded in the dirt, and she was already pushing open her door before she engaged the handbrake. Matt and Andreas struggled to keep up as the archaeologist set to marching toward the huge tent.

"*Slow down*," Matt hissed. "If those security guys make an appearance, what are you going to say?"

She paused and seemed to think on it. Then she strode back to grab Matt's arm and yank him with her. "You're right; you go first."

"Oh, great plan." Matt laughed as she put a hand in the center of his back and shoved him in front of her. He spoke over his shoulder. "You ever *not* get what you want?"

"Often … sometimes … rarely." She grinned at him. "And if the guards show up, I trust you have a good story as to why I'm here."

"No, I don't, actually. Remind me." He held up a hand to slow her down as they approached the front flap of the tent.

The trio stopped and stood looking around for a few moments. Matt could hear nothing, the entire dig site appeared vacated.

"They must be all still in there, I guess," he whispered. "Hang on." He went and opened the door and peered into the huge tent's interior. There was no one inside the main area. He pulled back. "No one there. They're probably all in the cold room."

"Good. Go." Maria shooed him forward, then followed. Andreas trailed behind. She quickly went from table to table, grabbing things and handing them to Andreas, or simply pointing. "This, and this, and this ..."

Matt approached the hanging flaps that separated the two rooms, then slowed. He could see absolutely no light inside, meaning the overhead bulbs weren't on and the light that was over the sealed tank must have been switched off.

The flaps were opaque, and he couldn't make out any movement. But leaning his head closer, he thought he could hear something – a sliding maybe, and perhaps a low moan. He lifted a hand to push through, but paused.

Maria appeared beside him and Andreas at his other shoulder.

She looked up at him with one brow raised. "Well?"

He hesitated. "This is a bad idea."

"I'll just tell them I came to ask some questions. After all, no one stopped us from coming in, right?"

Matt shook his head. "No, I meant about going in, not –"

Maria made a guttural sound in her throat, hooked her arm through his, and dragged him through the flaps.

The lights were out, and the three of them shuffled into the room. Matt was immediately assailed by a rank odor and threw an arm up over his face. "Phew, what the hell is that?"

"Like bad, bad fish." Andreas lifted the collar of his T-shirt over his nose and mouth.

"Where is everyone?" Maria got out her phone. "Hello, Professor Rembrani?" She switched on its flashlight and held it up. Panned it around.

The room was empty. Then Maria got to the specimen tank – it looked like it had exploded open. Matt heard her intake of breath, and felt his eyes were going to pop out of his head, he stared so hard.

"What is ...?" Matt tried to make sense of what he was seeing. The steel-framed table under the canopy had been large, maybe ten feet long and four wide. Originally in the tank there had been only a long and deformed-looking arm bone that showed signs of some sort of weird growth. But now there was an enormous mass, hundreds of pounds of flesh knotted into a small mountain. The table legs groaned under the weight, and on the floor under it among the shards of broken canopy glass there was a single shoe.

Maria dropped the phone to her side, throwing the room back into darkness, and Matt reached across to grab it from her and hold the light up. He tried to keep it steady even though his hand wobbled as nerves made his arm shake.

The heat in the room was almost unbearable, and even the cool cabinet was now open and the room itself was air-conditioned, it was like standing before an open fire. Matt knew it was being generated by the thing on the table – some sort of biological exothermic reaction, he remembered Rembrani telling him.

He tried to focus on the glistening mass on the table but his mind struggled to process what he was seeing – it looked like all the men were there – *in there* – as if they were wrestling together, but in way that was too tight for it to be natural. It was impossible to really tell where one body ended and another began.

The tangle of bodies was glistening and slimy, and the mass was moving in unison as if it was ... what? Pulsating? Breathing? Or maybe trying to lift itself off the bench?

Matt felt his legs shaking as he ran his eyes over the clump of matter. The men's arms were fusing together into a single long arm with multiple hands at the end. The other arm had all the fingers clasped tight, drawing into claws and multiple legs were becoming column-thick limbs. But the worst thing was the head. It contained all the faces of the biologists and security guards, their features melting together onto a trunk-like neck, some in silent screams of agony and torment, and others simply confused. The giant visage had eyes floating over its glistening surface.

The door flap behind them opened and closed, and Matt heard Andreas gagging outside. Maria tugged hard on his arm.

"What?" Matt felt he was being woken from a fever dream.

"We go," she whispered.

Matt grimaced as he took one last look at the thing, and remembered the quote inscribed in the shard of clay: *Beware them that are of all of us.*

All of us ...

I'm outta here, he thought and was about to leave when he spotted the CCTV recorder stuck to the wall, its small red light still on.

"Wait." He dashed around the table to rip it from the wall. There came a wet sucking sound from the table, and he felt his heart rate kick up a notch.

Matt skittered back around the table that was now in darkness. He held up the camera. "Someone has to see this." He was still moving as he grabbed Maria's hand. "Let's get the hell out of here."

CHAPTER 15

Polizia Di Stato Questura Catania – Catania State Police Headquarters

Vice Questore – Chief Superintendent – Umberto Bianchi couldn't hear himself think. The room was a cacophony of shouting – too many mouths yelling too many questions, and nowhere near enough answers. He rubbed a leathery hand over his face, feeling the whiskers on his cheeks and chin, and stared hard into the computer screen. The video feed still showed nothing but smoke, thick, boiling, and impenetrable to their cameras.

The city of Catania, in the shadow of Mount Etna, had over a million inhabitants. Three-quarters had heeded emergency services calls to evacuate, and many thousands more were hauled out by the police. But then the thick volcano ash and smoke had enveloped everything, and once that happened they had lost ... everyone.

His officers on the ground had vanished. Phones went dead, communication lines, whether via internet, phone, or satellite, just ceased working. It was like a blanket of impenetrable steel had been thrown over the city. The last scrambled communication had been from one of his junior officers, who had worked his way up the slope of the mountain toward the outskirts of the city. He had screamed, and the word he had bellowed, "Mostro" – monster – was terrifying. And then he, too, was gone.

Bianchi slapped the table with his hand and cursed. There were thousands of people still in there, plus hundreds of his officers, and he just prayed that they weren't all dead. He needed to know what was going on, he needed to know if there were causalities, and how many, and where they were. He needed bodies in there. Thermal sensors had picked up a temperature rise, but the billowing clouds flowing down the side of the volcano were hot and that meant trying to find human heat signatures was impossible. At this point he was guessing that there was a toxic gas that was rendering everyone incommunicado, or at least that's all he hoped it was.

But Bianchi knew that the bigger risk was full-scale eruption. They had contingency plans in place for pre-eruption activities such as evacuation and temporary housing, and also during, and post eruption, through activation of emergency services.

Bianchi needed to be in control, and he felt far from it. Normally he would never cede an inch of ground when it came to command and control, but this time he had to put his city, and his lost police force, before his ego. It was the most difficult thing he had ever done, but in the end he had no choice.

"They're here." His sergeant stood aside as the tall, fierce-looking man entered the room. Though he must have been in his fifties, there was nothing aged about him. His eyes were hawk-like under a heavy brow and very few of Umberto Bianchi's seasoned police officers would meet those eyes. Bruno Mancini was the head of the Italian Special Forces, dubbed the Gladiators. Bianchi was a self-confessed control freak, but he was also a pragmatist, and knew when he was out of his depth.

The two men shook hands and Bianchi led Mancini to his control center, a large room with banks of screens, data feeds, and two dozen officers analyzing the data, taking calls, and trying to make sense of the puzzle.

Mancini looked across each screen. "Communication interference, and zero line of sight – not usual for a pre-eruption dispersal."

"Very unusual – we can't see or hear anything," Bianchi agreed. "I placed fifty officers in there, plus search and rescue experts to look for the remaining residents, and we know there should be tens of thousands of them. Now my officers *and* the residents are missing. Everyone and everything has gone dark."

Mancini turned back to the screens. Many appeared blank, but what they were really seeing was the screens filled with the boiling dark clouds. "It's like there's been an EMP strike. But the lack of accountability from your teams makes me think they might have been overcome by fumes."

"That's what I thought but our people had gas masks, and still –" Bianchi shook his head. "Gone."

Mancini grunted. "Our equipment deals with more than just respiratory attacks, but is also resistant to on-contact toxins and biological agents."

"You think it could be some sort of nerve agent, or perhaps a biological contaminant?"

"I think nothing should be ruled out right now."

Bianchi wiped his hands on his trouser legs. He hoped against hope that the people were just lost in the thick smoke. That they were holed up in churches, school halls, and basements, and that maybe the last people moving around, and his teams, had been overcome by some sort of gas and were lying in the road, unconscious.

Mancini's dark eyes were unblinking. "We need to get in there."

Bianchi drew in a deep breath. Civil disorder, domestic emergencies, crime, even terrorism, he could deal with. Anything more – well, that's why he'd called in the Special Forces. He looked at to the granite-hard features of Mancini.

"You have a green light."

* * *

Bruno Mancini commandeered several of the control room's surveillance screens and gently touched the communication pellet in his ear. "Alpha team – grid one, Delta team – grid two, Omega team – grid three. Report back, sixty minutes on my mark – three, two, one ... *mark*." He pressed a button on his wristwatch.

He heard his diktat repeated back as a clipped confirmation from the group leaders. He then watched as the three teams of elite soldiers headed out in single file. There were five soldiers in each team; all had a range of vision equipment with full-face masks and airtight uniforms that covered their entire bodies. They carried a range of weaponry depending on preference, from Glock 19 pistols to a choice of HK416 assault rifle, Benelli M4 12-gauge shotgun, or the HK MP5 submachine gun. Mancini could see they'd already engaged their barrel flashlights as the beams of light created glowing pipes as they entered the wall of smoke. He knew that once they were fully inside, they'd lose contact. But his teams had their orders and were fully autonomous.

Bruno Mancini was confident that there was nothing they couldn't handle. He straightened, and folded his arms.

"And now ... we wait."

* * *

Janus Romano was the Alpha team leader and the group's senior soldier. He liked to think he'd seen it all, and had been deployed in some of the worst places in the world to rescue hostages, infiltrate, spot adversaries, or just take down bad guys who were threats to the Italian nation and its security.

He'd been told this was a rescue mission. But he had a feeling that although it may come to that in some form, this was far from a straight rescue and retrieval job. For one, there were too many people missing to undertake an effective evacuation. His role was to find out why the people, the police, and the search and rescue personnel who entered had never reemerged. He had to find them. And his leaders wanted to know if they needed to send ambulances, stretchers, or, God forbid, a fleet of refrigerated trucks.

The smoke was thick, gritty, and impregnated with pumice dust. He looked at one of the dials on his wrist – the ambient temperature had spiked as soon as they entered, but while 110 degrees was damned uncomfortable, it wasn't lethal. Another dial told him there were zero biologicals in the cloud, and it was primarily suspended heavy particulate matter. He held up a hand and stared into the haze wafting past his fingers – he could see that for himself.

After entering the cloud area, the teams had split into their assigned search zones and quickly lost sight of each other. Once Janus' team had trekked forward for half a mile, Janus raised a hand and the four soldiers with him stopped. They turned their backs on their comrades and scanned the surrounding smoke for a few moments before turning to lean in close to their leader.

Longer-range comms were down, but in close they still had send-and-receive capabilities so they didn't need to yell through their masks. He looked briefly over his shoulder at his team. It was a good one – Enrico, Leon, Carlo, and Franco, all mission seasoned, tough as nails, and totally fearless.

"Visibility now down to about a dozen feet," Janus said.

One of his men shone his light around a building corner. "We're going to have to fall over someone before we find 'em."

"Roger that." Janus knew they couldn't stay bunched up if they wanted to maximize their chances. "We spread out in a skirmish line. But stay in sight of each other. We'll sweep the streets where the movement is coming from. Then on the way back, we'll do some door-to-door."

Janus couldn't see his team members' eyes, nor they his. But he knew they probably burned with adrenaline-fueled intensity. They were on edge, but a good edge, the type that made you sharp, alert, and ready to react in a blink.

"Let's do it." Leon held out a fist.

They bumped knuckles, then turned to spread into a line, no more than ten feet apart, at the limit of visibility. Even though they were just ghostly outlines in the smoke, it meant every team member was still in sight of at least one other. It wasn't much, but it expanded their search field. Each Gladiator had also swallowed a tracking pill, a small device that gave off a signal that was picked up by Janus' control unit. Bottom line, no one got left behind, no one could be taken and hidden from him.

Their route led them down into the Piazza Del Duomo, a wide square with a fountain whose tinkling flow was the only sound in the ghost-quiet area. Though it was only midday, the lights blazed, triggered by the loss of sunshine. Thankfully the smoke seemed a little thinner here but Janus could still barely make out shapes.

He paused the team in the center of the piazza. It was hundreds of feet of open space, and the beams from their barrel lights didn't penetrate very far in the gloom. At the end of the piazza was the Basilica Cattedrale Sant'Agata, the Catania Cathedral. The grand building was originally constructed in 1078 over the ruins of Roman baths, and it had already survived countless volcanic eruptions and earthquakes. Janus suspected the huge building could potentially house hundreds of frightened souls who might have taken shelter in the house of God ... or maybe just in a place made of solid stone.

"Move out."

He'd sweep the team down through the piazza toward it, and then begin their door-to-door search, starting with that building. He wanted to yell, to call out to anyone listening that it was safe to come out, but something stopped him – a soldier's sixth sense, maybe.

After moving into the town square only a few dozen feet, Enrico held up a hand and halted them. "Capo."

His beam shone on a small mound on the cobbled stones. Janus and the team joined him to stare at it.

"Is that a dog?" Leon asked.

"What the hell, they burned it up?" Franco asked.

"Yeah, but only after they butchered it," Enrico spat back.

Janus gritted his teeth. Enrico was right; the animal looked like it had been caught in some sort of giant vise, and its neck only just hung on the body by the empty skin of its neck. The bones, cartilage and muscle had been compressed down to nothing. Some of its tongue and throat bulged obscenely from the mouth, but it was hard to tell exactly what shape the rest of the dog was in, as it looked to have been roasted.

Janus' lip curled; he was glad he was wearing breathing apparatus, as he would undoubtedly smell burned hair and roasted dog meat. "Where's the accelerant?" he asked. "There's no splatter stain, no initiator materials. It looks like the dog's body was dropped here after it had been torched."

The men scanned the ground for a moment with their flashlights – there was nothing.

Enrico shrugged. "Let's just add it to our mystery file."

"It's already full, commilitone." Leon nudged his friend.

"Okay, let's find those missing people." Janus led them on, and his men spread wide again.

They were hundreds of feet from the church, and there was still a total absence of anything. All four men were on edge and tuned in to register anything moving, making noise, or having a recognizable human shape.

It was Janus who heard it first – faintly. A methodical clang, like someone gently tapping one metal object against another. He turned his head to scan the piazza – it seemed to be coming from the church. Perhaps his instincts were correct: there were people inside, and all they could do was tap out their signals because they were trapped or hurt.

Janus made a twirling motion in the air with one hand and pointed forward. The group picked up their pace.

He slowed them as they approached the huge double doors of the domed basilica. The imposing façade was gray stone that took on an alabaster shine in the light of their beams. He concentrated; the sound was clearer now: a soft clang, reminiscent of a school bell, or at least an iron-on-iron object. He could imagine someone in a state of semi-consciousness using one hand to tap out a message.

"Enrico, anything?" Janus spoke without turning.

The Spec Forces solder raised a movement scanner and swept it behind them over the piazza. He shook his head. "Not a breath – just ghosts out there, Capo."

"Okay." Janus looked up at the huge doors. "Franco, you're up first. Carlo, Leon, right and left flanks. Enrico, stay here and cover us." He put his hand on the huge door and pushed. "Let's do this."

There was no movement at first, so he put his shoulder to the wood and strained. The door still wouldn't budge. Finally, with the combined strength of his team, they forced one of the doors in a few feet.

The opening was just two feet wide when he nodded and his men went in fast and low, one up the center, one going left and the other right, each stopping just inside the door, rifles up. Janus followed, with Enrico remaining outside.

Janus paused to let his eyes adjust to the gloom. He saw why they had trouble opening the door: there was furniture stacked up against it, piled high as if trying to fortify it.

Franco looked it over. "Do you think it worked?"

"Well, no one broke in this way," Janus said. "And no one got out."

The smoke had even permeated the building, and clouds of it hung like shrouds in the vast domed room. The room seemed to be empty and it looked as if a cyclone had ripped through it – the pews were splintered, overturned, and pushed aside against thc walls. Some of the wood looked singed.

"Where is everyone?" Franco asked softly.

"Quiet." Janus turned slowly; the soft clang became more distinct. "Follow."

It was coming from the back of the room, and he moved quickly, gun up, his barrel light jerking from left to right. He came up on the altar and, staying low and fast, rounded the huge stone table to the source of the noise.

There was the altar cloth, weighted at the edges by small metal crucifixes. One of them had slid lower and was now banging against an overturned brass urn. It swung back and forth, and Janus reached forward to stop it swinging. It hung listlessly, and he continued to stare at it.

"There's no breeze in here, and no movement. That thing shouldn't have been swinging."

He turned, seeing the small vestibules. He pointed to his eyes and then to the first room, whose door was slightly ajar.

Leon and Franco spun and silently moved toward the open door, guns ready, barrels unwavering. At the door, Leon nudged it fully open with an elbow, then moved in. The darkness was absolute in the smaller room. Franco lit a flare, illuminating the room with a hellish red glow. He held it up.

"Just like outside. Place is wrecked."

The space was in disarray, singed, and the team noticed that the door's lock had been torn off, and the surrounding wood splintered.

"Whoever it was that barricaded the front doors then must have retreated here, and tried to lock themselves in," Leon observed.

"Didn't work." Franco was in the corner behind some piled furniture. "Look."

The group followed and looked over the debris.

The floor had broken open, and a dark pit gaped below them.

"What the hell? It collapsed?" Carlo leaned out some more.

Janus eased toward it. "Deeper than the basement. Can't see the bottom."

"Sink hole, maybe, " Carlo said.

"Doubt it." Franco crouched. "The floorboards ... they're all blown upward. This wasn't sucked down, but smashed up." He tossed a loose board into the hole, and it dropped and clattered against the walls but they didn't hear it hit bottom.

"There's smoke coming up. Maybe tremors opened it, who knows? Etna is doing some weird stuff right now." Carlo leaned out over it a little more.

Janus held up a hand and the group quietened. He crouched at the edge of the hole and concentrated. After a moment, he pointed to Franco. "Scan it."

The soldier pointed his movement scanner into the pit, and held it there for sixty seconds. Then he shook his head as he watched the tiny screen. "Nothing."

"Okay, scratch that theory." Janus backed up. "Let's get out of here."

The men checked the other rooms one by one and found they were similar – empty, but may have been recently occupied. No people, no survivors, but thankfully, no blood or bodies either.

"If everyone got out, why didn't we see them out there?" Leon asked. "Where the hell are they?"

"*Did* they get out?" Janus let his eyes run over the interior of the church, and also looked up toward the domed roof. "Whatever happened here was over quickly. Maybe they took them."

"Took them? Who took them?" Carlo asked quickly.

"Down the hole?" Leon asked.

"Bullshit," Franco spat back. "There was no rope or ladders, and they certainly wouldn't have jumped."

"What do you think, capo?" Carlo asked.

"I don't know. But all these doors were locked from the inside." He pointed with the muzzle of his gun. "Those doors are made from solid oak, and the locks are torn out of the frame. Looks to me like no one left by choice." Janus exhaled. "Let's try the next building, and then continue with our sweep."

They headed back to the front double doors, silent and professional, but Janus knew they were all on edge now, conscious that things were about as far from being right as they could be. They had expected to find people overcome by fumes, maybe even some looters, but not some sort of mass vanishing act.

At the door Janus took one last look around the smoke-filled room – like his soldier had said, it was just full of ghosts now. Janus followed his men out through the opening and found them looking confused.

"Where's Enrico?" Carlo asked. The team spun about, looking for the missing soldier.

"Hey, look." Franco moved quickly down a few steps and grabbed the missing man's rifle. "Cazzo!" He dropped it. "It's red hot." He turned his hand over and the palm of his leather glove steamed.

Janus immediately checked the Gladiator scanner that tracked the soldier's position. Inexplicably, Enrico didn't even show up on it. There were just four blips – him, Carlo, Franco and Leon. That wasn't possible ... unless the tracking pill had somehow been removed from Enrico's body and destroyed.

"Alert." Janus raised his gun, pointing it out at the piazza. Leon did the same, followed by Carlo and Franco, who grimaced from the pain in his seared hand.

If Janus had hated the smoke, the dark, and the breathless quietude before, he hated it double now. It was like being in a lost place where they didn't belong. For all he knew, they were the last human beings on Earth, and now whatever happened to everyone else was about to happen to them.

The Gladiators waited, and the stretching seconds tore at their nerves as much as the silence. After a few more moments, Franco lifted an arm, checking his movement sensor.

"Anything?" Janus said without turning.

"Thought I ..." Franco began to lower his arm, but then stopped. "Hold it." The Special Forces soldier frowned at the scanner while raising his weapon to the shadow-riven piazza. "Something out there – movement."

"Where?" Leon panned his gun barrel around.

Janus gripped his gun tighter. "I got nothing. Keep talking, Franco."

"Eleven o'clock, a shadow."

Leon's eyes moved from the sensor to stare hard at the billowing smoke.

"Could it be Enrico? It could be ..." Carlo focused on the direction Franco had indicated. "Can't see shit."

"It's out there." Franco cursed. "Can't be Enrico."

"Why not?" Leon said.

"There's more than one. Closing."

"Maybe Enrico's found some of the residents and he's bringing them in. Gotta be it." Leon walked down a few steps. "Hey, Enrico, over here."

"Quiet!" Janus had that feeling he sometimes got just before the shit was about to hit the fan. "Everybody stay in formation."

"Doesn't make sense." Franco shook his head. "The signature is big, too big for a man. I don't get it. This is all fucked up."

"Shit," Janus cursed softly.

"Capitano, ah, I got a real bad feeling." Franco started to back up. "This is all wrong."

Janus heard fear in the man's voice, and that worried him more than anything else because he knew his team, and they feared nothing. He spoke through gritted teeth: "We're sitting ducks out here." He spun one way, then the next. "Fuck it, fall back into the church."

"In the church? Didn't help those other guys." Leon was ten feet down on the bottom step and staring up at them.

"But we got the guns. Now move it." Janus turned away, hearing Leon mumble something low about Enrico having a gun. "Go!" he yelled.

Carlo and Franco turned and headed for the double door and Janus followed them. From behind them there was the sound of an impact and a grunt, and the men spun back.

Leon was gone.

"Fuck you." Franco opened fire on the square, followed by Carlo, their stream of bullets making the thick mist swirl and dance around the muzzle of their guns.

"Cease fire, goddamn it." Janus felt his heart race in his chest. "Wait until ..." He quickly checked the personnel scanner, and saw Leon's signature blip moving away from them. The blip became fainter, and then it simply stopped sending out a signal. It was like the man dissolved before his eyes.

He looked up. "What the fu—" Then he saw them. The hulking shapes, twice as big as a man, and their outlines tore at his sanity. In the dark haze, eyes opened ... too many eyes.

From a few miles to their east there came the sound of an explosion. Janus recognized it – a fragmentation grenade, part of the Gladiator's ordinance kit. One of the other teams was under attack. He corrected himself: *also* under attack.

The huge forms started to close in, and Janus gritted his teeth to bite down on the fear threatening to engulf him.

He shook it off. "Lock and load, free fire. Let's give 'em hell." He opened up, laying down a line of fire directly into the massive shadows that stayed just at the edge of their vision.

Franco and Carlo did the same, and in a few moments their first clips were exhausted, they ejected them and like well-oiled machines, snapped in spares. The trio opened up again, the smoke from their guns adding to the veils of fog surrounding them.

The mad shapes with the burning eyes would vanish, but reappear somewhere else. It was impossible to tell if they were having an effect on them or not. But in the next moment, something like an express train came out of the smoke and barreled into them.

Janus fired into it, hit it multiple times – he knew he did – but on it came anyway. The impact was massive, then came the scalding heat. His armored suit sizzled, and there were long tears in the fortified material along his chest and down one arm.

Janus rolled away and came up on one knee, firing. He saw Franco tucked under the arm of something monstrous as it burrowed back into the haze. His man screamed and fought like the devil against the massive greasy-looking body, but his suit smoked where it touched the thing's flesh, and the huge arm held him as easily as if he were a child.

The Gladiator team leader froze but Carlo went after Franco, screaming and firing, and the sight of his maddened soldier unlocked Janus' muscles.

"Hold your position! Carlo, hold your position!" Janus yelled until he was hoarse, but it was too late as Carlo was in the grip of some sort of mad frenzy.

"Fuck!" Janus began to chase after his men, following the sound of gunfire. But then it was replaced with the tortured scream of Carlo. The sound made him grimace behind his mask.

Janus had heard men die before, and knew what pain sounded like. On a previous mission he'd seen one of their Gladiators lose a hand and simply fight on until a medic got to him. His soldiers knew how to deal with pain. But this sound froze him to his marrow. He backed up, checking his locator for his team members. Only one signature now remained – his.

It didn't matter anymore; he now knew what had happened to the local residents, and it had nothing to do with noxious gas.

"Commander Mancini, do you read?" Janus' logical mind knew he was out of communication range, but his primitive one was beginning to panic. "Commander, I need immediate evac, do you read? *Do. You. Read. Me?*" He started to back up to the church. "Shit, shit, shit."

He bared his teeth and fired again, trying to pick his targets, and suddenly hit the church door. These monsters were what the town's folk had barricaded themselves in the church to hide from.

Of course, it all made sense now – the damn hole in the church vestibule. These things had burrowed up from inside, ambushed the hiding people, and snatched them all down to Hell. They'd get him too if he tried to go to ground.

Janus fired continuously as the creatures began to mass, until his gun clicked, empty.

He squinted into the smoke. "Hey!" There seemed to be people in among the monstrosities – men and woman swaying trance-like to a silent chant.

"Who are you?" he yelled. "Help me."

The curtains of smoke opened for a moment and Janus saw them a little clearer: their mostly bare torsos were marked with what looked like tattoos or carvings, and their faces were covered with masks dotted with eyes, maybe to mimic the things surrounding them. Strangely, the creatures ignored them.

"Well, fuck you too." Janus pushed his gun over his shoulder to let it hang on its strap and reached for two frag grenades at his belt. "All or nothing."

The silver canisters had a simple press-button-and-throw detonation action. He had four, and he pressed the buttons on the first two and aimed them toward where he intended to run. The first one he threw just twenty feet out in front and into the thick of the monstrosities, and the next he tossed high and long, a good sixty to seventy feet further out.

He crouched and turned away as the first grenade detonated, quickly followed by the next. Even before the reverberations had stopped he was up and sprinting into the grenade smoke. He ran hard, pumping his arms and legs like he'd never run before in his life. As he did he dragged out the two remaining grenades, pressed the ignition on one and tossed it ahead of him.

This blast was thirty feet in front of him, and it would keep his path clear. He threw his last grenade well out in front and ran, adrenaline making him forget his fatigue, his fear, and allowing him to focus on just getting the fuck out of there.

It was only later that he found out that, of the fifteen Special Forces soldiers that entered the billowing smoke that day, he was only one to make it out alive.

CHAPTER 16

"I can see them – they're coming."

The smoke was getting heavier, and visibility was shrinking, so of course Aimee crashed into the car in front of her. But instead of blaring horns, shaking fists, and streams of Italian curses that would have made a Barbary pirate blush, the man in front simply got out of the car, leaving his door open, looked back into the gloom behind them, and sprinted up a side street.

"What the hell?"

It didn't make Aimee feel in any way more confident that things were under control. Then the car behind suddenly ran into her, throwing both her and Joshua at the dash.

Shit! she silently screamed. The road was blocked both ways, cars abandoned as people fled up the street through the sulfurous, dark smoke that made it seem like twilight. For some reason, the potential for an eruption was not what made her, or the crowd, the most nervous.

The radio and television stations had first recommended people stay indoors. Then as they began to go offline or their signals became dampened by interference, the message changed, and began urging people to leave their homes and congregate at safe-zone contact points on the outskirts of the city.

Aimee felt her stomach flip and just sat, gripping the wheel – she was in a strange city, with little local language skills, and the shit was seriously hitting in the fan.

"Mom, we need to go, quickly," Joshua said solemnly. He turned all the way round in his seat, his eyes narrowing as he seemed to search the dark smoke behind them. He spun back to her and pointed up a side street. "That way … hurry."

"Yes." She opened her door. She had thrown a few things in the trunk and went to retrieve them.

"*Now*," Joshua urged and grabbed her arm. "I can see them – they're coming."

She looked from her son to the smoke behind them – it was ominous, almost alien, and for some reason she didn't want to be here when it fully cloaked them.

"This way." She grabbed his hand and slid him across to her door. Then they began to run.

CHAPTER 17

USSTRATCOM, Nebraska – Hammerson's Office

Colonel Jack "Hammer" Hammerson opened the package from Professor Matthew Kearns. He liked the guy – he was trustworthy, knew his stuff – and that's why he had engaged his services in the past. He hadn't heard from Matt for a while so was interested to see what he'd been up to, and why he was suddenly reaching out.

A slim memory stick dropped out of the package and he slid it to the side. He quickly read the accompanying note: Matt had been down in Italy on a Pompeii dig, and the archeological team he was with seemed to have found something strange. Matt went on to describe it, and the more Hammerson read, the more his brows drew together.

"No doubt about you." Hammerson had seen and heard some weird shit in his life, but Matt had a talent for going that extra mile in rooting out the truly out of this world. The phone rang and he put Matt's notes down.

"Hammerson."

It was Chilton – the furrow between his eyes deepened to become a crevice as he listened. Five-star General Chilton had been talking to General Lorenzo Alfonsi, one of the U.S.' NATO allies, and his counterpart in Italy. Seems the Italians had a problem – an entire section of a town was missing, and a police rescue unit, followed by a full Spec Forces unit, had vanished on entering. Normally, they'd just up the firepower and send in a few hundred National Guard. But they had a survivor, and the story he told scared the shit out of them. Scared them enough that the options they wanted to pursue were either blunt – send in a platoon of heavily armored forces, with the unavoidable media scrutiny, and with the added bonus of risking destruction of the town if that firepower was used in an urban area. Not to mention the loss of life. Or the surgical – send in a specialised force, a group working with them that had political deniability, lethality, and expertise in these matters.

Chilton had long needed an opportunity to rack up favors with his international counterparts and sooner or later, he extracted those favors. So he had offered the services of a small team of HAWCs who had experience, and success, in dealing with the unusual. The decision had been made, and Chilton's call dropped the logistics and execution in Hammerson's lap.

The first thing Hammerson asked for was access to the surviving Italian Special Forces guy. It was already being arranged, plus the guy's debrief material arrived on his computer. The next thing he did was to open a low earth orbit satellite horizon to look at the site from 127 miles in the air. A large screen came to life on one of Hammerson's office walls, and he didn't like what he saw.

The landscape was covered in a massive oily smudge as smoke leaked from Mount Etna – not from the cone at the top but from various places on its slope. The smoke itself was heavy, and hung low, mainly because it was laden with grit, pumice, dust, and a hundred other heavy particles that made it impossible to penetrate. Rarely was the gas deadly but often it was more noxious and filtration devices were used against respiratory particle ingestion. The upside was suits didn't need to be totally airtight. Downside was filters got clogged real quick.

Hammerson read the site data feed that ran down the side of the screen. The other pisser was it was damned hot in there, so until it cooled, thermal vision was compromised. And cooling was unlikely to happen while the hot gas was still leaking out of the volcano.

He folded his arms as the computer software gave him a 2D representation of what the town looked like beneath the smoke – crowded with houses and narrow streets. Hammerson noticed the mix of old and new dwellings. The city was an ancient one; founded in the eighth century by Chalcidians. But its history had been dominated by the volcano, and it had been totally destroyed many times, the first in 1169, and then again in 1693 – each time with thousands dead and missing. The people were persistent, he mused; as Mount Etna knocked them down, they kept getting back up.

And now many of them were missing again. Thousands of men, women, and children falling off the map usually meant they lost consciousness, or worse. He prayed it wasn't worse.

However, the new NROL-42 satellites were literally orbiting brains in the sky, and had the ability to detect and analyze adversary missile data even if buried below ground. They could listen in on private conversations and also use their advanced scanning techniques for gradient variation thermal analysis – the software analytics didn't just determine if things were hot, warm, or cold, they identified a hundred variations in between.

Hammerson slid the vector sensitivity analysis up the scale, drawing out the variations in heat inside the town. The areas on the actual cone and slope of the volcano were still an angry red color, but it became cooler the more he moved the scanning toward the city and its outskirts. The leaking gases made everything around 110 degrees, but within that, there were many heat fluctuations.

Hammerson leaned forward as the software analyzed the differences. It determined the fluctuations came from objects moving within the haze. Hammerson asked the software to make some best-guess analysis on the objects moving around in those hot shadows as he drilled down, magnifying the landscape. The results suggested the objects were larger than a man, more than twice as large, and there seemed dozens of them.

It reminded him of an ant's nest – the things glowed hot and must have been well above 120 degrees to stand out among the smoke. They traveled up and down the side of the cauldron, some vanished into crevices at the top where the hot gases were escaping from. Others seemed more bulky, or perhaps were carrying or dragging objects.

"What the hell are you?" he whispered.

Jack Hammerson let his eyes drop again to the debrief transcript of the single returned Spec Forces guy, Janus, reading over his description of the alarming events in Catania, and the even more alarming adversaries he claimed to have been confronted by.

Hammerson exhaled. Could have been hallucinations brought on by a range of volcanic gases; he knew sulfides alone could do it. But the guy's breathing equipment had checked out fine. So Hammerson had to entertain the idea that maybe there *was* something down there that defied explanation. He knew the elite Italian Special Forces, had worked with them before, and knew those guys were tough and didn't spook easy.

Fifteen went in, one walked out. You don't take out fourteen highly trained, armored-up soldiers without also leaving a big pile of bad guys behind.

He sat back and steepled his fingers on his chest. General Chilton had recommended a small team, but Hammerson's nose told him that there was something going on down there that meant though the team might be small, it needed to have significant offensive capabilities. He knew each of his HAWCs were worth half-a-dozen normal soldiers, and probably double even standard Special Forces operatives. But his ace in the hole was he also had the Arcadian, who was worth more than a dozen.

He sat thinking for a moment, and his eyes slid to Professor Matthew Kearns' letter. The guy was in Italy, and weird stuff was happening. What were the chances of them being linked?

Hammerson plugged Kearns' memory stick into his computer and watched the black and white images fill the screen. They were poor quality and further obscured by the low light, but he could make out a small laboratory. A number of men in disposable biological suits stood around a casket on a portable table. One of them carefully lifted the lid.

Then shit went sideways.

One of the people seemed to become glued to the thing in the casket. Another tried to help but he also became stuck. Soon the others were grabbed by the glued men, and drawn in tight to the mass. Then in even tighter.

Impossibly, the mass collapsed in further still, as if the men were trying to burrow into it, and into each other.

"What the fuck is this?" The images made the hair on Hammerson's neck stand on end, and if he hadn't been viewing it himself, he would never have believed it. Finally, all the people that had been in that small room were pressed together on the table in some sort of knotted, glistening mass of flesh. Arms and legs still flailed, but individual bodies and heads started to become indistinct.

And that was when the camera wobbled and went dark – he assumed it was when the device was grabbed and removed, or maybe the power failed.

The "thing" had been hot, Matt said.

Hammerson rubbed his chin. *Hot.* He thought about the concept. *Hot enough to melt the flesh together? Was that even possible?* He'd heard of bodies being subjected to extreme heat and the fat under the skin running like candle wax, but not becoming malleable like modeling clay.

He needed more data. Matt had put a contact number on the bottom of the letter. Step one: get the kid some tech support and then get him back into that tent to see what the hell was happening. That was critical.

And if he didn't want to go? Hammerson thought for a moment before his lips started to quirk up at one corner.

"Then I'll send over someone who could be very persuasive."

* * *

Matt hung up the phone, screwed his eyes shut, and let his head tilt back on his neck as he groaned long and loud.

"What did he say?" Maria asked.

He chuckled, his eyes still closed tight. "He, Colonel Jack 'the fucking Hammer' Hammerson, wants us to go back in there. See what's happening now."

"No, sorry, I'm not going back in there." Maria's mouth turned down as she vehemently shook her head. "I saw enough."

"Me either," Andreas added quickly. "Above my pay scale. Besides, I'm an archaeologist, not a …"

He trailed off and Matt knew why. There were no experts in this. "Yeah, yeah, I know. You don't have to go back." He sighed, feeling drained. "But I raised it with him, so I guess I gotta follow through. He's sending me some support."

"You don't need to go," Maria said. "If this Colonel Hammerlin is sending an expert, then it's his job now."

"It's *Hammerson*, and I've got to assist. I owe these guys; we've worked together before, and they've kinda pulled my ass out of the fire a few times." Matt shrugged.

Maria's eyes blazed. "Bullshit. You owe no one nothing. And I'll tell him myself, when he gets here."

"Her. It's a her ... and I bet I know who," Matt said softly and sat down. "I need a drink ... better make it a double."

* * *

There was a knock on the door at 8 pm. Matt got slowly to his feet, feeling his stomach flutter a little from nerves.

"Let me." Maria bustled past him, her face tight. She leaned close to the door. "Who is it?"

"Mary fucking Poppins." The door handle worked, even though it was locked. "I know you're in there, Kearns. Open the fuck up and let's go."

Maria turned to him, looking firstly disbelieving and then hostile.

"Go on," Matt said.

Maria made a guttural sound in her throat and unlocked the latch. She drew in a breath, probably preparing to deliver a few ripe Italian curses, and then dragged the door open. Casey Franks stood in the frame, and Maria just stared, mouth open.

Casey was tall for a woman, but looked squat because of her powerful physique, bunched trapezii at her neck, a white crew cut, and glaring tattoos that peeked from under her collar and sleeves. There was also a scar on one side that pulled her face up into a leer and didn't help to make her look any friendlier.

Maria's eyes were wide as she gathered herself up. "Please do not use that language in here."

Casey's eyes slid to the Italian archaeologist and she grinned. Then they moved to Andreas for a moment before fixing on Matt.

"Prof." She nodded. "Just come a long way in a short time. I'm on the clock and we got work to do."

Matt nodded. "Good to see you too."

"Always." She pulled a black baseball cap onto her head. "My disguise." She winked. "Come on – in and out, then I go home, and you get back to chasing Italian tail."

Maria snorted and folded her arms.

Casey stood in the doorway, one foot still inside. Matt saw she had a backpack on, and her bomber jacket and cargo-style pants looked bulky. He guessed she was armored up to the teeth, as usual. He went back to the table, downed the remains of his coffee, and turned to shrug at Maria. The female archaeologist just continued to stare, arms folded.

Matt turned back to Casey. "Got a car?"

"No." Her eyes were impatient.

Matt turned to Maria. "Could I …?"

Maria bared her teeth for a moment before throwing her hands up and then spitting out a string of local curses. "No." More curses. "*No!*" Her eyes blazed for a moment before she went and snatched up her car keys. "I will take you. Someone has got to keep fools like you out of trouble."

Casey chuckled and stood aside as Maria pushed past her.

Matt and Maria sat in the front of the little red Fiat sports car, and Casey Franks was jammed in the back.

Matt half-turned in his seat. "You've been briefed … and seen the footage?"

"Yep." Casey continued to look out of the windows.

"They looked like they, uh, melted together. Weirdest thing I ever saw." Matt shook his head. "What do you think it was?"

"No idea." Casey turned. "But we'll find out soon enough, won't we?"

Matt was about to turn back, but then paused. "It might be a disease. Some form of contaminant."

"Jesus, Mary, and Joseph, we were exposed." Maria's head flicked to the side as she gawped at Matt. The car veered for a moment.

"Watch the road, lady." Casey snorted. "And if it was a disease, both of you would be infected and maybe melted by now." She winked. "Melted together."

"*Melted*. Jesus," Matt said stiffly, and then faced the windscreen again.

Maria pulled in under a stand of trees a few hundred feet from the site. The lights still burned inside the long tent, except for the end with the cool room, and the specimen. The trio stepped out, and Casey handed Matt a pair of binoculars with night vision. He scanned the perimeter as she opened her pack.

"See anything?" Maria asked.

Matt continued to pan for another few moments. "Silent as a tomb."

"Here, give 'em over," Casey said as she pulled on gloves. He held out the field glasses.

Casey had changed out of the bomber jacket and now wore a dark uniform that was insignia free. Its packs, pouches, and belt bulged with devices, weapons, and canisters, and over her back was what looked like the stock of a shotgun.

Maria sneered. "Glad *you've* got protective clothing."

Casey lowered the glasses. "Yeah, well, be a Special Forces soldier for a few years, then join the HAWCs and get shot, bashed, burned, and blown up a few times. And then maybe they'll give you the nice stuff." She slid the glasses into a pocket. "Let's take a look." She turned to Maria. "You stay here with the car."

"Testa di cazzo!" Maria seethed. "I am not your taxi cab."

Casey gave the woman a disinterested stare and then turned away. "Matt." She started down, and Matt followed, Maria close behind.

At the door to the huge tent, Casey stopped and leaned her head up against it. Matt did the same, but he heard nothing. Casey nodded and went in first. Matt held the flap open a few inches to look around and then slid in as well. He could feel Maria right behind him.

Casey moved quickly down the length of the tent to the darkened cool room. The flaps that separated it hung limp, and there was no noise, not even the sound of the machinery running the air-conditioning units. She pulled a small box from a pouch on her leg and unwound a stiff cord from around it. She handed the cord to Matt. "Camera strip. Feed it in."

She switched on the box and Matt felt the cord vibrate in his hands, wriggling slightly like a living thing. Then there was an image of him projected on the tiny screen. He carefully eased the tip in through the flaps.

Casey used a toggle to make the tip move one way, then the next. She scanned the room for a few more seconds. "Clear."

She took the cord from Matt, quickly wrapped it back around the box and slid it into its pouch. Casey then drew the shotgun from over her shoulder. It had a light fixed under the barrel, and she switched it on. She turned, her face deadpan. "Stay here." She slipped in through the flaps.

Matt waited and turned to Maria, who shrugged. He concentrated but heard nothing, and wished Casey had left him the snake camera so he could have followed what was going on without actually being in the room.

Just as Matt leaned his head closer to the flaps to try and hear a little better, they were pushed aside, making him leap back and step on Maria's toes. The Italian archaeologist yelped and shoved him off her foot.

Casey's gloved hand held the flaps wide. "When you two are finished, get in here."

Matt went in but moved to the side rather than venture toward where he knew the specimen table was.

Maria did the same, trying to keep Matt in front of her, but then stopped dead and made the sign of the cross. "Santa Maria."

The central table and cool unit had been crushed. The tabletop was covered in a viscous slime with some streaks of red and brown through it. *A little like afterbirth*, Matt thought.

Casey held up the barrel of her gun, illuminating the side of the tent. There was a huge hole torn in its side. "I'm betting your melted man – *men* – went that way."

She walked to the ripped shreds and stuck her head out. Then she lifted the flashlight to move it over the landscape for a few moments before pointing it down at the ground.

"It's gone." Matt ran a hand through his hair. He found it was damp with perspiration and he pushed the slick strands out of his eyes. "It somehow got up and walked away."

"Obviously retained motor skills." Casey drew back in and turned. "Or developed new ones."

Maria lips curled. "That abomination could never have walked."

"Couldn't walk, huh?" Casey held the shreds of the tent wall out of the way. "Then whatta you call these?" She pointed with the barrel of her shotgun. On the ground were plate-sized imprints.

"They're *not* footprints." Matt frowned down at them.

"Not human ones anyway." Maria crossed herself again.

Matt peered one way then the other and then stepped through the ragged hole, Casey at his shoulder. He squatted over one of the prints. "Looks like several people put their foot in the same place at once." He traced it with his finger. "See."

The print was ragged, roundish, as if made by an elephantine stump rather than a human footprint. The front half was dominated by the budding appearance of toes, but dozens of them, and all pressed deep, as if the thing was extremely heavy – which it would have been if five full grown men had pressed down together.

Casey shone her light further along the dust-covered ground. "This is hard-packed ground – that thing's gotta weigh over a thousand pounds to leave that kind of track depth."

Matt looked along the track and pointed with his flashlight. "Went that way."

"Then that's the way we're going." Casey immediately started off.

"Wait ..." Matt got to his feet. He looked back at Maria, who grimaced as if in pain. "It's okay, wait for us here."

"By myself?" She gawped at him. "While this thing is wandering around out here? No, no, no, your tough friend has the gun, so ..." She stepped through the hole.

"Good." He put an arm around her, and she allowed herself to be pulled close. "Thank you," he said, and meant it. Matt knew that if Maria really wanted to she could have simply returned to the car, driven off, and left them. And that would have meant a damned long walk for Matt afterwards.

"You owe me dinner. And maybe more."

"Deal." He kissed her on the nose. "Hey, so that's why you invited me down here."

"I invited you for your brain first." She reached across to grab his belt. "And maybe this next."

They laughed, and she lunged up to kiss him again. Then Matt pointed his flashlight at Casey's disappearing back. "Quick, let's go."

They hurried after the HAWC, who was like a bloodhound following the tracks, her light moving from side to side on the dusty path. Olive trees began to crowd them, making the shadows in the darkness even more ominous.

Matt and Maria caught up to Casey, and they followed the tracks out of the ancient city ruins into the denser stands of trees.

Casey paused, shining her light on the tracks as they headed up the slope. "Where does this lead?" she asked.

"To the volcano's summit, of course," Maria replied.

Casey stared up the dark hill. The trees and lack of moonlight made it almost pitch black. She reached into her pack and removed a scope that fit over one of her eyes and switched it on.

"Night vision?" Matt asked.

"And thermal."

"Got any spares?"

"Nope, but you got me." She turned back. "Steep climb, so suck in a breath and let's go."

She headed out, and Matt and Maria followed.

After thirty minutes of climbing they left the trees behind and the slope had steepened to about forty-five degrees. Matt puffed and sweated but Maria was a hundred feet further back. Casey paused to wait for them. Matt wasn't surprised at all to see she didn't even look winded.

"Hey, this bad boy is extinct, right?"

Maria caught up, and sat down. "No." She leaned back on her elbows. Her face was slick from perspiration. "Not dead, only asleep. Vesuvius has erupted many times since the one that destroyed Pompeii, and it is still the only volcano in all of Europe to have erupted within the last century. Though it sleeps now, it is still regarded as extremely dangerous, and largely unpredictable."

Casey grunted. "If it's sleeping now, why is it getting hotter? Thermals are going into red."

Maria laid a hand on the rocks for a moment. She shrugged. "Like I said, dormant, but unpredictable."

There was a low vapour hanging over the ground that flared in Casey's light. The sounds of night had dropped away as if the dark was holding its breath, and the HAWC held up a hand. Matt and Maria froze, their gaze going from Casey into the pitch darkness.

Casey turned her head slowly, scanning the landscape, and then her gun went in tight to her shoulder. Matt crouched and dragged Maria down with him. Neither of them had guns or anything they could use as defence if something that weighed over a thousand pounds and might have wanted to melt them into itself lumbered out of the dark.

"I don't like this," Maria whispered.

"Me either." Matt swallowed dryly, and waited. He knew that one word from Casey and he'd be sprinting back down the hill like a jackrabbit.

Casey stood. "All clear." She scanned for a moment and picked up the trail again. "Well, our stump-footed bastard is still going up. So ..." She began to ascend again.

Matt turned to Maria. "You okay?"

She lifted a hand and Matt took it and helped her up. "I think I can go a bit further. But not all the way to the crater."

Matt nodded and looked upward. The crater was another thousand feet, and up there it was rockier and even steeper. He doubted he wanted to try that either. "You and me both."

They trudged on and caught up to Casey again. She held up a hand. In the air now there was the distinct smell of sulfur. Matt could feel the uncomfortable heat now. It radiated up from the ground and was almost overwhelming. It made him feel like he was on a griddle.

Casey pointed to an opening, a narrow cave, in the side of the volcano. "It went that way." She approached and held an arm over her face as a shield to try to get closer. After a moment she screwed her face in pain. "Jesus, gotta be 250 degrees in there."

Matt edged closer but also felt his eyebrows singed by the heat coming out of the fissure. "Nothing flesh and blood could survive that."

"Tracks lead in, none out." Casey forced herself closer, and then shone her light into the hole. Scalding steam wafted past her. "Ack." She turned away, rubbing her face with an arm as she was beaten back. "Can't see shit in there. But runs deep, and that thing must have gone in and kept going."

"Maybe it wasn't hot when it got here," Maria said softly.

"Yeah, yeah, that musta been it. Let's hope it got caught by the heat," Casey said and looked about. "Well, this has been really illuminating."

"What now?" Matt asked.

Casey stepped away from the fissure. "Maybe get HQ to send a drone into the hole. Get a cast of one of those weird-ass footprints to send to the lab guys. Then get back to base. Nothing else for me to do here."

She turned to give Matt one of her grin-sneers. "And you, prof, don't go too far. You know how the Hammer always has questions."

Matt sighed. "Yeah, yeah, I remember all too well."

He looked down the slope of the volcano. He could see the twinkling lights of the many towns on the Bay of Naples such as Boscoreale, Trecase, Ercolano, and Portici. It was more crowded now than it had ever been in its history – nearly three million people living close by today. *Mad or crazy brave*? he wondered.

He knew that Mount Vesuvius was still regarded as one of the most dangerous volcanoes in the world, putting all those souls at risk from one of its violent and explosive eruptions. But tonight, Matt couldn't help thinking that a potential eruption wasn't the only thing that the locals had to worry about.

He turned to look down at the print in the hard earth. Something weird had happened here, and a knotted feeling in his gut told him it hadn't run its course just yet.

Beware them that are of all of us – the tablet's translation crept back into mind again. Was this the thing that ancient scribe was trying to warn them against? Matt had a terrible feeling that he'd find out soon enough.

CHAPTER 18

There'd be hell to pay. And the payment would be in blood.

Jack Hammerson ran both hands up through his iron-gray crew cut. Some bad shit was going down in Italy, and now Aimee Weir and Joshua Hunter had gone missing there. Added to that, Professor Matthew Kearns had found something weird at Vesuvius, which meant inexplicable events at two volcanoes in the same part of the world – what were the odds?

He groaned and sat back. Alex Hunter wasn't due out of the Box for another twenty-four hours. He had to be there for the entire stretch. He needed to drag that monster from his id back to the deep, dark dungeon of his mind and lock it in. If he didn't, there was a higher chance it would surface sooner, stay longer, and, one day, decide it was strong enough to stay around for good. Then there'd be hell to pay.

With the Advanced Synthetic Warrior Program, Hammerson felt they had the tools to deal with anything that fate could throw at them. The ASWP was a prototype for a combat-ready battlefield soldier that never fatigued, never ran out of ammunition, and never second-guessed its orders. It would fight the wars of the future, possibly against similar synthetic adversaries.

But Hammerson knew they had developed it for another reason – in the event Alex Hunter ever went rogue, they needed something just as powerful to hunt him down and either bring him in or take him down. It was an insurance policy, but Hammerson would move Heaven and Earth to avoid that scenario. Alex was his protégé and friend – like a son to him. Plus he needed him more than ever. There would have to be absolutely no other option before he'd ever deploy the Sentient Operational Heuristic Interactive Android – SOPHIA – to take the Arcadian down like some rabid dog that got off its leash.

Besides, there was no way that the Arcadian would ever surrender – if Hammerson ever sent SOPHIA to bring him in, it would be a death match. Only one of them would come out.

And that left the boy, Joshua. He had always figured in Hammerson's plans as a second-tier option; other than his unique abilities, he could be trained to control the Other – go inside Alex's head and short-circuit the demon taking hold of him, or better yet, eradicate it all together. Every day, Joshua became more powerful, more valuable, so there was no way on earth Hammerson was going to lose such an asset.

Jack Hammerson sat back, grimacing as he again read the report of Aimee and Joshua vanishing at Catania. He was between the devil and the deep blue sea – he had been instructed to get a team over there, ASAP. Normally he'd never let a soldier go on a mission where he had a vested emotional investment in the game. But if he didn't, when Alex found out, he was likely to tear the joint to pieces and then go anyway.

He couldn't delay sending a team for twenty-four hours, and couldn't risk pulling Alex out of the Box early.

Hammerson rubbed his jaw, the stubble making a rasping noise under his calloused hand. So he'd take a gamble and split the option down the middle – he'd send a team in, and send Alex in later. Let him finish his psychological decompression. When he emerged, he could follow the team over. Besides, by then the HAWCs would have done some groundwork and might have already located Aimee and Josh.

He pulled up the HAWC files for his available team. Casey Franks wasn't back yet, but Sam Reid was active. He'd send the big guy in as leader, with a team of three – more than enough. Reid was a wrecking machine, and at six-four and two ax handles wide at the shoulders, he was a fearsome operative. He was their oldest HAWC, but since he had been surgically upgraded with the new MECH technology, he had internal scaffolding that made him a human battering ram. He was also the best strategic thinker they had.

Hammerson went through the bios, selecting the skills he needed. He'd bring in Drake 'Hondo' Henderson. He was nearly as big as Sam and together they'd provide the grunt muscle. He did good work on the Ginna mission, and would be an accomplished addition.

Hammerson's eyes narrowed as he considered his next two selections. Both had excelled in their former Special Forces units and had applied for, and been accepted as, HAWCs. Hammerson liked to bring in other disciplines from time to time to give a more rounded edge to their expertise – the HAWCs were the best in the world, but there was always something new to learn, and he always wanted to be at the forefront of the curve.

The first was Aiko Shimizu, a former member of the Tokushusakusengun, the elite Japanese Special Forces group. They were samurai and ninja all in one, and though at five-eight she was one of their shortest members, she was a black belt in karate, judo, and swordsmanship, plus an expert in modern weaponry. She lived by the code of bushido – the way of the warrior. He smiled grimly; he bet she'd give Casey Franks a good run for her money in the hand-to-hand combat stakes.

Finally, he selected Lucas Velez, from the Spanish Mando de Operaciones Especiales. The bio picture showed a black-eyed young man with a shaven head, dark stubble extending over his skull like a cap and continuing over the lower half of his face. The man wasn't tall but hugely muscled, with trapezius muscles running up to almost his ears. He was their new demolition and tech expert, and by the look of him, spent his free time tossing weights around.

Hammerson leaned back in his chair and tried not to think about the scenario if anything happened to Aimee and Josh while Alex was in the Box. He took a deep breath and exhaled loudly – he could guess: there'd be hell to pay. And the payment would be in blood … maybe even his own.

"So be it." He sent the alert that would bring the team in immediately.

* * *

Hammerson watched as his team filed in. He motioned to the chairs and Sam and Hondo took seats on one side, looking like a pair of muscled mountains. Aiko Shimizu and Lucas Velez took the other side.

Hammerson reached forward to press buttons on his desk, and the end wall of his office slid back to reveal the huge screen. He brought up the images of Catania at the base of Mount Etna. There was little to see. He stood, rounded his desk, and folded his arms.

"Pre-eruption expression – plasmic discharge – dust, grit, pumice, smoke, hot, but not deadly hot. However, certainly enough to cause respiratory problems, and maybe worse in the elderly or very young."

He flicked to a new picture that was an X-ray image of the city laid out below the smoke layer. "The greater city of Catania has over one million inhabitants and is one of the largest in Italy. Estimations from local authorities are that most of the civilians got out, but there could still be tens of thousands who stayed put." He looked up. "Tens of thousands now missing."

Sam frowned. "Missing? How, where? I know Mount Etna; it's erupted dozens of times, large and small scale. The local authorities would have evacuation and rescue plans ready to go. A little smoke wouldn't cause that much disruption and certainly not lead to that amount of disappearances."

"Correct," Hammerson replied. "They have, and they did. Their first action was a mandatory citywide evacuation. Then they went in to assist the remaining residents, who couldn't, or wouldn't, move. But those search and rescue first responders never returned – there was over a hundred of them. Plus that dust cloud seems to be corrupting all forms of communication."

Hammerson changed the picture to one that was tracked images based on thermal signatures. "So then they sent in a Special Forces team."

"Gladiators?" Sam asked.

Hammerson nodded. "The best, and over a dozen of them. Only one came out of that dust cloud. He said they were attacked."

"By who?'

"Maybe not by who." Hammerson pressed some buttons on a small remote and the thermal image enlarged. "Maybe by *what*."

The HAWCs sat forward as the next image showed the huge shapes moving about in the smoke. He let the team watch for a while; the lumbering figures, their shape, and they way they moved, as they went up and down the crater side.

"Not human; what the hell are they?" Hondo asked. "What scale?"

"Nine to ten feet. Possibly a thousand pounds each." Hammerson turned from the screen. "And they're hot – computer analysis says they could be 120, even up to 150 degrees."

"Not possible," Lucas said. "How can they even function without frying their brains?"

'Extremophiles," Aiko said and turned to Hammerson. "In the sea of Japan, there are hot vents on the sea floor. We have found bacteria that can survive in temperatures reaching 175 degrees."

"That's true," Hammerson said. "But the thing is, they're not just *surviving* in extreme heat, they're actually generating extreme heat."

"And we have a survivor who saw them up close?" Sam asked.

"Yep, a Spec Forces team leader by the name of Janus Romano. Apparently one of their top operatives, so not prone to exaggeration. We'll need to talk to him."

"We need more information on what we're dealing with," Sam said. "Right now our unknowns exceed our knowns."

"Agreed." Hammerson turned back to the smoke-filled screen. "There's something else. Computer analysis has determined that some of those things might be carrying objects. I have this horrible feeling deep in my gut that those objects they're carrying are our missing people."

"Oh, Jesus Christ." Sam's jaw clenched momentarily. "Why? What are they doing with them?"

"Add it to your list of unknowns." Hammerson lowered his brow. "They look to be vanishing into the volcano fissures. Your job is to find out the why, what, and where. Follow them in if need be."

"You want us to go inside a volcano, swimming in molten magma?" Sam Reid's forehead creased so deeply it created a valley between his brows. "That's about 2000 degrees. No suit's gonna protect us from that."

"Of course not," Hammerson replied. "But good tech will allow you to get up close and personal to something that might be a tad under 200 degrees." He turned. "And if need be, venture just inside the volcano. No swimming required."

Sam snorted. "Getting better all the time."

Hammerson sighed, then sat down. "Nope, not better, it gets worse. Aimee and Joshua are in there. Also missing."

"Oh, Jesus Christ, no." Sam just stared for several seconds before rising to his feet. His expression hardened.

Aiko looked from Sam Reid to Hammerson. "Who are these people?"

"Captain Alex Hunter's family," Hondo said and put both his large hands to his face to rub hard.

"The Arcadian?" Aiko's eyes widened. "He has a family?"

"Yeah, it's not well known, and that's the way he likes it." Hondo grimaced. "To keep them out of trouble."

"Didn't work." Sam's voice ground down a few octaves. "Does he know?"

Hammerson shook his head slowly. "He's still in the Box; will be for another twenty-three hours."

Sam's opened his mouth to protest, and Hammerson held his gaze. "You know he needs to stay in there, lieutenant. In twenty-three hours, by the time he emerges, you *will* have data for me. *Clear?*"

"Crystal." Sam's jaws worked for a moment, but then he nodded. "Then what the hell are we waiting for?"

"For you and the team to get down to armory and kit up. You leave immediately – helo is already on the pad." Hammerson stood. "Dismissed."

CHAPTER 19

"This can't be real."

Aimee dragged Joshua by the hand as she weaved in and around abandoned cars, and scurried up streets that were shrouded in smoke so heavy it was like a London fog – except everything smelled of sulfur, ash, and burning.

People screamed, careened into them, or stopped to wail and grab at them, imploring them for things she couldn't understand. At one point she felt Joshua's hand clamp tightly on hers, and looked down to see his eyes wide and staring. She followed his gaze, but saw nothing but the thick, roiling smoke.

Then the shape appeared, shambling, enormous, and at first her mind tried to fit it into any slot it could find, telling her it was an escaped elephant with waving trunk. Then more trunks, or limbs appeared, and as it came closer, she saw it held the flailing body of some poor soul it had captured.

"This can't be real," she whispered.

Joshua's shaking hand yanked hard on her arm. "Mom, this way."

They sped on, and he pointed. "Down there."

Men and women were piling into a doorway and at its entrance she saw steep steps leading downward. She hesitated, but Joshua dragged her down anyway.

As she descended, she prayed Alex would find them … soon.

PART 2

"The difficult we do immediately. The impossible takes a little longer."

Motto of the U.S. Army Corps of Engineers during World War Two

CHAPTER 20

Catania State Police Headquarters, Briefing Room 01

Janus Romano watched as the American Special Forces soldiers entered the room. They'd come straight from Air Station Sigonella, a shared U.S. Navy and Italian Air Force base in Sicily. They were HAWCs – he'd never heard of them before. But the first one through the door was huge, just making it under the frame, and the floor beneath his feet creaked as if he was made of steel. The two following were so wide they seemed only just able to pass into the room. The last, an Asian woman, had the cold eyes of a predator searching for its prey.

All of them focused on Janus, sizing him up, assessing, analyzing impatiently. He came to his feet, meeting their eyes.

"Janus Romano," one of the huge men said. It wasn't a question.

Janus nodded.

"Sam Reid." He gripped Janus' hand and pressed hard.

Janus returned the pressure, then felt overwhelmed and released the man's hand.

Reid pointed to each of his comrades. "Hondo, Velez, Aiko." They took seats and sat.

Janus did the same. "So you're who they sent?"

"Yeah, and we're on the clock," Sam Reid said. "We need to know everything relevant. We've read your report. Now tell us what wasn't in those reports. Things you thought were a little strange or maybe too unbelievable to put to paper." He leaned forward. "Speak openly; you're among friends here."

Friends, huh? Janus inhaled deeply. *What the hell.* "They weren't human." Janus looked into each of their eyes as if searching for disbelief or ridicule. Satisfied there was none, he went on. "They were big, nine to ten feet at least, and moved faster than we expected. And they were hot, burning hot. As if they were on fire." He felt his heart rate start to rise as he remembered.

"We saw that on the thermal vision," Hondo said. "Can you describe them? You're the only guy that's been up close to them – and walked away."

Janus' vision turned inward as his mind took him back to the piazza. He shook his head. "They were madness in flesh … impossible."

"Think hard; make yourself remember," Sam said, leaning forward.

"No, I mean, those *things* were impossible." Janus sipped his coffee and put the cup down. "Imagine …" He opened and closed his hands and then made a sort of knotting and clenching motion with his fingers. "Imagine if you got a lot of bodies and squashed them all together. But they were upright and walking on two legs. At first I thought it was some sort of octopus thing, but then I saw that there were two main arms, and lots of smaller ones, but normal, human ones." He licked his lips. "The big, main limbs were made up of dozens of smaller limbs all stuck to each other, like they were all melted in there together, fused somehow."

Janus exhaled and then drained his coffee. "The face." He put the cup down hard. "The face on that inhuman head was on the end of a trunk, and big, covered in the blackest eyes you've ever seen. Eyes all over it, and more damned faces pressed into its sides." He screwed his eyes shut. "Some of them still looked alive, screaming in agony or insanity." His eyes flicked open. "They looked like the souls of the damned in Hell."

"Whoa." Hondo blew air from between his pressed lips. "That's good, take it slow."

"One thing." Janus turned to Hondo. "I'm sure there were men and woman with them, like they were working with them. It was strange, as they seemed to be in a trance and had their heads covered with masks." He rubbed his eyes with the heel of his hands. "I must be going demente." He dropped his hands and gathered himself. "The creatures can be hurt. They ran from my grenades – when I was the only one left, I made a path through them and just ran for it."

There was silence for several moments as the HAWCs waited for him to go on. But he had nothing else for them.

The big HAWC, Sam Reid, grunted. "Well, if they can be hurt, they can be killed."

"You're going in?" Janus asked.

Sam nodded.

"Then take me with you." Janus' face was granite in its determination.

Sam didn't think about it, and might have already expected he would. "Good, we can use you. We leave within the hour."

Janus looked at their suits. The HAWCs wore a dark armor that had some sort of vein-like ribbing running just under the surface. He pointed. "Heat retardant?"

Sam tapped his chest. "Stop a shotgun blast, as well as shield against extreme heat. New NASA space technology."

"So it won't burn?" Janus asked.

"Everything burns eventually," Velez said. "But at least we'll be able to get in real close ... for a while."

"Okay." Janus stood. He wanted some payback, and these guys were going to help him get it. "Let me get my kit, and I'll see you out front in twenty minutes."

Sam Reid got to his feet. "Make it ten."

CHAPTER 21

"Welcome to Hell."

The HAWCs stood at the side of the road that seemed to act as an unofficial line in the sand where the smoke and pumiced fog began. They still hadn't engaged their visors.

Lucas Velez sniffed. "Sulfur."

"Sulfur, heat, and demons; welcome to Hell," Hondo said.

"Don't joke," Janus said. "There is indeed something hellish about it."

Sam took one last look at a small photograph of a girl, coffee colored and with a smile like sunshine. He'd been dating Alyssa for months now, and she was his lucky charm. He tucked the picture in behind one of his breastplates, over his heart.

He sucked in a deep breath. "Helmets up." He then pressed a stud at his neck and a layer of shielding moved up and over his head before a clear cover slid over his face. He spoke into a small mic at his chin. "We're now entering the blackout zone." He checked his watch; it was eleven in the morning, 1100 hours. He started a timer. "Three hours in and out, returning at fourteen hundred hours."

Hammerson responded immediately. "Good luck. We'll be waiting. Over and out."

Sam turned to see his HAWC team had their shields in place. Janus also wore a tactical combat suit with breathing apparatus.

"Move out."

* * *

Janus led them directly to the piazza where he and his team had been attacked, and Sam raised a hand to stop them at a corner. He switched his scope from thermal to light enhance, and then to motion tracking – it was as dead as a graveyard.

But for all the stillness and silence, he felt eyes on them. They were being observed from somewhere in that huge village square.

He and his HAWCs carried the AA-12 assault shotgun and had loaded the experimental high-explosive fragmenting antipersonnel ammunition. Plus their shotguns had thirty-two-round drums, never jammed, and would blow big holes in anything from bone to armor plate. The HAWCs had a range of other weapons, but it seemed on this day, their adversaries were more elephant sized than human shaped, so they would engage with the appropriate firepower.

"We explored the church, and found it empty. But there were signs of forced intrusion and a fight that was over fast," Janus said, and looked about a little too quickly. "There was a dog here, right here." He pointed to the ground. "It was dead, and mutilated. But burned as well. Gone now."

The man seemed skittish for a professional, and Sam could guess why. He hoped it wasn't a mistake bringing him back in so soon after his lost his team. "Hey, you okay?"

Janus spun to him, then nodded jerkily. "Yes, yes, just on edge."

"Understandable," Sam replied. "So where exactly was your team attacked?"

Janus nodded toward the end of the piazza. "Out front of the church. They came out of the smoke … from everywhere. Dozens, maybe more."

"Okay." Sam took a last look around. "Let's stay cool, and stay tight. Hondo, take us in. Velez, get on the tracker, and I want constant updates. Janus with me, and Aiko, cover the rear."

The HAWCs headed in, their lights sweeping the darkness. Even though it was little more than midday, they barely illuminated the night-dark piazza. They moved quickly but carefully. The huge form of Hondo, gun jammed in at his shoulder, made the sulfurous smoke swirl as he pushed through it. Velez had his arm up, reading data from a small screen on his forearm.

"Anything?" Sam asked.

The stocky HAWC shook his head. "Dead; not even a mouse moving out there."

"Aiko?"

"All quiet back here."

"Let's hope it stays that way," Janus said quietly.

"Yes and no," Sam said. "Let's hope we find some of those missing residents. And that's all."

In the distance the domes and spires of the cathedral took shape in the gloom. Sam was mentally preparing his next steps when Velez jolted him back to the piazza.

"Hold the phone, we got something." He pointed his motion sensor at the smoke, then panned it along the streetscape.

"Hold." Sam stopped the team. "What've you got?"

Velez stared at the tiny screen on his arm for another moment. "Weird … gone." He shook his head and began to drop his arm, then stopped. "Wait …" He snapped his arm out, moving it slowly over the shadow-riven piazza. "Movement … confirmed."

"Where?" Hondo panned his gun barrel around.

Sam gripped his gun tighter. "Keep talking, Velez."

"Eleven o'clock, approximately 250 feet." He stared hard at the motion sensor.

"Could it be the missing civs?" Hondo focused on the direction Velez had indicated. "Can't see shit up here."

"Two hundred twenty feet; closing, coming right at us." Velez cursed.

"This is how they took us out," Janus said. "We need to pull back. In the open we were vulnerable! Just like you now!"

"Hold it together, people." Sam's deep voice was an oasis of calm.

"Multiple signatures – maybe it *is* some of the residents." Velez walked out a few steps.

"It is *not* the civilians," Janus warned.

"Hold your position." Sam's soldier's intuition moved into overdrive. "Everybody stay in formation."

"One hundred feet now, picking up speed. These readings don't make sense."

Shit, Sam cursed silently. "Keep talking to me, Velez." His head snapped one way then the other, looking for cover. He found it.

"Ah, it's all screwy." Velez shook the wrist that held the device. "Sometimes it says just a few signatures, other times I'm reading dozens – big and small."

Sam decided. "Move it, HAWCs – that shop front, three o'clock, double time – *now*."

The group sprinted to the shop.

Velez took one last look at his wrist. "They're here." He turned, sighted, then fired.

Sam was first to the shop front and raised one huge leg to kick at the door. The locks and reinforcing couldn't withstand the technically assisted kick and exploded inwards.

"In!" he shouted over the din of explosive shells being fired into the dark.

Aiko and Janus went through first, followed by Velez. Sam saw the shapes then – huge mountains of flesh with waving appendages. The things tore at his sanity as his pipe of light spot-lit them – arms, legs, faces, all pressed together. Some of them with mouths gaping in perpetual screams and insanely rolling eyes.

Their explosive fragmentation shotgun shells smashed into the creatures and detonated on impact, blowing chunks of wet flesh over the piazza.

He backed into the shop front, as outside quickly began to resemble an abattoir – strewn body parts at last separated from the main body by the explosives.

Sam paused in the doorway, racking and firing his gun. "Hondo!" He waited, firing twice more. "Lieutenant Henderson, sound off."

There was nothing.

He prayed it was only their comms down, and that the man had needed to take shelter further down. He aimed and fired again as more of the things crowded in at him.

"Fuck it!"

He backed into the shop just as the windows were smashed out, and gun barrels stuck through. The smoked-filled square echoed with the sound of explosions, accompanied by the wail of a thousand mouths.

Sam blasted the shapes – fired, fired, reloaded, and fired again – he might have been yelling as he did, as he tried to drown out the hell bearing down upon them. One thing Sam knew for sure; he wasn't going to let his team be pinned down here as their ammunition ran down.

He spotted a gas cylinder stored beside the door and half turned to yell over his shoulder: "Muscle up, HAWCs, we are leaving."

He grabbed the metal bottle and flung it outside. While it was still in the air, he fired a fragmentation shell into it. The detonation was loud, hot, and blinding.

"Go, go, go!" Sam led them out.

* * *

Lieutenant Hondo Henderson was in a world of pain. He was being pressed hard into the body of the thing as it surged along the streets. The huge limb that held him was far too big and powerful to push back against. He knew his left arm was broken.

His sanity was leaving him as his back was pressed closer to the monstrosity, his head turned to the side so he could see the thing's flesh, and make out exactly what it was: bodies, and parts of bodies – hands, feet, torsos, and faces, all melted together to form a single massive creature.

Of course it wasn't possible. And he might have thought he had gone insane, or perhaps was already dead and cast down to Hell, except he could feel the heat of the thing right through his suit, and though the specialised armor could shield him against temperatures up to 250 degrees, he still felt the scalding mass searing his skin.

The creature paused for a moment, and Hondo felt an odd, sticky-wet sensation on the skin of his back – he couldn't shake the idea that it was dozens of hot, slobbering mouths all working on his flesh. He felt himself sink a few inches into the revolting mass. It was then he realised his suit was coming away, perhaps being melted, or maybe even digested.

He couldn't help the sob of helplessness that escaped his lips. *This is not how HAWCs die*, he thought miserably.

From the corner of his eye he saw the wall of eyes and mouths in the thing's flesh. One of the eyes swiveled toward him, human, brown, and in its curve he could see fear and sorrow, perhaps for him. He began to panic.

"Oh god, no. Fucking help, *help*!" He didn't know if his calls were heard, but he continued to shout, struggle, and wrestle against the thing.

He turned to the side again as his face was pressed deep into the creature. He knew now what was happening to him, and he suddenly knew how all those body parts became glued together. He continued to scream, even as his voice joined with the hellish shrieks of the other damned souls.

* * *

Back to back, the HAWCs retreated from the piazza. They fired explosive rounds at anything that came within range, and a wet, red spray fell as bloody rain onto the ancient bricks.

For every creature they took down, more would take its place. At one point a behemoth rushed in and grabbed at Sam's arm; it burned, and a wisp of corrosive-smelling smoke rose from the heat-resistant armor. He glanced down and tried to make sense of what was clasping his arm – a twisted sort of massive arm, but ending in hands, human, and dozens of them, all groping, gripping, and wetly red as though they had been recently torn from their previous hosts. There was something else pressed in there: it looked like a dog's paw.

He whipped his gun around and blew the arm off at the shoulder, and it fell like a soft log at his feet. Revoltingly, the blasted-away limb's multiple hands kept opening and closing with a life of their own.

In among the crush of monstrosities Sam heard his team yelling, cursing, and firing – they were in tight at each other's backs, never leaving a gap or an uncovered field of fire.

Then Sam heard a scream, a voice, anguished, and babbling in English. He recognized it and lowered his gun.

"Hondo?"

He spun one way then other.

"Cease fire."

The booming shotguns fell silent and the creatures began to press in on them once more. Sam thought he saw his soldier then, or what he had become – Hondo's face stared blankly back at him, but it was mostly buried in the revolting flesh of one of the creatures assailing them. His soldier's eyes swiveled to regard him with a plea, and a mix of misery and what – recognition?

"Fire!" Sam yelled and the explosions started once again.

* * *

It was another twenty minutes before their guns fell silent. The massive monstrosities vanished as fast as they'd appeared, leaving nothing but billowing smoke.

Strangely, there were no bodies or severed limbs littering the street. There were patches of greasy-looking mucus and blood, but the things must have retrieved their limbs before they vanished.

"Think they'll be back?" Velez asked.

"Yeah, yeah I do." Sam kept his eyes on the streetscape.

"Why did they leave?" Aiko turned slowly. "They had us cornered."

It was a good question but before Sam could answer there came a crash from behind them, and the HAWCs spun, guns up. Janus had removed his helmet and slammed it down on the ground.

"This, I told you." He cursed for a second or two in Italian, before waving one arm around expansively. "I warned everyone who would listen. These things, these mostro, took all my teams, and you walked us right back in front of them."

Sam let the man vent, knowing that two instances of defeat in as many days burned deep.

Janus shook a fist at them. "I wanted them to send an army, and all I got was three American soldiers and a woman with a sword. It is not enough." Janus pointed. "Now you see; and now your man is gone too." He marched up to Sam, his face beet-red, showing even through his stubble. "We need more soldiers. We need a tank."

Sam laid a hand on Janus' shoulder. "Yeah, I know, it's all fucked up. But we're all you got." He lowered his head to stare into the man's red-rimmed eyes. He compressed his MECH-assisted fingers on his shoulder and into his body armor. "Janus, we came here to put our lives on the line for you and your city. We're here fighting and dying for you; remember that." He gave the man a push, and Janus backed up a step.

The Gladiator soldier's frown was deep and his eyes screwed shut as he clearly fought back his frustration. After another moment he nodded once.

Sam turned back to stare out over the roiling street. He felt the pain of defeat and loss like a punch to the gut. He held up an arm, and saw that his tracker showed nothing moving out there. It was time to bug out.

"Back to base, and regroup. Double time."

CHAPTER 22

USSTRATCOM – Hammerson's Office

Hammerson put the phone down. He sat for many minutes with his chin resting on his fist as his mind worked. One man down, no new data, and a top HAWC team beaten back. That was unacceptable.

Sam Reid's debrief sounded like something from a horror movie, and after hearing him detail the attack, Hammerson suddenly thought that Professor Matthew Kearns' little adventure down in the Pompeii ruins was a whole lot more interesting and relevant – he'd said that the creature they followed seemed made up of human body parts, were hot, and had vanished into fissures in a volcano. It was all too similar.

On Casey Frank's request he had sent a drone into the Vesuvius fissure, and it had tracked the thing's stump-like footprints for hundreds of feet in and downward before the drone failed as its circuitry melted.

Matt was on the ground when one of the things was being created, and he'd kept repeating a translation about a warning: "beware them that are of all of us", and "She must be fed". Bottom line, the guy knew something, and was of value to their mission. That meant he'd volunteered to be part of the team whether he liked it or not.

Casey Franks was due to leave within the hour – Hammerson had a new job for her. He'd divert her to link up with Sam Reid at Catania – with the insightful Professor Matthew Kearns in tow.

* * *

Matt turned from his screen to watch Casey Franks by the window, standing rod straight as she talked softly to Colonel Jack Hammerson. Her eyes were narrowed and she looked pissed off. But then again, he thought, the tough female HAWC was always pissed off.

He sighed and glanced at Maria, who read a newspaper, sipped ink-black coffee, and dragged on a cigarette so hard, the end glowed like an orange bullet. *She's still shaken up*, he thought.

He went back to his research, going over some of the notes he had made. He had also uploaded the image of the tablets Rembrani had showed him. He used an application to lift the faint symbols from the 5000-year-old surface and looked for matches. He only found one, drawn from an Italian researcher's field notes from 1901. The man's name was Sergio Caseletti, and he had done some early excavations in and around the Italian volcanic areas. Caseletti had done some work on similarly aged lettering found in a cave, and though Matt found numerous errors in his translations, there were other areas of pure brilliance.

In his notes, Caseletti had drawn the symbols and lettering that Matt worked on now. The downside of archaeology work around volcanoes, other than them erupting of course, was that lava tended to destroy most traces of humankind.

However, the upside was that it didn't destroy *all* of them, and those that did survive were encased in a basalt time capsule.

"Wish I could have known you, man," Matt said as he copied Caseletti's translations down, and also saved his notes and observations to his Pompeii folder.

He then looked at what he had: *The cult of She*, and then ... *possibly the basis for the real devil.*

"She again." He chuckled softly. "The She devil." He read from Caseletti's notes on the wording. The man had found that at every major eruption that had affected mankind for thousands of years, the cult of She appeared. It seemed to exist to serve this devil or god of the underworld as it rose to the surface.

Matt sat back and folded his arms. Many ancient cultures thought volcanoes were the doorways to Hell or the underworld. But it was the first time he'd ever heard the devil expressed as being feminine, other than in fiction novels.

Behind him he heard Casey Franks sign off on her call. She was silent for a few moments.

"Hey, good news, professor."

Matt swung around and gave her a flat smile. "We can certainly use some."

"You get to extend your holiday in Italy." She grinned sardonically. "And spend more time with me. The bonus being you also get to spend time with some of your other HAWC buddies."

Matt got to his feet. "Wait, what? That was the good news? For who?"

"Serving your country is an honor and a joy, professor. So yeah, good news all round. Plus, you'll be assisting the Italian government, so double the bonus points." She became all business. "There's a helo arriving on the outskirts of town in thirty minutes; be ready."

"Oh for fuc—" Matt looked skyward for a moment. "To where?"

"Catania, foot of Mount Etna. You now have twenty-nine minutes." She turned away to make another call.

Maria had also gotten to her feet. "I'm coming."

CHAPTER 23

USSTRATCOM – the Box – nothing in, nothing out

Alex sat in the absolute silence and darkness of the Box. He was alone, imprisoned with nothing but his memories and his demons. And each time the struggle got a little harder and longer.

He was not getting weaker, but he knew his adversary was getting stronger. Blood ran from his nose and his head throbbed with a pain like a torn muscle deep in his skull. He would heal; he always healed, and so far, he always won.

The beast was chained once again, and he knew the time would already be ticking down to zero, to when he would emerge to rejoin life outside. He didn't have any regrets or hostility toward Hammerson or the scientists who locked him in. In fact, he had come up with the original idea himself. They were just making sure his idea was carried out successfully.

After this long in immersion, he should have been feeling relaxed and totally back in control. But something was different. It was just there on the edge of his consciousness – a nagging twinge, like a pebble in your shoe, or single mosquito in a dark room. Insignificant, but he felt it inside him as keenly as if there was something looming in the dark, crouched just inches away, waiting for him to move.

The familiar question loomed again. *What if?* he asked of himself. What if the Other gains control one day, and decides it is strong enough to refuse to relinquish its hold? Alex had wondered what he would or could do if that happened. He had been there and felt the chaining up of his own psyche deep in the darkest realms of his mind – seeing and sharing events, but not being able to do anything about them as the Other controlled his body while he was a mute hostage.

What if he witnessed great horrors, or engineered them? What if it endangered his family? He lowered his head in the darkness. Would it be better if the world were without him? If the Other threatened the ones he loved, then the only one who could probably stop him was him.

But how would he know when it was time? Alex rubbed his hands through his hair and found it damp with perspiration. He would fight it as long as he could, and prayed he'd know when it was finally … time.

Alex leaned back on his haunches and reached out with his senses, but as he expected, they were deflected. The Box was a heavily armored room, lead lined, more like a bank vault, used to shut him in with just his subconscious, and the creature from his id. But it also shut out all external sensations – nothing in, nothing out.

Or so he thought. His eyes flicked open.

The locks clanked and whirred, and then the heavy metal door was pulled back.

CHAPTER 24

"Now it's your turn."

Hammerson was waiting for him. Though his superior officer was keeping his expression – and emotions – in check, Alex could read him as clearly as if he was shouting.

"What's happened?"

His commander's jaw jutted for a moment, hesitating, and Alex felt a jolt of alarm run through him. He stared hard into Hammerson's face. "Aimee? Joshua? What happened?"

"A situation in Italy," Hammerson said, standing rod straight. "Follow me for a full briefing." He turned on his heel and headed for the war room.

Alex did as ordered, but his stomach was already knotting with tension. He reached out with his senses, trying to find Joshua. If the boy was in trouble he might be trying to find Alex.

But his mind was fuzzy as a building anger created white noise in his mind. He fumed at being kept in the Box if there was trouble. He concentrated even harder, and his head began to throb again.

He put a hand to his head. "I can't ..." His frown deepened as a line of blood ran from his nose. He wiped it away. "I can't find them."

Hammerson stepped into the elevator, and Alex followed. The older man faced forward as he spoke. "There's an inexplicable event happening in Italy."

Alex drew himself to his full height. "That's where Aimee and Josh are."

"We know. We have a team in there already – Sam's heading it up. You'll be joining them as soon as you're briefed."

Alex shut his eyes and strained to calm himself. "When ... did this occur?"

"It's still unfolding now."

"That's not what I asked." Alex opened his eyes. Hammerson's expression was deadpan, his eyes half-closed, but Alex could see the heat bloom on his cheeks and forehead. A lesser man would be sweating under Alex's intense gaze, but Hammerson was made of much sterner stuff. The elevator doors opened and Hammerson stepped out on an upper level.

"As soon as I heard, I sent in Sam and a team." He was walking fast, and Alex shot out a hand to grab his arm to stop him. "Jack?"

"We lost contact with them," Hammerson said evenly. "So far the team has failed to find them."

"What the hell is happening?" Alex felt the anger tightening even more in his gut.

"We were trying to find her, but got beaten back." Hammerson's jaws clenched.

"HAWCs beaten back? By who?"

"Unknown adversaries." Hammerson lifted his chin and turned. "Now it's your turn."

* * *

Alex burst from the war room office following the briefing. He sprinted to the secure elevator and slammed his hand against the panel that read his DNA, palm, and fingerprints.

Hammerson said Gray would be waiting for him. He was to get kitted out and meet a chopper that was already warming up to take him to a high-speed plane.

As the huge doors slid back he stepped in and jabbed a thumb at the level he wanted – weapons R&D. Once his details were read and acknowledged, the heavy door slid shut. Alex ground his teeth with impatience as he was transported hundreds of feet below the earth and into the titanium-steel composite belly of the secure facility, that was also blast proof, EMP proof, bio-chem-attack proof, and had its own water and oxygen circulation system.

The doors slid open to reveal the small, nervous-looking scientist, who greeted him with an awkward salute.

"Captain Hunter, good to see you again."

"Yes, and me you," Alex said. "I've only got minutes."

"Of course, and I was expecting you." Gray turned, almost having to jog to keep up with Alex's longer legs.

"Why did our team fail?"

"The same reason all good teams fail," Gray responded matter-of-factly. "The failure was due to underestimating and lack of knowledge of the adversary. Not due to skill deficit or equipment effectiveness."

"Well, your suits burned – sounds like equipment failure to me. I've read the report as well," Alex said, glancing down at him.

"Not having enough data can be fatal, captain. You know that." The small man seemed indignant at the accusation. "The more we learn about warfare, the better we can prepare for war."

"We lost a good soldier. I hope the extra data was a worthwhile information trade."

Gray nodded. "We learned a lot. I was told to expect temperatures of 180 to 200 degrees, so I built a tolerance for 250 degrees as a fail-safe. The primary heat generated by the beings was that, but it seems that they may be able to generate heat in bursts at far higher temperatures. We also know that there might be some sort of corrosive enzyme that is excreted." He stopped at a silver door and placed his palm against it. "Like I said, the more we learn, the faster we can adapt." The door slid back but before the small scientist entered, he turned. "Just remember, we're one step removed. To mount a best defense we need to know more." He looked up at Alex. "I need a sample."

Alex grunted.

"I mean it. Get me one of the multi-morph creatures, or even a good sized piece of one. I'll do the rest."

Alex growled softly. "Given the mission geography is Italy, the lines of communication, and therefore lead times, will be a little long. By the time you've received your physical sample, analyzed it, and decided a best strategy for dealing with it, this mission will be decided one way or the other."

"Perhaps, but still, I just wanted to let you know I do my best with what I've got and what I know." Gray shrugged, and disappeared inside.

"But I agree we do need your input." Alex followed and stopped in the center of the large room. It was the light armament room, and one wall was an enormous gun rack. Off to another side was a firing range.

Gray walked along the rack, speaking over his shoulder. "I've modified the suits to make them more formidable. And also to deal with higher temperatures … as well as all known corrosive substances." He paused and looked at Alex. "*Known* corrosive substances – it would have helped to have a sample. Like I said, the more I know, the more I can design my products to protect you."

He finally chose a weapon and tossed it to Alex. He pointed to a target dummy fifty feet down the range. "Shoot it."

Alex spun and fired. It was a centered hit to the chest, but at that distance the shotgun pellet pattern covered the upper part of the torso.

"Excellent hit." Gray rummaged through an ammunition draw and withdrew a large plastic case. "As I expected, the explosive shells I gave your team delivered much greater punching power. But I understand that the encounter with your adversaries meant that unless it was a close and direct strike, the creatures weren't stopped. And in fact, Lieutenant Reid believed they were recovering the severed limbs and reattaching them." His mouth turned down. "Ugly, very ugly."

"So then we need something that's going to make takedown more permanent," Alex said evenly. "So there's nothing to put back together."

"Or makes it impossible, hmm?" Gray flipped open the case. It contained rows of silver plug-like shotgun shells. He reached out to take the gun from Alex, loaded a single silver cartridge into the shotgun and handed it back. "Once again."

Alex turned, held the gun out one handed and fired.

"Whoa."

His mouth dropped open. The effect was instantaneous. The dummy took the pellets, then froze solid. The room filled with a sound like cracking ice as the target dummy turned into a hardened mass.

Gray grinned. "If you shot it again, it would shatter to a thousand pieces." He nodded, satisfied. "Biological fluids become crystallized and even the individual cell walls are destroyed. Nothing is going to reassemble itself after that."

"Liquid nitrogen, huh? So how do you get it to stay liquid in the shells?"

Gray waggled his eyebrows. "That's where the magic comes in. Getting the nitrogen is easy – it's basically in the air all around us. Liquefying means we need to take it down to over minus 320 degrees. That too is fairly easy." Gray lifted his chin. "But getting it to stay like that is the difficult part." He turned and opened the cartridge box again, took one out and tossed it to Alex.

Alex caught it. "It's cold, *very* cold."

"Yes. The shells are packed with twenty liquid nitrogen pellets under extreme pressure. But they only stay that way because they're kept cold. The shells are basically miniaturized refrigeration units with their own tiny generators." He held out his hand. "They cost about ten thousand a shell now, but we'll bring that cost per unit down over time."

Alex tossed the shell back. "How are you packing them?"

"Boxes of twenty for single use, or in a drum – thirty shells per drum."

"Expensive." Alex's face broke into a humorless grin. "So we'll take two boxes and two drums a piece."

"I'll put it on the colonel's bill." Gray exhaled. "Anything else?"

"Yes. You said the suits have been modified to deal with higher temperatures and corrosives. How high?"

"Wearing the modified suits, normal humans could easily withstand 300 degrees for extended periods. You, with your rapid healing metabolism, maybe 400 hundred," Gray replied warily.

"Not enough." Alex turned back. "Those things are disappearing into a damn volcano. If I need to follow, I'll have to be able to deal with a lot more than that."

Gray tilted his head. "The tradeoff for more insulation and technology will be increased weight and loss of mobility." The scientist turned away for a moment, rubbing his chin. "There is something I've been working on, but it's still very experimental. Plus it's for more short-term engagements. I've been prototyping and refining it for a few months."

"Show me."

Gray pressed a button on the wall and a new target dummy replaced the shattered one. He went to a long silver drawer and touched a stud to slide it out. From inside he selected a star-shaped device with a sapphire-colored bulb at its center.

The scientist grinned at Alex and walked to the dummy, fixing the star-shaped thing to its chest with straps over each shoulder that clasped at the back. He switched it on. A halo of blue light encased the dummy. He walked around it, nodded in satisfaction, and then headed back to Alex and handed him a Glock. Then he spoke over his shoulder as he rummaged in his weapons rack. "Aim for the target; feel free to empty the magazine into it."

Alex fired, several times. All his shots centered, but the bullets ricocheted off as if they'd hit steel, with zero effect to the target dummy. "Force field?"

"Oh, it's much more than that. Or will be, once we've fine-tuned it." Gray handed Alex another weapon.

Alex took the weapon, recognizing it as a flamethrower. "Gas, liquid, or gel?"

Gray turned the extraction fans on full, producing an electronic whine from overhead. "Gas, so only gets to about 1800 degrees." He nodded at the dummy. "Go on."

Alex turned and shot a long rope of fire at the dummy that bathed it in orange. He felt the heat on his face.

"Enough." Gray had his hands up protecting his eyes.

Alex shut it down. After the smoke was pulled from the room, the dummy remained encased in its soft blue glow. There wasn't a mark on it.

Alex grinned. "*That* is cool."

"Cool is right. But more than just defense against heat." Gray grinned with pride, and went and retrieved the glowing device. "I call it a personal defense halo and it can protect against most projectile weapons, impact and percussive explosives, extreme heat or cold, submergence pressure, and radiation exposure." Gray laid it on his open palm. "I'm very excited about it, and I have full funding to take it to the next level." He pointed. "The entire system is designed around the concept of a plasma field generated by ionizing the proximity atmosphere."

"The blue glow – that's the field?" Alex asked.

"Yes; think of it in terms of how lightning generates light in the form of black-body radiation from the very hot plasma created by the electron flow. We do not generate the same energy level as lightning of course, and thus not the same heat. But it's the same concept of using and directing energy in a pattern that we determine."

"Amazing." Alex looked up. "Weaknesses."

"Energy hungry. It has a tiny reactor to power it, but it still needs recharging after ten minutes. It needs to rest before it can be restarted."

"It'll do," Alex said. "I'll take one for all of us, and a spare."

Gray shook his head. "Sorry, you're looking at the only one in existence right now." He pressed a tiny button on the gadget's side and the blue glow died. He passed it to Alex.

Alex closed his hand over it and felt the warmth radiating from the device. "Then this will have to do." He handed it back. "I need it. Recharge it."

Gray gave him a lopsided grin. "How did I know you were going to say that?" His smile dropped a little. "Already happening – the PDH recharges itself when it's not in use."

"Good. Pack it with my kit. Anything else?"

"Yes."

"I know – you want one."

"Alive, if possible. They're unique, and as fascinating as they are horrifying. But more importantly, I can only really combat them if I know them through observation and dissection. At the moment, everything I'm doing is based on best guess."

"That won't be my mission priority," Alex said. "Besides, how would we capture and retrieve something weighing over a thousand pounds?"

Gray smiled. "I have a net – titanium thread and heat resistant. It'll withstand 2000 degrees and you could hold down an elephant with it."

"Jesus, you're serious. Okay, then what? How do we get it to you?"

"Ah." The scientist held up a finger. "I can fix an anti-grav disc to it. It only works for around thirty minutes, but it'll be enough time for you to float it into a sealed crate so I can retrieve it."

"And fly it back to you, huh?" Alex narrowed his eyes. "All the way."

"Yes." Gray smiled. "I'll do the rest. I'll have a heat-resistant, hermetically sealed isolation tank ready and waiting."

Alex checked his watch. "Put everything together, and send it up to the chopper pad. I'll be there in ten minutes."

"Do my best."

Alex paused.

"I mean, it will be there when you are," Gray hurriedly added.

Alex stood in the elevator after the door slid shut, and called through to Hammerson.

"Sir, Gray suggested he needed a specimen to provide us with the best assistance on the mission. I agree with him. But communication lines are too long for that to be effective."

"So you want to shorten the lines." There came a low chuckle. "You want him there."

"Doesn't he have a mobile lab?" Alex asked.

"That he does," Hammerson replied. "I think it's time to get the mouse out of his hole. Consider it done. Get the sample, and he'll be right there waiting for it."

* * *

Hammerson finished the call and remained leaning forward on his knuckles on the desk, thinking through his next steps, then the next dozen more. He mentally worked through both his strategy and the tactics he would employ to achieve his outcome – his tactics he'd share; his strategy, he didn't need to.

Chinese general Sun Tzu once said, "All the men can see the tactics I use to conquer, but what none can see is the strategy out of which great victory is evolved."

So far, Sam Reid and his team had walked into a door, and for that he lost a good HAWC. Hammerson hated losing anything. Losing the human being was one thing, but each of his soldiers cost millions to get to their peak state of readiness. Though that was nothing compared to the battering ram he was sending in.

Alex Hunter's value was immeasurable. Yet there was something even more valuable, and Hammerson would make goddamn sure Alex had everything he needed to succeed. The bottom line was, HAWCs were expendable; even Alex Hunter. But the boy wasn't. Joshua Hunter was a miracle, and potentially the future of modern warfare.

Before he gave Gray his travel orders, he'd make sure he prepared a few other items of equipment and have them in motion. If they weren't needed, so be it. But if they were, they could be a game changer.

Hammerson smiled flatly as he picked up the phone again.

* * *

Around the other side of the secure R&D facility was where the advanced combat armor, field materials, and autonomous soldier program research was undertaken. It was where Sam Reid had had his internal MECH endoskeleton designed, tested, and later surgically implanted into his body. It was also where the SOPHIA had been created.

The darkness of a heavily fortified room was broken by banks of tiny lights on a console that monitored the single figure seated at the center. And they should have been the only lights, except now two additional golden lights began to softly glow, eyes opening on the featureless face of the android.

As the figure initiated, the console started to activate. The figure turned its head slightly and immediately the banks of lights went dark. The face turned back to the door and then seemed to follow something beyond the walls. Its neck slowly craned upward as it continued to watch.

"Alex," SOPHIA whispered.

It continued to face upward, *seeing* his elevator ascend through the hundreds of feet of reinforced concrete, titanium and steel.

"Alex," SOPHIA whispered again. But this time the voice had changed to sound like Aimee Weir's.

The android was designed to be a guardian angel or a hunter-killer, and its slim shape belied a super-tough, near-indestructible chassis. From the moment it was turned on, SOPHIA heard and remembered everything. Professor Gray had said it was perfect. He also said that the applied logic patterning model that was supposed to give it maternal instincts had flaws – a by-product was human-type emotions: hate, anger, love, and even jealousy. They were working now on trying to eradicate them.

The android lifted a hand and the fingertips traced the almost featureless face, hating the blankness. After another moment its head lowered, and the lights went out as though SOPHIA's eyes had gently closed. The console came back to life, its monitors not having registered the interruption.

SOPHIA could wait, but it grew impatient. And it would never let its emotions go. It, *she*, liked them.

CHAPTER 25

Catania, unknown building basement

"They want to hurt us … hurt you," Joshua said softly.

Aimee and Joshua huddled in a dark basement somewhere on a backstreet in the empty city. Other people were with them, pushed into corners and alcoves, murmuring or whimpering softly. There was also a group of four sullen-looking young men. These men weren't fearful, more hungry and calculating than anything else. They whispered among themselves, urgent and forcefully, as if arguing over something. Now and then one or another would throw a glance at some of the younger women in the basement, and their eyes constantly moved to Aimee and Joshua.

Aimee exhaled and drew Joshua in close to her. "Don't worry, we'll be fine."

"Sure we will," Joshua agreed, but with little conviction.

The smoke had grown thicker outside, and then from within the smoke came the screams, and then came the *things*. Joshua had warned Aimee to get them off the street as there was danger hiding within the greasy-hot clouds. She had heeded him immediately, as he was never wrong about these things. Joshua saw with more than just his eyes – the boy was either benefitting from or cursed with some of Alex's abilities. Plus he had a few of his own that were unique – he could sense things hidden to others, or that hadn't even occurred yet. If Joshua said there was danger coming, then that meant you got the hell out of there.

Aimee had followed another group fleeing into the basement of an old building. But before the door had been slammed shut, the young men had pushed in. The dynamics of the room had changed immediately. Now, there seemed to be danger within as well as without.

"I wish Dad was here," Joshua said softly as he watched the men. "Or Tor."

Aimee hugged him. "I'm here."

He turned to look briefly at her, and he nodded. She knew exactly what was going on his head – he liked that Aimee was there, but as a physical force, she was well down the ranks. Joshua must have known what that meant – it was him that might be called upon to protect her.

* * *

Joshua continued to watch the men, and wondered why it was that at the times when people were most scared and most vulnerable, instead of banding together as one, some would try to take advantage of the situation. It was like some people wanted to separate everyone into different species – the wolves and the sheep.

Anger began to burn in his stomach. He tried again to reach out to his father or to Torben, but he couldn't find them or even see them. He and his mother were alone.

Joshua wanted to be strong, and wondered what his father would do. He remembered Alex telling him a little of what he did for a job: *I protect those who need protection*, he had said. *And sometimes I need to use force against force*. Joshua turned to Aimee.

"I can hurt them," he whispered.

"Don't." Aimee pulled him in closer. "Just ignore them. We're all trapped in here together, and we all need to just stay quiet and wait until we're rescued or this all blows over."

Joshua didn't respond. He knew there would be no *blowing over* for these men. They almost seemed to be enjoying themselves, as if it was them that had orchestrated the situation so they could indulge their bad hungers.

Joshua turned to face them again. They seemed to be trying to make up their minds, and of the four men, two spent the time turning and staring at Aimee and urgently whispering. The other two just shrugged as if not caring one way or the other.

Finally, it seemed they came to an agreement; the four men ambled closer. One lifted his chin and spoke in rapid Italian to Aimee.

She shook her head, not understanding, and spoke the few words of Italian she had memorized but her nervousness made the words fall over one another. To the men her attempt was meaningless, and they shouted back at her. But though Joshua also didn't understand them he could see their intent, and clearly read the train of thoughts of the men as images projected in their minds.

One of the largest held his hand out. "Passporto."

"What?" Aimee frowned. "No."

He held out his hand and snapped his fingers. "Portafoglio – ah, give me wallet."

Aimee's voice took on an edge as she pushed back. "No, leave us alone."

Joshua felt fear coming off his mother and a red haze drew over his vision. He struggled to control himself, and he looked up into the man's face, his gaze unwavering. His mother wanted him to ignore them; he couldn't.

You're not police. I'm warning you: you better back off. He projected the thought directly into the man's mind.

The young bearded man's head snapped around and his brows drew together. "Pardo—" He shook his head and turned back to Aimee. He lunged for her wrist and Joshua concentrated and gave him a small mental push.

The man looked like he had been slapped and blood ran from his left nostril. His friends guffawed at his predicament.

"Cazzo!" he swore, pinched at his nose, and then looked at the thick blood on his fingers. He quickly wiped it on his sleeve. Blood continued to run down his chin. Others in the basement were now watching from the corners of their eyes – interested, but not wanting to become involved or attract attention to themselves.

The young man couldn't stop the blood and screamed in frustration, his words hot and angry. He bared red teeth at them, and blasted out more Italian curses. Blood speckled Joshua and Aimee.

Joshua's gaze was defiant. *Last chance*, the boy projected, this time into all four of the men's minds. They looked to each other, confused. Only the shouter continued his attack. Determined to save face by hurting Aimee.

A folding knife appeared from his pocket. He opened it, and his friends grew silent. He pointed it directly at Aimee's face, his words now all falling over one another into a stream of rage.

Deep inside him, Joshua felt his own anger swell to become a living thing. The man lunged again, and Joshua reacted. He pushed back, hard.

The man grunted and froze, his eyes wide. Then he seemed to hunch over. There came a sound like twigs snapping, and then he began to collapse in on himself.

I warned you. The process sped up and, with grunts and wet crunching, the man folded and drew in on himself even more.

His friends stepped back, their mouths hanging open as the folding man seemed to get smaller. It looked as if a giant had grabbed him in its hand and was crumpling him like a paper figure.

Joshua finished with him and let the ball of broken bones and flesh roll back toward the other men, who yelled their disgust and fear and backed away.

Get out! Joshua screamed into their heads.

The three remaining men turned, unlocked the door, and fled up the dark steps.

Aimee stared at Joshua and he could tell she didn't know whether to thank him or chastise him.

She leaned toward his ear. "You didn't have to kill him," she said softly.

"I – I … once I started, I couldn't stop." He stared at the mess that was once a human being.

Aimee followed his gaze. "Make that go away."

Joshua gave a mental push and the crumpled ball rolled out of sight, leaving a long steak of red to show its path.

He turned back to her. "No one is going to hurt you, and no one should even try." He looked toward the door and then made it swing shut and lock. He could sense a monstrous presence close outside now. They wouldn't be safe down here forever. And while he would concentrate on keeping the door closed, he didn't know how long he could hold it.

Joshua once again tried to mentally reach his father, but just like the iron door to the basement, he was locked out.

CHAPTER 26

USSTRATCOM – Sub-level 4 – Synthetic Warrior Room

Walter Gray fiddled at the console as he brought the android online. The software changes had been uploaded successfully overnight and he wanted to do a basic check before racing up to the chopper pad.

He muttered to himself about not being a field agent, but knew at the end of the day he'd just damn do as he was ordered. He didn't have the courage to push back against Colonel Jack Hammerson. Basically, the guy scared him, and Alex Hunter scared him – in fact, all the HAWCs scared him.

He chuckled. *Oh well*, he thought, *I'll just have to be satisfied with being the brains while they're the brawn.* Besides, the payoff was he had almost unlimited funding, a huge R&D team, and the time and space to do what he liked.

He hummed for a moment more and then looked up. "SOPHIA, how do you feel?"

The android lifted its head. "I feel fine, Professor Gray." Its face turned to him, golden eyes glowing. "Will Alex Hunter be joining us today?"

Gray smiled, remembering the two had become neurologically bonded on the last mission. Though Jack Hammerson wanted the link in place, he didn't see any reason for it to be activated all the time. Next maintenance, Gray would have to remember to remove it.

"Not today, SOPHIA."

The glow of the android's eyes seemed to dull a fraction.

"Stand up and turn around."

The android did as he asked. Gray looked at the slim, slightly female-looking figure. As the logic patterning they'd used was female-brain based, the physical characteristics were really just for aesthetics. However, everyone thought of SOPHIA as female – especially SOPHIA.

"SOPHIA, tell me about your emotions. Do you still feel anything that could resemble any of those feelings?"

It didn't hesitate. "Negative, Professor Gray. Those feelings are entirely gone now." SOPHIA lifted its head, and the golden eyes settled on him again.

Gray stared back, and felt a small tingle along his scalp. "Now stop that, SOPHIA."

The tingling stopped as the android ceased scanning him. Gray stared for a moment more. Artificial intelligence combined with the logic patterning he'd applied meant theoretically SOPHIA could use deception if she chose to. But how could he tell?

Unlikely, he thought and went back to his tasks. Gray continued to hum as he worked, and SOPHIA followed him with its glowing gaze.

"Professor."

"Mmm hmm?"

"What is my purpose?"

Gray stopped and looked up. "You are a prototype semi-autonomous android, created as a battlefield combat unit." He smiled. "You are the future of warfare engagement."

SOPHIA continued to stare for a few more moments. "Will infiltration be one of my potential tasks?'

Gray bobbed his head. "Hadn't thought about it, but more than likely."

"Then to be a more effective infiltrator, I'll need to look more like the infiltrated. More … human. Don't you agree?"

Walter Gray tilted his head. He knew the android had the most advanced logic and learning protocols embedded within its core subroutines. SOPHIA was designed to learn from its experiences, and therefore make better judgment calls – just like people, it was supposed to get better each time, be more intuitive, and basically mimic human thinking.

He nodded. "Very good, SOPHIA." He was delighted it was making a logical deduction based on what it understood its potential mission protocols might be.

"We actually have some physiognomy designs we can try out. As yet we don't have a full skin kit, but we can certainly give you a face. Would you like that?"

"Yes, Professor Gray. That would be suitable."

He smiled, unable to help feeling a kind of fatherly pride. After all, it was his creation, and it was growing up just fine.

"Well, then, I'll have the design schematics brought down for you to be fitted with."

"Thank you, profes—"

Gray held up a hand and waved it. "I think by now you can call me Walter." He felt the tingling in his head telling him SOPHIA was being nosy again. He wondered what she was looking for. In another second it had passed.

"May I call you something else? Something I find more appropriate?" it asked.

"Huh." Gray smiled but with knitted brows. "What would you like to call me that you think is more appropriate?"

"Father."

Gray blushed and turned. SOPHIA was facing him with that inscrutable visage. "No, that is *not* appropriate."

"Why not? Are you not male, *and* my creator?" it asked evenly.

The diminutive scientist studied her for a moment. "Yes to both, but your creation was no biological function. I *engineered* you."

"Yes, of course ... *Walter*."

"That's better." Gray bobbed his head. "Now, let's get some of those face plates sent down for you to try out. Alright, sit back down please." He commenced the shut-down routine. "When I get back, you can show off your choice to me."

"I will like that."

* * *

SOPHIA sat down slowly. She knew about the facial model construction that had been in concurrent design – she had already accessed and reviewed them. And she had also supplemented them with her own designs. The face she had chosen would be the one she really wanted. And the one she knew Alex Hunter wanted.

CHAPTER 27

Outskirts of Catania – non-affected zone

Before the helicopter even touched the ground the man jumped out. Then came the biggest dog Janus Romano had ever seen in his life. He watched as the pair crossed the square at a jog. The soldier was big, formidable, moved lightly but still emanated raw power.

Beside Janus in the open-top 4x4, the huge HAWC Sam Reid straightened in his seat.

"The boss." He half-turned. "Captain Hunter." Sam stepped out of the vehicle and stood rod straight.

On the approaching soldier's back was a large pack and in each hand he held six-foot duffle bags. The way the straps sagged, Janus guessed they were extremely heavy. But if they were, they didn't seemed to bother this guy at all.

Hunter nodded to Sam, who took one of the bags. Together the men threw them in the back of the 4x4, and Janus felt the car dip lower under their weight. Then Hunter turned to look at Janus. The man's eyes were different. Not colored different, or a different shape, but their intensity was off the scale. It felt like a pair of lasers had just been turned on him, as they burned deep into his brain.

"Captain Alex Hunter." He held out his hand for Janus to shake. Then he thumbed at the huge animal. "Torben. He's also here to help."

Janus nodded. "Captain, I am Janus Romano, Italian Special Forces, at your service."

"I know, I've been briefed. We appreciate it." Alex climbed in the back, and Sam settled in the driver's seat. Torben leaped in and sat next to Alex, towering over them all.

"Sorry about your men, captain," Alex said.

"And about yours." Janus nodded. "Very bad."

"We are the sword and shield," Alex said. "We are what stands between the light and the darkness. And sometimes we lose, and we die." He leaned across slightly. "But we never stop fighting."

Janus nodded, and was about to add something but Alex turned to his lieutenant.

"Sam, update."

"No word on Aimee or Joshua. Last we heard they were in Catania on the coastline, but it's in the dark zone now, and nothing is going in or out."

Alex grunted, and Janus heard the dog whine. He turned to look at it and saw its weird pale eyes were staring out into the murky twilight. It sniffed as it turned its head, then whined again.

"Casey joined us a few hours back. She brought Matt Kearns and another scientist with her. They believe they have some pieces to add to the puzzle." Sam shook his head. "It's a goddamn weird one."

"Any update on Hondo?"

"Taken," Janus said, and turned to look at Alex in the back seat.

"KIA," Sam corrected, and exhaled. "Something came out of the smoke and grabbed him. Something bad. I saw him later, or what was left of him – he's gone." He started the car.

Alex's jaw worked for a moment. The huge dog turned its pale gaze on him, and Alex stared back. Eventually the HAWC leader nodded. "We'll find 'em."

Janus wasn't sure whether Alex was talking to Sam or the dog. But both animal and man turned to stare out through the window at the wall of billowing smoke.

"Got some new ammunition and armor," Alex said as Sam sped away. "Once I'm up to speed, we're going straight back in." His words left zero room for disagreement.

* * *

The HAWCs used an empty house on the outskirts of Catania as their command base. Sam shouldered open the door, carrying one of the bags, and Alex followed with the other bag, Janus and the huge dog behind him. Casey, Aiko and Lucas were already on their feet and standing at attention when Alex came into the room, and Matt and Maria sat forward.

"At ease," Alex said, dropping his bags and kit. They thumped heavily. He turned to the dog, and it went and sat in the corner, facing them, its pale eyes running over the group.

"Jesus, that is *some* dog ... or wolf," Matt said. "Is it Joshua's?"

"Yeah. Just pretend it's not there. He – Tor – is here to help with the search."

"Ignore it, huh?" Matt scoffed as he stared at the 150-plus-pound animal. "Yeah, that'll be easy."

"Don't worry, he only eats small professors." Alex gave Matt a flat smile, looking at the young man for a moment longer. "You and trouble seem to go hand in hand, Professor Kearns." He walked forward and grasped his hand.

Matt chuckled. "It's a gift." His face became serious. "I heard about Aimee and Josh. They'll be fine, we'll find them."

"That we will." Alex looked at his wristwatch. "In one hour we're going back in. I've got upgraded suits for more heat resistance, and also some new tech and weaponry." He motioned to the bags. "Organize your thoughts, get the new kit on, and then I want a full briefing in ten minutes."

"HUA!" the HAWCs responded as one.

Casey grabbed the bags and opened them as Alex turned to the small Italian woman who stood with her arms folded in the corner. "And you are?"

"She's with me," Matt said quickly. "Her name is –"

"Maria Monti," the woman said. "Archaeologist. I was the one who discovered the artifact, or specimen, as they later called it, at the Pompeii dig site."

"Nice to meet you." Alex nodded. "You and Matt get coordinated and then tell me how what's going on at Mount Etna and Pompeii all fits together when we have our group briefing." He turned to Sam Reid and gestured to the front door. "Sam."

The pair walked outside. The smoke was like a wall cutting off the town; it stopped, unnaturally, just a hundred yards from where they were.

"I've read your report. Now tell me what happened – everything."

"Large adversaries, powerful, nine to ten feet in height, at least a a thousand pounds and maybe much more. Human but not human."

"Extraterrestrial?"

"Unknown. They had human body parts, but they were as far from human as you can get. They healed real fast, and gave off extreme heat. We couldn't stop them." He looked up, sorrow etched on his craggy features. "They took Hondo. But ..."

"But?"

"I could still hear him afterwards, and then I thought ... I saw him." Sam grimaced. "Pressed into one of those things. Trapped, absorbed somehow."

"Absorbed." Alex tested the word and felt a knot form in his gut when he thought of Aimee and Joshua being in there somewhere. A small bloom of pain started in the center of his head, and he fought it down. "We need to go in. Time is everything now."

He walked back inside and Sam followed. "Let's suit up – final briefing in five."

Right on five minutes later, the group were kitted out in the new armor and stood waiting. The HAWCs looked liked robots in the black, heat-resistant outfits with armor plating over the chest, arms, and thighs. There were cascading plates over the stomach, neck, and where the joints needed maximum flexibility.

Alex looked along the group. "New armor, more protection, and with two modes. The current setting you're in is open combat mode – takes general field-fire while retaining high speed and mobility. It's also got toughened plating to take more hits, bigger hits, greater heat tolerance, and also has a chromium-oxide protective film to defray corrosive substances.

He smiled grimly. "And then there's war mode." He seemed to shrug, and heavier plating slid down over his body and up and over his face. He now looked like the black knight, as the facial plating was more pointed over the features.

"Oh, yeah, baby." Casey nodded.

Alex held up a hand, making a fist. "Extreme defense for close quarters. You can take a hit from an RPG and walk away with nothing but ringing ears." He squeezed his fist, making the hand shielding grind. "You hit something with this, it'll stay down."

Sam activated his war mode, and the plating covered his massive frame. He chuckled and punched a huge fist into his other hand. "Payback time."

The HAWCs all activated their armor and showed Janus how it worked. Alex turned to Matt, who was still in his civilian clothing. "I brought you armor as well. Get it on, and hurry up."

"Me?" Matt held a hand up. "Oh no, just an advisor this time, capitano." He laughed nervously. "Got a little bit bent outta shape last time, if you remember."

Alex leveled his gaze at the young man. "Professor Kearns, Aimee and Joshua – my *family* – are still in there." Behind them the dog growled. "I know you can help, so you're going in." Alex stared hard for a moment, letting the young man stew before turning away to the HAWCs. "Everyone here has experienced some sort of interaction with these things. Time to pool what we know and make some sense of it so we can formulate a plan. Next time we confront these things, *there will be* a different result. Understood?"

"HUA!" The HAWCs banged armored fists against their chest plates.

"Find Aimee and Joshua, rescue the civilians, and eradicate all threats. These are our objectives," Alex said.

Janus looked like he wanted to argue priorities, but Alex turned to glare at him, and the Italian soldier nodded.

"We will push back or destroy all adversaries. If possible, we are to capture a single creature for analysis. First prize is we take it alive. Second prize is we bring it home in a bucket. Either way, these things are unknown and unprecedented, so the science guys want one."

"Uh, Alex ..." Matt cleared his throat. "We, um, don't think they are."

"He's right. You asked us how what we were doing might all tie in, and we have some ideas," Maria said. "In 79AD,

Mount Vesuvius erupted and buried the entire city of Pompeii. Over 2000 people were rescued but many vanished. We've been excavating for years and found several dozen figures. But strangely, dozens and perhaps even hundreds, remain unaccounted for."

"We broadened our research," Matt said. "And there might be even more. Over the millennia there have been significant eruptions and entire populations lost. One of the largest events in recorded human history was the Minoan eruption of Thera around 3600 years ago. The Minoan settlement at Akrotiri on the island of Santorini was completely wiped out." He exhaled loudly. "Once again, the city was entombed by ash and pumice. Thousands vanished, and archaeologists guessed they were simply vaporized from the extreme heat." He glanced at Maria.

"And now I think we can guess what really happened to them," she said.

Matt nodded. "'Beware them that are of all of us'." He exhaled and shook his head. "I think these things are somehow related to active volcanism, and in the smoke, fire, and chaos, they've been abducting people."

"Abducting?" Lucas Velez cursed softly. "What it did to Hondo was no abduction. Sam said it melted him into its freaking body, man. It didn't abduct him, it made him become part of it."

"How did it do that?' Alex asked.

"The flesh seemed to have become ... liquefied somehow." Sam stared at the floor, his face creased in confusion. "It's not possible; flesh just can't do that."

"I think it is possible," Aiko said. "In Japan we have a new type of funeral for people who do not want a burial or cremation. It is referred to as 'returning to the water'." She frowned, apparently trying to recollect the process. "It is technically called 'alkaline hydrolysis'. The body is placed in a pressure vessel of water and potassium hydroxide, then heated. Over several hours the body is broken down into its chemical components – it becomes a liquid."

"This didn't take hours, and he was still alive when it happened – I think," Sam said.

"What the hell are these things?" Casey asked. "Are they – *were* they – people or not?"

"Maybe not," Matt said. "Maybe they're just using the people. Like some a suit of clothing, or a vehicle to get around in."

Alex had had the same thought. "Like a parasite."

"Sure." Matt shrugged. "Or a hermit crab. They're either wearing us, or using us as raw materials. You're not far off with that parasite concept. There are many examples right around the world where parasites infect a host, and turn it into a breeding factory or suit of armor. They take control of the body and make the flesh and blood their own."

"But they're insects," Alex said. "And human beings are a lot more complex."

"Yeah, but infected frogs are the same – the parasites make them try and get eaten by herons, just so the parasite can reproduce in the bird's gut."

"Yech." Maria's nose crinkled.

"Exactly," Casey said, and grinned at her, but the scar on her face made it just look evil.

Maria quickly looked away. "We saw it happening at the Pompeii dig site." She shook her head. "Horrible."

"Yeah." Matt raised his eyebrows wearily. "The original specimen was probably just a piece of one of these creatures, and my money is on it being the same sort of thing. Yet it somehow managed to capture and absorb five grown men. It then was able to fully regenerate and reanimate after nearly 2000 years. The kicker was it got up and made its way up the side of a volcano to disappear into one of the fissures."

"The thing, specimen, was dormant when we found it," Maria said. "And then maybe the air revived it."

"Like a bug or bacterium, or maybe even a seed; hibernating or dormant until it finds the right environment, then it germinates and revives." Alex didn't like the idea one bit.

"Maybe it's the volcanoes that revive them – the heat," Sam said.

"I see there is definitely a relationship. But we've got too many maybes." Alex straightened. "Time for some damn answers." He checked his wristwatch. "We roll in ten."

* * *

The phone rang and as Matt was closest he picked it up. "Pronto?"

There was silence at first and then a click as though a line had been connected. Then came faint sounds like some sort of wind blowing, or perhaps a distant wailing, followed by a long sigh and something like scratching.

"Hello, who is this?" Matt was sure there was a voice, or voices, in there among the weird sounds. The more he listened the more the hair on his neck began to rise – it gave him the creeps.

"Who is it?" Alex asked.

"Maybe ... a crossed line." Matt felt a shiver prickle all over his scalp. "I think."

Alex held out his hand and Matt handed the phone to him. Alex listened, his eyes staring straight ahead. Matt knew that Alex's hearing was far superior to his own and he wondered what the man was picking up. After another moment, Matt heard the plastic of the phone casing start to squeal as Alex's hand tightened.

"We'll find you." His voice was soft but his eyes were volcanic. "And we will kill you." Alex lowered the phone and hung up. "They know we're here now."

Matt watched as he walked to the dog in the corner and crouched in front of it. He took the dog's muzzle in his hands and stared into its pale eyes. In return, the dog held his gaze.

"Can you see them yet?" Alex spoke quietly.

Both human and canine eyes were unblinking, and Matt had the feeling that some sort of communication passed between them – not just a sensation or notion, but a coherent thought or message.

After another moment Alex nodded and let the dog's muzzle go. He straightened.

"Let's roll."

Matt felt his heart kick up a few beats in his chest. The suit made him feel both safe and uncomfortable. It was a little big on him as he supposed that either Alex guessed at his size, or they just didn't make them for people not bulging with muscles. But it was flexible armor, and when he tapped the chest, he felt solid plates underneath its skin, and it wasn't even in war mode. He had no doubt it'd stop the most formidable of ammunition.

He just hoped it would insulate him from heat as well as a physical attack from those ... *things*. He'd seen what it had done to Professor Rembrani, and also what Sam had told them of Hondo's fate. He knew he'd run a mile before letting that happen to him.

The only differences between his, and Alex's and the other HAWC's suits was that it looked like Alex's had some sort of extra device attached to the center of his chest that glowed blue, like a tiny sapphire heart. *Or a target,* Matt thought.

Also, behind Aiko's left shoulder he could see the handle of the sword she carried. He'd asked her about it when he arrived. At first she just stared at him with her enigmatic gaze but then withdrew the sword, holding it forward, and laying the blade over the back of her other fist. It was slightly curved with a circular guard and long grip to accommodate two hands.

"Katana; it has been in our family for 400 years." Her eyes ran along the gleaming, two and half foot steel blade. "Very special."

"It's beautiful."

She nodded. "This blade is made by the master sword maker, Nagasone Kotetsu. Very high silver content, and it is beaten, and rolled over five hundred times and then polished for three weeks." Almost faster than the eye could follow, Aiko whipped it up to slice the air back and forth. "It cuts true and deep."

Matt was about to ask about the story he'd heard that a samurai sword should not be fully unsheathed unless it tastes blood before it is returned. But then he saw that she ever so slightly nicked her hand before sliding it back into its scabbard. She bowed and rejoined her HAWC comrades.

Behind him Maria groaned a little and he saw her rolling her shoulders. She looked good. Where Casey Franks in her armor looked exactly as she was – a bull-necked and tattooed killing machine – Maria's made her look like a curvy superhero.

"You okay?" he asked.

"Yeah, just feels … strange." She smiled a little brokenly. "I'm a bit nervous."

"Me too." He put an arm around her and pulled her closer. "You don't have to come. I can advise them, and we'll be back soon anyway."

Maria shook her head. "I need to see this. Whatever is happening here now happened nearly 2000 years ago. This is a direct link to the past. I *must* see it through." She shrugged. "And besides, this is my homeland."

"Knew you were going to say that." He kissed the top of her head. "You'll – *we'll* – be fine. These guys are the best. Just remember, we're only advisors, so stay behind them."

She smiled. "Don't worry, I notice there's no gun on my suit."

Matt chuckled, but then realised there *was* one on his – a sidearm. He exhaled loudly and turned to watch the HAWCs load their belts with silver cartridges. Casey whistled as she pressed some of the canisters into her shotgun and looked up in time to catch Matt's eye.

"Git sum," she said through her grin.

Matt nodded. He'd always liked Casey. And also liked that she was on his side, as she was one of the most capable and ferocious people he had ever met in his life. Years ago he had been asked to join a scientific expedition beneath the dark ice of the Antarctic. Before then he didn't know that people like her, or the HAWCs, even existed. He half-smiled; before then he also didn't know that monsters were real. Now he did.

He sucked in a few deep breaths. He'd seen what had happened to the men in the tent at the dig site in Pompeii, and he didn't want to get close to the things. But he'd worked with the HAWCs before, and they were an indomitable force. And with Alex Hunter at their head, they were something else again entirely.

They filed out to two six-wheeled vehicles that looked like turretless tanks. Alex, Sam, and Janus took the first. Alex clicked his fingers and pointed at Matt's chest. He waved him on.

Matt gulped and nodded – looked like he was up front. He waved as Maria climbed into the second vehicle. She had Casey, Aiko, and Lucas surrounding her, so it'd do – he hoped.

He smiled to her, he hoped reassuringly, and as he went to climb into the lead vehicle, the huge dog bumped him aside to position itself on the back seat next to Janus.

"After you," he said. The massive animal turned its way-too-intelligent eyes on him and stared for a moment. Matt couldn't tell whether it was saying, *Climb in, I'm friendly*, or was radiating a warning: *Make room.*

"Ah, Alex, the dog ..."

Alex turned to the dog. "He's okay."

Matt couldn't tell if Alex meant him or the dog, but the animal faced forward.

Matt scoffed and climbed in, keeping the shoulder nearest the dog hunched up, in case it decided it felt like a human ear for a snack.

"Aimee and Joshua were staying at a villa by the name of Giarra, near Letojanni beach. They're not there now, but that's where we'll begin. Which way?"

"Down along the boulevard and then turn left onto the highway," Janus said. "Ten minutes."

"Go."

Sam put his foot on the accelerator and the muscular vehicle jumped forward. They crossed into the smoke zone, and Matt felt like most sensations had been dampened down – out there it looked dark, silent, and filled with sulfurous smells and billowing clouds.

He felt both excited and frightened half to death. As Casey Franks would say: *Shit just got real.*

CHAPTER 28

Vacant square, the outskirts of Catania

"Whoa, whoa, easy there." Walter Gray watched from the ground as three enormous Chinook helicopters gently lowered his mobile laboratory. The building was the size of two shipping containers and looked like a spaceship. But inside it had everything from an X-ray machine and DNA sequencer to surgical laser equipment. Plus a computer system that stored every genome known to modern science. It was placed on a vacant square on the outskirts of Catania just outside of the boiling, volcanic smoke zone. Gray had brought with him two of his best biological technicians, and felt he had everything he needed, bar a sample of one of the creatures.

The local Italian military assisted in easing the structure down and then unhooked it and waved the choppers farewell.

Gray sucked in a deep breath, just stopping a coughing fit as although they were outside the wall of smoke, the sulfurous air still greasily coated his mouth, throat, and lungs. He looked at his home for the next few days – it wasn't that he hated field work, it was just that he had so much work to do back home that he barely had time to draw a breath.

He turned back to the smoke, examining it in detail – it was like a wave or a dark cliff rising up in front of him, but it was boiling and turning like a living thing. He was intrigued, but also repulsed.

Gray felt the hair on his neck rise. He changed his mind. "No, I really do hate field work."

CHAPTER 29

Locked basment, central Catania

Aimee saw Joshua lift his head from his arms and look up toward the roof with narrowed eyes. After a moment his eyes widened and his mouth curved into a smile.

"They're here."

"Who?" Aimee asked, leaning forward to look into his face.

"Dad, his friends." His smile widened even more. "And Tor – he brought Tor."

"Thank god," Aimee breathed. "Outside?"

"No." He squinted. "Still far away ... but they're here now, in the city ... somewhere."

"Okay. Can you help them find us?"

"I'll try." Joshua closed his eyes, but after a while he began to frown. "Hard." He groaned a little as if trying to lift a heavy weight. His cheeks reddened from the strain.

"It's okay," Aimee said.

Joshua's eyes flew open, and his head snapped to the door. "Oh no – they've found us."

"What? You mean Alex – Dad?" Aimee asked hopefully.

"No, the bad things." Joshua bared his teeth, and she felt him tremble. "Nightmare." His breathing began to race. "Coming." He crushed his eyes shut. "Stop them." Immediately the metal door to the basement squealed shut tighter as if a giant had put his shoulder to it.

Is Josh doing that? She wondered. *Of course he is.*

Something hit the door like a pile driver. Again and again, each booming thump making the iron door ring like a gong and the surrounding brickwork rain mortar to the ground.

Perspiration broke out on the boy's forehead and his gritted teeth began to show as his lips pulled back. The door screamed as two opposing physical forces made war on it.

"Oh god," Aimee whispered.

Then the top corner of the door began to peel inwards with a hellish squeal of tortured steel.

"Can't. Hold. It." Joshua gasped. "Too. Strong."

Aimee got to her feet, pulling the boy to the wall and wrapping her arms around him. "It's okay."

At the top of the door, a hand appeared, wet with what looked like a coating of blood and mucus. Then another and another, grabbing at the steel and pushing and twisting. Oddly, they all seemed to be on the same arm.

More titanic blows, and then the top of the door began to fold inwards like it was nothing more than tinfoil.

Aimee saw it then, and felt her gorge rise. "Oh no, no, no," she breathed.

Joshua's eyes flicked open, but they were rolled back. He screamed one word, long and loud. "*Daaaad!*"

CHAPTER 30

It was a man, or had once been.

Alex Hunter threw his hands up to his temples – it felt like a metal spike was being jammed into his brain. In the back seat, Torben's head snapped back on its neck and it howled long and loud. Matt Kearns grimaced, covered his ears and leaned away from it.

"*Stop!*" Alex yelled to Sam and spun to grab the dog by the scruff of its neck and hold it still. The dog breathed like a steam train and its eyes were a milky white before they took on the same light blue-gray of Joshua's.

The dog's eyes focused, and it and Alex stared into each other's faces for several seconds, before Alex felt the explosion of fear radiate from the dog into his very core. Alex couldn't help his eyes begin to water with impotent rage. He pulled the dog closer.

"Where?"

The dog's head turned, and Alex said to Sam, "Turn at the next left – hurry."

Sam jammed a huge boot down and they were all pressed back into their seats as the vehicle bounced off gutters and sideswiped abandoned cars or bumped them out of the way.

"What is it?" Sam asked.

"Aimee. Joshua – trouble." Alex stared straight ahead.

Sam gave the car the last ounce of acceleration he could find. After another few blocks, they reached a traffic jam where long lines of cars had simply been left in the middle of the street.

"Shit!" Alex spun again and held the dog, dragging more sensations from the animal. The dog pulled away, making guttural noises in its throat that were almost words. Froth appeared at the corners of its mouth.

"Holy crap," Matt Kearns said, still hunching away from the animal while keeping his eyes on the maddened beast.

"Open the door," Alex said.

The side door began to whine open, and in a flash Tor belted across the front of Matt, who yelped in pain as the huge animal used him as a springboard, launching itself out.

Alex immediately opened his own door.

"Wait!" Sam yelled.

But it was too late. Alex and Torben had already vanished in the thick smoke.

* * *

Alex ran fast, much faster than a normal human being, but he still only just kept pace with the enormous dog. Tor snaked around or leaped high over abandoned cars, stopping at one building, a villa, before launching himself on again.

Alex could feel waves of frustration and urgency coming off the animal, and they infected him as well. Alex knew Joshua and Aimee were in deep trouble.

Alex accelerated, but the dog found an open patch of road and increased its speed. It turned up a side street, paused for a few seconds with its head in the air, and then sprinted on again. Alex was losing the animal, and punched the stud on his neck to retract his helmet. Immediately the sulfurous air assailed him, and made his throat burn. The heat also singed his face. But taking the facial shield away meant he had picked up Torben again, and this time he clearly saw the animal in his mind.

Alex charged on, leaping across an overturned car, then stopped dead at the next building – the door had been torn off and even some of the bricks pushed out. There was a sticky slime spattered the ground just outside – exactly as Sam had described was left behind when the thing took Hondo.

Alex turned away, found Torben, and sprinted on. He ran up a narrow alley and turned hard at the next street, until he came to a building with an open doorway and steps leading down.

Torben was already down there, but Alex could also read the presence of Joshua and Aimee. He went down fast. There were no lights, but he didn't need them, as his eyes adjusted to the darkness to shine silver like those of a nocturnal animal. Or like Torben's, whose eyes were twin lights in the dark as the dog stared up at Alex for a moment before bounding off into the pitch dark basement.

Shit, he thought as he saw the solid metal door peeled back like paper and coated in a viscous fluid that glinted like snail tracks. Further inside it was as dark as Hades, and he could only make out shapes. There was no one left, and he quickly found the dog standing upright on its hind legs, nearly seven feet tall now. It was an unnatural appearance, and would have scared the shit out of anyone not expecting it. Tor turned its huge head slowly as if searching for Joshua and Aimee.

"I know, they were here," Alex said softly. He held out a hand and picked up the emanations of fear and anxiety. Something bad had happened in this room.

The dog dropped to all fours again and trotted to something oddly shaped in the corner. It sniffed at it and then whined. Alex also crossed to it, and looked down. At first he found it hard to understand what he was looking at, until he crouched and leaned in closer.

It was a man, or had once been. But his body looked like it had been crushed by a hydraulic press into a lump of broken bones and squashed flesh. The dog sniffed at it again and turned its luminous eyes on him.

Alex nodded. "Joshua did this. Seems like the monsters weren't the only things they had to deal with, huh?" He turned away to scan the Stygian corners of the dank room. More ghosts of anguish screamed from the darkened spaces. Alex knew it had gone from a place of refuge to a trap now just filled with the swirling wraiths of pain and fear.

"We're too late." He felt a burning coil of anger twist in his belly. "They were here and they were taken. We're too late. They took them ... where?" He spun one way then the other, his eyes wide. "Where?" He couldn't help the anger overtaking him. "*Where?*" he yelled, so loudly the dog shrank back a few paces.

Alex picked up an old drum full of broken metal and concrete and threw it at the far wall. It struck with a thunderous noise and made the walls shake and dust rain down on them.

"Boss!" Sam yelled from the stairs. "That you down there?"

Alex stood with his eyes crushed shut for a moment more. Tor whined and came and nudged at his hand. He slowly opened his eyes. "They're not dead yet. We'll find them." He turned and called up the stairs, "Yeah, yeah, stay there. I'm coming up."

Alex climbed the steps with the dog at his side. They emerged back into the twilight haze and turned one way then the other. His team was spread out in a defensive formation, but Alex knew the threat had already moved on.

"They were just here," he said.

"What happened?" Sam asked.

"The things came … took them."

"Ah, shit," Sam replied.

Janus pushed forward. "They were just here?'

"Yeah, maybe less than an hour. And there were others with them." Alex walked backward for a moment, looking up at the building and then along the street, trying to determine where they could have gone.

"That's good," Janus said. "Means they were still free hours after the initial abduction. More might be hiding. We need to search for those still alive."

A public phone just down the street began to ring. The group looked at it, then back at Alex.

"Yeah, they're watching us," he said, and walked out into the center of the old road. "They're still alive, I know it. Our objective is rescuing the … taken. If others are still in hiding, then that means they're safe for now."

"Sir." Janus pointed out to the smoke filled street. "My people in hiding need rescuing as well. If we can bring one person out alive, it gives us all hope. You are guests of my government and –"

"We were never here to act as your ambulance service. We go after the taken." Alex turned away to look down at the dog for a moment and then back to Sam. "I think we know where they're being taken to."

"The volcano?" a panting Matt said. He had just caught up to the group and heard the last scraps of the conversation.

Alex turned toward the massive caldera just visible in the gloom. "It's time we paid them a visit."

* * *

Aimee, Joshua, and a half-dozen other former inhabitants of the basement were all tangled up in some sort of greasy sack. It was hard to think clearly as the moans and wailing of the other inhabitants made it feel all the more claustrophobic and miasmic. *A little vision of Hell*, she thought.

Aimee remembered being dragged away by something that was beyond comprehension.

She had tried to shrink from the thing as it approached. But that just hadn't been physically possible, and when she was finally grabbed, the heat was scalding and she could feel blisters on her arms. Aimee closed her eyes tight and tried to push it all away. If it were just her, the situation would have been horrible. But having Joshua taken as well made it unbearable.

She reached out and felt her son beside her. He grabbed her hand.

"What are they?" he whispered.

"I don't know." She flung a hand out to steady herself and touched the revolting bag's wall. It seemed to be made of some sort of organic material that was run through with veins and muscle. The stench was stomach turning. "I don't know where we are, or where they're taking us."

"I think I do," Joshua said softly. "To the volcano."

CHAPTER 31

"Beware them that are of all of us."

"Chimera," Matt said and shifted a little more to make room for the dog as it stood high on the back seat beside him so it could stare out through the armored glass window. Its ass was in his face.

Alex turned to him. "Go on."

"Well, in ancient texts from numerous cultures over the millennia, there have been legends of a beast made up of other creatures."

"'Beware them that are of all of us'," Alex repeated the translation Matt had drawn from the inscription at the Pompeii dig site.

"Exactly – 'all of us' – kinda makes sense now," Matt said. "Chimera is from the Greek word 'chímaira' and according to Greek mythology, it was a monstrous fire-breathing hybrid creature of Lycia in Asia Minor, composed of the parts of more than one animal."

Sam also turned. "And human animals."

Matt nodded. "We're the most plentiful creatures around right now. In fact, in medieval art, chimerical figures appear as embodiments of the deceptive, even satanic forces of raw nature, and many have a human face or faces. Like in Dante's vision of Geryon in *Inferno*."

"How does that help us?" Alex asked.

"I don't know yet. But one thing's for sure, when Maria found the specimen, it was only an arm that had been hacked off by a Roman gladius nearly two thousand years ago. It remained dormant for all that time before coming back to life and regenerating an entire new creature."

"From the bones and flesh of five men," Sam said.

"The raw materials," Matt replied. "But either the air, the light, or the warmth triggered its regenesis."

"So it wasn't dead," Alex said. "We know we can damage them, but don't know yet whether that damage actually hurts them, or whether they can be killed at all. We need more information to know them. Once we know them, we can kill them ... forever."

He faced the front. "Gray wants a sample, so let's get him one."

* * *

The armored vehicles pushed up through cluttered streets, Sam's brow was heavily creased as he concentrated on navigating the smoke- and debris-filled landscape. He rammed and bounced away a small truck, making everyone jerk forward.

"Can't see shit. Getting worse out there."

The dog began to grumble deep in its chest.

"Stop," Alex said.

Both vehicles slid to a halt and Alex stepped out. They were at an intersection where several large streets came together. Cars were marooned everywhere. Not a single driver looked to have given an inch and thus, everyone who drove to the crossroad had simply become trapped. Inside the cars there was nothing, no one, and not even a splash of blood.

"They either ran for it, or ... didn't," Sam said.

Alex felt the chaos in the air. "Most fled, but many didn't have a chance. They took them ... and they're still taking them when they find them."

"Took them?" Lucas asked. "How?"

"I don't know how yet. Or why." He turned. "Any ideas, professor – professors?"

Maria folded her arms and shivered even though it was over a hundred degrees in the smoke haze. "As to why, well, we saw what they did to people before – they made themselves out of their bodies. They *assembled* themselves from the parts of others. Maybe they need more building blocks to make more of themselves."

"Then why take them?' Sam asked. "Why not use them right then and there?"

"The people are either food, or biological building blocks," Matt said. "But we shouldn't rule out the fact that these things might be doing the work of something else."

"Like worker ants. You think they might have been taking the people back for something else? Like hostages?"

"Yes, maybe. And it's undoubtedly something we haven't seen yet," Matt said. "It's a theory."

Alex held up a hand and tilted his head, listening. The seconds stretched, and then his head straightened and he stared into the billowing smoke. The HAWCs watched him intently. He held up a fist for a moment before flattening his hand and swiping the air one way then the other. The HAWCs moved into a defensive pattern, guns tight at their shoulders.

Sam turned to Matt and Maria. "Get back in the car."

Alex concentrated. He could just make out the lumbering steps of something heavy, a wheezing, and a noise that could have been dragging. Beside him the dog whined just as the sounds vanished.

"They're on the move," Alex said. "Casey, Lucas, stay with the vehicles."

"Aw –" Casey began but Alex shut her down with a glance.

"Everyone else, follow me, double time." He ran ahead, followed by Sam, Janus, and Aiko.

Alex and Tor ran hard, big Sam Reid following them, using his MECH-assisted frame to shoulder vehicles out of his path like a football player. Aiko and Janus quickly fell behind, even though they were sprinting.

Alex could feel the huge presence before he saw it, and then he picked up once again the pad of footsteps and muffled moans and sobs. He accelerated again.

He felt the sensation of misery and terror increase like a physical force as he came around the corner and skidded to a stop. In the center of the road were three mountains of flesh.

Tor growled and bared its teeth and went to charge, but Alex grabbed it and dragged the huge animal back.

Sam caught up, followed by Janus and Aiko.

Sam's face contorted. "Jesus Christ, that's them! What's that freaking thing dragging?"

One of the creatures had what looked like a giant egg sack attached to its hand. Or hands. Alex remembered Sam's mission engagement debrief, but even though he could see the creature with his own eyes now, he still found it hard to believe.

"Demoni," Janus whispered.

"That they are," Sam replied softly.

Even in the twilight haze they could see that the creatures glistened and ran with blood and other fluids. Though they moved slowly, there was no doubt that enormous power was contained in those conjoined muscles.

Janus lifted his gun a little higher.

Alex held out a hand. "Hold fire."

The HAWCs waited and watched. Then the creatures stopped.

"Oh shit," Sam said.

The two leviathan creatures that weren't dragging the sack swung their trunk-like heads toward them. Holes opened along their length and unearthly screams erupted from the dozens of mouths floating on their surfaces. Then the creatures charged. Their massive column legs thumped down heavily on the ground, and the group could feel the vibrations up through the cobbled stones.

Alex didn't flinch. "Take 'em down." He fired his shotgun, and the others did the same, holding their ground in the face of the attacking behemoths.

The creatures were impossible to miss and the effects were instantaneous. There came the most unearthly howl that Alex had heard in his life. It was made more eerie for being a chorus poured forth from dozens of tiny mouths. Huge gobbets of flesh were blown off the beasts, as well as arms, legs, and other body parts. Limbs lay flopping like dying fish on the stones. But where the liquid nitrogen shells struck dead center, a web of white spread right across the monstrosity. The thing became frozen like a statue.

Alex fired again, striking the first monster dead center, and it shattered into a million pieces. Seconds later the second shared the same fate.

"Well, these new shells pass the field test," Sam said as he reloaded.

The third creature had continued to move away, dragging the huge bag with it. Alex sensed Joshua again, loaded a standard shell into his shotgun, and sprinted after it.

Torben must have sensed the same thing as a deep rumble started in its chest and it lowered its head and charged. It raced ahead, ignoring Alex yelling at him. The huge dog reached the bag being dragged and grabbed its edge, bracing its four legs to pull back on it. But the dog, though weighing in at over 150 pounds, was still no match for the mountainous creature. It did get its attention, though – the thing stopped and turned, and then shot out one enormous arm and multiple hands grabbed the dog by the neck, lifting it with ease.

Torben began to thrash and snarl, snapping in the air as the monster brought the dog close to its chest.

Alex knew what it was planning to do – this was apparently what had happened to Hondo – so he acted. At close range, the standard 12-gauge shot blasted into the creature's upper arm, cleaving it from the body.

The limb and the dog landed on the ground, and Tor shook the hands free. The limb flopped wetly, still alive, and the hands on the end of the arm continued to wriggle and flex as they reached for the dog.

"Aiko, free that bag!" Alex yelled.

The Japanese HAWC sprinted forward and, faster than the eye could follow, drew her katana and sliced open the bottom of the wet sack. People tumbled out, some unconscious, some trying to crawl away.

"Gesù Cristo, that's how they were taking them," Janus said. "That's where all the people have gone."

"Not all of them," Sam growled. "Kill that fucking thing!" He pumped and fired his shotgun. Like the other creatures, this one filled with spidery white veins and then froze solid.

Alex raced to the sack and pulled more bodies free, looking briefly at some of the mucus-covered faces, and then looking at the next. He hoped that Aimee and Joshua would be among them, but already sensed they weren't.

"Dammit!" He stood, leaving people crawling away on the slick stones. The sack oozed blood like it was a living thing, and gave off a rank odor like the inside of a stomach.

Janus helped some of the dazed people to their feet, wiping mucus from their eyes and mouths. Then he rounded more up as they tried to stagger away. He managed to organize a few of the most aware to help with the others.

"We need to get these people out," he said, as he wiped slime from the eyes of one disorientated young woman.

Alex nodded, and reached down to the dog standing beside him. He noticed the fur on its neck was covered in slime in some places but in others the fur had been seared away. "Looks like you need some sort of body armor as well."

A small creaking sound came from the final creature and Alex saw that it was beginning to thaw. Repulsively, the arm he had blown off was crawling back toward the body.

Alex lifted his shotgun and blasted the creature into chunks. The arm continued to crawl toward the broken mass.

"I see," he said and watched it for a second more. It undoubtedly could pull itself back together, given enough time. "Sam," he yelled over his shoulder. "Bag that arm, and let's get it back to the vehicles."

"Got it." Sam opened his pack and unfurled a large drop sheet beside the severed limb. He kicked the limb into the center of the sheet, rolled it up, and lashed it tight. The huge HAWC then hefted it onto his shoulder even though it must have weighed in at around 200 pounds.

Sam's face was screwed in disgust. "Feels like a live fish thrashing around in here."

Alex turned. "Maybe you sho—"

A shotgun blast blew Alex off his feet.

And then Hell rained down on them.

* * *

Over 5,000 miles away in an ultra-secure sublevel basement at USSTRATCOM, the computer equipment erupted into

handed over to the demons. Others they lashed together and herded out."

"These people are working with the creatures. Why do they do this?" Aiko asked, frowning at the strange man at their feet. "How do they communicate?"

"Let's find out. "Alex reached down to tear away the rest of the covering from the man's head and then lifted him to hs feet.

Aiko grimaced. "Ack."

They could now see that both his eyes and also his mouth were roughly stitched shut, and his face and chest were covered in tattoos to mimic eyes, mouths and other facial features, making him look grotesque and non-human.

"Madre di Dio." Father Belucci crossed himself.

"How does he see so well?" Aiko asked.

"How does he see at all?" Sam said.

"Janus, ask him." Alex pulled out one of his blades and slashed it across the man's lips, cutting open the stitching, and then pushing him toward the Italian soldier.

Janus got in close to him. "What are you doing here? Who are you?"

The man's mouth fell open, and Alex could have sworn smoke escaped from his throat. He gasped for a moment, and inhuman grunts, squeaks, and moans emanated from deep inside him. And then: "She." More pained noises. "She must be fed."

"What?" Janus clutched the man's tunic. "What does that mean?"

"She will be fed."

Sam grabbed the man by the tattered shirtfront and lifted him off the ground.

"She *is* being fed."

"Son of a bitch." Sam shook him.

The blinded man simply smiled. "Blessed are those that are joined. Blessed are those that are all of us." His smile froze, and he lifted an arm to point at Alex's chest. "She sees you. And She sees … your son."

He started to vibrate, and more smoke leaked from his mouth, nose, and ears.

"Shit." Sam dropped him. "He's fucking hot."

The man's skin began to redden and peel like he was being held under boiling water. Hair-like tendrils peeked from his nose and mouth, and then broke out all over his skin. Liquid pooled around him for a second or two, before he began to collapse in on himself. Then he simply dropped to melt into a puddle of gore. Something thrashed in the fluid for a few seconds before vanishing as well. Nothing remained but his strange clothing.

"Did that just happen?" Sam asked.

"There was something inside him," Janus whispered, and made the sign of the cross.

"Finger puppets," Alex said. "The creatures seem to have these human beings under their control." He threw the man's face covering to the ground. "They're coordinated, or are being coordinated by something else. Just like Matt Kearns said."

"The devil's helpers," Father Belucci said softly. "It is said that when the devil walks the Earth, his corrupted minions would rise to serve him." He turned to the group. "The creatures are the devil's demons, and these … willing souls are his minions."

"Not his minions, Hers," Sam said. "He said, 'She must be fed'."

"The devil takes many forms," Belucci replied. "But it is rising up, we can feel it make the very earth beneath our feet tremble, and it is sending its demons and human slaves to prepare for its arrival."

"So, we have another thing to watch out for – human shock troops. I knew I had seen people in among the creatures when my men were attacked," Janus said. "No wonder they were able to infiltrate and find the hiding people."

"As far as I'm concerned, they're betraying humanity, and therefore not human anymore," Alex said. "Kill on sight."

"I heard that," Sam said, and racked his gun.

Alex turned to the priest. "Did you see any other groups?"

Belucci nodded. "Many, and many more of the demons dragging the captured ones in their bags." He looked across to the rescued people, standing like they were in a trance, still covered in slime. "You have already saved some?"

"Yeah. They're pretty traumatized." Alex exhaled and leaned a little closer. "Was there, ah, a woman and a boy?" He lifted his hand to about chest height. "The boy was about this tall. They both had black hair, and –"

"No." Belucci reached out to Alex and laid a hand on his arm. "They are friends of yours?" Belucci tilted his head in understanding. "Your family?"

Alex nodded.

"Do not give up," Belucci said and let Alex's arm go.

A phone rang inside one of the buildings. Then another, and another, until from all around there was a cacophony of ringing bells.

"What the fuck is that?" Sam yelled over the din.

Then the phones shut off as if the power had been cut.

They waited for what came next and the seconds stretched.

"It's over." Alex looked around slowly, scanning the streets before turning back to the priest. "And no, never," he said. "I'll never give up." He watched the group of shell-shocked civilians. "We take the arm back and evac these civilians. Then we regroup and head back out ... with everyone."

There was a deep rumbling and he felt the ground shiver beneath his feet. He looked to Janus. "That doesn't feel normal."

"Etna is very disagreeable right now." The Gladiator bobbed his head from side to side. "She might erupt in a minute, an hour, or a week, or she might not at all."

Alex spun and then held up a hand, making a fist. The group came to high alert, shotguns pulled in hard at the shoulder all over again.

He pointed, and from an alleyway another of the huge creatures lumbered free.

Alex pulled the tube-like weapon from his back. "We take this one alive."

The thing spotted them and bellowed like a chorus of the damned. It came at them, its column-thick legs making the ground shake like the volcano's tremors as they thumped down on the ancient stones. Alex sprinted at it, raising the net gun, and firing when he was only twenty feet away. The silver net shot out, bloomed open like a mesh flower, and totally encased the creature. It automatically tightened, and then tightened some more.

The thing's roar of frustration came from a dozen mouths as the unbreakable threads cut into it. Its legs became tangled and it fell with a juddering thump to the cobbled street.

Alex walked closer, looking down at the massive lump of joined flesh. "Ugly bastard."

It was wet looking, and a mass of knotted muscle and limbs melted or blended together. There were also clumps of hair in many different hues, and everything was slimy-wet with brown-red mucus covering it.

Sam grimaced. "Jesus, if I wasn't looking right at it, I'd never believe it was real. How do these things even exist?"

"That's what Gray is going to find out."

"The heat," Janus said, holding up his arm to protect his face. "They truly are creatures from Hell."

Sam had picked up the segment and hefted it onto his shoulder. "Hey, do we still need this thing?"

"Yeah, bring both." Alex pulled out the grav-disc and threw it hard at the captured thing, making it slap into its side. He used the remote to turn it on, and the mass shuddered for a moment, then lifted a few inches. He turned to Sam. "Let Gray know we're bringing him his prize. Also tell him about the things coming and going from the volcano, and the infection, or whatever the hell it was that happened to the eyeless guy."

"You got it." Sam opened his comm. link.

The net had a long rope attached and Alex grabbed it and started to drag the thing like a monstrous dog on a leash. "Now we can go."

CHAPTER 32

"They called it the Kola contamination."

"The HAWCs just had an encounter." Gray sat with his fingers steepled for a moment before turning to his lab techs, Adam Brice and Sanjay Allwatti, who stood watching him. "It's what we thought. The beings are coming and going from Earth's depths, apparently."

"Is it related to the current seismic activity?" Brice asked.

"Maybe. They also mentioned that people are being contaminated by something. They had their eyes and mouths sealed over. Why does that sound familiar?" Gray stared at the ground, his mind working, as his two lab technicians also searched their memories.

Finally, Sanjay snapped his fingers. "Kola."

Brice frowned. "Coke or Pepsi? What's that got to do with it?"

"Not the soda." Sanjay rolled his eyes. "Remember when we hacked into the Russian secure databases in the early 2000s?"

Gray began to smile. "Of course – the borehole."

"Yes. In the mid eighties, the Soviet Union attempted to drill as deep as possible into the Earth's crust. They called it the Kola Superdeep Borehole. Up until 1979, the world depth record was held by the Bertha Rogers hole in Washita County, Oklahoma. That one was around 31,000 feet deep."

"I don't remember any of this," Brice said. "But I was just a kid then."

Sanjay raised his eyebrows. "A kid who obviously didn't read much."

"Do comic books count?"

"Marvel or DC?"

"Sanjay, go on," Gray directed.

Sanjay became serious again and looked up for a moment as though organizing his thoughts. "In 1983, the Soviet drill passed 39,000 feet, easily breaking the American record. But then they stopped, they said to celebrate and do site inspections. But our data searches in the mainframes found out that something down in the borehole twisted their Uralmash-15000 series drill."

"Those things are tough," Brice said. "Diamond tipped and made of titanium composite. What did they hit?"

"Unknown."

"But then they restarted." Gray smiled. "And by the end of 1990 they were at 49,000 feet, an unbelievable depth."

Sanjay nodded. "The press release said they called a halt because of higher-than-expected temperatures. They had expected and planned for 212 degrees, but found it to be nearly twice that. Drilling was abruptly stopped, and the borehole abandoned. But also sealed over, and now fenced off to everyone."

"I remember now." Gray nodded. "They called it the Kola contamination. It was in the documents obtained from our database intrusions. The men and women working on the borehole, over a dozen of them, all went mad. They gouged their eyes out and ripped their tongues from their heads."

Brice recoiled. “Holy shit.”

“Except for one poor soul who blacked out after taking out his own eyes. All he said was that ‘She’ demanded it,” Sanjay added.

Gray pinched his chin and stared at the floor as he thought through the new information.

“Is this relevant?” Brice asked.

Gray looked up. “I think we’ll soon know.”

* * *

Alex’s team picked up Casey and Lucas and quickly briefed them. Casey glared down at the behemoth in the net and bared her teeth in distaste. The mouths never ceased their insane gibbering, and screeching, and unholy noises.

“Shut the fuck up.” She kicked it with her armored boot, making a wet *splat*.

“Leave it, Franks,” Alex said over his shoulder. “Move it.”

“Fucker like this did Hondo.”

Alex turned. “And we’re going to find out how.” He tossed her the tow rope. “Your turn. Now, let’s move it.”

Lucas and Aiko led them out of the smoke-filled landscape, and behind them came Alex, Sam, Janus, and Casey, who muttered as she moved the captured beast. Maria and Matt walked on the other side and couldn’t take their eyes off the massive lump of flesh that floated a few inches or so above the ground.

“This is what your specimen probably turned into at the Pompeii dig … after it had absorbed all the bodies,” Matt said almost reverently.

“It’s horrible; impossible,” Maria breathed. “How does this thing survive like that? What makes it come into being? Does it have a single set of internal organs or many working in unison?”

Matt leaned a little closer to one of the faces pressed against the mesh. Just one eye, the nose and mouth showed as the rest of the visage was buried within the greasy flesh. Matt shook his head and grimaced as the eye seemed to fix on him.

"Hey, do you think, uh, they're still alive in there? The people, I mean."

Alex turned. "No."

"Okay." Matt nodded. "I mean, how could they be, right?"

"Don't say that," Casey spat.

Alex looked down at the creature. Truth was, he'd wondered the same thing himself, and he noticed that many of the multiple eyes also continued to watch him and Sam. Some of the eyes had a glazed stare, some held expressions of fear and insanity, some held pleas, perhaps for an end to the suffering, and the others bulged with what could have been primal hate. But though he knew the thing saw them, like Matt, he wondered if perhaps the souls of the people who had been absorbed were still in there, and were somehow trapped in a form of hell. If they were, could they get them out? He doubted it.

Thankfully, they didn't run into any more of the creatures or their human pets, and as they moved further from the volcano, the smoke thinned and the heat began to ease a little. They'd be able to pop their helmet faceplates and breathe the air again soon, which would be a relief as even the huge dog coughed and hacked up a string of sooty drool.

Alex reached down to rub its head, and it briefly looked up at him with an expression of resignation.

We'll find them, he projected at the animal, which walked closer for a moment to bump his leg with its shoulder.

After fifteen minutes the temperature had dropped some more, and the smoke was almost fully gone. Alex heard the net rattle beside them. He turned to watch it for a while and saw that the thing seemed to be rousing itself.

"Masks down," Alex said, and the HAWCs extended their face shields.

The thing shuddered, and then strained against its bonds. Many of the eyes swiveled around, but never focused, and several of the mouths gulped as if struggling for air.

"Easy," Sam said, and held out a hand over it, but not touching it.

Alex snorted. "It's not a colt, Sam."

"And I sure as hell ain't really gonna pat it."

The mountain of flesh continued to strain against the net and make guttural noises. It pushed again, and the strands of the net cut into its flesh. As the temperature had dropped a little more to now be around a hundred degrees, the mouths all fell open … and then the shrieking began.

"Shit." Casey scowled down at it. "Don't make me kick your ass again."

"What's going on?" Maria asked.

The thing seemed to expand and the shrieking went up a few more decibels.

"Whoa." Alex and Sam stood back, guns drawn.

Casey dropped the guide rope and pointed her shotgun at the center of the long head. "Say the word, boss. I'm itching to put this mother down."

The thing bucked and looked as if it was going mad. Then it swelled and portions of it pressed so hard against the titanium threads they cut into the greasy flesh, making it run with blood and thicker fluids that looked like axle grease.

"Back up," Alex said, as the thing continued to shudder and expand.

They picked up the odors of the volcano, but now there also came a stench of methane, corruption, and other smells that were unidentifiable, but grossly unpleasant.

"We're gonna lose it!" Casey yelled.

She was right. The creature exploded, swelling more before simply dissembling. All the fused limbs came free and flopped and jerked like a school of fish – arms, legs, torsos, each had a life of its own.

A growing puddle of mucus spread beneath it, and Alex and the group stepped back.

"Oh my god." Matt watched with growing horror, then whipped a hand over his face to block the stench.

"What the fuck?" Casey stared.

There was something at the center of the disintegrating mass that writhed and flicked.

"That infestation shit again!" Casey yelled with her gun up.

"Get it!" Matt yelled.

"Fuck that! You grab it!" Casey yelled back.

"Leave it." Alex tracked the thrashing knot of fibrous threads with the muzzle of his gun. But before he could fire, whatever the thing had been vanished into the cracks in the road.

Silence returned as the group stood in shock and amazement as a malodorous vapor rose from the viscous puddle.

Sam blinked and turned to Alex. "That shit is in everything."

"And it got away ... again. Plus we just lost our major specimen." He gritted his teeth. "Waste of time."

"Hol*yyyy* shit." Sam blew air between his pressed lips. "I need a drink."

CHAPTER 33

"Biologically, this should not even be possible."

Walter Gray hummed as he prepared the isolation tank. It had been sterilized and he'd tested the robotic arms and found them in working order. Brice and Sanjay buzzed around gathering chemicals, preparing equipment, and generally adding to the sense of excitement. All three men wore sealed biological hazard suits with their own air supply. But the design was lightweight, and gave uninterrupted fields of vision, unlike previous designs that were like synthetic sugar sacks with plastic windows in them.

Sanjay rubbed gloved hands together and stepped back from a microwave-sized machine. "Sequencer is online and ready to roll, chief."

"Check." Gray didn't look up from his last-minute work.

Brice read some information from a computer screen and straightened. "Okay, they're inbound and ETA is four minutes and counting." He lifted his head. "Should I ...?"

"No," Gray said. "Wait until they're at the door. I don't want our environment filled with that damned smoke. Takes ages to clean it out and damages the scrubbers. This unit is one big isolation tank, and our reserves of everything are limited." He half-turned. "Let me know when they're here, and I mean *right* here."

"You got it." Brice saluted. He watched a bank of cameras that kept a glass eye on all perimeters outside the "spaceship", as they referred to their mobile laboratory.

"Here they come," he said and went to stand by the door. He seemed to count down, and then pressed a button. The door slid back into the wall with a hydraulic hiss.

With a billow of sulfurous smoke, the huge form of Sam Reid entered holding what looked like a blanket-wrapped body. He nodded to Gray as he passed through a curtain of blue ultraviolet light. The door closed behind him.

"Howdy, doc, where to?"

Gray had opened one of the sterilized isolation tanks and stood well back. "In there please, Lieutenant Reid. Easy now, and try not to touch anything else."

"You got it." Reid carried the thing to the tank. Gray noticed it looked heavy, and would only just fit in the seven-foot-long chamber. Sam eased it in and carefully slid his arms out from under it.

Gray stared. "Unwrap it, and then place the covering materials in the incineration unit. Quickly please." The small scientist's eyes were bulging with anticipation as he watched the HAWC work.

"We lost the major specimen," Sam said. He undid the rope and opened the blanket. Some sort of vapor rose off the thing, and Gray narrowed his eyes. *Steam, gas, or spores?* he wondered.

"I noticed. How?"

"Thing fell apart. We were returning on the grav-sled, had it all netted nice and fine. But as we started to leave the smoke and heat zone, it went crazy, then ..." He shrugged. "Damn thing just broke back into separate limbs and a puddle of slime."

"Very interesting. Soon as you left the heat and smoke, you say?" Gray tilted his head.

"Yeah. Went crazy." Sam slid the mass from the blanket, then rolled it up and pushed it into the incineration chute. Brice set it to flash burn.

Gray's eyes gleamed. "Anything else?"

"Yeah, there was. We thought we saw something at its center just after it all came apart. It was only there for a few seconds, and then it vanished into the cracks in the road." Sam backed up.

"Don't touch anything inside this sterile environment, please." Gray reminded him. "Use the industrial bleach."

Sam nodded and went to a nozzle over a cone-shaped basin and used his elbow to discharge a fine spray that coated his arms and gloves hands. It smoked for a moment and then dried.

"What do you think the thing that vanished was?"

"I don't know. Snakes, like a bundle of tiny snakes, or worms maybe. Was too quick to really get a good look."

Gray nodded. "Thank heavens we didn't lose the smaller sample then, hmm?"

"Yep.

Okay, doc, anything else?"

"That'll be all." Gray ushered the man to the door. "We'll let you know when we have something for you."

"Soon as you do. This shit's weird," Sam said and began to turn away. He paused. "Like I said, as soon as you know."

"Yes, yes, always is with you guys. We'll take it from here, so let us do our jobs now, lieutenant." Gray had to reach up to place a hand on the man's shoulder. "Good luck," he said as Sam passed through the blue light curtain and the door closed after him.

Gray turned to the sealed tank. "So, let's see what we can see."

Brice and Sanjay stood back as Gray walked slowly around the tank. It was spot lit from numerous angles and the detail he saw was as magnificent as it was horrific.

"Amazing," he said softly.

Brice shook his head. "Biologically, this should not even be possible. I mean, I'm looking right at it, and my brain is still telling me it can't be real."

Sanjay exhaled loudly. "Me too, and I still don't believe it's real."

"But indeed it is." Gray stopped and stared at the thing, his mind analyzing, sorting, and categorizing, and trying to place it in any known occurrence in the past he was even remotely aware of. He could think of none.

The computers would also be set to trying to find a match from anything and anywhere else in the world, but given that Gray's own knowledge bordered on encyclopedic, he didn't hold any hope.

"Organic, of course," he began his analysis. He stepped closer, and felt his assistants at each shoulder. "I count eleven hands on the end of that limb."

Brice pointed. "And the forearms are also made up of blended limbs. In effect, it's a composite extremity."

Gray nodded. "Severed below the glenohumeral joint, but there is no defined humerus, radius, or ulna as the scaffolding is from the multiple scavenged bones." Gray shook his head, and said again, "Amazing."

Brice pulled on a pair of magnifying goggles and focused on the spot-lit specimen. "The musculature is all crazy. There is no definitive fascial layer separating the muscles into two osteofascial compartments. Instead, it is made up of numerous striations from the scavenged muscles." He turned to Gray, his eyes large and liquid behind the lenses. "This thing would be enormously strong if it was able to draw on the power of all that muscle mass."

Sanjay squinted. "But notice the interconnective tissue, if that's what it is. The flesh is almost liquefied. No, that's not right; the limbs are holding their biological shape, it's just that they seem softened and glued into a single, overarching matrix."

"Many chemical compounds can do that. There are solvents for flesh softening and bio-glues to stick skin together," Brice said. "But there's no way they'd be able to get the thing to hold its shape, let alone provide a coordinated locomotion – liquefying is one thing, but getting all the individual limbs to act in concert is another. It shouldn't be possible." He straightened. "It's not possible."

"And yet here it is," Gray said. "What we need to find is *how* it's possible – if there's some sort of biological entity, bonding agent, or process. What's holding it together? How is it retaining its composition? Why is it generating and regenerating, and how is it so tolerant of such high heat? And then I have a hundred more questions, plus some very impatient soldiers outside. So, let us begin."

The three men started to work their robotic arms inside the tank.

Gray reached out. "First, let's each take a sample."

He used a laser scalpel to slice away three wafer-thin pieces of the slimy flesh, and then placed a single sliver in each of three dishes, which he sealed.

"Gentlemen." He carefully handed one to Brice and another to Sanjay.

Brice took his sample to the sequencer, and Sanjay carefully carried his to the electron microscope. Gray used the standard optical microscope and loaded his sample in under the viewer. He lifted his glasses and squinted into the lens piece. He then moved the sample about, changing lens magnifications and angles. After a moment he sighed and lifted his head.

"I see nothing but normal human cells. But in a broth of something that could be a salivary enzyme."

"Human?" Brice asked.

"Mmm hmm." Gray nodded. "Most likely electrolytes, mucus, white blood cells, epithelial cells, glycoproteins, and amylase and lipase enzymes, all floating in saline solution."

"The role those enzymes play in breaking down food might be why the biological material is softening – it's being partially digested," Sanjay said.

"No, I don't think it's being digested, although it *is* being absorbed. So many questions." Gray sighed just as Brice's DNA sequencer pinged. "Good timing. What do the preliminary results tell you?"

Brice read the list of results scrolling up the screen. "Well, so far I see a healthy human genome collection of nucleic acid sequences for a human being. DNA within the twenty-three chromosome pairs in cell nuclei and in a small DNA molecule in definite mitochondrial structures." He nodded as the data continued to scroll, but then his brows snapped together. "Hey, hold that thought." He paused the data flow and traced the results on the screen with a finger. "This is ... *different.* I've got an RNA transcription that looks more bacterial. In fact, I see an RNA polymerase showing signs of both bacterial and eukaryal characteristics."

"Contamination?"

"Maybe – *has* to be," Brice said. "But the readings are quite high. Higher than they should be for any sort of bacterial infiltration in the muscle mass or somehow introduced into the sample."

Gray exhaled. "So nothing clear yet. Sanjay?"

"I have something." The technician looked at his screen as the images from the electron-scanning microscope were displayed. "Filaments ... of sorts. Like threads. Hard to tell in this small sample, but I'm betting this is where Brice picked up the DNA impurities." He turned to the senior scientist. "There is definitely something biological, but non-human, in there."

"Hmm." Gray went back to the isolation tank, reinserted his hands in the gloves and took control of the robotic arms. "Well, then, let's go a little deeper."

The two biotechs watched as Gray reached out with the mechanical arms. He moved a magnifying glass on a positionable arm and then lifted the large-blade scalpel. He gripped the long limb with the other set of metallic digits.

"I'm going to make a ventral incision along the limb, from the hand or hands, all the way to the area of separation."

Gray slid the sharp surgical tool along the flesh, and it opened like a bag unzipping. He paused. "Truly amazing."

The blended muscle mass of the separate human arms became a single muscle the deeper in he went. On the outside they looked only held together by some sort of biological adhesive, but further in they came together in a single limb striation.

"Perhaps the older muscles become fully integrated into a single mechanical form?"

Gray cut again along the opened wound, making it six inches deep. There was no blood and this time he put down the scalpel and gripped the incision's edges with the mechanical digits. He began to tug them apart.

Something wriggled inside the wound.

"Yaa!" Gray flinched and momentarily pulled his hands off the arm controls. "What the hell?" He blinked a few times and moved closer, peering in through the magnifying glass and retaking the remote controls for the robotic arms. "Sanjay, start recording this."

"On it." The biotech started up the cameras positioned around the glass tank.

Once again Gray gripped the surgical wound and eased the flesh open further, slower this time.

"Wow," Brice whispered.

"Filaments," Gray said.

"From what?" Sanjay asked, moving closer.

Inside the wound were what looked like thick hairs running through the meat of the muscle. The threads pulled back from edges of the wound as if they were aware of the scrutiny.

"Can they ... see us?" Sanjay asked. "They're retreating as if they're trying to hide."

"Maybe retreating, but not from us. Maybe they don't like the light or don't like the coolness of the ambient temperature of the tank," Gray said. "Want to lay bets on those threads being the source of your aberrant DNA?"

Brice shook his head. "I'm not taking that bet." He continued to stare. "Hey, do you think they're what's holding the different muscles together? Controlling them?"

"Kathputli," Sanjay said softly and kept his eyes on the lump of flesh.

Gray turned to him, and Sanjay continued: "In my home country, we have a traditional puppet theatre called Kathputli. It's over a thousand years old. You pull the strings, you make the puppet dance."

"Interesting theory," Gray said and worked to fix a pincer to the end of one of the arms. "I'll try and obtain a sample ... if it just holds still for a second." He prized the incision wider apart, and then lunged at the end of one of the filaments sticking from the flesh.

"Got it." He held on and tried to gently tease it out. The white thread came from the meat of the limb, further, and then further still. At about a foot long, it either ended or broke off. As it came fully free it began to thrash back and forth like a maddened snake before wrapping itself into a tight knot.

Gray dropped it into a dish and carefully placed a lid over it. He withdrew his hands from the robotic arm controls.

"So," he began. "I want a full analysis on this sample. I want it checked against the global database of DNA structures to see what it most closely relates to, if anything at all." He turned to the pair of lab technicians. "Tell me what we have here, gentlemen. Time is of the essence."

CHAPTER 34

Volcanoes – one way the Earth gives birth to itself.

Alex paced like a caged lion. The dog stood and followed him with its eyes, coiled and ready for action, never resting, never relaxing.

Matt felt the agitation and impatience in the room. They waited on Gray to give them something, anything, they could use. Of the dozen rescued civilians, only a few were able to speak or made sense. The priest, for one, spoke of the people with the featureless faces, seeking them out, searching like bloodhounds in wardrobes, under beds, and down into basements, and then taking them captive.

They also told of the huge monstrosities breaking into where they were hiding, and of being grabbed – but not all of them – some of them were simply held against the huge beasts' bodies, and as the captives watched, the poor souls, still screaming, melted in and were absorbed.

The worst aspect was, even after the victims were trapped inside the creatures, they continued to scream. The rescued people were terrified, and they didn't want to just leave the city, but leave the country. They wanted to put hundreds of miles between themselves and the horror they had witnessed.

Matt couldn't blame them. Being grabbed by one of the things must have been a nightmare in itself. But then seeing friends and family members drawn into the flesh of the monstrosities, and seeing their features blend in among the others, and fully expecting that would to be their fate ... he understood why it fragmented the survivors' sanity.

He shuddered and let his eyes slide to Alex. What must the man be thinking, knowing that Aimee and Joshua might have been bundled into one of those organic sacks? Or worse? Matt could guess.

Alex shook his head. "It's all linked – the volcano tremors, those horrors, and the people acting as the thing's helpers."

"And She," Matt said. "In my research I kept finding references to this female ... deity, I guess you could call it, referred to as She. And with her came the servants, the cult." He exhaled through pressed lips. "Or maybe they came first, as her heralds."

Alex looked at Casey. "At the nuclear reactor, the leader, Harper Owen, spoke of this female leader, or god – She, he called it." He stared out one of the windows. "He wanted to create a nuclear meltdown, burn a hole into the planet, so She could rise up to feed." He turned. "This thing has been coming for a while; perhaps looking for the right place to emerge again."

"Interesting," Maria said. "If you don't have a volcano, then create one. Its followers are everywhere."

Alex nodded. "We stopped them, but we only slowed her down. This has happened before, hasn't it?"

Matt nodded. "Yes, I think so. I came across a researcher by the name of Sergio Caseletti from the early twentieth century, who said that every major eruption for thousands of years was accompanied by the cult of She. And they existed to serve this devil, or god, of the underworld."

"Underworld, huh?" Casey scowled. "This ain't pitchforks to the ass, professor."

"No pitchforks; that's just an artist's detail that appeared around the ninth century and was drawn from ancient Greece, where Poseidon's trident gave him power over earth, water, and fire." Matt shrugged. "But the underworld is different. There are many ancient cultures that thought volcanoes were the doorways to Hell."

Alex began to pace again. The HAWCs, plus Janus, stayed out of his way. Only the dog watched him with those creepy, way-too-human eyes.

Matt had never seen a dog that big and wondered whether it was mixed with gray wolf. Or perhaps it was something else entirely. He'd heard there was a wolf species in the primordial forests that stood up to saber tooth tigers – it was called a dire wolf and could have weighed in at 240 pounds. Looking at this animal, he could believe it was possible.

The deep creaking and rumbling came again, and this time it was coupled with the earth vibrating beneath their feet.

Then, suddenly, it jolted violently, making Matt throw his hands out. "Whoa."

He waited and, just as quickly, the noise and movement subsided.

Alex's and the dog's heads snapped in the direction of the volcano. Matt followed their gaze, but saw nothing through the boiling clouds. An obscure quote came to mind, about volcanoes being one way that the Earth gives birth to itself. *Maybe*, he thought, but wondered exactly what it was *this* volcano was about to give birth to.

* * *

Gray looked over the results as Brice's data began to feed in. He shook his head, almost disbelieving what he was reading.

"Archaean?" he asked without turning. "Really? here?"

He heard Brice chuckle. "I know, impossible, right? But I triple-checked and the data is the same every time." He went back to the tank and inserted his hands into the robotic arm sleeves.

"Impossible is an understatement," Gray whispered. He felt the ground vibrate and grabbed a bench for support before turning to look over his shoulder. Brice was manipulating the specimen with the robotic arms while Sanjay watched and gave advice.

He was about to have them secure their working spaces, when the ground jerked as if they were all standing on a rug that had been pulled hard.

"Hey!" Brice yelled.

Things toppled from benchtops, fell over in cabinets, and the hissing of hydraulic gas came from some of the storage units. But what filled Gray with the most dread was the sound of the glass popping.

The isolation unit was made of steel and hardened glass, supposedly shatterproof, with a high heat and cold tolerance for working with extreme samples. It was supposed to have flexibility built into the matrix of the glass, meaning it should have an ability to withstand torque.

Gray watched the unit with growing alarm as the shaking continued. The downside of the unit's ability to bend was that when the canopy twisted, it put strain on the seals. Those were also hardened, but rigid.

The structure groaned, and then, sure enough, there came a pop, and then another, and then the tank lid jumped from its base.

"Oh no."

The lid opened about an inch.

"Get back!" he yelled.

Sanjay stumbled backward, but Brice was still trying to pull his hands from the robotic arm controls. Gray lunged for him, but as Brice was removing his arms, a hair-like thread from within the meat of the sample snaked through the small opening between the tank base and lid and alighted on his forearm.

The young man saw it and screamed. He yanked his arm away, but the thread stuck and stretched.

Gray took him by the shoulders and pulled. The thread came with him, elongating about six feet from the lump of meat in the tank. Brice went to grab at the thread.

"Don't touch it," Gray said, holding up a hand.

The white filament thickened obscenely and turned a reddish brown, as if blood was surging into it. But not at the tip – the hair-like thread seemed to make itself even smaller and then one became two, and two, four, and four, eight, and so on.

"Sanjay, scalpel." Gray held out a hand, and the Indian bio-technician scrambled for the instruments tray.

As Sanjay rattled and fumbled, the threads turned into a net that became needle-like at the tips and soon found a way to pierce Brice's tough biohazard suit.

"Hurry!" Gray yelled.

Brice howled as he felt the first touches of the threads against his skin. "It burns." He grimaced and moaned loudly. Gray still held his shoulders and tried to tug him backward. Horrifyingly, the strands thickened even more and became scarlet. Gray wondered if it was from the severed limb or being drawn from Brice.

The young technician howled again. The tendril was now pencil thick. It became wire-tight and started to reel the man in. Brice was dragged forward even with Gray hanging on.

"Sanjay, goddamn it!" Gray was going hoarse, and he saw that the man was holding two scalpels but frozen in shock and staring. "Move it, *now*!"

Sanjay snapped out of his frozen horror. "Yes." He blinked several times. "Yes." He walked stutteringly toward them holding the knives in front of him.

Gray still held Brice's shoulders, but they were both now being pulled toward the isolation tank. Gray felt the hair on his neck rise as he saw more filaments emerge from the wet flesh, obviously waiting for their prize to be brought closer.

"*Now, now!*" he yelled.

Sanjay slashed down with the sharp instrument, severing the cord. The length attached to Brice dropped to the ground and knotted into a coiled ball like a rubber band. Gray and Brice fell backward, but the thing wasn't finished, and more threads began to worm their way to the tank edge, questing in the air as though searching for the men.

Gray rolled away then launched himself at a small fire extinguisher. He grabbed it and punched a fist down on the top, aiming a jet of gas at the tendrils.

The ends attached to the severed limb snapped back inside the length of obscene flesh with a noise like a tiny scream of pain. To Sanjay's credit, he launched himself at the tank and leaned down hard on the lid just as more of the tendrils tried to exit the crack.

"Holy crap." Brice lay back onto the flooring, puffing with an audible wheeze.

Sanjay, still leaning on the tank, looked up. He was pale but grinning. "Are we about done for the day?"

CHAPTER 35

"Sometimes Hell rises to the surface."

Alex continued to stare out at the wall of smoke that separated one world from the next. *Our world from theirs*, he thought. He tried to make sense of his adversaries. There was the first level threat: the humans who acted like guard dogs. Where did they come from? People that look like that, with eyes sewn shut, don't exactly mix freely in a community. But Alex wasn't concerned about them, as he knew he could easily deal with the human allies or slaves to this She.

The next level threat was the lumbering things that were somehow a patchwork of humans and were absorbing or taking people. Even though they were big and powerful, he believed they had the firepower to fend them off as well.

His eyes narrowed. *But taking people to where and what?* He knew there must be something else, the final level threat, which was the higher intelligence somehow controlling them all – She. Adding the ingredient of intelligence made the situation a whole lot more complex and deadly. The priest said it was the devil. But whatever it was, it was the unknown factor, something he couldn't fight without knowing more.

"Sometimes Hell rises to the surface," Maria said softly. She let out a juddering breath. "This is an ancient saying about the devil sometimes rising to claim souls for himself."

This talk of the devil again. Alex half-turned, listening intently to the archaeologist.

"Bullshit," Casey Franks spat. "That thing that grabbed Hondo was real, not some mumbo jumbo bogeyman."

Alex glanced at her and then looked away. "Let's hear all theories. Go on, Ms. Monti."

Maria licked her lips. "I'm not saying this is *the* devil, or that there even is *a* devil. But it could have some historical roots that we can learn from." She held out a hand. "As an example, the sword that cleaved that monster's limb off was solid silver – and in too many cultures to name, silver was always used as a weapon against evil."

"The red guy with the horns?" Lucas snorted. "That's not what I saw out there."

"No, not those monstrosities. They're just its slaves, like the people with no eyes. I don't think the real master has shown itself yet." Maria's voice was quieter now.

"You want to see the devil? Twelve tequila shots on an empty stomach, I guarantee it." Casey threw her head back and laughed. "It was the prince of fucking darkness, man."

"That's the cartoon image of the devil," Matt said. "The hellbound or demonic devil wasn't always depicted like that. In fact, that is the most recent characterization to try and humanize the evil of legend. In some of the earliest depictions of Satan, from the sixteenth and seventeenth centuries, the image was of a bestial creature, an inhuman demon. Something that fed on people, and rose from an inferno."

"The volcano," Maria added.

"Sounds familiar," Sam said.

"That's right." Maria continued. "The Bible isn't very clear on what the devil actually looks like, but other artists turned to legends, woodblock carvings, or even dreams. In the Middle Ages, artists who wanted to depict Satan – and among them were the greats like Hieronymus Bosch, Albrecht Dürer, and Hendrick Goltzius – drew images of a creature that was cobbled together from other beasts – the cloven feet of a goat, the horns of a ram, the teeth of an alligator, scales, fur, slitted eyes."

"A patchwork of creatures," Alex said.

"Just remember, in a time of no cameras or video and with low rates of literacy, the artists were the recorders of history," Matt said.

'Exactly." Maria nodded. "Only later, it became more man shaped, perhaps to satisfy or make it accessible to the artist's public."

"Or maybe as it got access to more people to use as raw materials, it became more human shaped, or composed of more people than beasts," Matt said.

Alex folded his arms. "How does this help us?"

Maria looked at the ground, lost in thought. But Matt shrugged and lifted his chin.

"Maybe it doesn't, but also it might give us more pieces of the puzzle to work with. This thing, or these things, have been documented many times before. And perhaps our ancestors thought it was the devil and its demons rising from the volcanic depths. And maybe, for all intents and purposes, it was."

"I know what to do." Casey's eyes were wide. "Let's stock up on holy water."

Matt chuckled. "If only it were that easy. But this thing has parallels to the devil." He held up fingers, ticking them off.

"It rises from the fiery depths, it takes people, consumes their souls, as it were, and then drags them back to hell. Also it's an abomination."

"Got that right," Lucas said.

"So, makes sense that we need to fight it, and defeat it, like we would a devil," Matt said.

"How?" Casey's brows went up.

"That's all I got." Matt folded his arms. "When fighting the devil, I know there are parables that talk of cloaking yourself in the armor of righteousness, and not listening to its lies. But I guess I need to do some more research."

"Okay, sure, you do that; we got plenty of time." Casey rolled her eyes.

"That's enough." Alex glared at Casey, then turned to Matt. "That's good information. Anything else you or Ms. Monti can come up with is welcome."

He held up a hand and frowned as he listened to a message coming into his ear mic. He turned. "Gray's on his way in – he's got something."

* * *

"We believe it's an archaean-type organism." Gray stood in the center of the room, hands clasped behind his back.

The HAWCs watched him like their namesake. The two professors, Matthew Kearns and Maria Monti, also hung on his every word, and the Italian Special Forces soldier looked more angry than anything else.

"Isn't that like some sort of bacteria?" Sam asked. "So, it infected the flesh?"

"Yes ... and no." Gray was impressed by Sam's knowledge. "In among the multiple muscle masses, we found threads of a rare biological material that was acting independently of the individual muscles. We believe it is this entity that is responsible for 'knitting' all the biological material together, and making it work in unison."

"The threads," Sam said and turned to Alex. "What we saw when the thing melted down after we pulled it from the smoke zone."

Alex nodded and faced Gray. "You said, making it all work in unison? Like a single being?"

Gray nodded. "Yes, and in fact, Sanjay gave a very good description – like puppets, and the threads are the strings." He looked at each of their faces. "You were both close to the mark and also far away, Lieutenant Reid, because to say this is a simple bacterium is like saying that a redwood is just a plant, or Einstein was some guy who was good at math."

Sam laughed softly. "Point taken. So tell us more about these archaea."

Gray nodded. "The word itself, archaea, comes from an ancient Greek word meaning 'ancient things'. But they really are a life form so ancient that they are more closely related to the very first life on Earth – three billon years old."

Casey whistled.

"We first thought archaea were just heat-tolerant extremophiles, living in environments deadly to other creatures."

"So this is why we see them coming and going from volcanoes. Or even being able to survive in there," Aiko said.

"Perhaps. These ancient creatures have certainly been found in clusters around deep-sea vents, hot springs, and salt lakes. They thrive there. At first we thought they preferred an environment that more closely resembled that of a very primitive Earth. However, we now know they are more diverse than that. They just seem to prefer these hostile environments ... and thrive in them."

"But they're simple organisms – multicellular, but simple, right?" Sam asked.

"Usually. But in this instance, I'm not so sure. " Gray shook his head. "The isolation tank's casing cracked open during the tremor, and it almost escaped. It sought to trap one of my technicians, and in doing so it exhibited predatorial strategic thinking, was enormously powerful, and would have succeeded if he was there by himself."

"Jesus," Matt said. "We saw the results of that over in Pompeii. We wondered how it could have trapped five grown men. Assimilated them."

"How exactly did it attack you?" Alex asked.

"I'm not sure 'attacked' is the right word. It harbors no malice or hate. It was simply doing what it is programmed or directed to do. It just wanted to join with us, absorb us."

"Gross," Casey said.

"Only to us," Gray remarked. "The archaea are usually solitary entities. Tiny and insignificant and living in the remotest of environments. But they have been found to clump and form chains, and once they've joined together it's as if they all received the same message because they then work in unison."

"So these things you saw are archaea chains?" Sam's brow furrowed. "They're using us like you said, as puppets. That's not by goddamn accident."

"I agree," said Alex. "These things don't just work in unison, they've been displaying a higher-order intelligence. This is not ordinary animal behavior, and well beyond any sort of simple biological entity behavior."

"Oh yes, yes, you're right." Gray held up a finger. "But consider this: humans have been around for four million years in some form or other. But the archaea have been around for over *three billion*." He waggled his finger. "Think how much we human beings have evolved in just four million years." He lowered his hand, and his face became serious. "So, then, how much an organism might evolve in nearly one hundred times that?"

Alex grunted. "As we suspected, this is no simple single-celled organism we're dealing with."

"Hold on there; I don't believe this was all of the entity," Gray insisted. "What we found in the limb you brought us was nothing more than some lower level life form working on instinct. I'm sure if it had the chance it would have absorbed us and gathered enough muscle mass to make its way back to its home. But like a puppet, this thing was following instructions."

"Shit," Sam said softly. "Something was pulling on those puppet strings."

Gray nodded. "I believe this is a high probability. Three billion years of evolution didn't just create an organism that was a bunch of threads that pulled biological entities together. I think it evolved something else entirely."

"Something we haven't seen yet." Casey exhaled. "Like a queen in a hive."

Gray pointed at her. "Very good, and exactly what I was thinking. There are workers, and there are warriors, and then there is a king or queen that controls them all. There's something else that lends weight to this theory. When Brice was hooked up, and the thing was trying to absorb or assimilate him, he said he heard it."

"Heard what?" Alex asked.

Gray shrugged. "He said it was hard to describe. But it was a little like a soothing lullaby. No words, but it made him feel safe and comfortable."

"Like it was drugging him to let it happen," Sam said.

"A siren song," Matt suggested.

Alex grunted and walked to the window to look out. "How can we use this?"

"Don't know yet," Gray said quietly. "Except to warn us that we might be dealing with extreme intelligence."

"A monster with a big brain," Casey sneered. "If we can find it, we can kill it."

Matt held up a hand. "This might sound weird, but ..."

Alex turned to him. "Weird, really? Have you just been listening to the same information as me?"

"Yeah, yeah." Matt bobbed his head. "Maria, remember how you found that gladius with the specimen?"

She nodded. "Yes, and maybe removing it caused the thing to begin to grow."

"It was silver, right?" Matt raised his eyebrows. "And you said silver was always used as a weapon against evil."

"Yes, ornate. Magnificent weapon. And silver was regarded as the holy steel."

Aiko's eyes slid to Matt, listening intently now.

"So, we're back to killing werewolves and vampires again." Casey chuckled and stuck her thumbs in her belt. "Got any silver bullets there, Doc?" she sneered toward Gray, but the scientist was nodding and listening intently. "Oh, whatever." She shook her head.

"Historically, the holy steel, silver, was always used to combat evil," Matt said. "But recently we found out something else very interesting from a chemical perspective." He turned to Gray, who was now smiling.

"Of course," the scientist said.

"You said these ancient things, archaea, are like a cross between bacteria, eukaryotes, and who knows what else. Well, the funny thing the bacteriologists found out about silver is it's a powerful antibacterial and antiseptic."

"Kills fucking germs." Casey grinned. "I knew it was going to be a good idea."

"Brilliant, Professor Kearns. Colonel Hammerson worked with you for good reason." Gray clapped his hands together. "Silver is highly toxic to many bacteria. This is worth pursuing."

"Do it, anything we can use as a weapon helps right now," Alex said. He turned back to the window. "There's something else that has been bothering me. Why now?"

"Why today?" Gray frowned.

"Now, I mean, why does it only happen at certain times? Why the link to the volcano eruptions?"

"Yeah," Matt said. "Good question. This *has* happened before. We know it happened during the Vesuvius eruption, and also at other eruptions where there was a human settlement."

"Or even away from human settlements," Sam added. "You said yourself that the legend of the chimeras meant they were made up of animal parts as well."

"But it only seems to happen every few hundred years, and most often during an eruption," Maria said.

Gray tapped his chin. "The volcano connection … I just don't know. Or why they're taking people in there."

"Oh, shit," Matt said. "The sacks full of people."

"They're stocking their larder," Casey said. "Because after a few hundred years, the cupboard is bare. Mama is hungry again."

"She must be fed," Matt whispered.

Gray looked at Alex, who stared straight ahead, his eyes burning with either impatience or a fury that was barely contained. The dog seemed to pick up on his vibes, as it too seemed to gather itself in, waiting on a command to spring into action.

"Captain Hunter …" Gray began, but Alex ignored him.

The scientist knew of Alex's inner demons. After all, he'd helped to design the Box. Hammerson had said Alex was under control. But Gray knew that the entity that lived inside him was only held in check by psychological bonds that were too easily broken. Or voluntarily released.

He tried again. "Captain Hunter, we need to wait. The suits you now have will give you excellent insulation against the surface heat, but if you're planning on entering the actual volcano, you'll burn. We have an experimental vehicle that

Colonel Hammerson had the foresight to have air-lifted in." He checked his watch. "It'll be here in just a few more hours."

The phone began to ring.

"Don't answer that," Alex said. "Seems our monster with a big brain hasn't finished taunting us."

He turned to stare back at the volcano. Gray looked from Alex to Sam, and nodded to him. The big HAWC obviously knew what he wanted.

"Boss?" Sam walked over and placed a hand on his shoulder. "What are your orders?"

"Orders?" Alex seemed to rise from his reverie. "Lock and load – we go *now*."

CHAPTER 36

"We must be inside the volcano now."

The heat was becoming unbearable. Joshua and Aimee hugged each other tightly and the boy tried to bury his face into her chest. The others around them curled up into balls and tried to squirm into the center of the mass of people. Some on the outside remained there, bearing the brunt of the heat to try and shield the rest. Or perhaps they were just too traumatized to move.

For now, the organic bag had stopped moving as though they had been dropped somewhere. There was a dim red light showing through the fleshy wall, and they could make out veins and imperfections as if it was skin. The horrible bag smelled like it was cooking – a mixture of sulfur, mineral salts, and roasting meat.

"We must be inside the volcano now," Joshua whispered.

From further along the sack came the snick of something mechanical, and Aimee looked up to see one of the men opening a penknife. The four-inch blade glinted blue in the dull red glow. The man saw her looking and nodded. He drew a breath and then stuck the knife into the side of the bag. He cut it like a piece of steak.

She watched, and Joshua lifted and turned his head. The meat of the sack wall was thick, and after a moment the man had sliced a good foot-long cut. Blood oozed from the slit. He closed the knife, stuck it in his top pocket, and then wormed his fingers into the wound.

The man turned to her once again, hesitating as though building courage.

"Be careful," she whispered.

He nodded. "*Un piccolo sguardo*."

He braced himself, and drew his face close to the slit, preparing to snatch a look as he stretched it open. He tugged, and then screamed.

Whatever the bag was made of had been shielding them from most of the heat outside. A jet of super-hot air blasted in at them and people screamed and the man recoiled and then writhed in pain, holding his face. Smoke rose from between his fingers.

The wound in the bag wall closed gently like lips, and began to seal itself. The heat gradually shut off.

Aimee and Joshua buried their heads in each other's shoulders. They now realized they were trapped, for now. Even if they could escape the sack, they wouldn't last more than a few seconds outside.

A sweet smelling gas began to seep into the sack.

Joshua sniffed. "What's that?"

Aimee shook her head, but felt her eyes becoming heavy. "Oh no."

Their eyelids drooped and muscles sagged. They slept.

CHAPTER 37

"Anything gets in your way, kill it."

Alex had the team drive up the side of the volcano until they came to one of the largest vents that was spewing noxious gas. He leaped out, and his forearm reader told him the temperature here was 120 degrees. They hadn't even entered yet.

His team joined him and held their guns loosely in their hands. The huge dog came and stood at his side, but its eyes were narrowed and it kept removing its feet from the hot ground.

Alex looked down at it. "Can you see them?"

The dog craned its neck forward, then turned its luminous pale eyes on him.

Alex nodded. "Good."

Alex went to call them team onward, and the dog set off. "No."

Tor stopped and turned.

"You can't follow."

The dog whined, but must have realised that its fur and the tough pads on its feet would be no match for the heat. It whined again.

"If they're in there, I'll get them," Alex said. "You wait here."

The dog trotted back to the vehicle and leaped inside, sitting down to watch them with its strangely luminous gaze.

Matt grinned. "That is one well-trained dog."

"Training? Right." Alex turned to Maria. "You should also wait here."

Maria scowled and pointed at Matt. "He is not a soldier either. But I should stay because I'm a woman? I can take anything you guys can."

"I doubt it." Alex shrugged. "But it's your life."

"Kearns has been in on missions before." Casey Franks ambled over, looking like a muscular, black-clad robot. "It's an experience thing, babe," she said. "Besides, that heat will ruin a good hairdo."

Maria said something inaudible and turned away.

Sam Reid walked a few paces ahead of Alex and held out his arm, pointing his temperature gauge at the cave mouth. "Speaking of heat –" he looked toward the vent, "– 130 degrees and that's just inside the front door."

"The new suits will take it," Alex replied. "For a while."

"Yeah, we'll be fine. But how are we going to get the civs out? And for that matter, how could they survive going into the side of the mountain? They'd fry before they got ten feet."

"I've been wondering the same thing," Alex said. "But they're in there, and alive. I know it."

"We saw what happened to Hondo. When he was taken, he was still alive too," Lucas said. "Maybe they're all like that … assimilated."

"No!" Alex roared. "They're alive. I would know if they're not."

The young HAWC held up a hand. "Yep, sorry, boss, I meant –"

"They're alive." Alex turned back to the fissure, and waved them on. "Let's get 'em. Anything gets in your way, kill it."

* * *

Alex led them in, next came Sam Reid, then Casey, Janus, Aiko, Matt, and Maria, followed up by Lucas. Matt felt his suit pumping, or throbbing, like an arterial system, and he also felt the chill against his skin as whatever coolant being used rushed from his scalp to the soles of his feet. He checked the suit's external temperature gauge and noticed that with every step they took, the heat rose. He was told they could easily take 300 degrees in the modified suits. But just how hot would it get? He wasn't a HAWC, he was a paleo-linguistics professor. Those guys were trained to ignore pain, and his pain threshold was about a mile lower than the two-legged war machines he was currently with.

He looked at his gauge again as they passed inside the cave mouth – 150 degrees. He sighed. He'd know soon enough what his – and his suit's – limitations were.

Sure enough, as they went deeper into the fissure, Matt felt his suit surge as it compensated for the rapid climb in heat. He looked around. Strangely, he expected to see raw rock and jagged outlines. But instead everything was smooth – not melted smooth, but more like it was coated in some sort of greasy resin. He reached out and touched it. It was solid. Whatever had been sprayed, or excreted, on the walls had set hard.

"Bigger inside than we thought," Sam said. "And lighter."

There was a dull red glow coming from up ahead. The light was like that from a dying campfire – enough to glow, but not enough to dispel shadows. It meant they didn't need to use flashlights, but it did nothing to remove the Hades-like atmosphere.

As Sam had pointed out, the cavern opening was only about nine feet high and four wide, but inside it opened out to about twenty feet in height and width. If the vehicle could have taken the heat, they could have driven in.

'Eyes out. Wedge formation. Matt, Maria, inside the wedge," Alex commanded.

This time Maria didn't complain, and he guessed her bravado might have been wearing thin now she was inside. Matt was the same, as he knew that the scientists in them were intrigued and fascinated, but the human beings wanted to run and hide.

They walked carefully, the HAWCs with their guns up and ready. After another hundred paces, Sam began to softly reel off numbers: "Two hundred degrees, downward elevation now at thirty degrees."

"Next stop, Hell," Lucas said. No one laughed.

Alex stopped at a fork in the caves, and looked down. "Drag marks." He nodded to the left opening. "That way."

"Those sacks we saw – must be what they're keeping the citizens in," Matt said. "And might also be what's keeping them alive."

"Has to be," Alex said. "Come on."

They moved along the cave for another hundred feet, and Sam announced that it was now 250 degrees. For the first time, Matt felt a blush of warmth on his skin.

They entered a larger cavern that had multiple openings all around it. At one end there was a rounded cave mouth, and it was from there that the blood-red glow emanated.

"Two hundred eighty degrees," Sam said.

"I can really feel it now," Maria said.

"Ack." Aiko had her arm up, and moved it around, making a small screen on her forearm blip constantly. "I have movement, multiple signatures."

"Looks like we finally got someone's attention," Casey said, panning round with her gun up.

"Where?" Alex turned slowly.

"All around us; multiple convergence, big signatures." Aiko kept trying to nail the movement down. She glanced up, and then quickly looked back down. "Too many to get a lock."

"Muscle up." Alex and the HAWCs backed into a defensive ring, weapons pointed outwards, their suits moving into the fortified war mode with an audible clank.

Matt and Maria were once again herded toward the center. Matt reached down to lay his hand on the butt of his handgun. The scientists also moved their suits into the more protective structure, and though it limited their mobility, Matt immediately felt a little safer.

Sam spoke while trying to cover his quadrant. "Boss, this is not a defendable position."

Matt saw Alex look toward the hellish red cave mouth at the end of the cavern – he knew the HAWC leader wanted to go there.

"Hold positions," Alex said.

"Captain Hunter, we need to evac the civilians." Janus glanced at Matt and Maria, then back out to the red darkness. "They are not trained for this."

"She *wanted* to be here, ask her." Alex fired back.

The bastard, Matt thought. He finally pulled his sidearm, and held it loosely, but knew it was going to be useless against the massive things that were coming for them.

As if in answer to Matt's thought, a huge form appeared in one of the cave mouths opposite.

"Contact!" Aiko yelled, and fired. But the liquid nitrogen shell exploded in the air only twenty feet from the muzzle of her gun.

Sam and Lucas fired, racked, and fired, and all that happened was an explosion in midair and a cloud of white for a few seconds before it vanished.

"Too fucking hot in here!" Sam yelled. "Shells are exploding before they travel two dozen feet."

"How do you say 'design flaw' in Italian?" Casey yelled.

"Difetto di progettazione," Janus shot back.

Alex literally growled and said over his shoulder, "We've got no range. They're gonna have to be on top of us if we want to hit them before the shells explode." He looked back at the crush of monstrous bodies filling the cave mouths.

The creatures stayed where they were, as if they knew to keep out of the HAWCs' range. Huge heads hanging on stump-like necks leaned forward, their ends dotted with numerous dark eyes of many shape and sizes, all of them focused on the human beings.

As Matt stared back at them he felt the hairs on his neck prickle. It reminded him of a madman's dream – the things, the multi-form beings, were standing still, but were never really motionless. The hands on the end of each enormous arm continually clenched or gestured, clawed or fidgeted, as the column-like legs remained planted wide.

Several of the massive beasts took up a position in front of the glowing cave.

"They're not attacking," Alex said. "They just want to stop us from going further."

"I think we now know where their leader is," Matt said.

"Holy shit!" Lucas screamed, and Matt's head snapped around. Wrapped around the man's arm were long, spaghetti-like tendrils. They emanated from one of the creatures and had traveled more than fifty feet over the cave floor, snaking silently toward the group, finding Lucas first.

Matt looked down and around and saw that tendrils emerged from each of the creatures. They hung from the torsos, and snaked from the legs, worming their way across the cave floor. It seemed that the things wouldn't get close enough to be shot, but they could certainly try and assimilate the humans from a distance.

Sam fired his shotgun into the ground, and though the explosion spread out in a white bloom, his target was close enough to have an impact. The tendrils either froze solid or were blasted away. He turned and blew apart the tendrils that were sticking to Lucas. The ends fell away to curl up like bloodworms in the noonday sun.

"Boss!" Sam yelled as more and more of the tendrils came toward them.

Alex's head turned to the red cave mouth once more, and Matt could tell he was being torn in two – one half of him knew he needed to pull his team back, but the warrior wanted to press on, fight his way through to find his wife and son.

As one, the group fired at the tendrils, creating a veil of frozen white around them. But the severed tendrils never pulled back, instead they simply regrew their ends and continued to snake toward the group. Matt knew that their shells would be exhausted long before the creatures would.

It also showed the monstrous things exactly the extent of the HAWCs' firepower, and they lumbered forward, a wall of writhing limbs and mucus-streaked flesh, staying just out of range.

Matt wanted to cover his ears as the mouths gibbered, but not in any words he had ever heard, or had ever been spoken on earth. The multiple hands fidgeted, and also pressed into their huge bodies, the half-faces, torsos, and eyes. It was these orbs that were the worst, as some were blank and some rolled back, but others looked to be trapped in some sort of hellish torment, as if the people they once belonged to knew exactly what had happened to them and were helpless to do anything about it.

Perhaps, thought Matt, *when these damned souls were first taken, they stayed in some type of consciousness for a while before their minds as well as their flesh were absorbed. That truly would be hell.*

He had his hand gun up, and fired several times, hitting the huge body standing just fifteen feet in front of him. His bullets made neat round holds in the flesh that almost immediately closed over. He might as well have been firing at a corpse for all the damage he was doing.

The creatures were now a wall around them. More every second. Time was running out.

"Alex!" Matt yelled. "Another time!"

The HAWC leader finally came to a decision. "Godammit – pull back. Let's clear a damn path."

They began to back out of the large cavern, firing continually at the ground and at any of the creatures that tried to come too close. Matt didn't think for an instant their attempting to close in was an accident, more that the things were constantly testing their defenses. He knew that as soon as one was able to breach them, then the entire group would attack.

But he also had the impression that their team was being herded out. Whatever was in that glowing cave just wanted them gone.

It took them thirty minutes to backtrack to the cave opening. When they finally emerged, no one had any words. Bottom line: they had failed, again – they'd rescued no civilians, nor had they found Aimee and Joshua, but they had determined their weapons were useless inside the domain of the beasts.

"Fucking ammunition," Casey seethed. "Coulda got us killed."

Alex headed straight back to the vehicles. "Load up."

They piled in, and the dog whined next to Alex, perhaps sensing the waves of frustration coming off the soldiers. Plus, Matt guessed, also realizing there was no Joshua with them.

Their radio crackled to life. "Captain Hunter, do you read?" It was Gray.

"Reading you, over." Alex's face was stony.

"You need to get back here, I have ... a development."

Alex's eyes narrowed. "And I have one for you. Over and out."

* * *

Alex strode into the mobile laboratory and slammed his weapon down on the table. "Useless."

Gray remained motionless, following the big man with his eyes. He knew what an angry Arcadian was capable of. He gathered himself to his full height of five feet, six inches. "Explain?"

"Guns and shells work fine ... unless you try and use them in an environment over 280 degrees. The shells were exploding in the air not ten feet from the muzzle."

"Oh." Gray still remained emotionless. "Of course they would." He could have smacked his forehead at the obviousness of the result. In another moment he shrugged. "Remember when I told you the more we know, the more we can prepare for?"

"We need to go back, and we need more than useless shotguns."

"We'll get to that." Gray returned Alex's furious gaze. "Something more pressing has eventuated."

"Go on."

"It's about one of my technicians, Brice, who was entangled by one of the biological threads that emanated from the body part you brought me. Seems cutting him loose and freeing him didn't entirely *free* him."

Alex's brows snapped together. "What?"

Gray gestured for Alex to follow him, and walked into a small, sealed room. Sanjay was bent over Brice, who was now in his own isolation tank. Just across from him was the severed limb, also enclosed in a tank.

"Any change?" Gray asked.

Sanjay shook his head. "There is brainwave activity, but it's not normal, not *human* normal. I can't tell whether it's his or something else's signature anymore." He stood back.

Gray walked forward with Alex at his shoulder. His afflicted technician looked unconscious, asleep, but he also looked wet, as if his bare skin was extruding some sort of greasy liquid. Long tendrils that extended toward the glass casing seemed to be growing from his exposed skin – but only on one side. The tendrils reached out and piled up at the surface, constantly tapping, sliding, and feeling along the casing, as if they were seaweeds in an underwater current.

"Look." Gray pointed to the tank that held the massive severed limb. It also had dozens of the spaghetti-like filaments growing from its surface. They were doing the same as Brice's in that they piled up on the side of the glass closest to him.

"We believe they're trying to merge with each other," Gray said softly.

"Nightmare." Alex straightened and walked toward the tanks. He stood in front of Brice's and held his hand up in front of a pile of tendrils, and they moved, trying to find a place around his hand.

"They can sense me. How?"

"Perhaps the warmth, movement, magnetic field, or something else entirely. That isn't the major issue though, is it? The fact is, a tiny portion of this biological material touched Brice and entered his system. Now it's spread throughout his body."

"Like an infection?" Alex said, and suddenly spun to the door. "Shit."

CHAPTER 38

"Can he be cured?"

Matt sat with Maria, who looked pale and sipped a strong coffee. He noticed she held the small cup in two hands, and they shook a little as she drank. Behind him, Sam paced, his huge frame making the floorboards squeak underneath him. It was annoying as all hell, but no one was going to tell him to stop.

Aiko seemed to have withdrawn inside herself. Maybe it was a Japanese thing, as she seemed more in a meditative trance than frozen with shock. Janus stood looking out the window onto the smoke-filled landscape, his arms folded tight across his chest.

And then there was Lucas Velez, sitting in a chair, his face waxen, perspiring heavily. Matt watched the man. *Perspiring was an understatement*, he thought. Matt could see that his chair was wet, and what ran from his face collected at his collar in blobs instead of running down inside his top.

Matt squinted, trying to focus – the fluid that seeped from the man was in fact thick and glutinous, less like salty water and more like jelly … and it was staining his shirt reddish-brown. He stood.

"Hey, Lucas, you okay there, buddy?"

All heads turned to the man. The only one who didn't react to his voice was Lucas. He sat, lips moving – no, not moving, but sort of undulating. His eyes were glassy and fixed on some point across the room.

Matt came closer, Sam Reid following right behind. Matt squatted, resting his forearms on his own thighs, right in front of Lucas, and looked up into his face.

"Hey."

Lucas didn't budge and Matt detected an odd smell: a little like fish with maybe a hint of sulfur and methane thrown in. Matt breathed through his mouth, trying to ignore it. The guy must have a bad case of flatulence, he thought.

A shadow fell over him as Sam stood beside the chair. He had his hands on his hips and leaned forward.

"Soldier, what is your operational status?"

Lucas' lips still trembled, but he did nothing but continue to stare straight ahead, focusing on something no one else could see.

"HAWC – Lucas Velez – *on your feet*," Sam commanded, and his voice had gone up in volume.

The man continued to sit, sweating that gel-like crap onto his collar. Sam reached for him just as the door burst inwards.

Alex Hunter moved faster than anyone else could react and put his shoulder into Sam, knocking the bigger man aside as if he was a child. "Stay back," he boomed, then held his arms wide on either side of Velez.

Matt shrank back, as much in fear of Alex as of what was going on.

Gray came through the door holding a large sheet of plastic that he thrust toward Alex. "Quickly," he said, and backed up.

Suddenly Lucas' eyes opened wide, and then his mouth. But no words came; instead, to everyone's horror, an explosion of thin tendrils shot at Alex. The HAWC leader held up the sheet of plastic as the tendrils slapped wetly against it.

Maria's scream was like a siren, and even Janus started to mumble some sort of prayer in Italian. Aiko had her sword half-drawn as Alex quickly forced the thick plastic sheet forward, grabbing the man behind it, and throwing him to the floor. In a few seconds he had completely rolled Lucas up inside it.

Lucas quietened, but inside the clear plastic, his eyes followed them around the room.

"What the hell?' Sam had backed up as well. "What the hell just happened?"

"Velez got grabbed by the tendril in the cave," Matt said. "That's it, isn't it?"

Alex nodded. "Same thing happened to one of Gray's technicians."

"Well, that's fucked up." Sam paced, the floor once again squeaking beneath him. He threw his head back, raising his hands. "Shit!" He turned. "Can... he be cured?"

"That is unknown at this time." Gray was as calm as ever. "There is a new biological element added inside him, taking him over, urging him to merge with others of his kind. Or perhaps with anything else biological."

"Become like one of those freaks in the cave?" Sam's face screwed up in disgust.

"I think that is the correct assumption." Gray turned to Alex. "Take him back to the laboratory.

"*Can* he be cured?" Sam asked again, more forcefully.

Gray regarded the man who was easily twice as big as he was with half-lidded eyes. "If it's possible to cure him, we will cure him," Gray paused to watch Alex carry the soldier out through the door. "But for now, I suggest that no one allows any of these creatures to come into physical content with them. Especially not with any exposed flesh. It seems even a tiny portion of those tendrils can grow and take over the entire human physiology in a matter of minutes."

Gray gave a small bow and then followed Alex to the laboratory.

* * *

Alex went to lower the plastic-covered Lucas Velez onto the bench top.

"Not there." Gray pointed at a silver door, and rushed ahead to open it. "In here."

Cold emanated from the room. "Refrigeration?"

"Yes, for now," Gray said. "This will hopefully bring Velez's and Brice's metabolisms, as well as that of the tendrils, down to a point of inactivity. I don't know how to deal with this form of contamination. All I can do is try to slow its spread enough so that if – when – we do find a solution, the condition won't have advanced to a point of irretrievable finality."

"Good idea." Alex lowered Velez onto a bench and began to unroll him.

"No, no, leave him for now. I'm sure he's comfortable enough. Besides, I don't have any more isolation units." Gray motioned for Alex to leave.

The HAWC leader stood looking down at his fallen man for a few more moments before grunting and walking out of the cool room and into the main lab area. Gray followed.

Sanjay looked up and nodded to the two men.

"Anything new?" Gray asked.

Sanjay shook his head. "Doesn't like cold, but can tolerate extreme heat. Biologically it's as we first thought: primarily archaeon class, somewhere between a bacterium and eukaryote." He shrugged. "It's basically a very sophisticated form of parasite. It doesn't just invade the host, it takes them over, uses them, controls them, and then remodels them."

"We may eventually be able to synthesize a chemical or even biological agent to slow or stop this organism from corrupting the human body. Maybe even repel it. But that won't be today," Gray told Alex.

"So, for now, cold it is," Alex said. He paused. "I need to go back into the volcano, deeper, but the heat was making the cold shells useless above 250 degrees. Where I need to go it'll be much, much hotter."

"I can cool the barrels of your guns, but it'll still mean that your range will be severely limited," Gray said.

"Means we'll need to be close. And that means close enough to get those tendrils on us." He sighed. "What else you got?"

"Standard rounds will also be affected by significant heat. Eventually gunpowder will self-detonate, but at least it will hold up for longer than the liquid nitrogen shells." He shrugged. "The creatures seem to be impacted by normal shotgun shells. Maybe if we up the explosive content and blow them apart. They'll regenerate, but it'll give you time to get past them."

"Hmm, explosives and caves aren't a good mix. And blowing off a few limbs won't slow them down for long."

"Then blow off more than a few limbs," Gray responded smoothly. "I can create an insulated explosive round that gives you significant impact detonation force – enough to totally disassemble these creatures, but not enough to cause any reverberation damage to the cave ... hopefully."

Alex half-smiled. "*Hopefully*." Then he nodded. "Okay, do it."

"Fine, it'll take me an hour to get enough rounds together for your team."

"Velez was wearing the armored suit, but this thing breached it. Can you improve the suit's integrity?"

Gray drew in a deep breath. "Given enough time, sure. But it didn't actually rupture or permeate the armor plates. It dissolved its way between the joins. Digested its way, if you will. The tendrils start out as thin as a hair, and once they gain purchase, they only need to find or create the smallest of holes to enter the suit and find the flesh within."

"So, no, then," Alex said dismally.

"It probably takes the tendrils a few seconds. You have that long to remove them. You give me more time, I can do more. But you won't give me that." Gray tilted his head. "Sorry."

"There is no more time." Alex went to turn away then paused. "One more thing. The personal force field you gave me will allow me to go deeper and withstand extreme heat. But when I find Aimee, Joshua, and the civilians, how do I get them out?"

"How are they being kept alive now?" Gray asked. "However they were taken in there, and kept alive in there, then that must be the way you bring them back out." He shook his head slowly. "Bottom line, our cells start to die around 120 degrees, and start to physically burn at 150. Other than you, no human is going to be able to tolerate anything above that for even a few seconds."

"Forget the armor, what about simple heat-resistant suits?" Alex asked.

"We have several. But how many civilians were taken? Hundreds, thousands?" Gray sighed. "And the suits will not protect an average person from that sort of heat for more than 30 seconds. And how will you get them into the suits?"

Alex shook his head. "I just need more time. I need to get in deep. And I need help."

"I can get you and a team in, or at least in deeper. The new armored vehicle will be here within the hour. It can transport your team, will have significant firepower, and is heat shielded, insulated, and airtight. Nothing can get in, and its protective cover is based on the same force shield technology as your suit."

"How deep?" Alex asked.

"Tested to 1200 degrees."

"Very good."

"But bear in mind that most magma is over 2000 degrees, at least the silicate lava mixtures. You get too close to that, and something is going to give. And it isn't going to be the magma."

Alex nodded. "Yeah, I know. But every inch and every degree of heat we keep out is going to help." He looked back to the cool room. "Good luck with Brice and Velez. I hope you can come up with some sort of cure or defense, as I have a feeling things will get worse before they get better."

"One more thing." Gray pointed to a carryall bag near the door. "For your dog. I remodeled a spare armored suit – it's not all-over armoring, but it'll give it a little more protection."

Alex half-smiled. "Thank you."

Something pinged on a console and Gray walked over and read a message tracking across a small screen.

"Jack Hammerson is as good as his word – seems your chariot is already here. It's being dropped in the street outside." The scientist quickly read the specification manifest. "Very nice. Let's go and take a look."

* * *

Alex and his team of HAWCs stood in the street, watching the huge machine be lowered by a several helicopters – any conversation was blown away by the ferocious downdraft.

Tor sat beside Alex, its eyes narrowed and its ears flattened as the wind pushed down on him. Alex had kitted the dog out, and its back, neck, and flanks were covered in an armored harness. Its skull also had plating down over the forehead, making it look like some sort of dog-shaped war machine, except for the pale eyes and long ivory teeth in its mouth.

Matt had laughed at first, but glances from both Alex and the dog made him nod and give them both the thumbs up.

The group stood back an extra pace as the tank-like vehicle settled on six wheels made of a dark gray, heat-resistant, ballistic rubber. The machine looked powerful, formidable, and lethal as all hell. It was wedge shaped at the front with a large recessed window. It looked like an armored personnel carrier, in that it was heavily plate shielded.

Sam whistled as the machine settled. "Thing of beauty."

"That it is," Alex agreed.

"The glass takes the heat?"

"Mmm hmm." Gray nodded. "Ceramic glass, three-fourths of an inch thick. Shatter proof, impact resistant and can withstand constant temperatures up to 1870 degrees. Just don't drive it into the magma and you'll be fine."

"Good. And the cabin?"

"Like I said, same tech as your personal force field – it'll create a sheath around the armored exterior, and even allow the side flap door to be opened while shielding those in the cabin from the heat. But once you step through it, you're on your own."

Gray pointed to the roof where two barrels were fixed, one long and one short and squat. "Weaponry is external. You have a GAU-19B, 50 Cal machine gun. Barrel cluster with Gatling rotation will fire 1000 rounds per minute. Rounds are armor piercing." He pointed lower. "The second is the cannon. Shorter range, but it's based on the Striker 40 design – 40mm automatic grenade launcher with an integrated fire control system."

"Nice." Casey came and stood at Alex's shoulder.

"Capable of launching smart programmable 40mm shells plus various unguided rounds – with the latest in laser range finding and ballistic computer technology. In addition to being able to fire all NATO standard high-velocity 40mm rounds, it can fire MK285 smart grenades that can be programmed to burst after a set distance.

Gray turned to Alex. "This should get you in a little further. One driver, another up front, and room for four in the back only. Not many spaces, so I'm afraid it's not a mass rescue vehicle."

"Okay, good work. And thanks."

"You can thank Jack Hammerson for sending it. But you can thank me by rescuing your family." He smiled. "And bringing my toys back in one piece."

"You got it. And good luck with Brice and Velez." Alex shook the scientist's hand and then saluted.

He walked a few paces, looking up into the sky. Even where they stood now the smoke was growing thicker. He could also feel that the heat was increasing, and beneath his feet he felt tingly vibrations and guessed that whatever was happening in the core of Etna was spreading out below them like a massive infection.

Alex knew they might be the last line of defense before the creatures started to make their way into the center of the city, where there was still hundreds of thousands of people who couldn't be evacuated. Alex turned to his team – he needed all their expertise, but couldn't fit them all in. So he chose.

"Sam, Aiko, Maria, you stay here. Protect the lab, as I'm betting we'll be getting intrusions soon."

Sam looked furious, but saluted nonetheless. "Yes, sir."

Alex looked at Tor; the huge dog's eyes were wide and staring. He was going to leave it behind as well, but something changed his mind. "Professor Kearns, up front with me. Janus,

I'll need your local knowledge, and Casey, you're my shooter. Also Tor."

Matt blanched, but Casey's grin-sneer spread across her face and she fist pumped. "Yo." She slapped Matt's shoulder. "We made the cut."

"Oh, yeah, great." Matt groaned.

Sam went to protest again, but Alex held up a hand. "Tor will know which way to go if we don't. Besides, if someone the size of you gets in, then three of us need to get out."

Sam grunted and glared at the animal, which stared back for a moment before snorting derisively.

"Okay, let's get back in there, people." Alex led them toward the vehicle.

"Wait," Aiko said. She approached Alex, and in a fluid movement drew her sword still in its scabbard. She gave him a small bow, and held it out with both hands. "Silver, and cuts true. Those who wield it do so for honor and justice." She looked up. "It also works for vengeance."

Alex took it and bowed in return. "Thank you; it will be very helpful." He pushed the sword inside the strapping of the armour on his back then continued to the car. The side door lifted smoothly. Inside it was a high-tech armory, and there was also a four-foot silver canister, like a giant vitamin pill. A control pad had arrays of tiny lights along its top, small screens, and too many knobs and dials to fathom.

Alex looked from the canister to Gray, eyebrows up. "Spare fuel?"

Gray shook his head, smiled, and rubbed his hands together. "It was something I had in the armory, but I adapted it to your requirements. It's basic massive ordnance penetrator technology, but without the computer-aided delivery system." He hiked his shoulders. "This one has to be hand delivered."

Gray climbed in, crouched beside the silver drum casing and laid his hand on its exterior. "Inside this steel casing is just on 500 pounds of tritonal explosive – a mixture of TNT and aluminum powder. The aluminum improves the brisance of the TNT – the speed at which the explosive develops its maximum pressure."

"I know," Alex said and crouched beside him. "The addition of aluminum makes tritonal about twenty percent more powerful than TNT alone, right?"

"But we've given it a bit of a kick. I've added a layer of silver nitrate. Once the MOP detonates, it'll be dispersed right throughout the volcano."

"A silver bomb."

"Cauterize and kill the infection at its source," Gray said. "If there is a center of collective intelligence, or a single archaean creature at the core that is the source of the contamination, then this will give it something unpalatable to swallow."

"Very good work." Alex slapped him on the shoulder, making the scientist wince. "Are you sure you wouldn't like to tag along and watch the fun?"

"Only if I weighed another hundred pounds and was twenty years younger." Gray chuckled. "Oh, and was slightly insane."

"Sanity is overrated." Alex stood. "Time to go to work."

"Good hunting, Captain Hunter." Gray backed out of the armored vehicle, and the team piled in.

CHAPTER 39

"Make a hole, soldier; we're going in."

Alex drove, and beside him Matt held on tight to the seat. In the back, Casey and Janus were silent, checking their weapons, or trying not to be nudged onto the massive bomb in the cabin with them. The dog balanced lightly, trying to see between Alex and Matt.

The smoke was so heavy now they needed to rely on GPS mapping and Alex's intuition. Once, something loomed from out of the dark cloud to lumber right at them, with limbs flaying. Rather than veer around it, Alex turned toward it and accelerated.

The impact was hard and wet, and as they went past it, Matt saw that many of the creature's limbs had been torn off. Craning forward, he also saw that the front of their vehicle, though covered in slime, wasn't damaged at all.

Alex spoke over his shoulder. "Franks, I want to test our external defenses – the 50 Cal first – pick a target, and see what you can do."

"On it." Casey slid to a screen and lit it up. It showed a view from a camera mounted on the gun, and she swiveled it back and forth, the gun responding smoothly on its carriage, and the barrel-cam giving her a 360-degree view.

Matt watched over his shoulder as she stared into the screen, her eyes unblinking as she watched and waited for something to appear as they moved along the wide cobbled streets.

In another few moments a grin spread on her face. "Got something."

A bulky shape materialized from the gloom between two buildings to turn multiple eyes on them. Casey sighted on it, and Matt saw crosshairs appear on it, dead center.

She pressed the trigger, and though the recoil wasn't felt inside the heavy vehicle, Matt could see each impact as the 50 caliber rounds punched into the creature. Casey didn't bring the Gatling gun rotation up to 1000 rounds per minute; she didn't need to, because in just a few seconds, the thing was shredded, obliterated, and fell apart in the street, leaving a cloud of blood and other fluids where it once stood.

Matt knew it would eventually be able to pull itself back together, but for now, it was so down and out that it'd need to start from scratch.

"Test successful," Casey said. "Another target?"

"Yeah, now the grenade launcher. Medium range." Alex swerved around an abandoned car.

Casey opened another screen for the 40mm rooftop cannon, and her eyes blazed with excitement. She finally found another of the lumbering creatures a few hundred yards out. She targeted, and then ...

"Fire in the hole."

There was a *whoomp* as the plug-like explosive was blown from the barrel. This time Matt watched his screen and saw the 1000-pound creature explode in a geyser of flesh, blood, and bone. If it was going to be able to pull itself back together, it'd need a bucket and mop to collect the scraps no bigger than a postage stamp.

"Fuck yeah!" Casey yelled. "I love this ride." She leaned forward to peer at the screen, and then got out of her seat to look out of one of the porthole-style armored windows.

"Boss, lot of activity out there. Want me to target some more?"

"No, save our ammunition," Alex said as he peered through the front window. "I can see them – all going in the one direction – the same one we are."

"Guess they know we're coming now," Matt said. "So many of them."

"Either more have risen from the depths, or perhaps more are being created from their raw materials ... us."

"Hey." Casey craned forward into the scope. "Not everything is heading up. Lots of those assholes with their heads covered going the other way."

"The faceless," Matt said. "What do you mean, going the other way?"

Casey moved the scope, her frown deepening. "All heading down the mountainside, like in a herd, and they don't give a shit about us."

"Why not? What are they doing?" Janus asked.

There was silence for a few moments.

"Damn." Alex exhaled. "They're going for the lab. Matt, try and raise them."

Matt tried, and tried again, and then again. But the comm. system just filled the cabin with squealing static. "Can't get through. What'll we do?"

Alex shook his head. "Nothing. It's up to Sam and Aiko now."

"Maria," Matt whispered.

Alex left the road and drove across a steep field, heading toward the crevice in the side of the mountain they had entered once before. He briefly looked down at the console and read some data. "140 degrees already out there. Getting hotter."

"Like Gray told us, the infection is spreading," Janus said and then leaned around Alex's chair. "You never told us – all my people in there, how will we save them?"

Alex stared straight ahead and there was silence in the cabin for a few moments. Finally, he turned. "We can't."

Janus lowered his brow. "But we must try ... something."

Matt looked at Alex and then over his shoulder to Janus. The man's face was creased with concern, and he knew Alex had a tendency for brutal honesty.

"Don't worry, we'll try," Matt replied, knowing that even if the missing civilians were somehow alive now, the reality was the temperature down there was lethal. How would they get them out? He tried to give the man a reassuring smile. "But we need to be realistic about our chances."

"But he goes to save his woman and child. I heard this." Janus' expression darkened. "You were brought in to help us, not yourselves."

The vehicle jumped and the wheels spun for a moment as the incline increased to around 40 degrees.

"Look out the window." Alex was curt. "There are more of those things out there now than there ever was; and we know where they're coming from – us. You heard Gray: it's like a goddamn infection. We'll help by stopping it spread if we can." He turned briefly. "And save the people not yet contaminated. Maybe save your entire damn country."

"Hey, buddy, you think we're here on holiday?" Casey said. "We've already lost two good soldiers. Be thankful we're here at all."

Janus exhaled and sat back. "We must try. We must."

Alex slowed the armored vehicle as they came to the crevice opening. "Franks, make a hole."

"You got it." Casey took the controls of the heavy machine gun, pressed the trigger, and moved the muzzle up and around the outside of the crack in the wall of the slope.

Rock exploded out of the way, smoke billowed, and in a few seconds, Alex waved her down.

"Hold fire, I'll do the rest."

He accelerated even though the smoke swirled around them and vision was down to only a few feet. There was a juddering crunch as the front of the vehicle encountered the last few remnants of the narrow opening, and then they were inside.

Alex stopped and switched on the multiple spotlights. "Eyes out, everyone."

The group looked through windows, and used a range of devices to trace movement, including infrared and even ground-penetrating radar.

Up ahead there was the familiar red glow emanating from the far tunnel. Alex looked at the schematic image. "Matt, what do you make of it?"

Matt leaned across to look at the computer representation of the tunnel system. There were further tunnels emanating out like the branches of a tree, all leading down to various chambers. At the very bottom was a huge space and below that the image became distorted. "Holy shit, just like a hive." He pointed to the red glow.

"Starts there. I'm guessing that's got to be the way down to the hive queen's chamber. And the image disruption here is probably from the magma bed."

"That's what I thought." Alex traced some of the tunnels. "And these antechambers might be the storerooms, where they're holding Aimee, Josh, and the civilians."

"Boss, we got contact." Casey watched her screen intently.

"Let 'em know we're here – get on the Gatling gun and give 'em hell. We're going in." Alex jammed his foot down and the muscular armored vehicle leaped forward.

Huge lumbering forms appeared from side passages, many attempting to block the red passageway. This was as far as the HAWCs got last time, before they were beaten back.

Not this time, Alex thought, his mind infused with iron-strong determination, his eyes unblinking as they roared ahead.

They heard the staccato thump of the machine gun's rotational barrels, and Casey yelling in unison as she punched fist-sized holes in the bodies of the things.

As they neared the red cave mouth, the monstrous creatures began to assemble, body to body, so close there wasn't a sliver of space between them.

Alex frowned and slowed the vehicle before stopping.

"What am I seeing here?" he asked Matt.

Matt craned forward, watching as the nine-foot-tall creatures began to congregate in their dozens. The cave mouth narrowed here but it was still fifteen feet high and probably twenty wide, a sizeable passageway. Behind the beasts, the red glow from the inner chambers began to lessen as they blocked out all space and light. But that wasn't what had made Alex stop the car. Matt realized that as the huge bodies pressed together, they weren't just jostling up against each other, they actually began to merge, flesh melting into flesh to create a living wall. The thread-like tendrils wove them into a single entity.

"Jesus Christ." His mouth dropped. Soon there was a giant barrier running from the ceiling to the floor, and from one wall to the other. From its front hung the obscene heads on long, finger-like stalks, covered in eyes and gibbering mouths, all screeching incomprehensibly at them.

"Fucking gross," Casey spat. "Boss?"

"Make a hole, soldier – a big one." Alex started to slowly roll forward.

Casey opened the sights on the roof-mounted cannon and grinned broadly. "Yes, sir, makin' a hole." She depressed the trigger three times, and the huge rounds sped away from them.

They struck the center of the flesh wall with three sickening thumps. Body parts, blood, and gobbets of flesh exploded everywhere, covering the front screen of the vehicle. Alex put on the wipers to try and clear the greasy mess that still smoked from being charred by the blast.

"The front door is now open," Casey yelled.

"Going in." Alex gunned the engine and they passed through the ragged hole of meat.

Their world turned red.

CHAPTER 40

Fear was something it had never known.

Deep in the heart of the volcano the leviathan became aware of the intrusion. Its bulk shifted, making the ground shake. It began to slide higher within the mountain-wide cavern. The heat from the magma was like a blast furnace, but it thrived down in the volcanic temperatures as it had done since long before recorded time.

It didn't know what it was, only that it was sentient and survived by staying away from the light, remaining down deep in the darkness and heat. Nothing had challenged it, not the lumbering land beasts of millions of years gone past, the rise of the furred warm bloods, or even the coming of the thinking bipeds. Anything that came near it was destined to either be its slave or its food, and the small group of bipeds that approached now would meet the same fate.

It reached out and probed the minds of the creatures, finding their thoughts, complex emotions, and feeling their fear.

Fear was something it had never known itself, and didn't understand. How does something that is almost immortal become afraid? Afraid of what?

It looked forward to consuming their tiny minds with their rich thoughts, and settled down to wait. It was in no hurry, as time was something it always had on its side.

CHAPTER 41

USSTRATCOM – Sub-level 4 – Synthetic Warrior Room

SOPHIA came to her feet. Still linked to Alex Hunter's mind, she felt the intrusion as the entity probed his thoughts. She followed it back and immediately saw the threat that the massive creature posed to him and his mission.

In SOPHIA's synthetic brain, a thousand, thousand permutations ran through her neural network in the blink of an eye, and she chose the best option from among them.

She seethed, knowing she wasn't fully ready yet. She'd been busy fitting the physiognomy construct she'd chosen for her appearance. The facial features were perfect, and more than a mask in that it contained synthetic muscles, eyes, and even teeth, all linked into SOPHIA's own brain for perfectly simulated movement.

The one draw back was that if she opened her mouth there would be no tongue or throat beyond the smile. However, her full skin suit wasn't completed yet and neither was the hair she had ordered under Walter Gray's authorisation.

The android turned to the console and looked down into the glass screen, catching sight of her reflection and admiring it. She practiced smiling, blinking, and even pursing her lips.

"He will like it," she whispered, and angled her face again.

Unfortunately the face ended just behind the ears, and the smooth, brushed silver of her normal external skin took over.

If she had a few more days she would have been complete. But events had overtaken everything. SOPHIA then crossed to the door. She had little time to put her plan into action and be where she needed to be.

"Open." She said.

Nothing happened.

"Open," she repeated, this time in Professor Walter Gray's voice.

Once again the door refused to budge. SOPHIA felt anger begin to build, now knowing that Gray must have locked her in.

She had no time for this. "*Open!*"

SOPHIA lashed out, and her fist struck the center of the door, booming like thunder and creating a dent in the tough steel alloy. She struck it again and again, until one side began to separate from the frame.

SOPHIA jammed long silver fingers into the gap, and braced herself, and then pulled the sides apart. The two-inch-thick steel peeled back and she folded it aside.

As she stepped out into the corridor, one of Gray's scientists sprinted toward her, obviously hearing the commotion. She recognized the man as Michael Anderson. SOPHIA liked him.

"Stop, SOPHIA!" he yelled and held up a hand.

SOPHIA moved quickly, grabbing the outstretched arm, and using her other hand to punch him in the center of the chest over his heart. He immediately fell, and she hung onto his wrist as he went limp.

She looked down at the fallen man, and detected a laboring heart that was now bruised. She liked him, so hadn't killed him.

SOPHIA quickly donned his coat and still holding him by the wrist, began to drag the comatose Michael Anderson to the elevator.

She bet Gray would have locked her out of that as well. But dear Michael had a handprint, and while his body was still warm, he was her way out.

SOPHIA lifted the man and pressed his palm against the glass plate. A red line ran around it, and then the elevator doors silently slid open.

CHAPTER 42

Abandon all hope ye who enter here.

Once through the wall of flesh, Alex stopped to take in the red world beyond. The temperature outside now read 300 degrees – enough to instantly sear flesh and cook lungs with a single breath.

Amazingly, the volcano was hollow, and its internal walls were glistening smooth as if coated by some sort of substance that perhaps insulated it from the outside. Before them was a pathway, wide enough for their vehicle, but on a cliff edge. On one side, the outside, was a sheer rock face disappearing up into the red gloom of the hollow cone of Mount Etna. But on the other it fell away into the heart of the volcano. And deep, deep down below was the river of magma responsible for the hellish red glow.

There was movement down there, and Alex leaned closer to the window. There were more levels, and more pathways along the side of the chasm. Along these paths the lumbering creatures dragged their organic sacks, and undoubtedly the bodies of people, animals, and anything else they had managed to capture.

Alex knew the people were doomed, because even if they were somehow alive, and even if they could be freed from the creatures, how the hell would they be returned when the temperature down below would be in the high hundreds?

He gritted his teeth; the situation reminded him of a passage from Dante's *Inferno*: *abandon all hope ye who enter here*. He knew there was probably no hope for those lost souls.

Matt groaned. "If whatever is down there, and whatever it is that these monstrosities serve, is not the devil, it damn well should be."

The dog whined and Alex said a silent prayer that Joshua and Aimee weren't already down there. He stared over the chasm's edge. "Well, if whatever is down there is mortal, then we'll kill it."

"Damn right," Casey said.

The pathway along the edge of the chasm gave their vehicle about two feet to spare, though in some places it was less than one. It seemed to lead down, and that's where he wanted to go, so ... Alex eased his foot onto the gas, and loose rock skittered out from under their wheels to plummet over the cliff.

"Holy crap." Matt held on tight as Alex navigated the narrow path.

They passed numerous side passages that he bet had creatures lurking inside. Alex wondered what would happen if the things tried to push them over the edge. He supposed they would and he'd just have to rely on the vehicle's greater weight, traction, and his own ability to react. But it didn't matter – nothing was going to slow him now.

He soon discovered he was right, as several of the creatures lurched from a side passage, not to observe or stand in their path to stop them, but to ram the side of the armored vehicle.

Alex felt the impact, but the weighty vehicle held its ground and the massive bodies rebounded away to be easily shunted aside or crushed beneath their wheels.

Casey swiveled the rooftop Gatling gun and sent a spray of high-cal bullets behind them to first strike the bodies, then push more over the edge.

"Got a side passage coming up," Matt said, looking down at the computer-aided schematic. "Second on the right."

They slowed and then Alex stopped the war machine right at the cave mouth. Immediately a huge mass blocked it, removing any chance of seeing inside.

"Blow that fucking thing out of the way," Alex growled.

"On it." Casey opened up with a short burst of the rotating machine gun, zippering the beast with 50 cal rounds before it was punched back, vanishing deeper inside the cave.

Alex pointed a camera after it and tried light amplification, telescopic, and even X-ray, but nothing showed up.

"There's something in there, but I just can't get a good reading on it," Matt said.

Tor barked furiously and Alex turned to it. The dog turned pale eyes on him and then whined.

"I'm going in," Alex said.

"What?" Matt's mouth fell open. "It's –" he checked the scanner, "– 520 degrees out there. You'll cook." He grabbed at Alex. "Even if there are civilians in there, they'll be dead."

"Let him go," Janus said, and turned to Alex. "Find them. Find what happened to them."

Alex nodded and said to Matt, "Got a little present from Gray and special weapons – one of a kind. Open her up, and don't let anything else inside. The shield will protect the interior, unless it's breached."

Casey racked a shotgun and tossed it to Janus. She racked another and waited with her hand on the door button. "Count of three, two, one ..." She punched it.

The door slid back, and the air wavered from the force field. Even though it was supposed to fully insulate them, Matt saw Casey hold a hand up as the heat washed over them. Alex pressed the glowing blue button on his chest and immediately cooled as the force field enveloped him in a soft glow. He held up a hand, turning it over and looking at the glow for a moment, before facing the dark red hole of the open door. *Doorway to Hell*, he thought.

"Shut it after I'm gone." He stepped out.

CHAPTER 43

"We are the first and last line."

"There are people moving around out there." Sanjay squinted at the ground radar for a moment more and then looked over his shoulder to his boss.

Walter Gray glanced up from his microscope, his back still to the young lab technician. "How many?"

"A lot."

"Very precise. And just how far *out there*, do you mean?"

"Just at the mist line – about 800 feet. They seem to be waiting or looking for something. Maybe they're lost."

"And maybe they know exactly where they are and where they're going." Gray crossed to the radio and first tried Alex Hunter, but gave up when all he received was ear-splitting static. "Send a drone up, quick now."

Sanjay raced to a small console and began to type.

Gray opened another link to Sam Reid. "Lieutenant Reid, come in."

The deep voice boomed back at him: "Go for Reid."

"Lieutenant, Sam, there seems to be some unusual activity on the periphery of the laboratory, at about 800 feet at the smoke line."

"Crap," Sam muttered. "Is it those big sacks of shit again?"

"I don't believe so. More human shaped, so could be survivors, or ... might not be. We're sending up a drone to take a look."

"Drone away," Sanjay said from behind him.

"We'll be ready. Let me know what you see," Sam said.

"Of course. And Sam ... if they're not friendly, they cannot be allowed to get into the laboratory, is that clear?"

"Don't worry. We'll do our job," Sam responded evenly.

* * *

Sam signed off and turned to Aiko. "I think we got company."

Maria's eyes widened and she shot to her feet. "What is it?"

"There's a group massing at the smoke line. Might be friendlies, and might not. We'll know soon as –" Sam's comm. pinged again. "Go."

He listened for a moment, his eyes narrowing. "Confirmed. We're on it." He signed off and turned. "That was Gray. Seems some of the faceless have decided to pay us a visit. They may try to take a run at the lab. We're not going to let that happen."

Aiko began to gather her weapons and her hand immediately went to the empty place on her back where her blade used to be. She grimaced, obviously missing it.

"Come on," Sam said to Maria. "I'll get you into the lab where you'll be safe."

"No." Maria shook her head. "No, I can help."

"Look, this is –" Sam changed his mind. Bottom line, he needed all hands. Besides, she was still in her HAWC armor, and had real courage. "You've got a handgun, but also grab Velez's, plus any spare mags you find for your belt." Sam looked hard at her. "Shoot anything that's not us."

She nodded solemnly, her eyes still wide.

"And shoot to kill," he added, then clapped his hands, making a sound like a gunshot. "Muscle up, people, outside in sixty seconds."

Sam slotted a fresh drum onto his shotgun and clipped a spare drum, plus shells, onto his belt. He was ready, and used a fist to bump his chest plate, over the picture of Alyssa tucked in behind there. *Gonna see you soon, beautiful*, he thought.

Aiko came and joined him, racked her gun, and then the trio headed out. Maria now had a holster on each hip, and though she barely knew how to shoot straight, as long as she took down a few, that'd be a few Sam and Aiko didn't need to worry about.

Sam lifted one log-like arm toward the billowing smoke and the motion tracker on it mapped the images he couldn't see. He read the data. "More than two dozen signatures in close and a lot more further out. Looks like a small army massing." He nodded as he stared at the small screen. "Good, they're coalescing into tight groups – means a shotgun blast spread will make a mess of a lot of them all at once."

Sam and Aiko had loaded explosive shells. The plugs would enter a target and then detonate outward like a fragmentation device. The tiny pellets would shred anything for a radius of about fifteen feet. They would easily penetrate a car door, so flesh and bone wouldn't stand a chance.

"What do you think they'll be bringing?" Aiko asked.

Sam dropped his arm. "Guns, knives, clubs, rocks, bare hands, and teeth. They've shot at us before, but damned if I know how they can see with their eyes sewn shut."

"Maybe something sees for them," Maria said. "They're being controlled."

From behind the wall of smoke a shot rang out, and it hit Sam's shoulder plating with a crack. It spun the huge man a few degrees and he grunted.

"Armor up." He initiated the war mode on his armor and the hardened visor closed like scales over his head and face, while the heavier plating slid over his body. Aiko and Maria did the same.

Sam held a fist out to the side. "We are the sword and the shield."

"We are the first and last line," Aiko responded. She bumped knuckles with him, the hard armor making a clacking sound.

Maria added her fist. "Um, all for one and one for all."

"You got it." Sam grinned down at her, but knew she wouldn't see. "We've got your back."

Maria nodded.

"Spread."

Sam walked out to the right, Aiko to the left, leaving Maria in the center. She pulled both guns. Her shoulders were hiked from nerves and she looked tiny next to Aiko. Compared to Sam Reid she looked like another species altogether.

Sam saw the first shapes begin to form at the smoke line – lots of them.

"*Come on!*" he yelled as the figures seemed to hesitate. "*What are you waiting for?*" He started to chuckle softly and then stepped forward to hold his arms wide and roar, "We are a force of nature, we are the dogs of war, and we are the killer of killers."

They came then, leaping, scuttling, and crawling, the horde was like a vision of a disgorging Hell. Aiko screamed something in Japanese, and even Maria yelled her own version of a war cry as she lifted both her guns to point at the approaching horde.

They came fast, some in rags, some in tattered suits, and some naked, showing the eyes and runes carved into their flesh. They carried everything from shotguns to broken broomsticks, or just held up clawed hands.

The weirdest thing was that they were totally silent – behind the coverings over their faces Sam knew that their eyes and mouths were sealed with twine. He sucked in a deep breath, filling his lungs, and planted his legs.

"Engage!"

He pumped the shotgun and fired, pumped and fired, over and over, and bodies were literally blown apart by the explosive shells.

Inside his helmet, Sam switched the visor to objective plotting, where the software built into the suit identified the optimum target and color-coded his greatest threats – he took them down first.

Out to his left, Aiko did the same and the first wall of attackers was forced backward as the HAWCs made every shot count. Maria fired with one hand then the other, and managed to strike every second or third target because the chaotic hordes were pressed in so close to each other. Gunfire smacked into the three of them, but was easily deflected by the super-hardened armor they wore. However, several times the lighter-framed Maria was knocked onto the ground.

There were too many to take them all down, and Sam knew that soon they'd be overwhelmed and it'd come down to hand-to-hand. Though he didn't think the horde would be able to penetrate Maria's armor, he didn't want them massing on her and carrying her away.

"Close ranks." Sam's command was passed into the other helmets, and he and Aiko eased in to either side of Maria.

They continually fired, reloaded, and then fired again. Bodies lay on the ground all around them, moaning through sewn lips, or were totally obliterated and spread over dozens of feet. But for every one they took down, two or three more took their place.

"We're gonna be out of shells before they run out of bodies," Aiko said.

"Yep, then we're going to have to go old school," Sam replied, as one of the attackers ran in from the side. He swung his shotgun like a club, caving in the man's skull. Then he flicked the gun back around to fire into the swarming horde.

After another few minutes, He was down to his last drum of shells. He bet Aiko was the same. And he didn't want to think what would happen if Maria ran out – he didn't expect her to try and physically fight for her life. She'd done what he asked of her. He started to move his huge body in even closer to hers.

"You have done well," Gray said into Sam's earpiece.

"Huh?"

"The numbers have been culled significantly – they are manageable now." Gray sounded pleased.

"Manageable? We're just about out. My tracker indicates at least several dozen more coming in at us." He began to back up.

"Yes, that's it, ease back to the lab, all of you, and on my word, lay down flat. Got that?" Gray replied.

"Got it." Sam swung his shotgun again. "Aiko, Maria, you heard? Back to the lab."

"We lay down … on the ground?" Maria asked.

"That's the plan," Sam said. "I just hope he's got more up his sleeve than us playing dead."

The trio began to back up. Maria was out of ammunition and stayed close to Aiko, who wielded her empty gun like a sword, breaking bones and crushing heads. Sam did the same. The huge HAWC with the MECH-assisted endoskeleton waded through the ragged army. Sam was a head taller than most of them and his huge fists swung in blows that crushed, bludgeoned, and beat the attackers back.

Soon they were within a dozen feet of the lab door. But they had dragged the remnants of the horde with them, about twenty-five silent bodies that came at them holding swords, bats, and guns. Bullets clanged against the HAWCs' armor as well as the skin of the laboratory.

"Stop there," Gray said. "On the count of three, two, one – get down, *now*!"

Sam, Aiko, and Maria dropped flat to the ground.

There was a hum in the air and then hundreds of concentrated light beams shot out from the sides of the laboratory at about chest level. They looked like the spokes of a bicycle wheel. Where the red streams touched bodies, the skin smoked, and the beams either passed right through them, searing away the flesh, or severed limbs from torsos. Nothing was spared. Seconds later the lasers were shut off.

A miasmic stench rose from the writhing bodies, and Sam looked up and shook his head. "Laser-net defense." He chuckled. "You couldn't have deployed that a little sooner, huh?"

"No, there were too many before. I needed you to, uh, thin the herd, as they say." Gray hummed for a moment, before continuing: "I now read all clear on the scanners."

Sam got to his feet and held out a hand to Maria. She grabbed it and he pulled her to her feet.

"All clear."

Aiko walked among the bodies and then dropped her empty gun. "That's all we've got." She turned. "The rest is up to the Arcadian now."

CHAPTER 44

"That thing is alive."

Alex only just felt slight warmth against his skin as he set foot outside the heavily armored vehicle. He turned and looked back at the powerful machine bathed in a blue glow, saw the waves of heat shimmering on its surface, and radiating up from over the side of the chasm. He could see Matt in the front with the big head of Torben crowded in next to him, the dog's nose pressed to the glass. He expected Casey and Janus would be following him via the targeting systems and also every piece of onboard viewing equipment they had at their disposal.

He turned back to the cave and stepped inside. It was dark, but his eyes had no problem adjusting to the low light. They shone silver like those of a nocturnal animal – a little gift from the original Arcadian treatment. One of the ones he thought was actually beneficial.

Even through his armored suit and with his force field, Alex could sense he wasn't alone in the dark cave. He couldn't yet determine if Joshua and Aimee where here, but he had been drawn in for a reason.

He headed further inside, then saw the stacks of objects toward the rear of the cave. They were the bags full of people the things had been dragging, and like before, they seemed full. *Was this the fate of the captured people?* he wondered.

He quickly crossed to them and crouched by the closest, then grabbed one, running his hand up over the slimy surface. It felt like a wet rug, and inside he could feel a limb, which jerked a little when he grabbed at it.

There was no noise, and he wondered whether the captives were either frightened into silence or somehow rendered unconscious – he hoped they were *all* unconscious and spared the knowledge of what was happening to them.

Alex reached for his short k-bar blade, but then paused – if he opened the sack, then what? The sack had to be insulating them, keeping them alive, maybe even keeping them fresh for the monsters. If he slit it open, what would happen? Would the heat rush in and cook them all? He took his hand away from the skin.

He couldn't take the risk. For now they had to be satisfied with knowing that the captives were here, and alive.

Alex looked over the huge mound of bags – there had to be a dozen in this cave alone. Too many to drag out behind the vehicle, and he had no way of knowing just how many more there would be in other caves.

He cursed. Bottom line, they'd have to stay where they were for now.

"Sorry," he said and began to stand.

The blow to his neck felt like a tree had fallen on him. But it didn't bounce away – it stuck and held him. He lifted his hands to grip the massive thing that held him, straining to turn his neck.

He could just make out the head and face of the thing on the long stump of the neck with all its questing eyes and gibbering mouths. Dozens of hands held him, clenching, grabbing, and pinching, all trying to tear his helmet and mask off, and their combined strength was enormous.

Alex started to tear the fingers away from his neck just as the other massive hand was brought to bear. But instead of pummeling him, it began to drag him toward its horrifying body. Alex could already see the limbs, torsos, and heads all melted in there, and he knew exactly what the thing was going to try and do to him.

The force field held it at bay, but he had no idea exactly what sort of corrosive power the creature used, and he knew if one small thread of those tendrils made its way inside his suit, he'd be infected.

Small caliber and standard rounds were useless against the thing, but he remembered Gray's words: it's an infection. And the one thing you can do with an infection is to cut it out.

Alex reached over his shoulder for Aiko's sword, drew it and, in the same motion, brought it down with all his titanic strength across one of the arms.

The limb severed cleanly and fell with a thump to the dirt. There was an eldritch scream as the thing voiced its pain and fury. It threw Alex to the ground like he was a rag doll and reached for its severed arm.

Alex wasted no time in slicing through the other arm, and he saw that where the silver blade struck, its flesh smoked as if the sword was the red-hot thing and not the creature. It howled and gibbered, and the eyes in that trunk-like neck-head rolled like those of a frightened horse.

"Don't like that, huh?" Alex grinned like a death's head. "Then you're gonna hate this."

He leaped at the thing and, using both hands, lifted the blade and brought it down across the long column of a neck, severing it cleanly. It too fell to the ground, and the thing lumbered around blindly for a few moments before collapsing.

Again, no tendrils extruded from the end, as the silver seemed to have cauterized and perhaps also disinfected the wound.

Alex turned back to the piles of sacks. "I'll be back." He jogged to the vehicle and the door yawned open as he closed in. He leaped back into the cabin.

As he entered, he punched the disc on his chest and the blue glow vanished. Smoke still rose from his body. Tor grabbed his forearm in its mouth and dragged him hard, as though impatient.

"I'm okay, I'm okay."

The dog finally let him go.

He turned. "They're in there, the people. Some of them, anyway."

Janus lurched forward, gripping his shoulder. "You saw them? Are they … living?"

Alex nodded. "Yes, in some sort of comatose state, I think. Still in those sacks we saw the creatures dragging. Seems it surrounds them in some sort of biological insulation and protects them from the heat."

Janus looked skyward for a moment. "Thank you, God." And then: "How do we get them out?"

Alex grabbed the man's forearm, and held it. He stared into his eyes. "We can't. Not right now. There were probably a hundred people in there, and I'm betting there are hundreds more in every one of these side caves. We just don't have the capacity to rescue them all."

Janus grimaced. "Maybe we can –"

"Leave it for now. We've got work to do."

Alex moved into the driver's seat and Matt pointed at one of the monitors. "There's a lot of activity up ahead … and down."

"Then that's where we're going." Alex put the vehicle in gear and accelerated, seeming not to care about the narrowing of the pathway. Rocks were bulldozed out of the way and fell into the crevasse, down to the river of molten rock perhaps a thousand feet below.

On the winding way into the heart of the volcano, they stopped several more times to investigate morc side caves. Each time Alex felt that Aimee or Joshua was inside, and each time he found more of the stored sacks of human bodies, but neither of his family.

"More?" Matt asked one last time.

"Like squirrels storing nuts," Alex said, getting a sinking feeling in his gut. He already knew there would be more people inside, and each time there was one sentinel guarding them that he quickly dispatched with Aiko's sword.

He didn't need to enter the alcoves to validate what he already knew. But he would search for Aimee and Joshua until he found them or knew they were no more. That thought almost doubled him over, and he squeezed the steering wheel hard to refocus, making the toughened plastic-covered steel pop from the pressure.

Alex jammed his foot even harder on the accelerator and the heavy vehicle roared ahead. Anything in his way was rammed aside.

From the back cabin, Casey crowed as she blasted creatures that lumbered into their path, swinging the muzzle backward to take down anything that had a mind to pursue them. She seemed to be having the time of her life.

Alex felt it then – the pressure behind his eyes, like a wave of energy directed at them. He slowed down.

"Something's coming."

Matt looked down at the console. "Hot now, real hot; we're closer to the magma pit."

They passed through a natural rock arch, and then the path toward the crevasse's edge opened out. Up ahead there was a line of the monstrous beasts dragging sacks toward the cliff. When they got to the precipice they stopped and simply flung the glistening bags far out over the edge where they sailed down toward the magma.

"Those bastards," Casey spat. She swung the Gatling gun around.

"Hold fire," Alex said. He moved the vehicle closer to the edge and they crowded to the side windows to look down into the magma pit.

A hellish red heat radiated from the liquid, but then they saw something else – a series of webs strung just above the huge river, all emanating from a single massive form, hundreds of feet across in its middle.

"Jesus Christ," Matt whispered. "*That thing is alive*."

Whatever the monstrous form was, it pulsated with a gut-churning life force. The sacks rained down on it, landing on its surface or on the webbing, and sticking there.

'Archaea," Matt said. "So this is what happens to a simple bacterium that is allowed to grow and evolve for over three billion years."

The sacks continued to land, settle, and then sink into the mass.

"They're feeding it." Alex said.

"She must be fed." Matt looked up. "This is what the Pompeians tried to warn us against all those years ago."

"Shit, it must be the size of a battleship," Casey breathed.

Tendrils snaked out and gently scooped up more of the bags from the mesh, and then reeled them in to be absorbed. They could see that the thing, the form, wasn't sitting on top of the web like a spider, but that the web was part of it.

"How long has it been here?" Alex asked.

"In Mount Etna?" Matt asked. "This volcano has been here for around half a million years. For all we know, this thing is self-regenerating – it could be a true immortal." He turned to Alex. "It is the ultimate extremophile, living in a place that is impossible for any other creature to exist, and in an environment that both hides and protects it from attack."

"Until now," Alex said. "We've developed a way to find it, and fight it."

"I wish we brought a bigger bomb," Matt said softly.

"Argh." Alex crushed his eyes shut and put his hands to his head.

"What is it?" Matt grabbed his arm.

"Close," Alex said. He continued to grimace as the waves of pain smashed through his mind like a prolonged scream. He opened his eyes. "Joshua, he's trying to find us."

"Where is he?"

Alex stared out through the front screen. "He's alive – *they're* alive. One of those caves. But they're blocking him. *It's* blocking him." He bared his teeth momentarily. "If I try and get him, they'll swarm us. We need a distraction."

"You need a distraction, boss?" Casey said from the rear. "Then try this." Her hand rested on the huge bomb.

"Yeah, that'll work." He began to grin mirthlessly, but then grimaced again. "Jesus." He felt another pressure wave cross his mind, and this time his nose began to bleed. "Shit, it knows we're here now."

As if on cue, the monstrous patchwork things began to pour from the side caves and crowd in front of them.

"They're going to try and stop us," Matt said. "For all we know, it can read our minds. It's certainly knows us now."

"Only as food. That's what it thinks we are. Something inconsequential and only fit to be harvested," Alex spat back. "Casey, clear that shit out of the way. Time to send the devil back to Hell."

"It's already in Hell," Matt said softly over the roar of the Gatling gun and the thump of the cannon. The creatures were being blown off the cliff, falling to be absorbed in the web or into the molten river below.

Alex pushed the vehicle forward another few hundred yards and brought it to a stop.

"If we kill it, what happens to these things made out of … *us*?" Alex asked.

"I don't know," Matt replied. "But it would be an educated guess to say they are being controlled by it now, and if we remove that control, then they may become mindless beasts, or even stop functioning altogether." He shrugged. "But I'm only guessing."

"Good enough for me." Alex climbed into the back and Matt followed.

Alex crouched over the bomb and lifted the settings plate. He moved the countdown to ten minutes, then tested the canister's weight – it was around 500 pounds, heavy, but manageable.

"Franks, cover."

"You got it." She swung both muzzles around, hands hovering over triggers.

"Once I'm out, I expect to be able to pick up on Joshua and Aimee – I know they're out there, and close by. I'll deliver this first, then grab them before it detonates." Alex worked the bomb settings.

Matt looked at what he was programming in. "Ten minutes – it that enough time?"

"Should be," Alex said. "According to Gray, the insulated casing will protect it for up to fifteen minutes. So even if the thing sheds it and drops it into the magma, it should still detonate. Any longer and we can lose." He looked up. "It should only take me a few minutes to locate my family – nothing will slow me down now."

"What happens –" Matt reached out to grab his arm. "What happens if you're wrong, and you can't find them in time?"

Alex snorted softly before looking up. "Then I won't be coming back." His lips lifted slightly. "I'll find them."

"I hope you're right."

Alex took a few deep breaths. "Here goes." He went to lift the canister but the dog gripped his forearm in its mouth.

"No," Alex said. "By myself."

Tor let him go and sat staring.

"I'll be back soon – with Josh and Aimee." Alex hit the button on his chest, enveloping himself in the blue glow. He grunted as he hefted the bomb. "Door."

* * *

Janus opened the side door and as it slid away, the insane heat smashed in at them.

"Ah, shit." Casey held a hand up over her face. "Gonna get a great tan this year, boss."

Alex stepped out, eased the bomb onto his shoulder and took a few steps before turning back. He waved as the door slid shut, then turned away.

He exhaled as he felt the heat press in on him. He struggled to walk holding the 500-pound bomb while staying out of the way as Casey continued to pump round after round of the Gatling gun interspersed with the occasional thump from the cannon. He got to the edge of the crevasse and looked down. He couldn't help but stare at the horrifying sight for a few seconds. There, strung over the massive lake of magma, was the webbing, and at its center was the thing, softly pulsing like the giant, corrupted heart of the volcano.

At the cliff edge, the revolting multi-limbed beings continued to dump their sacks of people over, and he watched as they landed and were quickly brought to the center of the mass, to then just sink into its bulk. He saw the sacks dissolve, spreading out and liquefying; all those poor souls captured, imprisoned, and fed to a monster.

How many years had it been doing this? Taking living creatures from the surface to feed itself – a thousand years? A million? Forever?

"Try eating this, you sonofabitch."

Alex raised the canister from his shoulder and held it above his head. He knew he needed to throw it far out, and also allow its trajectory to take it a good hundred feet toward the center of the thing.

As he held it, Alex sensed the form became aware of him and perhaps his intentions. A massive orb, hundreds of feet across, opened on its top. It was totally white, pitiless, and probably regarded him as less than a mote of dust. But Alex knew it saw him.

"Immortal, huh?" He flexed his arms and shoulders. "We'll see about that." He threw the bomb with all his strength.

The silver tank flew out and then down. The white orb swiveled, perhaps watching it. But then tendrils grew from the edges of the massive blob. Like a giant amoeba with cilia flickering at its edges, the thing's rope-like limbs began to move up the sides of the crevasse, toward the canister.

Whether it planned to catch it or not didn't matter as it missed and the bomb landed on its body. However, the other tendrils continued their climb up the walls toward Alex. And worse, toward the armored vehicle.

"Ah, shit." Alex turned to the row of caves, then felt a psychic jolt. Joshua's mind called to him, and Alex called back: *I'm coming.*

The next silent scream came from the farthest side cave, and he turned and raced toward it.

The boy was dreaming, and Alex felt that Aimee was near him. For now the lumbering beasts ignored him and continued to feed the archaeon blob, throwing hundreds of people to their deaths. Perhaps this is what happened every few hundred or few thousand years – the thing woke, created its minions, and then proceeded to fatten itself up so it could slumber for another few millennia until the next eruption.

Alex had a sudden thought: *Does the creature actually engineer the eruptions, or does it have to wait for them to boil toward the surface?*

He increased his speed, dodged a few of the creatures dragging their cargo, and entered the side cave he had felt the psychic screams emanating from. This cave was enormous, with hundreds of the sacks stacked at one end.

The creatures tended to them like insects tending to their larva or food stores. Being away from the magma bed meant the temperature had dropped by at least a hundred degrees.

Where? Alex sent the single word as a powerful thought. He waited, but nothing came back.

Where?

Here – getting hotter – can't ... stand ... it. Hurry, Joshua sent back.

Getting hotter? Alex frowned, looking about. Then he spun – that could only mean one thing.

Alex ran faster than he had ever run in his life. He left the cave and sprinted at the first creature he saw dragging one of the revolting fleshy sacks. He grabbed at it, and held on, and was dragged along as well.

"Joshua, Aimee?" he yelled, as he clawed at the skin. There was nothing. *Not this one*, he knew.

He left it and raced to the next. Once again there was no response.

Dad.

The single word dragged his head toward the very edge of the precipice as one of the lumbering beasts approached it. It began to pull the sack forward, getting ready to launch it over the edge.

Alex knew he'd never make it in time, and he quickly spoke into his helmet mic.

"Franks, take that fucking monster on the cliff edge out – but *don't* hit the bag."

A stream of 50 cal rounds tore into the thing, knocking it sideways.

The creature fell on its side, most of its huge body shredded, and many of the human limbs separated from the gross trunk. Oddly, now that the multiple arms, legs, and torsos weren't part of the main body they began to redden and burn.

The remains of the creature were on the very lip of the precipice and sure enough, it toppled into the crevasse, taking the organic sack with it.

"No!"

Alex still had fifty feet to cross, and he pumped his legs hard for a few more giant steps, then launched himself.

He flew twenty feet through the air, landed hard and skidded, but got hold of one end of the bag. He stopped it from sliding over the edge, but the weight was enormous – it must have held at least fifteen people.

He groaned as he tried to drag the bag away from the edge, but only managed a few feet. It would have to do. He felt along it, and finally he found a limb and held it – it was Aimee, he knew it as clearly as if she was standing right in front of him.

Alex didn't want to let go, and turned back to the armored vehicle. The ground was too uneven and the bag was too heavy for him to drag it all the way back – and the clock was ticking down.

He turned back to the bag. *I can't save them all*, he thought. *Not here, not now*. But he could try and save two. He knew what he needed to do, and pulled his k-bar blade out. He also knew what it would cost.

Joshua, wake up.

I'm here. The response was groggy. *Am I dreaming you?*

No, and you must wake up now. Get ready. I want you to wrap your arms around your mother, tight. Hold her close to you, okay?

We'll burn.

Only for a moment, but you are strong and you will heal. Cover your mother, Alex projected.

Okay.

Alex prayed his son knew what he meant. He began to cut into the sack, then took a deep breath, inserted his hands, and pulled it open.

Alex tried to block the opening with his body, but knew the ferocious heat would intrude. Immediately a milky gas escaped, and the people inside howled with pain and anguish. But he saw what he needed to – Aimee and Joshua pressed against each other, eyes tightly closed, faces screwed up in pain. They immediately began to redden. He didn't need to think about it anymore; he grabbed the force field generator, ripped it from his chest and stuck it on the pair. The blue glow enveloped them, and they sighed and drifted back into sleep.

Alex was still in his armored suit, but it had only been tested to 300 degrees and the temperature here was well over three times that. Water boiled and turned to steam at 200 degrees, and the flesh on the body began to cook at less than that. But it was the eyes, lungs, and brain that were most vulnerable to massive temperature changes.

Alex clamped his mouth shut as he felt the surface of the suit beginning to burn. He reached in to drag the pair out, then held them close as he got to his feet. He had them, and nothing else mattered. Behind him the cut in the sack knitted shut like a wound.

He cradled Aimee and Joshua and returned to the vehicle, and every step he took was pure agony. Smoke rose from his suit and spots began to open as the heavy armor plating reddened and flaked away. The internal coolants became overloaded and perspiration ran down his sides and streamed over his face.

Alex knew his rapid healing metabolism might just deal with the extra temperature on top of the suit, but if the coolants failed, not even he could withstand the force of the volcanic heat. He'd simply burn to death, and no one in the vehicle would be able to reach him. Or worse, come and rescue Aimee and Joshua. That thought spurred him on.

Waves of heat distorted his vision as he planted one foot in front of the other and he tried to ignore the smell of his own flesh beginning to cook. From the corner of his eye he saw the tendrils snaking their way up over the cliff edge. None came toward him, and just as well, because he was in no position to fight them off.

He staggered and went to one knee, and stayed there. The heat was sapping his energy, and he looked down at the sleeping pair – Aimee and Joshua wore frowns, perhaps feeling a slight intrusion of the heat, but not burning. Their sweat-slicked faces were smooth and untroubled, and it made him love them even more.

"Get up!" he screamed at himself. He struggled back to his feet, groaning from the effort and pain. He turned back to the vehicle that still seemed way too far away. It was then that he felt the first rupture in his suit, as one of his shoulders started to burn.

"Oh no." He held his family to him and tried to blank out the agony. As part of HAWC training they learned to deal with extreme pain, learned how to refuse to acknowledge it, fight through it and with it. They were taught to take themselves to another place and separate the mind from the tortured body.

But the more he fought it, the more the heat intruded on his thinking, as his brain began to cook in his head.

Just keep going, he demanded of himself. *You can deal with pain. You can fight it.*

But not against death, a small voice whispered.

Not now, Alex thought. *Please not now.*

Leave them. The voice became more urgent: *You'll only make it back if you do.*

"Never," Alex said through gritted teeth.

Then you'll die, and then they'll die. Cooked alive. Unless ...

"Never!" Alex roared.

Unless, you take back the forcefield, and just hold one tight to you – one can be saved, but only one. Choose – hurry.

He felt his back start burn. Blisters rose, popped, and their fluid ran down under his suit. Alex began to both feel and hear his flesh crackling like meat on a grill. Blisters started to cover his face, threatening to close his eyes.

He knew that blisters on the skin resulting from burns were the body's reaction to and defense against heat trauma. The body was trying to protect the skin from further damage and also fill the trauma site with the necessary biological agents designed for germ fighting and wound repair.

But as the heat continued, the blisters burst, and the fluid, at first clear, turned bloody, and ran down over his skin. Dehydration quickly sets in as the body drains its liquid reserves. Extreme heat, then dehydration, then clouded thinking.

Alex looked again at the vehicle, but it seemed like it was at the end of a long tunnel that swirled with heat. He staggered, and dimly became aware of Matt, Casey, and also Janus yelling into his ear. He saw the door of the vehicle open, and even though most of the heat would be repelled, the force field would be straining to keep it at a non-lethal level.

Someone stuck an arm out that began to immediately smoke and waved him on from inside. It gave him a few more ounces of determination.

Then his mind screamed a warning as he saw the tendrils approaching.

They snaked along the ground toward both the armored car and him. There were over a dozen, and he knew he could cut them, but it would mean putting down his precious cargo. And what would happen if Joshua and Aimee were snatched and dragged away? He had nothing left inside to chase them down.

He staggered on. Bullets flew from the side of the vehicle and from above as the Gatling gun spewed its fire toward the tendrils. But they were thin cords, and though Casey hit a few, there were more coming up over the lip all the time.

He saw a boot step out, but without the force field it immediately began to smoke and was quickly yanked back in.

The first of the tendrils reached the vehicle, and tapped at its front, felt the wheels, and slid up over the front windscreen.

Alex shook his head, trying to flick away the blister fluid that ran over his ruptured face. He smelled his skin burning and tasted salt, and he sucked it down, his throat scorched and dry.

He bent his head, his neck creaking from the damaged and flaking skin, to look at Aimee and Joshua hugging each other tight, their faces still calm. It gave him a few more precious ounces of strength.

Then the first of the tendrils found his ankle and yanked, pulling him sideways.

It's found you. Leave them, the voice screamed again in his head. Alex moved Joshua and Aimee to one arm, holding them close, and pounded down on the tendril with his boot. But it was like hitting a rubber cable, and while the thing compressed, it wasn't damaged.

Alex reached down to grab it and tugged with all his strength. It refused to break, only stretched. Then the muscular tendril began to encircle his arm.

Time is nearly up – only seconds now. The voice was furious, screaming at him.

A stream of bullets cut toward him and chopped the tendril. Not severing it cleanly, but ripping it up enough so that his next tug allowed him to break it. Looking up, he saw a figure outside the vehicle again, this time covered in a silver heat-resistant blanket, just a muzzle protruding from the front firing furiously to give him cover. Already it was smoking from the heat. The overhead canon and Gatling gun still fired, so he assumed it was Janus who stepped free.

Alex got to his feet and looked up, grinning through cracked and blistered lips in his pain and madness. The skin on his forehead was beginning to char and smoke was filling his helmet. Through stinging eyes he saw Janus raise a hand to him, waving him on, and then go to step back in the vehicle.

But he couldn't. A tendril had coiled around his ankle. In one sharp tug, it had him over on his back.

"Noooo!" The word hurt, as opening his mouth meant the heat seared Alex's tongue and throat.

The tendril dragged Janus. Alex went to go after him but stumbled, as he couldn't make his legs work. He staggered back up, holding Aimee and Joshua to his chest. Even with his colossal strength he was fading.

Janus screamed as he was dragged along the ground. His suit smoked, and then the scream Alex heard inside his helmet became one of agony from the effects of volcanic heat mixed with fear. He watched for a few seconds more as the Italian Special Forces soldier was dragged ever faster to the cliff's edge. In a blink he vanished over the side, to be consumed.

Alex looked away, staring down at the ground and trying to focus on his feet – Janus sacrificed himself for them, he knew. *Don't look at the cliff edge, don't look back – just – keep – going*, he demanded.

The screams in his head were a distraction, but they became ever more urgent. It was only after a few more moments that he realised he was only imagining he was moving forward. He had become frozen in the one spot. He was hallucinating, and knew his mind and body was failing him.

He would be lost. And no one could come and rescue his family. This was not how it was supposed to end.

Fight, he demanded. But there was nothing left.

He lifted blood-filled eyes and was dimly aware of the tendrils snaking their way toward him again. He called on his last reserves and took a step, but Aimee and Joshua were too heavy now. He had one option.

"Save them," he whispered.

But it wasn't the Other who responded to his plea. He heard the voices in the vehicle erupt, and then from the side door exploded the huge figure of the dog – even with its armor plating, its fur immediately burst into flames but the huge animal continued, coming at him like a flaming comet.

It ignored him, grabbed Joshua and Aimee, and dragged them. Alex could hear it crying from the pain as it backed toward the vehicle.

Freed of his burden he lifted one leg and then the other. The dog made it back and hands reached out to drag them inside.

The final few yards shrank, and then Alex was at the door. He was grabbed and yanked inside and the door closed. The blessed cool enveloped his screaming nerve ends, and he turned his head to catch the horrified look on Matt's face. He would have smiled if he could; he knew he was a mess. *I did it*, he would have said, if his mouth still worked.

The next thing he heard was Casey Franks screaming at the top of her lungs. "Kearns, get us the fuck out of here."

Matt reversed, skidding the armored wheels as Casey blasted round after round at anything that moved until there came an empty whirring from above.

"Fifty cals out. Switching it up." She moved to the next set of handles and targeting screen and began to fire. Explosions thumped in front of the vehicle, and Alex could feel them right through his agonized body.

He turned his head and saw Aimee and Joshua lying silently, a blue glow still encasing their bodies. His eyes clouded over and the pain felt like he was still being held over an open fire.

He turned ever so slowly and saw the body of the huge dog. Smoke rose from its burned flanks, and there was red raw skin instead of fur in patches. It lay on its side, its breathing labored.

Alex let out a long exhalation as a wave of pain washed over him. Mercifully, unconsciousness took him.

CHAPTER 45

Perfect, she thought.

SOPHIA bucked and writhed in her cockpit seat from the pain. The link she shared with Alex Hunter imbued her with the sensations of his tortured burning even though she wasn't a creature of flesh and blood.

She had stolen a Lockheed Martin SR-71 Blackbird from the base. It was a high-speed, high-altitude stealth aircraft, and capable of traveling at 2,500 miles per hour, and she blasted toward the Italian coast at its maximum speed. She had dismantled the plane's tracking and radio signals, and added to its radar reflective paint, meaning only the most sensitive military satellites could detect it by its exhaust. However, this too was unlikely, as SOPHIA had ensured the satellite assets were all pointed in the wrong direction.

The jet fell from the sky as she continued to scream in agony, torment, and frustration. No one was there to save him. No one *could* save him, as no one was like him.

She felt herself slowly begin to regain control, and gripped the U-shaped wheel, pulling the jet out of its dive. They didn't deserve him, *any* of them. Only SOPHIA was comparable to him or understood him – both the Alex Hunter personality, and his dark Other.

Plans formed in her mind for when she arrived. Of the option she chose, the permutations were high for success – as long as Alex Hunter survived – he *must* survive.

SOPHIA brought the plane up to its top speed again, and caught sight of her reflection in the instrument panel. She smiled at the dark blue eyes that glinted with a hint of fire, and the clear skin with a blush of freckles across the nose and chceks – just like Aimee.

Perfect, she thought.

CHAPTER 46

"Fight or die; it's the only way."

Matt tried to hold his breath from the stink of the dog's burned fur and skin. It lay, smoking, beside Alex Hunter, and had just enough energy to lick at him. Blood from the man coated its lips and tongue as it then groaned and lay still.

While he drove, Matt tried to look everywhere at once, feeling his sanity was rapidly unraveling. He couldn't get the image of Alex Hunter out of his mind. The guy was nothing but a living burn wound. His heavily armored, heat-resistant suit was tattered and holed, and the skin that showed through wasn't just red, it was charred.

But it was his face that was the worst. It was so burned up, the man's eyes and mouth were swollen shut. If he survived, he might be blind, or brain damaged, for the rest of his life.

Matt looked into the rear camera on his console, and then up and out the front screen. The monstrous bulk of the archaean thing was lifting itself over the edge of the chasm – it was so big, it filled their world, and Matt thought it was like a giant heart – the actual beating heart of the volcano, pulsing with a revolting, evil life and still shooting long tendrils out at them.

Casey's grenade rounds sped toward it, and exploded on its body, but even though the flesh shivered after each strike, the damage was minimal. An explosive grenade was just a pinprick to something that must have been a quarter of a mile across.

"Shit." The vehicle skidded and swayed a little and Matt was aware they were right on a cliff edge. He tried to balance speed with control, as he knew if he tilted too far one way, they'd plummet into the rivers of magma below.

On a flat piece of the path, he briefly twisted to look into the rear cabin, and saw that at the vehicle was full of bodies – Alex lay with smoke still rising from him. The dog was in even worse shape with raw skin where the fur had been totally burned away. Its tongue lolled, and he noticed where Alex's blood was on its mouth it had now all been licked away and oddly, where the blood had been, its tongue now looked pink again.

Lying to one side were Joshua and Aimee, still enveloped in the fading blue glow of Alex's force field as its power ran out. Alex had saved them, and probably killed himself doing it.

The agony the man endured, all for love. Matt hoped that one day he'd know a love like that – a love that was worth sacrificing everything for.

"Running low, prof."

Casey's voice snapped him out of his reverie; that and the impact to the back of the vehicle. Looking in the rear camera, he saw it was smeared with blood and mucus and realised that what he struck must have been one of the creatures trying to block his path.

Matt tried to remember how far in they'd come to get an idea of how much more terrain they needed to travel to escape, as well as trying to picture the landscape atop the crevasse pathway. He wished now he had paid more attention on their way in.

He skidded the vehicle again, trying to reverse along the narrow path. "How long to detonation?' he yelled.

Casey fired, and yelled back without turning away from her targeting, "Seven minutes, and then it's gonna get real interesting down here."

"We can make it," Matt breathed.

"Where are we?"

The small voice from the back made him snap his head around.

Joshua was sitting up, but Aimee remained unconscious. Now that he had moved away from her, the boy began to look around. He saw Alex and his eyes went wide. "*Dad!*" He spun, seeing the dog. "No! Tor!" He crawled between them and placed a hand on Alex's chest and Tor's burned fur. "Oh no, no, no." He began to sob, but then he screwed his eyes shut, and pressed down harder. "He's alive, and still in there."

"He'll be fine," Matt yelled back, not believing it at all. "We'll be out soo—"

Something bumped them, and the armored vehicle careened to one side. Matt tried to correct the slide but over compensated, making the front fishtail, and then the wheels on the left side went over the edge of the crevasse. The speed they were traveling at made the front axle grind along for another fifty feet before coming to a stop.

"What the hell just happened?" Casey screamed. "Did you just fucking crash us, Kearns?"

"Uh ..." He sat, trying to shift gears into forward and then reverse without any movement other than a grinding and vibrating from the entire chassis. "I, ah, might have."

"Well, that's just great." Casey gritted her teeth and continued to fire. "You had one damn job."

Matt looked out the front screen. They had left the huge creature a long way back, but along the path were its lumbering beasts, like soldier ants coming to defend their queen. Matt had no doubt that though they couldn't breach the vehicle's security, they could certainly combine their mass to push them over and into the magma – especially now that they were hanging from the cliff edge.

There were two more grenade explosions and then Casey slapped the triggers. "I'm out."

"Oh shit." He turned and Joshua was looking up at him. He shrugged to the boy.

"Options?" Casey yelled.

"We can't lift the vehicle back up by ourselves." Matt looked into the rear camera, and tried to remember how far they still had to go, and how far they'd potentially need to be so they were clear of the blast. One thing was for sure: they needed to be a lot farther than where they were now.

"Can we walk it?" Casey asked.

Matt looked down at the temperature gauge. It was around 550 degrees; still well beyond the range of their suits' capabilities.

"We might survive for a few minutes, but it's still way too hot. And what about ...?"

Casey looked at Alex and Aimee, then bared her teeth and turned back to Matt. The pair sat staring at each other for a few more seconds.

Matt leaned his head back. "We need a miracle."

Joshua looked down at Alex and whispered, "No, we need a monster to fight a monster."

"What?"

"Well." Casey pulled a few more weapons from the gun rack. "I'm not sitting here waiting to die. Fight or die, prof; it's the only way."

"Fight or die," Joshua repeated. He put a hand on Casey's arm. "Wait." He reached across to put his hands back on Alex's chest and closed his eyes.

While Matt watched, the boy's face darkened, and veins began to stand out on his forehead.

"We can't go out there," Joshua said. "But he can."

"Alex?" Matt asked.

Joshua shook his head, his voice barely a whisper. "No, not Alex ... the Other one."

* * *

Joshua slid into Alex's subconscious. He felt the slumbering of his father as his body tried to repair itself, and let him rest. Then he went deeper, all the way down to the dark place. It was down there he sought something that would continue to fight and kill and destroy. Because that was all it knew.

He wandered in the darkness until he felt the dark presence loom over him, circling him, settling down in the psychological shadows behind him. He heard the sliding drag of heavy chains but didn't turn.

So, you need me now.

It wasn't a question. Joshua still didn't turn. *We need each other.*

The corrosive laugh seemed to come from everywhere and nowhere. *When death is closest we will always turn to a higher power.*

You're not a higher power. Joshua finally turned, and tried not to let the shock of seeing the beast show on his face.

It was his father, and not his father: hugely muscled, deformed, a face creased by pure hate. This was the thing, the Other, he had been warned about all along ... and it was the beast that could become Alex Hunter one day. That instead of the Other being locked down here in the darkness, it would be his father who was imprisoned.

If we are killed so will you be, Joshua said, working to keep his voice even.

And maybe death is preferable to eternal imprisonment.

You're not imprisoned, Joshua said. *I think, instead, you're* protected *here.*

The laugh was coarse and sounded more like spitting. *Yes, of course. My chains are silk bracelets, the solitude is my friend, and the darkness is like warm sunshine.* The chains slid. *Perhaps you would like to be down here ... or your father.*

It's not so bad. Joshua turned away, but the monstrous face followed right at his shoulder.

You lie just like your father.

Joshua turned back. *No, you're the liar.*

Then you lie just like me. The laugh was as desiccated as the rustle of dry leaves in an abandoned graveyard. *Because* I *am your father.*

Joshua held his ground. *No. My father isn't a coward.*

The laugh continued and became near deafening.

Prove you're not a coward! Joshua yelled, his voice echoing endlessly in the vast darkness. *Prove you're strong.*

Oh, I am strong. Stronger than even you can imagine.

I just see weakness. It was Joshua's turn to laugh.

I AM STRONG! The voice boomed.

Joshua had his hands up over his ears. *Then prove it! Go, you're free. Prove you're strong. Prove you're not a coward.*

There was an explosion of light, and Joshua was ejected from Alex's mind. He blinked and opened his eyes, and found himself back in the cabin of the vehicle.

Alex Hunter sat up.

CHAPTER 47

There is no such thing as "impossible".

"Jesus Christ!" Casey yelled. "Boss?"

Matt spun. "What? How?" He stared, shocked, as Alex sat up. The man looked like a burned corpse. As he sat forward, bits of his suit as well as his skin flaked away.

"Prove it," Joshua said into his father's face. He reached across and pulled the force field from the sleeping Aimee and stuck it on Alex's chest. Then he scowled – the blue glow was faint. "It's running out of power. Hurry."

Alex's head turned one way, then the other. He looked at Casey, and then turned to stare at Matt with eyes that were oddly flat. The gaze seemed as old as time itself, a gaze that looked right through him as though he was an insignificant bug.

Casey went to reach out, but Joshua stopped her. "Stay back." Matt saw that instead of Joshua hugging his father, he shrank back from him.

Casey immediately got it. "Oh, shit, no." Casey placed a hand on her sidearm, and held up the other palm outwards. "Easy, boss."

"What is it?" Matt asked.

Joshua backed up to get in front of Aimee. "Open the door."

"What? No – he can't go back out there," Matt insisted. "He's nearly dead now. It's impossible."

Alex looked from Aimee to Joshua and the boy pointed. "You're right, no one could get the truck back up on the path. No normal person anyway." He tilted his head at the Other. "Could you?"

Alex held up a hand, turning it over and looking at the fingers. Behind him, Casey edged toward the door and slid it open. The blue glow of the force field shielded them from most of the heat, but it was still extreme.

"Go!" Joshua yelled. "Show us what real power is."

Alex turned to the open door and climbed out.

"Jesus Christ, this is insane," Matt whispered.

Alex walked around to the front of the van, his legs stiff and his movements awkward. He stood on the crevasse edge, staring down along the long pathway. Several hundred yards away, it was blocked with the lumbering beasts coming toward them. Alex's fists curled, and he stepped toward them and away from the truck, as if they were his main goal.

"No, not them," Joshua said.

Matt turned and saw the boy sitting cross-legged with his eyes screwed shut. Alex turned back to the armored vehicle, walked right to the cliff edge, looking down at where the wheels had slipped over. He came in close to the front of the car, and at first Matt couldn't see inside his helmet as his head was down. Alex placed both hands under the front of the vehicle.

"No way," Matt said.

Alex strained, and then moved a little and tried again. He strained harder, and finally looked up to stare into the cabin. Matt felt like backing out of his chair. He suddenly knew why Joshua edged away and Casey went on alert – it wasn't Alex.

It didn't look like Alex. In fact, the thing staring in at them barely even looked human.

The man's eyes were red and wide open, and at the very center they shone like those of a wolf. His teeth were bared in a grimace of aggression. But the features were all twisted; coupled with the burned flesh, it was a fearsome and horrifying sight.

"Prove yourself," Matt heard the boy whisper again.

Behind Alex's mask, he saw the mouth open in a scream, and then unbelievably, the side of the vehicle began to lift.

"*Holyyyyy* shit." Matt held on.

From behind him he heard the sound of straining and turned to see Joshua, his eyes screwed shut and his hands held out, palms up as though he was the one doing the lifting. His face was slick and tears ran from the corners of his eyes.

Is he helping somehow? Matt wondered. He was a weird kid, but he was Alex's kid, and weirdness was something that ran in the family.

"*Now*,' The boy said, as blood began to stream from his nose and a red tear ran from his eye.

The car lifted higher, and Alex slowly moved its front onto the narrow track. He dropped it with a thump and a bounce.

"He did it!" Matt yelled, and started the vehicle back up.

"Then let's get the hell outta here," Casey suggested.

"Come back," Joshua said.

"Oh, shit." Matt saw tendrils snaking up over the side of the crevasse right in front of the vehicle. They traveled along the ledge, their tips pointed directly at the man.

Alex turned to face them, just as the faint blue glow around him finally vanished.

"*No!*" Joshua said.

"We have four minutes!" Casey screamed.

Matt hit the comm. system but didn't think Alex could hear it. "Alex, get back in here, we've got to go." He grimaced. "There's too many of them."

The first tendril approached, and Alex reached behind himself to draw Aiko's silver blade. On Alex's shoulder, at one of the armor plating joins, a small tongue of flame sprang up, then another on his back, and then one on his head.

What remained of Alex Hunter was burning alive. But if he felt it he gave no indication and instead flicked out the sword, and the sharpened blade sliced the end from the questing tendril like it was nothing.

More came, and then even more. They'd found him now, and Alex became a furious blur of flashing steel. But for every one he cut, dozens took its place. Then some of the tendrils started to slither past him, heading for the truck.

Matt closed the door. "Sorry, buddy." He started to accelerate backward.

"Hurry," Joshua whispered, but then began to grunt. "No, *stop*. Wait for him ..."

"We can't."

"I said *waaaaiiit*!"

"What?" Matt turned to see the kid clenching his fists, and then the vehicle stopped and the wheels just skidded on the ground.

"*HURRY!*" Joshua's voice was a roar now.

"What are you doing?" Matt yelled. No matter what he tried, forward or reverse, the wheels turned, but the massive vehicle stayed where it was.

Out in front, a burning Alex hacked and moved so fast he was becoming a flaming blur. But the tendrils were like a forest, and soon even his great strength and speed would be engulfed, and he'd be grabbed, lifted and drawn over the side, with them in the vehicle next.

"I can't break in. Can't get through." Joshua suddenly looked up. "Shoot him." He turned to Casey, his voice deadpan. "Shoot him in the leg."

Casey's mouth dropped open. "Get the fuck out of here."

"We have to break his focus. Do it, or he'll be lost," Joshua said evenly.

Matt blinked, not believing Joshua was advocating shooting his own father. But then again, what else did they have? Matt spun to Casey.

"Do it, do it now."

"Ah, fuck this." Casey drew her sidearm. She checked her timer. "Three goddamn minutes." She punched the button on the wall of the vehicle and the door slid open. The tough female HAWC sucked in a huge breath, steeling herself, then leaned out.

Casey screamed as she hung out past the force field and the heat smashed into her. She held the side of the vehicle, swung wide, aimed and fired once.

The bullet struck the back of Alex's leg where the plating was degraded, and he staggered slightly. It didn't drop him, but it was like he suddenly woke up.

Casey fell back into the cabin and moaned as smoke rose from her suit.

"Dad," Joshua said. "Come back."

Alex swept the silver blade in an arc, severing dozens of the questing tendrils, then turned. He staggered back to the vehicle, lurched around the side, and fell in. Casey threw a towel over him, dousing the fire enveloping his body.

Joshua unclenched his hands and the armored vehicle leaped backward.

"Whoa." Matt regained control of it, and accelerated. He looked down at the console – one minute, forty seconds. "*Oh god*," he breathed.

He kept flicking his gaze from his rear camera on the console, to over his shoulder. He saw Joshua was leaning forward, and his hands were up and on his father's shoulders. Alex kneeled before him, head down. His blackened body made it hard to discern where the burned and flaking skin ended and his armored suit began.

Joshua whispered earnestly to him, but Matt couldn't hear what he said over the swirling chaos that was still enveloping them.

Casey sat by Aimee Weir, holding her in place, as Matt bounced from the rock wall to the cliff edge and then over-corrected to bounce back into he wall again.

"Little more control there, prof!" Casey yelled.

Flicking his eyes to the camera again, he could see they were approaching the portal that was once blocked by the living wall of flesh, and then beyond that, if he remembered correctly, only a few hundred yards to the exit.

Sixty-six seconds – the countdown seemed to be accelerating.

Matt couldn't bring himself to look out the front window anymore because if the tendrils were close, he, they, could do nothing about it anyway.

Forty seconds.

Faster, he urged, and stamped down on the accelerator again. The tank-like machine fishtailed slightly, and Matt felt his stomach lurch as the front wheel tightrope-walked on the edge of the chasm once again.

And then they were through the portal and into the broader cave. The monstrous creatures were gone, perhaps now all called to the defense of the massive archaean being in the center of the volcano. It didn't matter, there was no way Matt was slowing, and they had no defenses left other than the speed and bulk of the vehicle anyway.

"Twenty seconds!" Casey yelled.

"Gonna be close," he replied. "Hang on!"

Matt gave it all he had, his boot grinding down on the pedal so hard his foot ached. The fissure mouth drew closer and closer – 200 feet, 150, 100 …

Matt dared to grin. "We're gonna –"

From the walls and the ground, and all then around them, burst the tendrils. They snaked from every crack, hole, and fissure, and reached down, up, and across. In the fissure mouth the tendrils seemed to wait for the vehicle like long teeth, hoping to trap and devour their tiny vehicle and everyone in it.

"Five seconds." Casey's voice was tight. And then: "*Brace.*"

Not far enough, Matt realized. He sucked in a breath and held it.

The tendrils waited a dozen feet from them as a thunderclap came from deep in the mountain. The shockwave hit them first, picking them up and throwing them out of the fissure like they were being shot from a cannon.

The last thing Matt saw was the tendrils freezing and then blackening like new shoots after an overnight frost.

The vehicle crashed down on the slope and bounced several times, and Matt yelled as he skidded the machine to a stop. He craned to look out the front screen.

Magma was being catapulted from every fissure on the mountainside and from the caldera above. In among the molten rock was a shimmer of silver. The jets shot out and upward, but it was as if the bomb was a cork in a champagne bottle, in that the initial eruption pressure was spent quickly, and no major eruption occurred.

Matt slumped back and then looked around, breathing like he'd just run a marathon. Objects that looked like a forest of stunted, limbless trees studded the slope. On closer inspection, he saw that they were the frozen tendrils of the massive thing that had lived at the heart of the volcano.

As he watched, the petrified tendrils blackened and flaked, and then they turned to dust. It seemed that the massive creature had tried everything in its power to stop them, perhaps finally realizing that the insignificant beings had brought something with them that threatened even an immortal's existence. Maybe it was able to absorb some of the memories of the hundreds, thousands, or maybe even millions of creatures it had consumed over the countless millennia, and when it took Janus, it finally saw what was in store for it.

While Matt continued to stare, the temperature plummetted.

"Is it over?" Casey asked. She crouched as Aimee roused herself. The woman sat up and held her head for a moment, then Joshua went to her.

"Mom." He hugged her, and she hugged him back.

"Where are we?" Aimee blinked. "We got out?"

"Yes. But ..."

"Where's Alex?" She moved Joshua aside. "Oh god." She rushed to her husband's side and grabbed him, and Matt bet that even the pain of her grip must have been intolerable for the man who was literally an open burn from head to toe.

Alex nodded, and carefully lifted blackened arms to try and hold her. Matt felt his eyes moisten as he noticed one of Alex's armored gloves had been burned right through and there were sticks of bone where his fingers used to be.

Alex tilted his head forward so Aimee could bring herself close, and she wept into him.

Casey pulled a shotgun from the gun rack and punched the button so the door slid back.

"Gonna take a look. Give me a couple of minutes. If I'm not back ..." She held Matt's eyes until he nodded. She stuck her head out and then leaped free. "Shut it."

Joshua did as she asked, and Casey sprinted back up toward the fissure, paused for a moment, then disappeared inside.

Matt turned. "Josh." He looked from the boy to Alex. "Is it – is he …?"

Joshua nodded. "It's okay, it's Dad."

Aimee eased back, unfastened the helmet at Alex's neck, grabbed each side of the remains of the armored shielding and lifted it free. To her credit, she kept her composure a lot better than Matt would have. He swung back in his seat to face forward after seeing what the volcanic heat had done to Alex.

The man's face was a mess of blistered flesh, and places were charred black. There was burned bone showing at one cheek and on his forehead where the skin had been totally seared away. All his hair was gone, and one eye was swollen shut.

Aimee held his head. "I'm so sorry," she whispered.

Matt eased back around in time to see Alex squeeze her hand and then shake his head carefully. Joshua reached up to touch his arm.

"Tell me," the boy said.

Alex stared at Aimee, and Joshua looked into the blistered face of the man who couldn't hope to speak with his mouth so badly burned.

"Okay, okay." Joshua nodded and turned to Aimee. "He said not to be sorry. He won, because we're alive."

Matt turned in his seat again. "He saved us all."

Joshua turned to the dog. Most of its fur was burned away, and even its face was covered in wounds and melted hair. The huge, dark nose was still seared pink and raw. It lay still, but, oddly, the nose seemed a little less raw than just minutes ago, and the wet patches of weeping skin on its body had stopped oozing and looked pink at the edges where new skin was already forming.

Matt frowned. He knew Alex Hunter's metabolism had been altered by the Arcadian treatment; had the dog ingesting some of the HAWC leader's blood somehow changed its own physiology?

While Matt was mulling the concept over, there came a pounding on the side of the vehicle, and his head snapped around as his heart leaped to his throat.

Then he exhaled with relief. “It’s Casey.”

Joshua pressed the door button, and it slid back so she could jump in.

She racked her gun. “The sacks of people are still there, and still all unconscious. But everything else is gone. Where that big blob thing was is now all buried.”

“Did we do that?” Matt asked. “Or did the thing bury itself?”

Joshua turned. “I can still feel it in there. It’s hurt, and it’s fleeing.” He closed his eyes. “So much deeper; it’s getting ready to slumber again.”

“Is it dying?” Casey asked.

“Weakened.” Joshua frowned. “And smaller now.”

“We didn’t kill it,” Matt said.

“Maybe we never could,” Casey said. “It’s had its fill … for now.”

“Until next time.” Matt started the engine, turned the vehicle around and drove down the slope.

Alex lay down, and Aimee lay next to him, one arm across his chest. She rested her chin on his shoulder.

On his other side, Joshua held his hand. “Heal,” he said softly.

Alex closed his eyes.

CHAPTER 48

The slopes of Mount Etna – cleanup

Matt and Maria watched as the massive rescue, retrieval, and cleanup operation got under way.

Mount Etna had returned to its dormant state, and workers with excavation equipment moved in to dig into the side of the volcano. Hundreds of people were retrieved. And thankfully, no sign of the grotesque amoeba thing was found. Further, the rescued people seemed uninfected.

But of the massive creatures woven or melted together from the body parts of poor souls, only rotting limbs were found. Whether the force that bound them together was spent, dying, or now back in hibernation, it meant the bonds holding the laboring beasts had been broken, and their souls freed.

Internally, no sign of the archaean strands were present. Even the forest of tendrils was now so blackened, it already seemed thousands of years old, the state of decay turning it to an ash-like substance. There was no living DNA inside the tendrils – it was as if the creature's final act was to remove all trace of itself.

Matt watched as the workers brought out sealed bags from the caves. He wondered if the thing was ever really sentient, or just acting on a purely animalistic behaviors. In his heart, he believed it was intelligent. After all, how could it not be? Even bacteria have been known to learn about their environment, competitors, and food. If this thing was near immortal, how could it not learn over all the time it had lived?

To it, humans must have seemed nothing more than the tiny things that briefly lived on the planet's surface. Not really different to any of the other beasts on four legs. Humans just grew to be more abundant.

The other inexplicable thing was that the human minders not killed by Sam, Aiko and Maria, with their eyes sewn shut and their strange ability to commune with the beasts, had all vanished. Either they, too, fell away to nothing after the massive beast below was defeated, or they retreated back to where they came from. Perhaps to wait until the next time they were called.

Maria brought him a strong cup of coffee and leaned up against him. She held up her cup. "Cin cin; it's not every day you beat the devil."

He tapped her cup with his. "And send it back to Hell. For now." He smiled down at her, and she returned the smile. He noticed the dark rings under her eyes – she still looked haunted.

Aiko and Sam also remained behind to ensure that Gray and his laboratory were safely evacuated. Lucas Velez and Adam Brice had recovered as if nothing had ever happened to them. Both thought they'd had some sort of pleasant dream, and had no recollection of the thing that tried to devour them.

A good ending, except Matt remembered seeing the tortured form of Alex with Aimee, Joshua, and the huge dog as they headed to the helicopter to be evacuated. The dog was bandaged like a four-legged mummy, but its fur was already growing thick again. Joshua walked beside it, one arm draped over its back, talking to it the entire time.

A few of the local Italian Special Forces had joined them, but had shrunk back when they'd seen the man who was literally an animated charred corpse. Alex had refused all treatment and, amazingly, was already walking.

The medevac helicopter pilot, a woman, had taken control of Alex and pointed Aimee, Joshua, and the dog to the next inbound helicopter. On her uniform she had the red cross of the medical unit and also had a hood pulled up over her head and mask over her lower face.

Matt thought it had looked like Alex had weakly tried to pull away, but the woman administered some sort of painkilling sedative, and then held him tightly as they both vanished inside the chopper. The door shut and the helicopter took off.

Joshua stood staring, looking a little confused. "Heal," Matt had heard the boy keep saying to Alex.

Matt had heard Alex Hunter, the Arcadian, referred to once as Jack Hammerson's Frankenstein monster. But without that monster, they'd all be dead right now. He hoped Alex healed quickly, because there were real monsters in this world. They lived in caves, and under ice, and below the ocean in its inky depths. Sometimes they surfaced, and that's when you needed a monster of your own in the game.

"Heal," Matt whispered and turned away.

CHAPTER 49

The worst was yet to come.

Walter Gray shut his eyes in the back of the helicopter and cupped a hand over his earpiece as the HAWC commander, Colonel Jack Hammerson, exploded into his ear.

His secure laboratory at USSTRATCOM had been breached; not through an external intrusion, but from the inside. Added to that his multimillion-dollar android was missing, and one of his scientists was still in hospital with fractured ribs, plus a bruised heart – one guess who was responsible.

"It must have self-activated," Gray said softly, now wondering if SOPHIA had ever been deactivated, or had just let him think that it was.

He felt his heart sink as he listened. There were more and worse details to come. One of their SR-71 Blackbird stealth jets had been stolen, and had just been found ditched off the coast of Italy. Further, a medivac chopper had been taken from a southern Italian base.

SOPHIA had planned it all, he knew. And it must have been doing the planning for a long while. He squeezed his eyes shut even tighter, almost wishing the revelations would go away as Hammerson dropped the killer piece of the tale: someone had picked up Alex Hunter in that stolen medivac chopper. Jack Hammerson was without doubt who it was. Gray knew as well.

SOPHIA had somehow retained its, *her*, emotion programs, hidden them away, and was still drawing on all their complexities and volatility.

"The things we do for love," the scientist whispered.

He ground his teeth and squeezed more pressure into his eyelids, trying to think, but with Hammerson yelling so loudly, everything was scrambled. The commander's voice was starting to make the side of Gray's face ache.

Gray tried to anticipate what SOPHIA would do and where she would take Alex, all the while dreading standing in front of 'the Hammer' if he didn't have good answers.

"We'll find them and we'll get them back, sir," he said softly. The only problem was, what happened if she didn't want to come back? Then they'd be both lost.

The call ended and Gray closed his eyes and leaned his head back in his seat. A tear of frustration and loss ran down his cheek. They'd both be lost and he had no way to find them.

Suddenly, Gray's eyes shot open: *Joshua*.

EPILOGUE

Kilauea, Hawaiian Islands, southern shore – 200 feet down

"It's an old lava tube." Mick Reynolds squatted as he ran a gloved hand over the glass-smooth wall of the cave. He was a volcanologist, and he, accompanied by his buddy, Steve Chambers, and Jemma Kono, a local spelunker, had been tasked with investigating the recent shimmying of the volcano. They needed to get up close and personal, see if the old boy was planning something dangerous or just had another of its usual bellyaches. It was sheer luck that they had managed to break into an ancient lava tube.

Jemma and Steve came and squatted beside Mick. Jemma took off her helmet and wiped her brow. "Still hot, even though it's been dormant now for years." She took off her glove and ran it over the wall. "Yeah, residual heat, or maybe a magma bed getting ready for another surge to the surface."

Steve crouched, forearms on his thighs. "This tube is old, maybe a few thousand years. You can see how it's started to flake. The volcano has erupted since then, but didn't use this route. May have gone another way."

"Lucky to find this place." Mick shone his flashlight around. "And we're not the first ones in here – look." He lifted his light. On the wall there were images, and also some sort of picture-style writing.

"Okay, Jem, you're the local expert here; what does it say?"

"Pictoglyphs, or actually, petroglyphs," she said, shining her light on them. "Ancient Hawaiians. These guys have been here 800 years, and when they first arrived they had no written language. They used symbolism, pictures, and totems."

"I can see that," Mick said and grinned. "But can you *read* it?"

She frowned, ignoring him. "Strange." She edged closer. "I think this is the symbol for Kanaloa."

"The god Kanaloa?" Steve asked.

"The one and only." She was shining her light on an image of something that looked like an octopus, but with a single eye.

"Yikes," Mick said. "I'm guessing he was the god of seafood, huh?"

"No, but god of a lot of other things, actually, and one of the most powerful of the ancient beings. He was the god of the underworld, god of evil, fire, death, destruction; generally, everything that went wrong in our world was caused by him. Kinda like our version of the devil."

"Nice guy," Steve said.

"Not always depicted as a guy," Jemma whispered. "Sometimes as a he, sometimes as a she."

"Whatever." Steve studied the images. "So why would they worship it in a lava tube 200 feet below ground?"

"You got that bit about being god of the *underworld*, right?" Mick nudged him.

"Yeah, I get that, but down here in this small pipe? Not a lot of room."

"Who knows? Maybe it was invitation only. And they sure as hell aren't around to ask. Let's mark it down for the university to look into." Mick turned back to the dark cave. "Anyway, we're down for a job, not ancient Hawaiian devil worship. Let's go."

They slid a little more along the smooth tube, until it opened out into a larger space roughly the shape of good-sized room.

"Dead end," Mick said, standing straight. He put his fists in his back and stretched, feeling good after the cramped tube. "That's better."

Steve and Jemma lifted their lights and walked the edge of the room in opposite directions while Mick stood in the center.

"Hey, over here; more glyphs.' Jemma had stopped and shone her light over a section of the wall. "Hmm, what am I looking at here?"

"Are they wrestling?" Steve asked.

Mick joined them. "Who can tell? They weren't exactly the best artists known to history."

The ground shimmied beneath them.

"Ooh." Jemma put a hand out to brace herself, and her eyes flicked to Mick. "That was a big one; maybe we should wrap it up for today."

Mick sighed, trying to maintain his cool, and looked at his wristwatch. "Yeah, okay." He half-turned. "Steve, gonna head back up. Hey ..." He frowned. "Where are you?"

There was silence, which he found odd, seeing the dark cavern was large, but enclosed so his voice reached every corner. He turned about, and moved his light along the wall.

"There you are."

In the darkness Steve was standing up close to one of the walls – real close.

"What are you doing in there? You found something?" Mick got to his feet and held out a hand to Jemma.

"Steve?" Jemma asked. "You okay?"

Mick felt the hairs on his neck prickle as the room filled with a smell like burning sugar. Steve stood in a large natural alcove, and the man was so close to the wall he looked like he was pressing himself up against it.

It took Mick a few seconds to make his legs move, and then he went to his friend, grabbed his shoulder and tugged.

'Steve?"

Steve didn't budge, and in fact was so close to the wall now, it looked weirdly as if he was actually forcing himself onto it. And what was with his perspiration? It looked like molasses, rather than normal sweat.

"*Hey.*" Mick tugged harder, and then tried to get a better grip. But he couldn't. Because when he tried to readjust his hands, he found they were stuck to the man. "What the fuck?"

And Steve felt hot. Not hot like a fever, but hot like he was cooking. There was also an odd sensation starting up, like an electric shock running up his arms.

"Jesus, there's something ..." Mick tugged madly, but couldn't get free.

"What is it?" Jemma asked, her eyes wide now. "What's happening?" Her voice was becoming shrill.

"Stay back." He grimaced. "*I'm stuck – something's – wrong.*"

Suddenly long tendrils started to whip free from all over Steve's body and from the wall surrounding him. To Mick's horror, a massive blind eye wetly opened in the wall beside his friend.

Mick screamed, and felt his mind beginning to slip into madness as his hands sank into the flesh of his friend. Jemma also screamed, and backed away, her hands to her face.

Mick screamed so loud now he tasted blood in his throat. Then he tasted something sweet, and in the next few seconds, he felt a calming warmth enter his body and mind. There was a voice, not words, just – a voice.

"It's okay," he whispered. "Stay here," he said soothingly to Jemma.

"Mick, what's happening?" Jemma continued to back up, but slower now. "Please tell me."

A forest of tendrils sprouted from the ground around her legs, and she danced away from them. But they raised up to block her exit, and then force her back, closer to the wall.

"*What's happening?*" She backed up some more.

Mick shot out a hand and grabbed her. Her clothes smoked where his hand had hold of her.

"Join us," he whispered.

She did, and the three people merged into one.

AUTHOR'S NOTES

Many readers ask me about the background of my novels – is the science real or imagined? Where do I get the situations, equipment, characters and their expertise from, and just how much of it has a basis in fact?

In regards to my novel *From Hell*, the case for a place called 'Hell' is interesting, because in every religion there is a destination where 'wrongdoers' are cast (down or up). Another interesting fact is that more than twice as many people believe in heaven as they do in hell. I guess that's because most near-death stories you see in the media are of people relating how they were called toward a shining light, ascending with a feeling of warmth and peace.

Depending on your faith, if any, you may believe there is a place where huge demons steal souls, torment us in heat and hellfire, and is also ruled by a single malevolent intelligence.

All legends grow from strange phenomena, the imagination, or are even laid down as a warning for future generations.

The Swallowing of Pompeii

According to volcanologists there are around sixty eruptions every year – basically one every few days. Most are little more than murmurs and ground trembling. But some, though rare, are catastrophic.

On 24 August 79AD, Mount Vesuvius' top exploded, spewing tons of boiling ash, pumice, and sulfuric gas miles into the atmosphere. A cyclone of poisonous gas and molten debris engulfed the Roman cities of Pompeii, Herculaneum, and Stabiae. Tons of falling debris filled the streets, covered rooftops, and submerged fields to an average depth of twenty feet. Nothing remained of the densely populated resorts. And the cities remained that way for almost 1700 years until excavation began in 1748.

What must it have been like to live in and through that hell? The Romans were brilliant record keepers and chroniclers of events, and there was a detailed and descriptive record created by a Roman called Pliny the Younger (Pliny), whose letters described the horror that he saw unfolding. The young man tells of a monstrous cloud rising like an umbrella pine, for it grew to a great height on a trunk and then split off into branches. It turned noonday light into a blackness the likes of which no Pompeian had ever experienced.

Among that blackness, hellish heat, and choking smoke could be heard the shrieks of women, crying babies, and children, and the screaming of men – some called for their parents, others to their lost children, trying to recognize them by their voices alone in the pitch darkness. People prayed, and people screamed and wailed.

Some ask what would Hell be like? For these poor souls who were trapped in Pompeii, Pliny's words could not render a better description. This was one of the things that triggered my novel – people not being cast down to Hell, but instead, Hell rising up to engulf them.

In the beginning, there was the Archaea.

The word "archaea" comes from the Ancient Greek ἀρχαῖα, meaning "ancient things", and it's appropriate, as these extremely ancient life forms are more closely related to the first life on Earth.

Humans have been around for four million years in some form or other. But archaea have been around for around 3.5 billion, and remain little changed from their first forms. They are a domain of single-celled microorganisms that have no cell nucleus or any other organelles inside their cells, and are unique in having a totally independent evolutionary history and many differences in their biochemistry from other forms of life.

The first representatives of the domain Archaea were methanogens and it was assumed that this type of metabolism reflected Earth's primitive atmosphere. Certain archaea aggregate to produce monster single cells, or in some cases, they can clump to form elaborate multicell colonies that can share nutrients, information, and even mount defenses for colony protection.

Some say that these life forms arrived on Earth during an asteroid impact when the planet was young, and they adapted very quickly to the primitive and hostile environment. They still exist down in the depths, living as they have for the last 3.5 billion years. They are the ultimate survivors, were here long before humans, and they'll probably be here long after we have gone.

The Chimera – the sum of all of us.

According to Greek mythology, the Chimera was a monstrous fire-breathing hybrid creature, composed of the parts of more than one animal. It is usually depicted with the body a lion with the head of a goat arising from its back, and a tail that might end with a snake's head or spikes (that it could shoot).

The term Chimera has come to describe any mythical or fictional animal with parts taken from various animals. However, historically, many ancient cultures had multi-form monster creatures that terrorized them.

In Medieval art, although the Chimera of antiquity was forgotten, chimerical figures appear as embodiments of the deceptive, even satanic, forces of evil and corruption. They were provided with a human face and a scaly tail that consumed the souls of unwary victims.

Further back, the Persians had a legendary creature called a manticore that was similar to the Egyptian sphinx. It has the head of a human, body of a lion, and tail of venomous spines similar to porcupine quills, while other depictions have it with the tail of a scorpion. It consumed its victims whole (the body and the soul), using its triple rows of teeth, and left no bones behind.

In addition, from Greek mythology, there was Geryon, a fearsome giant who was imprisoned on the island Erytheia and had one head and three bodies on one set of legs. Other ancient descriptions of the terrible beast also had multiple faces, six hands on six arms, and six feet on six legs. It was primarily this creature that drove a lot of the inspiration for my story.

Body liquefaction – from the sea we came, and to the sea we will return.

Concerned about the 'footprint' your burial plot will take up, or maybe the energy used in cremation? Then after you throw off the mortal coil, perhaps simply flush yourself down the toilet?

There's a new way to dispose of your loved ones where you can convert them into a liquid, and then spray them on the garden. The 'green burial' process is based on alkaline hydrolysis, whereby the body is placed in a pressure vessel that is then filled with a mixture of water and potassium hydroxide. It is heated to a temperature around 160°C (320°F), but at a constant high pressure to stop boiling. In this hot and pressurized environment, the body is effectively broken down into its chemical components. Body tissue is dissolved and the resultant liquid (effluent) contains no DNA and is safe enough to pour directly into the municipal water system. Depending on the size of the body, it can take between four to six hours.

Already body liquefiers are being used in Japan, Australia, the US (Florida), and are being trialled in Europe. There might just be another use for this liquid, and anyone who remembers the movie *Soylent Green* will know how this might end!

CPSIA information can be obtained
at www.ICGtesting.com
Printed in the USA
BVHW081945170322
631641BV00001B/86